HALF A PRAYER

THE TOME OF BILL - 6

RICK GUALTIERI

DEDICATION

For Cabot, Greg, Jake, Kurt, Mike, Paul, and Tony - my Friday night gaming crew. You guys are a constant source of inspiration in so many different ways.

ACKNOWLEDGEMENTS

Special thanks to: Alissa, Ruby, Jim, Chris, Jonathan, Evgenia, Todd and Solace for their awesome feedback. You guys help keep me (and Bill) on the straight and narrow, never cutting me slack for things I forgot four books ago.

PART I

1

WHEN A STRANGER COMES
KNOCKING

"Who the hell are *you*?"

"Excuse me?" the thin man asked, his brows furrowed behind his horn-rimmed glasses.

I sighed, disgusted at myself. I hadn't meant to immediately come across as an asshole. That was never a sound tactic for being welcomed with open arms at a stranger's doorway. Unfortunately, he'd surprised me. I'd been expecting a very different welcome.

Don't get me wrong, I'm not sure how things would have gone down otherwise. Best case would have been arms around my neck and luscious lips pressed against my own. Worst case would have found me immediately vaporized. What I hadn't been expecting, though, was that the person who would answer the door wouldn't be the blonde woman I was secretly - or not, depending on who you asked - in love with.

Turns out, I was batting zero.

"I think you have the wrong address," Horn-rims said as he began closing the door.

"Wait! I'm looking for Sheila." Saying her name aloud

3

was odd, almost wrong - as if I were a child caught saying a curse word. Although it was cool outside, pinpricks of sweat broke out on my brow. Name-dropping had the desired effect, though. Recognition flashed in the man's eyes and the door's progress paused.

I realized that wasn't necessarily a good thing. I'd stalked...err, followed...Sheila on Facebook for almost the entire duration we were coworkers at Hopskotchgames.com - long enough to know she didn't have a brother. This fucker wasn't old enough to be her dad. Thus, I held on to the thin hope that he was a visiting cousin or maybe some neighbor that had dropped by to borrow a cup of sugar and was just about to leave.

Yeah, I was grasping at straws.

The man looked at me expectantly. Blurting out nothing but a first name probably wasn't going to get me invited to dinner.

"Sheila O'Connell. I'm a friend of hers."

His beady green eyes narrowed behind the thick lenses and he frowned. "I'm sorry, but nobody by that name lives here. Now, if you'll excuse me, I have some work to do."

Duh! I guess it would make sense that she'd at least be using a different last name. Remington had figured out her identity and tried to use her family as a bargaining chip against her. It hadn't turned out so well for him and his team, but she had no way of knowing whether the information had been shared amongst her potential enemies. Also, it was quite possible she didn't trust me not to spill my guts about her.

"She might be using an alias." Even as the words left my mouth, I realized how utterly fucking stupid they sounded. I might as well have told this guy I was looking for Carlos the Jackal.

An unpleasant grimace creased his mouth and he sniffed the air. "Have you been drinking?"

"Um..." Oh crap. That sure as hell wasn't going to help things.

I'd circled the surrounding neighborhood several times over the past hour, working up the nerve to approach the house. When that hadn't panned out, I'd stopped at a strip mall a few blocks away and popped into a local chain restaurant - one that had a bar. A couple of shots of liquid courage were just what the doctor ordered.

In retrospect, it probably wasn't my smartest move. A tequila-soaked stranger standing on the front stoop well after dark was bad enough these days. Hell, that didn't even count the sword I was holding - wrapped in a towel, sure, but probably obvious to anyone with half a brain.

"Listen, pal, I don't know who you are, but you need to back up and leave quietly. We don't want any trouble here, but I won't hesitate to call the cops."

I couldn't blame this guy for wanting to slam the door in my face and then dial 911 as fast as he could. Wait a second...*we?*

"Hold that thought," I replied, reaching into my pocket.

His body tensed up and his eyes widened as his civilized brain tried to make sense of the fight or flight impulses racing through it. I'd been in his position not so long ago. Had I actually been packing a gun, his hesitation would have cost him.

It was going to cost him anyway, but in a slightly different manner.

I used the old vacuum cleaner salesman cliché and slid one foot over the threshold so he couldn't immediately slam the door in my face. It was your basic wooden model - nothing overly reinforced - and it wouldn't stop me if it came down to it, but I really didn't want to have to force the issue. If Sheila was indeed inside, the last thing I wanted was to come crashing in like a bull in a china shop.

That could spook her, a scenario that could end very badly for me.

What I had in mind, instead, was slightly more subtle, or so I hoped.

I pulled the glass vial from my pocket and held it up.

The look of tension eased from his face ever so slightly, only to be replaced with one of confusion. "Is that *blood*?"

"You betcha." I uncorked the stopper. "Bottoms up!"

And with that, I downed the contents and waited for it to work its magic on me.

It had only been three days since we'd returned from our epic ass-kicking up in Boston. Following the string of revelations that had followed, we'd all taken a day to get our respective thoughts back in order.

Though chaos began to reign in many places as the world edged ever closer to Armageddon, other areas hadn't quite caught the hint yet. Hell, sitting inside my apartment in Brooklyn, one could have almost been fooled into thinking things were pretty much normal. That is, if a vampire conversing over a couple of cups of blood-infused coffee with his human roommates was *normal*.

As it turned out, one of the seemingly monumental tasks before us was a bit less daunting than we had originally assumed. Upon learning that Sheila, the last Icon of Faith - a girl who was capable of melting my heart in more ways than one - was alive, I immediately formulated a plan to track her down.

Using my not-so-insignificant programming skills, I began to code up an algorithm that would search online newsfeeds for any mention of a blonde warrior glowing with a brilliant white light. Assuming the power grid didn't falter and she was keeping busy with saving people and other stereotypical Icon activities, I figured it wouldn't be long before we'd triangulate her position and make contact.

Even that was unnecessary, though.

I had just finished writing up a subroutine to filter out any fetish websites from the results when Ed finally spilled the beans: the dickhead had a phone number for her.

"The fuck, dude?" I had so eloquently responded.

"I'm only supposed to use it in an emergency."

"And the end of the world isn't an emergency?"

"A *company* emergency," he clarified. Ed ran Iconic Efficiencies, Sheila's company, in her stead. "Besides..."

"Let me guess. She didn't want you to tell me that either."

His silence was all the answer I needed. *Fuck!*

"If it helps, it's not a direct number; just a voicemail service. The point was for me to leave her a message and she'd call back."

Despite being royally pissed off, I had to grudgingly admire that. She was taking precautions - probably more than I would have. Well, okay; it was *definitely* more than I had. Upon escaping from Switzerland, the nerve center of the vampire world, I'd done little more than make a beeline straight for home.

Ed wasn't comfortable calling Sheila and outright asking where she was, and I was forced to agree it was probably a poor idea. If she truly was that squirrelly about the forces of darkness hunting her down, she'd uproot and run the second she smelled any deception - or so I assumed. A small part of me insisted that she was no more likely to go all black ops than I was, but the fantasy of her living out some Jason Bourne-style escape was too hot to resist.

Thankfully, my roommate was a lazy fuck at heart. All of his call logs were still on his cell phone. The concept of cleaning them out had seemingly never crossed his mind. A little online snooping confirmed that her calls had all come from payphones - jeez, I didn't even realize those still existed - from the area in and around Rochester.

That made sense. Sheila's family was originally from upstate New York. It wouldn't be too much of a stretch that she'd want to be close enough to them in case anything happened.

Sally had taken care of the rest, calling in a few favors with a coven up that way. She told them to keep an eye out for an escaped thrall that *coincidentally* happened to match Sheila's description.

I wasn't too happy with getting other vampires involved, but her logic was hard to argue with. They knew the place and had the numbers to canvas a wide area.

"What if they find her and get too close?" I asked.

"She's the Icon." Quite frankly, that was really all the answer I needed.

Suffice it to say, it was only a couple more days before we had an address.

"Are you sure you don't want me to come?"

I raised an eyebrow at the question, a smirk forming on my lips.

Sally gritted her teeth. "Before you continue along whatever sick train of thought you're following, let me make it very clear that the only one who would be screaming is you...and not in a good way."

"I have no idea what you're talking about," I lied, feigning innocence. "But to answer your question, I probably need to do this on my own."

"I'm not disagreeing. I just think it's stupid. You can barely say your own name around this girl, and yet, somehow, you think you're gonna convince her to not only trust you again, but to join us on a suicide mission to kill this Vehron fucker?"

I winced at the thought of the other Freewill, the one I'd accidentally set free, the one who was infinitely more badass than me, the one who'd killed a good friend of ours and badly beaten another.

Pouring salt in that otherwise unpleasant wound, Sally had continued. "Keep in mind it's also getting dicey heading north. Covens are dropping off the grid left and right. I have a feeling our friend has been recruiting."

"What about this Brighton Coven?" I asked, referring to the vamps who'd sniffed Sheila out. "Think they're still trustworthy?"

"Of course not. They're vampires."

"I mean, do you think he's gotten to them yet?"

"No."

"How can you be sure?"

"They answered my call."

She had a point there.

"Be careful, Bill," she said at last, her tone serious. "You just got back a few days ago, after being missing for months, and..."

"And...?" I asked, unable to help the grin on my face.

"*And* I just offered you a job in Pandora Coven. Pissing off your new master isn't a good way to start a working relationship."

"I'll be careful. I've got a plan."

"You? A plan?"

"Yes, it *is* possible."

"Fine, but just in case..."

It was then that she reached into her purse and handed the vial to me. It was sealed so there was no scent, but the sight of the red liquid inside immediately registered with my brain.

"Is that...?"

"My blood. It's not much, but it might be enough of a boost in case of emergency."

I hesitated for a moment before accepting it, a lump forming in my throat. For all of her queen bitch attitude, I sometimes forgot what a good friend Sally could be. "Thank y..."

Of course, then she had to go and ruin it. "And if you ever tell anyone what I just did, I will smash that thing and shove the broken glass so far up your ass that you'll be shitting sand for a month."

Ah yes, I was truly feeling the love.

2

SEND ME AN ANGEL

"That's it. I'm calling the cops..."

I concentrated my will toward Horn-rims and let loose with everything I had. "*SHUT THE FUCK UP AND INVITE ME IN!!*" As the compulsion left my mouth, it was like an invisible sledgehammer kicked me right in the frontal lobe.

Fuck! I'd known that compelling a human was much more demanding than controlling another vamp. I'd seen Sally do it a few times, only to get knocked on her ass from the effort. I just hadn't appreciated how difficult it really was.

My vision doubled and the next thing I knew, I was down on one knee, gripping the doorframe to keep from keeling over, and hoping that the owner...

Sheila's boyfriend.

...the owner didn't pick that moment to slam the door on my fingers.

I risked a look up to find glazed eyes staring back. He was holding the door open expectantly.

Holy shit, it had worked. Sure, this wasn't exactly what

II

Sally had in mind when she handed her blood to me, but the definition of emergency really was a subjective thing.

I staggered back to my feet, feeling like my head was gonna explode. *"**AND GET ME SOME ASPIRIN WHILE YOU'RE AT IT!!**"*

Motherfucker!

Okay, that second one definitely didn't help. Thankfully, I pitched forward onto a carpeted floor instead of back down the stairs.

As I inched my way in - dragging a concealed sword that suddenly seemed to weigh half a ton, the front door closed behind me.

"Thank you, Jeeves," I muttered into the carpet. "There'll be a generous tip for you come Christmas."

I heard my host's footsteps walking away. Realizing that I was being a poor guest, lying there and drooling on the floor, I crawled over to the couch and pulled myself up onto it.

Thankfully, absorbing Sally's strength also meant adding her healing ability to my own. By the time my bland-looking friend returned, holding a glass of water and a full bottle of Bufferin, the echoing in my head had died down to a dull roar.

After I'd chugged about a dozen of the pills - it's not like they could kill me - my senses finally calmed down and my thoughts became coherent.

Why the fuck was I here again?

Oh yeah, Sheila. Now where was...

"What are you doing here?"

Apparently, she was closer than I thought.

I should have replied with *something*, but my brain seemed to have shut itself completely down.

Sheila stood about fifteen feet away in a hallway leading from the living room. She was aglow with the flames of faith, blazing almost painfully bright - her eyes resembling miniature stars.

She was obviously a little bit annoyed.

She was also a *lot* undressed. Her damp hair hinted at the shower she'd just stepped out of...that, and the towel wrapped around her.

I was never much of a praying man, but in that moment, I sure as fuck believed in a god. And he was a good god to allow me such a sight. If I had died right then, it would have been a happy death.

She remained in a battle stance for a moment longer as my eyes continued to bug from my head - my brain in overdrive, attempting to etch this memory into my subconscious for all of eternity, if need be.

Apparently sensing that no battle was about to ensue, and no doubt noticing where my eyes were roaming, Sheila glanced down at her state of undress and immediately blushed - the little bit of color in her cheeks a beautiful contrast to the white fire that otherwise surrounded her.

A small part of me was tempted to flash my fangs and attack, if only because I had a feeling my life wasn't going to be getting better anytime soon. There's something to be said about going out on a high note.

Instead, she was the one to break the standoff, pointing a finger at me. "Don't move." She ducked inside a door, adding just before she slammed it shut, "And don't you dare hurt Robert."

"Who's Robert?" I muttered right before remembering the other person in the room. I glanced toward him. He stood there, eyes glazed and unmoving. Compelling a human had been a shitload more painful than I'd have guessed, but I could see how handy it was in certain situations.

It was tempting to compel him to go play in traffic or maybe find a nice friendly police officer to kick in the balls, but I stopped myself short. I didn't know this guy for shit. For all I knew, he was just a neighbor who had popped by to borrow some milk...and just so happened to hang around while she took a shower.

Grrr.

A darkness stirred deep inside of me and demanded I take some action - preferably the brutal kind.

No! That was a slippery slope. Plus, what had this poor schmuck done to deserve any of that? Nothing...except bone the one girl I had designs on.

Oh, fuck it.

I shook the rest of the pills from the aspirin bottle into my hand as I whisper-compelled, "***YOU HAVE EREC-TILE DYSFUNCTION!!***" The resulting kick to my head from the effort was well worth it.

"What was that?" Sheila stepped back out into the hall. She'd slipped on a t-shirt and pair of shorts. Not quite as nice as the towel, but pretty tasty nevertheless.

"Nothing. I was just remarking on how...functional the décor was."

She still looked somewhat wary, but the aura of faith around her had died down to a barely visible glow. It flared up again momentarily when she glanced in the direction of the guy I assumed to be Robert. He continued to stand there like some android awaiting instructions.

"What did you do to him?"

There was no point in lying to her. Hell, I wasn't even sure I'd allow myself to. "I compelled him to let me in. That's it." Well, okay; maybe I could lie a little bit.

"You can do that?"

"Not really. I had a bit of a boost...it's hard to explain."

"Is he going to be all right?" She walked up to him and waved her hands in front of his unblinking face.

"Yeah, he'll be fine. It'll wear off soon." I'd seen enough human compulsions to be pretty certain he'd snap out of it, but having never actually done it myself, I had no idea how long that might be.

A look of panic crossed her face and she closed her eyes. After a moment, even the soft glow around her faded to nothing. She turned toward me, a look of worry upon her face. "Is he aware? Will he remember this, seeing me like...that?"

That surprised me. "I'm not sure. I don't think so. He seems pretty far under to me. Wait; you mean he doesn't know?"

"No. I've been keeping it under control around him, at least until you showed up." That last part had a bit of an edge to it, enough so that I was surprised I didn't immediately start bleeding.

I probably deserved it anyway. After all, I'd originally dragged her into this mess, even if inadvertently. How was I supposed to know that a few compliments on my part would set in motion the chain of events that would turn her into the Icon, the legendary foe of vampire-kind? Shit like that didn't happen to most people.

Of course, I'm not most people. I had the *luck* of being the Freewill, equally legendary warrior of the undead. Or at least I used to be before accidentally setting that muscle-headed dick up in Boston loose upon the world. Now? Well, I had no idea what I was now and it probably wasn't the right time to wonder. "So...this is Robert?"

"Yes," she replied, looking somewhat uncomfortable. I could understand the sentiment. Fighting monsters of the night was easy as pie compared to some things.

"And he's..." I trailed off, hoping to hear cousin, friend, acquaintance, anything but...

"My boyfriend."

Fuck! "And you both live here?"

"Yes."

"Together?"

"Yes, together."

Double fuck!

I sat down and took a deep breath, resolving myself to get to the point of my visit. None of this was any of my business, after all. She was free to date who she wanted. It's not like we'd ever even kissed...minus one close call that ended with me on fire. Besides, we had bigger fish to fry. The end of the world was looming and we both needed to get our heads in the game.

"So isn't this a little sudden?" I asked, ignoring all of that shit.

"Sudden?"

"Yeah. I mean, it's only been a little over three months since..."

"Since I was hunted by a pack of murderous vampires?"

"Well..."

"Who killed all those Templar who'd taken me in?"

"I guess..."

"Including my friend Ben?"

"Yeah, I suppose that was..."

She raised a hand and pointed to her forehead. "And then ended things by trying to put a fifty-caliber bullet through my skull?"

"I can sorta understand your point."

"Then you can see why I needed a little bit of normalcy. I was alone, on the run, looking over my shoulder every five minutes..."

"And..."

"And Robert is a nice guy. He treats me well."

I couldn't argue there. At the end of the day, didn't she deserve at least that much?

"He's a good accountant too." She let out a laugh. "If things ever get back to normal, I might have to let him manage the books at Iconic Efficiencies."

"An accountant, eh?" I quipped, unable to help myself. "Must be a real wild man on Friday nights."

"That's kind of the point. Like I said, I needed a little normal."

Oh, fuck it, I needed to know. "So...do you..." I might have mumbled the rest.

"What?"

Gah! "Do you...love him?"

"He's a good man."

"That's not an answer."

"I didn't realize I answered to you. Are you going to try compelling me too?"

"No!" I cried defensively. "I couldn't even if I wanted to, and I don't. I would never..." I stopped as the smile crept onto her face.

"So why are you here, Bill?" She took a seat on the couch, opposite of where I still sat, and stared me in the eye. Needless to say, I looked away first. God, I'm such a fucking weenie.

"Don't you want to know how I found you?"

"Ed."

"That obvious, eh? Don't be mad at him."

"I'm not. It was only a matter of time before he spilled his guts...figuratively, I hope."

"He's fine. Well, not fine..."

"Wait? Is he okay? He seemed good the last time I spoke to him."

"You don't know?"

"Know what?" Concern filled her features. I wanted to

reach out and comfort her, but I hesitated. We probably weren't quite there yet.

I filled her in on Ed and his condition as best as I could. The truth was we still had no idea what had happened to him, how it worked, or if it was permanent. On the outside, he seemed to be fine. It was when you got to his creamy center that things got all explodey.

All the while, Robert continued to just stand there. It was starting to get a bit creepy. Sheila, oddly enough, seemed fine with it, though.

"So he really doesn't know?" I hooked a thumb at the bookkeeper. "Not even with the world going all batshit?"

"It's not going crazy everywhere."

"I noticed. This place seems pretty...well, normal."

Now it was her turn to avert her eyes.

"Your doing?"

Silence met my question.

"You know, I could have sworn I had seen mention on the news of a..."

"Fine," she snapped. "Yes, it's me. Robert works late, usually well after dark. By day, I can be Sheila Williams, a girl who works the register at the local pharmacy."

My thought process slammed to a screeching halt at that. *Williams?* My first name was William. Was it just a coincidence? Or was there something deeper that...?

"...good that he works long hours. It gives me a chance to go out at night and keep the neighborhood safe."

"Let me guess," I replied, trying to focus. "You kill any vamps that happen to get too close?"

"I'm not specifically hunting vampires, Bill. I'm keeping an eye out for anything that's *weird* in a bad way."

"Weird in a bad way, like vampires?"

"Yes, like vampires if I get the sense they're a danger. But the last several days, it's been other things as well."

"I can imagine. So...would you consider me weird in a bad way?"

There was an awkward pause in the room. Yeah, I'm good at killing meaningful conversation that way. It's not too hard to guess why I'm so popular with the ladies.

"I wouldn't," she finally said. That was a relief. "Normally."

Oh, fuck; here it comes.

"But Ed told me what happened...or at least, what he was told happened."

"You can't trust the telephone game," I countered lamely, fidgeting with my hands.

"Oh, so you didn't turn into some kind of mon... something else. Something that tore Remington limb from limb."

"I thought he killed you." There was an edge to my voice and I wouldn't have been surprised if my eyes momentarily turned black. It was not a pleasant memory for me to relive. "I kind of lost it."

"So when were you going to tell me?"

"Tell you what? That I killed Remington? I kind of thought you were dead these past three months."

"Not that. There was no way that guy was walking out of there alive, not after what he did. I don't care about that. When were you going to tell me that...?"

"That I'm a monster?"

"Pretty much."

"I would've gotten to it eventually."

She ignored my pathetic excuse and went on. "That's what worries me about you."

"That I can turn..."

"No. That you're not *you* when you do. I saw you fighting: against the Templar, those vampires, and even those witches. You didn't kill anyone you didn't have to. In fact, you went out of your way not to kill. You could have left people behind, but you didn't. You could have saved yourself a lot of trouble, but you were there for your friends."

"It's nothing anyone who's halfway decent wouldn't do."

"I know, but that thing isn't *you*. I asked Ed about it. He told me about Canada and, before that, with the Khan's assassins."

"He did?" Jeez, didn't the asshole have any of his own stories to tell?

"Yes, and it all points to the same thing: whatever mercy or goodness you have in you normally - it all goes right out the window when you change."

"You don't have to be afraid of me."

She looked directly at me, her strange silver eyes glimmering. "I'm not afraid of you."

"Oh."

"I'm afraid of what it is you turn into. I'm afraid of what could happen. And most of all..."

"Yes?" I prodded gently.

"I'm afraid of what I might have to do to stop you."

HOUSEWARMING GIFT

Robert began to stir, breaking the awkward silence. He blinked his eyes and moaned, beginning to wake from the power of the compulsion. Oh, crap.

Sheila's eyes opened wide in panic and mine quickly followed. When Robert last had his senses about him, he'd been ready to call the cops on me. I'd also spilled the beans about her using a fake name. This was going to require some pretty fast talking on both our parts.

"Do it again," she hissed.

"What?"

"Put him under again. Make him forget all of this."

"The world is coming apart at the seams," I argued. "He's gonna figure it out sooner or later."

"I'm not ready yet. *Please*, Bill."

Oh, fuck me. She could have added "tear off your own head while you're at it and put it on the mantle as a bookend" and I'd have still done so. There was no way I could resist her plea, and it had nothing to do with compulsion.

Speaking of which, I hoped I had enough of Sally's juice still running through my system.

"TAKE A LONG NAP!! THIS IS ALL JUST A BAD DREAM!!"

I don't know which of us hit the floor first or hardest. All I knew was that one second the compulsion came flying out of me, and the next I was studying the pattern of the ceiling tiles.

Much to my dismay, Sheila went and checked on Rob the Knob first. At least it gave me a moment to collect my thoughts.

She was right about everything she'd said. There *was* a monster in me. It didn't matter that at the moment I couldn't change into it. Dr. Death was still inside of me and could return at any time...albeit, knowing him, it wouldn't be at any time that was remotely convenient for me. My inner beast was both a killer and an asshole. Talk about pouring lemon juice on a paper cut.

It was weird. I'd never considered myself a likely candidate for having a split personality. My childhood wasn't all wine and roses, mind you, but it was pretty decent. I'd been an only child in a middle-class household. The closest my parents had come to being abusive had been the occasional bit of sarcasm from my father, and even that wasn't remotely close to the level I got from Sally most days. Who knew? Maybe I was more fucked in the head than I realized. Heh, if I actually managed to save the world, maybe I'd reward myself with a couple of rounds of psychoanalysis. That would be a hoot.

That would have to wait, though. I had a big mean motherfucker up in Boston to kill first, not to mention a worldwide supernatural war to stop. It was safe to say my dance card would be pretty full for the next few months.

I blinked a few times to clear my head and found my view of the ceiling blocked by one much more pleasant.

"Are you okay?"

"Nothing curling up in a corner and crying for several

hours won't fix," I muttered. "How's your boy toy?" Ugh, I should've waited to open my mouth until the room stopped spinning. It came out far more sarcastic than I'd meant.

"Sleeping like a baby, thanks." She raised one eyebrow at me - looking far sexier than Mr. Spock ever had a shot at. "Is that jealousy I detect in your voice?"

Yes! "No," I replied quickly, my voice still a bit slurred. "I just think you can..."

"Think I can *what?*"

Oh, crap. I needed to get back to my feet and clear the cobwebs out before I spilled my guts while lying there on her floor. "Think you can maybe help me up?"

She reached down and offered me a hand, which I took before I could think better of it. The moment my hand closed upon hers, I realized my mistake and immediately winced. A second passed and nothing happened, save maybe my palm sweating. There was no flash of light and, even better, no horrifically painful immolation of my body.

"I've been practicing," she explained.

"I can see that," I replied once back standing vertically. It was impressive. I'd seen her exercise control over her powers before, but it had taken some effort on her part. Now, though, she'd barely batted an eye. Harkening back to her question; hell yeah, I was jealous, and not just of Robert. It made me think of all the things I could do if Dr. Death and I could only come to some sort of agreement.

I pushed it from my mind. There I was, standing in the same room as the girl of my dreams - holding her hand, even. It was not exactly the time to be having a pity party.

I could have stood there like that for an eternity.

"So, you didn't come all this way just to compel my

boyfriend into letting you see me wearing only a towel, did you?"

"Um...no, of course not." I reluctantly let go of her hand, immediately missing the feel of her skin. I took a deep breath and forced myself to get down to business. "We need your help."

"We?"

"All of us: Me, Ed, Sally, Tom, Christy...Hell, maybe even the whole world."

"How is she doing?"

"Sally? Oh, she's as big of a bitch as..."

"No, Christy. She was a little freaked out when I met her. How's she doing with the baby?"

"Oh, fine. Interestingly enough, she freaked out again when she found out you were still alive." The resulting flare-up of her powers necessitated the use of a fire extinguisher to put out our couch. "But she's okay with it now."

"That's good to hear. Please send her my regards."

"Will do."

"So this help you need..."

"Yeah." I sat down. This was going to be fun. "You know how the world has been getting ready to shit a brick?"

"Believe me, I've noticed."

"Well, it's started."

"Noticed that too."

"Good...sorta. Anyway, remember that whole thing about us fighting to the death?"

"Yes. That girl - Gansetseg, wasn't it - seemed pretty convinced that you were going to kill me."

"Yeah, she's funny like that."

"I'm sorry, by the way."

"Huh?"

"She was a little...intense, but she didn't deserve what

she got. In the end, she helped us out, and that counts a lot in my book."

"Gan's fine," I interrupted offhandedly.

"She *is*?" The surprise was evident in her voice, minus the typical horror one normally expressed when they heard something like that. I had to remember she'd never seen Gan at her *finest*.

"Yeah. Apparently, the little psycho jumps off buildings all the time."

"Oh...that's..."

"Yeah, forget about her. Trust me, I'm trying to."

A sly smile played out over Sheila's face. "She has a crush on you, you know."

"Hence the trying to forget about her part."

"It's cute."

"She's a three-hundred-year-old mass murderer."

"Maybe a bit less than cute."

"Exactly." Gah! I was letting myself get sidetracked way too easily. If I kept this up, I'd keep talking to her until sunrise. That wasn't a bad thing, mind you. The problem was if that happened, I'd be stuck, and I was pretty sure Robert would eventually wake up. With no more of Sally's blood to swig down, I'd probably be forced to do things the old-fashioned way and punch him out...which would most likely go a long way toward undoing any trust I was trying to build up again with Sheila. As much as I hated to do so, I needed to focus and just blurt it out.

"We might not have to fight to determine the fate of the world." As far as pickup lines went, I'd used better.

"Well, that's good," she replied, bemused.

"No, you don't get it. This prophecy shit is pretty serious. I mean, I don't take it seriously, but a lot of folks do."

"So we just don't..."

"That's the problem. I'm not sure we *can* avoid it."

"Didn't you just say you don't take it seriously?"

"I know and I'm trying really hard not to, but everything I've done seems to draw me closer and closer to actually living it out. It's starting to make me paranoid."

"Okay, fine. The Templar were pretty convinced of that too. Let's pretend for a second that maybe they were right about some things."

"Good. Well, that's just the thing. See, our prophecy, the one the blind vampire seers made..."

"Blind vampire seers?"

"Yeah, they're fucking weirdos. I met them when I was trapped in Switzerland." I held up a hand. "I'll tell you all about it later. Anyway, long story short, there's another Freewill." She raised an eyebrow and I remembered that the Templar had drilled another name into her head. "Another *Night Spawn* like me." I really needed to remember that phrase more often. It was so much cooler than Freewill.

"Oh." Her eyes opened wide in surprise, but that was all. It was safe to say she was starting to come to grips with the various nasty surprises the supernatural world liked to toss out when one least expected it. "Are you sure he...or is it she..."

"It's a he, and yes, I'm sure. I'm doubly sure he's bad news. Let's just say he makes Remington's entire hit squad look like a Girl Scout troop in comparison."

"But how..."

"Because he kicked my ass six ways to Sunday. He turned my dungeon master and he ki..." I swallowed before saying it. Starlight's death still seemed far too surreal to be true. "He killed a good friend of mine."

Sheila was quiet for a moment, then she raised a hand and put it on my shoulder. It wasn't much, but at the same time, it was insanely, weirdly comforting. I wasn't sure if it was my feelings for her, something to do with her Iconhood, or maybe a bit of both. All I knew was that for a moment I felt warm inside, and not in an about to burn to a crisp sort of way. Sadly, I had to interrupt the moment. She had to know the danger.

"His name is Vehron..."

"That's a strange name."

"They call him Vehron the Destroyer, and believe me, it's not just some bullshit moniker to make him look cool. This guy is the real deal."

"Listen, Bill, I..."

"You don't understand. I mean it. He's over two thousand years old - a former vampire general who used to fuck up whole civilizations for shits and giggles. The guy has a rap sheet a mile long and..." I paused, unsure if I wanted to let her know of Vehron's other crimes - that he'd been responsible for the deaths of more than one Icon.

"If this guy's so old, then where has he been all this time?"

"He was a decapitated skull in Alexander the Great's closet. I sorta accidentally set him free when I bumped into his fish tank and..." The look on her face stopped me. "I can assure you I was not drunk at the time."

"I didn't say you were, but you have to understand how it sounds."

"Oh, believe me, I understand. Hell, I lived it and still don't quite believe it."

"Okay, fine. Let's say that's what happened. Did you track me down, drive all the way up here, just to break the news that I was fated to fight some *other* guy to the death?"

"Yes...no... not exactly. I mean, I didn't drive. I had a little help from..." I was rambling again. If we both lived to be a thousand, I had to wonder whether we'd ever hold a conversation without me sounding like a mumbling idiot. "No, I didn't come up here to tell you about your fate."

"Then why..."

"I'll show you." I looked around and spotted the wrapped sword still lying where I'd dropped it during my second or third compulsion - I didn't remember which. Reminding myself what it could do, I reached into my pocket and produced a pair of leather gloves.

Sheila stared, her eyes twinkling as I picked up what was rightfully hers and unwrapped it, being extra careful not to let the blade touch any of my skin. That would've fucking hurt.

I dropped the towel to the floor and lifted the weapon by the hilt. I don't know if it was some innate power in the sword or her close proximity, but the blade began to glow softly.

"Is that...?"

"The sword of Joan of Arc?" I asked. "Not anymore. It's the Icon's weapon - *your* weapon. You asked me why I came up here. Well, I'll tell you."

I held out the sword to her waiting hands. "I came here to recruit you."

4

SHOT DOWN AGAIN

The fire that had erupted from Sheila earlier was nothing compared to what happened when she grasped the hilt of the sword and held it up in front of her. It was like she became a being of pure energy. White fire engulfed her, so bright that I had to shield my eyes. That wasn't the worst of it, though. My skin began to blister from our proximity to each other. I backed up a step, and then added three more to it before I felt safe from immediately becoming a pile of Freewill dust.

It was impressive as all hell to watch, but then I realized that wasn't necessarily a good thing.

"Um, the shades are open," I pointed out.

"Huh? Oh..." A look of embarrassment passed over her face, then she closed her eyes and reined it all in. The white power of faith seemed to collapse in on itself until all that remained was a faint glow emanating from the blade.

"I think it's happy to be back with you."

"The feeling is mutual." She gave the weapon an experimental thrust, then brought it up behind her back and grabbed it with her other hand, swinging it forward again

29

with a skill that would've made Inigo Montoya jealous. "Funny to think that only a few months ago I could barely cut a cucumber without slicing my finger. Now...well, I didn't realize how naked I felt without it."

I found my mind wandering back to her clad in only a towel, almost making me wish I had held on to the sword for a little bit longer, but the daydreams could wait for a time when she wasn't right in front of me...like at night when I was sleeping alone and she was cuddled up next to...grr.

Once again, those violent impulses passed through my mind, Dr. Death stirring his ugly head, maybe? I couldn't be sure that it wasn't just me being a jealous prick. Oh well, depending on how thorough my earlier compulsion had been, cuddling would be all she and Robert would be doing. One needed to take comfort where one could get it.

"So, you were saying?"

"About what?" I asked, completely caught up in my thoughts.

"You said you were here to recruit me."

"Well, it's not so much recruiting as hoping you'll help."

She sat down, laying the sword across her lap - almost as if she were afraid I would take it back. As if I could even if I wanted to.

"Be careful with that thing. Don't let Robbie go and try hocking it at the next Comic Con."

"Don't worry. I have the perfect place to hide it. How'd you find it anyway? I thought you said something earlier about being trapped in Switzerland?"

"I was. Long story. Sally was actually holding on to it. Everyone thought you were..." I didn't want to go there again. "Anyway, she found it after the fight with

Remington and thought it deserved better than sitting in some evidence locker." I left out that her definition of *better* had turned out to be storing it in a smelly old duffle bag.

"Thank her for me, please."

"I will," I lied. "So about that recruiting part..."

I filled her in on my adventures with Vehron, how he'd kicked our asses all throughout the tri-state area, finally ending with the disastrous battle in Boston.

"So this James," she asked when I'd finished my tale, "he's one of those Draculas?"

"Yeah, one of the thirteen vamps in charge and the only good egg in the bunch, at least that I've met so far."

"Aren't they the same group that put a warrant out for my head?"

I guess some things were hard to forget, even after taking a subsonic chunk of metal to the skull. "Yeah. I'm still working out the details, but I'm thinking due to their general disposition toward you, we might have to play this one under the radar. Won't be too hard. This new Freewill has pretty much killed or enslaved everyone he could get his hands on."

She sat back and looked pensive. I could understand. Living life was so much easier when you didn't have vampire death squads hunting you down.

"I'll figure something out," I said, trying to sound reassuring. "I promise. Hell, James will be so happy to have Calibra back that he'll probably..."

She sat up straight. "Calibra?"

"She's the current Prefect in charge of Boston, assuming she's still alive. Anyway, James kinda likes her. I get the impression she's sort of his star pupil."

"Oh...okay." She sat back down, a frown creasing her lips.

"What's wrong?"

"I thought the name sounded familiar for a moment."

"Tall girl, thin, wears her hair in a tight bun and walks around like she has a stick jammed up her ass."

"Not that...never mind. It's probably nothing. The Templar used to drill me nonstop in their dogma. I think one of the things they mentioned had a similar name. That's all."

"Well, she could probably pass for the patron saint of office drones. Anyway, James might be able to put in a good word...maybe even get the Draculas off our asses."

"You mean *my* ass."

"Ours. Believe me, I'm not going to ditch you...and also, I have a feeling they'll be kinda pissed at me anyway. Seems they always are."

"Bill..."

"It's no big deal. I'm used to it by n..."

"I can't help you."

That stopped me mid-sentence. "What?"

"I can't help, at least not now."

"You don't have to be afraid of any of them."

"I'm not."

Oh, of course not. "And you'll be helping a lot of people out. What's left of my coven is enthralled by this asshole, not to mention a metric shit-ton of other vamps from the surrounding..."

"That's the problem." Her eyes momentarily flashed white. "They're not people; they're vampires."

"Yeah, I know. Wait, you do realize I'm a vampire, right?"

"It's not that. This isn't some stupid racist thing."

"Then what's the problem?"

She stood, placing the sword carefully onto the couch,

and began to pace. "I didn't agree with everything the Templar said or did. I know they weren't as righteous as they pretended to be, but there was one thing we did see eye to eye on. They continually told me that I was here, that I was given this power, to protect people - humans."

"The last defender of humanity," I muttered, reiterating yet another part of the prophecy that seemed to hang over our heads like a rapidly descending pendulum.

"That's what they said too. I'm still not sure I want to believe that part, but they were right about one thing: I have a gift and I want to use that gift to help those who can't fight back - to be a beacon of light in the darkness, or try to anyway."

I'd be lying if I said that her speech didn't give me some wood. To hear a goddess like her spout off what was essentially a superhero origin story was pretty goddamned hot. It took me a moment to focus again enough to speak. "That's cool. I want to help you help people too."

"But this won't be helping people."

"Sure it will. This asshole is enslaving covens left and right, turning them against..."

She walked over and knelt in front of where I sat, leveling her gaze with mine. To my surprise, she took my hands in hers. The slightest of sparks traveled up my arm at her touch, although I had no idea if it was her power or just wishful thinking on my part. "Listen to me, Bill. I know you mean well, but you're wrong about this."

"How so?"

"Say I go with you and we manage to defeat this Destroyer. Then what?"

"James can take over the Boston complex again and secure it against..."

"Against your enemies," she interrupted. "They'll lock it up tight again so they can fight this war you told me about...so they can win it. And what happens when they do? Are they going to go back to hiding in the shadows? Can you honestly tell me they're fighting this war so they can leave humanity alone?"

I didn't answer for several seconds. I saw where she was going and, deep down, knew she was right. Fighting for either the vamps or the Sasquatches meant only one thing: humanity was gonna get the short end of the stick. They might not go quietly and it might not be easy, but at the end of the day, I'd learned one thing from a lifetime of gaming and comic books - the beings with the super-powers usually won.

Still, I had no intention of letting any of that happen. Stopping Alex and his mad quest for world domination was at the top of my to-do list. The problem was that Sheila hadn't seen Vehron in action, but I had. That guy seriously needed to die. Otherwise, he was going to start resurrecting the dogma of his people, a bunch of psychos ridiculously called the Cult of Ib. I didn't know a lot about them, but I'd been told they wanted nothing less than to see the world burn.

"You don't understand." I held up a hand before she could speak, stopping myself short from placing a finger on her lips. That most certainly wouldn't have helped my concentration. "I don't want the vampires to win either. This guy, though, he's not going to stop. He's going to whittle away at both sides until..."

"You're not putting forth much of a convincing argument here."

"I know. What I'm trying to say is this guy scares the ever-living shit out of me. He's bad news for everyone: vampires, humans, and whatever the hell else is out there."

"I still don't..."

"Including you. He's already killed two Icons, and that's only the tip of this fucker's iceberg."

"Already?"

"I told you, this guy is old. He was razing kingdoms to the ground before either of us were gleams in our great-great-great-grandfathers' eyes."

"So you want me to fight..."

"I want *us* to fight him. Night Spawn and Icon together. We won't be alone either. We have Sally, Ed, Tom, and Christy."

"So...your roommates, a vampire fashion model, and a pregnant witch?"

"Well, yeah, although Sally's not really a fashion model, and I'm pretty sure Ed isn't fully human anymore."

"Fine. The six of us against this one vampire."

"And all the vamps he's bent to his will. And however many zombies he released onto the streets of Boston."

"Zombies?"

"Yep."

"And how many is that?"

"I...a few."

"A few?"

"A lot, maybe."

"Well, you're certainly ambitious, I'll give you that."

"One needs to have hobbies."

"I'll bet."

"So," I asked, looking her in her silver eyes. "Are you in?"

The pause between us grew longer by the second until it was almost painful. When at last she spoke, I'd already guessed what her answer would be. "I'm sorry, but I can't."

"Why?"

"I already told you. I'm not going to do anything to help the vampires, even inadvertently. From what you've told me, this guy has introduced a measure of chaos. As far as I can see, that might be a good thing. Let the vampires fight amongst themselves while trying to defend against their enemies..."

"Bigfoot."

"Of course. Regardless, all of this will give humanity time - time to adapt and defend itself. It'll give me time too."

"But if we take them out now..."

"And what if we fail? Don't you think I've thought of doing something like this, thought about striking at the heart of the vampire nation and ramming my fist through it?"

"It's in..."

"Switzerland. I heard you." She stood up, and I could tell by her stance that she was resolute in her decision. Fuck! "I'm supposed to be humanity's last defender. That means I protect people where I can and, if necessary, fight with my back against the wall. It's hard to explain, but that feels right to me. I don't put much stock in my supposed fate, but I know my gut, and it's telling me that I'm not supposed to go on the offensive. If I do that, I don't think things are going to work out."

"Listen, I know you're afraid. I am too."

"But I'm *not*. I'm cautious, wary, maybe even a little paranoid these days, but the one thing I'm not is afraid."

"Must be nice."

"No, it isn't. Because even though I'm not afraid for me, that doesn't mean I don't feel it for everyone else. I have to trust in my instincts here."

"But the prophecy states..."

"That me and this guy are going to duke it out in the end? If that's my destiny, then I accept that, but it will come at a time when the world needs me most - not when I decide to charge in like some half-baked General Custer."

I stood, sensing I wasn't going to change her mind. "When you're ready for your Little Big Horn, just remember you'll have some lieutenants backing you up."

"The battle is supposed to be..."

"Bullshit," I said, refusing to lower my gaze this time. "The prophecies say you're supposed to fight him. They don't say anything about not having backup or that it needs to be a fair fight. I checked on that much."

"If you say so," she replied with a sad smile.

I nodded knowingly, took a quick glance at Robert, and then said the words I thought I'd never purposely utter in her presence. "I should probably get going."

"Promise me you'll take care of yourself. There're some weird things going on."

"The world can't get rid of me that easily."

"I should think not," she replied with a sly smile that made my dead heart roll over in its grave.

I turned toward the door, my eyes drifting once more toward Robert, who was still out cold on the floor. He had no idea how lucky he was. "Keep an eye out should you head over to Brighton. I hear there's a coven there."

"I'll keep that in mind."

As I reached the exit, I turned back toward her. My tongue wasn't quite ready to let out those words I wanted to say without making me sound like an idiot, but maybe I could get close.

"Be safe. You might be humanity's last defender, but you're not invincible. Neither of us are and I...I can't watch you die again."

To my amazement, she broke into a wide grin.

"It'll be okay, Bill. You just need to have a little faith."

5

BEAM ME UP, SCOTTY

I might have been brokenhearted and rejected, but at least I didn't have to walk far. Originally, I'd asked Ed if I could borrow his car...or at least the rental he was using while his new car was being repaired. But he'd dissuaded me from that course of action with a very gentle, "Go fuck yourself!"

Thankfully, another of our ensemble had offered a slightly more direct method of conveyance.

I strolled to the end of Sheila's street and turned at the corner. A hundred yards down, a figure sat on a bench at a bus stop. She was pretending to read a book - probably on baby names - by the light of the nearby street lamps. Well, okay; maybe only partially pretending to read.

Who'd have thought that things could change so quickly? Less than six months ago, the sight of Christy would have caused me to hightail it in the opposite direction, then call up Tom and bitch him out for dating a witch with a death wish for me. Now, she and I were quite cool with each other - cool enough that she was able to take me at my word that Sheila had no intention of hurting her, her kind, or especially her unborn child.

I mean, yeah, she had certainly freaked out a bit when my roommates and I sat her down to tell her the Icon was alive and well. Sally had stood there smugly, latte in hand, as Christy's magic flared up, and Ed, Tom, and I dove for cover. In the end, though, she had calmed down and accepted it - well, after bitching Ed out for about an hour for keeping that knowledge from the rest of us. I took immense enjoyment at seeing someone else on the receiving end for a change. Hey, I never claimed not to be petty.

I'd told her how Sheila had made me promise to put her down should she ever start walking down the path of the Magi prophecy - the one that claimed the Icon would be the end of them all. That had seemed to settle her down, along with the fact that upon their first meeting, they had hit it off pretty well.

Christy's only caveat to this revelation was that her new coven not be told of this, at least until such time as it was painfully obvious. I could understand that. The last time mage and vampire alike had suspected the Icon had arisen, they had banded together in a joint hunting party of disastrous proportions.

After we'd gotten a reasonably good idea of where Sheila might be living, it had been Christy's idea to act as my backup on this mission. I wasn't overly pleased at the prospect of dragging her into things with me, since she was becoming increasingly heavy with child, but she was quick to point out the minimal danger of this operation.

"How many monsters do you think will be actively crawling around the Icon's home? If that were the case, the entire supernatural world would know by now. Since they don't, it's a safe bet that she's either really good at hiding or even better at making sure nothing gets out alive to spread the word."

It was hard to argue with that.

I approached openly and she waved when she saw me. While a part of me wanted to be stealthy - one could never be entirely sure who or what was watching - common sense dictated I not sneak up and risk a lightning bolt to the face. I sat down next to her on the bench. "Hey."

"Hey yourself." She put down the book.

"Any good ideas?"

"A few."

"I hear Bill is an awesomely studly name for babies these days."

"Not if it's a girl," she countered. I was tempted to point out former Doctor Who companion Billie Piper as an excellent example, but she continued, "And if it's a boy, I'm already leaning toward Harry."

"Ugh."

"I know you two had differences."

I turned and raised an eyebrow.

"Okay, some pretty major differences, but he was good to me up until he became obsessed. I prefer to remember and honor him for the father figure he was."

I wasn't in the mood to argue. "Whatever floats your boat. What's Tom's take on this?"

Her sigh relayed everything.

"Oh, come on. Starscream or Mumm-Ra might be perfectly serviceable middle names."

"Remind me not to invite either of you to the baby shower." She laughed, but then her expression turned serious. "How'd it go?"

"She said to say hi."

"You told her I was here?"

"No. It was just a general thing. Her passing on her regards."

"Good. She's going to be paranoid enough knowing one person can find her. If she thought another vampire and witch raiding party was on its way..." She trailed off, closing her eyes for a moment. The whole incident had been painful for her too. Both her master and the entirety of her old coven had been wiped out during it. "Oh well, I didn't really want to be invited in for tea anyway."

"You'd have liked the place; could have met her new boyfriend."

"Boyfriend? Oh, I'm so sorry, Bill."

"It's no big deal," I lied. "I mean, she's young and insanely attractive. I couldn't expect her to wait for me."

"Especially since she doesn't know she's waiting for you?" Christy teased.

"Don't start."

"What's he like?"

"Seemed like a decent enough fellow - nice and normal. An accountant, if you can believe it. You don't get any more banal than that. Pity he can't *rise* to the challenge."

"Rise?"

"Bump uglies, dance the horizontal mambo, make the beast with two backs." I looked at her and flashed my fangs. "Gotta love compulsions."

She sat bolt upright. "You didn't!"

"I might've."

"By the White Mother, that's just wrong." Her tone, however, indicated she didn't find this in the least bit surprising. Her time with Tom had well prepared her for such petty things by immature males. "How long is it going to last?"

I shrugged. "Could be a day, a week, or whenever. Don't know and really don't care."

"Some days, I'm so glad you're on our side. So what about her? Is she going to join us?"

"No," I replied bluntly. There wasn't any point in beating around the bush.

"Did she say...?" She paused and held up her hands. A

bandage was wrapped around one of them. "Just give me a moment." A deep purplish glow flashed around her, then just as quickly subsided. "Anyway..."

"Hold on. What was that?"

"Oh, don't worry about it. While you were in there, I set up warding glyphs at the four corners of this block."

"You don't say."

"Relax. It sets up a magical line in the sand of sorts - tingles in the back of my head if anything crosses it."

"So right now?"

"It was just a cat."

"By the way, what did you do to your hand?"

"Nothing serious. I cut it setting up the glyphs," she replied dismissively. "So did she say why?"

I relayed to her my discussion with Sheila, including her reasons for turning down my offer to go asshole-hunting.

When I finally finished, I expected Christy to share a similar sentiment with me that this was anything but...

"Good," she said.

"What?!"

"Not *good* that she's not going to help, but her choices are all for the right reasons. I think she's correct. The role of the Icon is to defend, not attack."

"Bullshit. All the Icons I've heard about: Achilles, Beowulf, Samson, Joan of..."

"All of them met with bad ends, most of which were the result of their own arrogance, if the stories are to be believed."

I thought about that for a moment. She had a point. Many of the heroes of old that we celebrated in myth, legend, and the occasional movie starring Brad Pitt - they made for an awesome adventure tale. In the end, however, they all died young, often in very violent scenarios. Even so... "I haven't heard of any Icons who did otherwise."

"I have," she replied. "Harry insisted I study the past - the *real* past - very carefully." She didn't need to elaborate much on that. History was written by the victors and then whitewashed by the victors' descendants. Magic and monsters had been neatly removed from the official histories. In the few places where they remained, they were assumed to be myth or allegory. "There were many Icons who stood tireless watch as defenders of kingdoms. You just don't know about them because..."

"Because they don't make for a good story?"

"Exactly. What would you rather read about - a stalwart defender who held the line and eventually died in his sleep at the age of ninety-nine or a manly action hero who went out in a blaze of glory?"

"You do have a point."

"I don't know exactly how the vampiric prophecy is worded, but I'm familiar with some versions of it. From what I know, the battle between the Icon and Freewill isn't supposed to be like some cheesy wrestling match."

"A pity. Throw some Jell-O into the mix and..."

"I'm *serious*. Both sides aren't supposed to come at each other in some macho, *mano-y-mano* slugfest. If I were to make my best guess, the Freewill is the aggressor with the Icon only taking the battlefield after all of humanity's other hope is lost. That she's taking this stand fills me with hope for her. She's not going out there headhunting to collect trophies. She's not doing this to get her name in the paper. She's doing this because she *has* to."

I may not be the most empathetic guy on the planet, but I sensed a bit of desperate hope in her words. I couldn't help but notice her hands went to her stomach as she spoke. It wasn't surprising. An Icon who was a conquering hero was bad news for her kind. An Icon just trying to stem the tide and save as many people as she could, well, that type of hero was far less likely to be in the market for baby-killing.

I put a hand on her shoulder, as comforting a move as a guy like me knew how to make. I was more used to confronting the impending darkness with some pithy comments. Stuff like this was out of my league. If she started crying now, I would have no choice but to panic.

We sat like that for a moment, both of us no doubt wondering how we could possibly stave off the cruel destinies fate seemed to have in store for us all.

Finally, I broke the silence. "Fine, Sheila's out. If this is the part she's going to play, I won't try to dissuade her from it." I left out that any such talking would likely include me mumbling like an idiot, all the while trying not to stare at her all doe-eyed. It really ruined the cool image of us as a badass supernatural couple.

Oh well, at least I had the memory of her in that towel to keep me going for a while as I charged headfirst into horrific danger - and that's certainly what I still aimed to do. Facing Vehron without her by my side was a prospect that was near pants-shittingly terrifying. Even so, it needed to be done. I'd released that genie from its bottle and, knowing how the vampire nation had reacted to such slights in the past, I had every reason to believe it was going to be up to me to put him back - preferably in as many little pieces as I could muster.

"It's gonna be tough without her," I said at last. "But the plan hasn't changed. We still need to find a way to take that asshole down. Let's get back to New York. Maybe between Sally and me..."

Christy eyed me skeptically. I got no respect whatsoever.

"Fine, mostly Sally. Let's just apparate out of here before I decide to go back and beg."

"I told you, that's just in the books. We don't apparate, we..." Her phone pinged, interrupting her.

"Something cross the magical barrier?"

She glanced at me like I had two heads. "It's a cell phone, not a magic wand. That was my text alert."

I turned away, caution draining from me in an instant. It was probably Tom asking her something unimportant - hopefully. I found myself silently praying it wasn't something else, like him sexting her. God, I *really* didn't need to know what he wanted to do to her with his tongue, as if he hadn't already shared such tidbits in gruesome detail.

I heard her typing in response, followed by another ping as the other party replied again. Oh, crap. I made it a point to keep my eyes away from the screen and to try to think of anything else.

Unfortunately, there was only one thing for me to think of. Despite everything - the war, the danger that Vehron represented, all of it - I couldn't focus on anything but *her*. There she was, just a couple hundred yards away. She had a house, a boyfriend, a *life*. I tried desperately to push down the jealousy I felt at both the normalcy of it all and the fact that someone else was sharing her bed. I wasn't sure if she was happy or not, but at least she was trying. And, by God, or whatever deities currently looked down upon me with raised boots, I reached deep down inside and found myself hoping that she succeeded. No matter what happened, I wanted her to be happy. If she could have that, then I could live vicariously through it - knowing that no matter what evils I faced, she was somewhere out there with a smile on her face.

In the meantime, I'd do whatever I could to shit on the papyrus the prophecies were printed on and make sure I went against whatever...

"Time to go," Christy said, putting her phone back in her purse.

"Huh?" I pulled myself from my reverie. "Please tell me he's not wearing a leopard print Speedo."

A look of confusion passed over her face. "What?"

"Never mind." I stood up and offered her a hand. "Shall we get our butts back to Brooklyn?"

She grasped my hand with hers, stood, and closed her eyes. "Nope. There's been a change in plans." A glow began to surround her...no, make that us.

"Wait...what?"

Unfortunately, a torrent of light swallowed up whatever answer she may have had as we were whisked away into the nothingness.

6

THE NEW DIGS

As usual, the feeling of being - oh fuck this, I didn't care what she called it - *apparated* was a bit disconcerting. Imagine being someplace one moment, then being nowhere the next. For just a split second, I was nothing but mist surrounded by more mist. Then, just like that, I was spit back out into the world as if being birthed through a pinhole. It was pretty fucking freaky.

I steadied myself, not wanting to look wobbly in front of a pregnant witch who seemed to take the entire experience in stride. I blinked, expecting to see my living room or some other familiar setting, but then I remembered Christy's statement just before we zapped out of existence. What the fuck had she meant by "change of plans?"

The room swam back into focus around us and I had to question her words even further. The grey walls, slop sink, various mops, and shelves of toiletries spoke of only one conclusion - we had reappeared inside of a janitor's closet. Was this some kind of joke by my roommates or, even worse - was it some sick kink of Tom's? If he thought

I was gonna stand around while he plowed his girlfriend in a bathroom stall, he was out of his fucking...

"Not bad. She did a halfway decent job," Christy commented.

"Huh?"

She glanced down in response and I followed her gaze. We were standing in a circle of sorts, drawn on the floor with what looked to be a Sharpie. There were four additional symbols drawn outside of it at equidistant points.

"The four elements at the four corners of..."

"It's a circle. It doesn't have corners."

"Hence why you would make a lousy mage," she shot back.

"Sorry, I don't dance naked in the moonlight."

"And for that, we are immensely grateful," a familiar voice said just as the door leading out of the small room opened from the outside.

"Let me guess," I said to Sally. "You wanted to help us come back, but also needed to take a massive shit and couldn't decide which was more important?"

She rolled her eyes, surveyed the rest of the room, then rolled them again. "Considering your conspicuous lack of the Icon, I'd say conjuring you up in the shitter was pretty damn prophetic of me."

"I can explain..."

"Do it later. Probably best we don't hang around here having a powwow." She turned and stepped out.

"Why?" I asked, following, but any other comment died in my throat. The *why* was pretty goddamned obvious. The distinct lack of urinals told me all I needed to know. Most women didn't take kindly to male intruders within the ladies' room.

Sally stopped to turn back and address Christy. "You're welcome to come along. You can stop in and say hi, rest up a bit, and grab a bite to eat before heading back."

I waited patiently for the punchline. It wasn't like Sally to just make a...well...*nice* offer without at least hinting at some horrific outcome. Much to my surprise, though, there was no snarky rider to what she'd said.

"Thanks, but I have enough juice to get back. Besides, I've been gone long enough already. My sisters are warding the apartment, but as priestess, I need to get back and oversee their work."

"You don't look like a reverend to me," I joked.

"It just means I'm the leader, the elder mentor of the coven." She turned back to Sally. "That other one is beginning to worry me. Please tell me you brought him with you."

"Yeah, about that..." Sally trailed off into silence, grinning in a way that said she'd screwed something up but didn't really care.

"Who are you talking about?" I asked. "Not Dave, right? He's..."

"Gone," Sally replied flatly. "Guess I should've reinforced a few extra compulsions into him. I didn't realize he'd just up and leave."

"He can't...he's not covened...he..."

"I know," she snapped, "but there isn't anything I can do about that right now. Orders are orders. He'll either be fine or he won't. It's out of our hands."

"What orders?"

Sally ignored my question and addressed Christy again. "Take care. Stay in touch. If anything gets too weird..."

"I know," Christy replied. "May the White Mother bless you both." She raised her arms and began to glow. "I think we'll need it," she added right before vanishing.

Sally stood and watched the light of the magic fade away. "I have a feeling we're gonna need a lot more than that. I hope her White Mother has a father, brother, and some cousins too." She turned and walked out, leaving me momentarily alone in the ladies' room.

Ah, the mysteries that were mine to explore. Sadly, I had no idea where we were, nor how long it would be until someone barged in, took a look at me, and called the cops to report a perv hiding in the stalls. Fuck! Why is it when I'm finally someplace cool, there's never any time to make good on it?

I quickly checked my pockets, but sadly didn't have a pen on me. Goddamn it! I couldn't even scrawl my cell phone number on the wall along with a message like *"Call Bill if you want cock for days."* I always wondered if something like that would work.

Oh well, I guess I'd have to keep wondering.

Thankfully, a quick check of the surroundings confirmed there was nobody but Sally present, so I stepped out of the restroom and moved away from the door to give myself some plausible deniability in case anyone showed up.

"Let's go." She started walking. "This place is supposed to be for employees only."

"Compulsion?"

"Nah. The only workers I ran into along the way were all male. No challenge required."

That wasn't too hard to imagine. Sally was a petite thing, just barely over five feet in heels, but she made up for it by being stacked in all the other places that counted. She was stylish, sexy, and had a body that I would've happily run my tongue over for hours - if I thought I could do so and live. Her blonde hair was slightly past shoulder length and usually highlighted with some color to give it a little zing. Electric blue seemed to be the highlight of the week, and I caught myself stealing glances at it - amongst other bits.

Sally wasn't just good looks, though. She also possessed a keenly dangerous mind and an attitude that could've sunk a destroyer faster than any torpedo. All combined, she put the fatal into femme fatale. I could only picture what a terror she must've been even as far back as high school - probably Kelly Bundy on amphetamines.

The nicest part of it all was that by walking alongside her, I probably automatically jumped up a few notches for any other woman who happened to notice us. Who says all side effects are bad?

We turned a corner and I could see that the hallway stopped ahead - the area beyond opening up, *way* up. I realized I still had no idea where we were. We had teleported out of my living room on my Sheila-quest and I'd expected to return there. Instead, I glanced at the throngs of people moving back and forth, the luggage in their hands, and the various signs pointing toward gates.

"Airport?"

"Yep." She kept walking, her pace deliberate, as if she knew where we were heading. Oh, fuck; not another plane. Since becoming one of the undead, my luck with airlines had been piss-poor at best. No matter where I was, no matter who I was with, I always seemed to end up traveling as a piece of fucking luggage. I'd wound up stuck in the freaking baggage hold for the entirety of the bumpy trip last time. First class it most certainly wasn't.

I was about to start grousing when we passed an interesting sight. It wasn't all of the old people sitting around that caught my eye. That in itself was pretty common. It was what they were sitting in front of that made me do a double take: a row of slot machines. I knew New York was always hard up for cash, but...oh crap. No way! We had work to do back east. We couldn't be where I thought we were.

"We're not in La Guardia, are we?"

"Nope."

"JFK, Newark...maybe one of those shitty little puddle jumper airports?"

Sally stopped in her tracks and raised an eyebrow, refusing to tell me what I suspected. Instead, she reached into her purse and produced a quarter, which she held out to me. "Might as well try your luck. Something's gotta eventually go in our favor."

Needless to say, I didn't walk out of McCarran International Airport, primary transportation hub of Las Vegas, Nevada, an instant millionaire. I did, though, manage to get some dirty looks from the old folks who'd been playing. Fucking geezers think they have squatters' rights to any one-armed bandits in sight.

Following my lost chance at an early retirement to a desert island where I might have ridden out the end of the world in peace, I stopped and asked Sally, "Why are we here?"

"I just arrived myself."

"Oh?"

"Yep, and the place we're headed is warded against sendings, so I figured beaming you guys here made sense."

"Yeah, let's get to that 'here' part. Spill."

She grinned shrewdly, the tips of her fangs barely poking out between her lips. "Doesn't work that way, I'm afraid. You first."

"But..."

"Seriously, what happened with your girlfriend?"

We stared at each other for a few moments in a silent battle of wills, her green eyes boring holes through mine. I had the feeling she'd stand there for an eternity rather than give way - goddamned stubborn bitch. Oh well, fuck that. I'm sure to some my going first would look like a sign of weakness - capitulation against a superior foe. However, it was a means to an end lest we wind up standing there all night looking like two star-crossed lovers refusing to say goodbye.

Oddly enough, that thought lingered in my head for longer than it should have. Oh well, it was probably a side effect of my heart being crushed like a paper cup. I quickly pushed it aside as I told her a greatly abbreviated version of my story, mostly sticking to Sheila's reasons for not wanting to join us. Unlike Christy, Sally didn't seem overly pleased at Sheila's logic. A look of annoyance showed on her face when I was finished.

"Fuck," she spat softly. "I was afraid she might do that. Doesn't help that she's probably still squirrely from our last little adventure."

"Yeah, I got a bit of a sense of that."

"Any trouble?"

"None at all."

"Good, then you still have that vial I gave you?"

"Uh...not exactly."

"What do you mean?"

"Well, there was a little bit of trouble."

"A little bit?" she asked dubiously.

"Yeah, she had a..." I mumbled the rest.

Her face stretched into a wide, shit-eating grin - enough so that I would have gladly staked her for that alone had I a weapon in hand. "She has a boyfriend?"

"Maybe."

"Her own personal pipe-layer."

"Listen..."

"A man willing to deliver the sausage whenever she gets a midnight craving."

"Okay, I get the point."

"So did you kill him?"

"What?!" I stopped and looked around. Thankfully, my little outburst hadn't attracted any attention. I lowered my voice. "No, I didn't kill him."

"Then what?"

"I might've...compelled him."

"That blood was only supposed to be for an emergency, Bill."

"What? Protecting the Icon's virtue sounded like a pretty big emergency to me."

She got a pretty good laugh out of it in the end. "There's hope for you yet."

"Maybe," I groused. "Just probably not with her."

"Her loss."

"Really?"

"No." Bitch! "It's probably for the best, though. If she'd said yes, we'd have been in a bit of a pickle."

"How so?"

Sally made it a point to weave into the densest part of the crowd as she spoke. It was all I could do to use my enhanced hearing to concentrate on weeding her voice out of the many others around us. "Orders from on high. They came in right after you left."

"On high?"

"The very top - the Draculas."

Oh, crap. "Who called?"

"Colin; who else?"

"Were these new orders from James?" We hadn't heard anything from him since he'd left my apartment, still nursing his wounds following the fall of the Boston complex. Mind you, that wasn't too surprising for me. I was lucky if I heard from him every other month. Sally, though, seemed to be able to reach him whenever she needed to. Go figure - when a perky blonde calls, guys answer.

"Nope." She stepped to the left to avoid a couple that was paying more attention to their squabbling kids than where they were going. "Colin made it a very specific point to let me know that this came from the First Coven as a whole."

"I bet he enjoyed that."

She glowered at me, her sour look saying it all. Colin was a grade-A dick. Even with the world crumbling around us, he was still more than willing to grease it up and stick it in whenever he could.

"I assume that has something to do with why I'm two thousand miles further west than I thought I'd be."

"They knew what we were planning to do."

"What? How?"

"Relax. Just us; nothing to do with who you were going to see. They assumed that we'd be working on a half-assed plan to head back north and put a shank in that asshole."

"Rightfully so," I pointed out.

"Yeah, I guess we're getting easy to read. Anyway, they were very specific. We were not to do anything of the sort."

"How specific?"

"Of the 'we're watching you and there will be consequences if you even think about it' variety. I was told we'd better have our asses on a plane heading west by the time he was finished hanging up on me."

The "we" part of that line caught my attention. That was good. It meant they hadn't been savvy to my plans to make contact with Sheila. Although I'd been uncomfortable including Christy, it had been the smart thing to do. If Colin had been telling the truth, and I had no real reason to doubt he was, and had I opted to drive to upstate New York, they'd have probably tailed my ass right to her doorstep.

How was that for irony? I'd been trying to tell Sheila she had nothing to fear from me, while at the same time, it had just been dumb luck that I hadn't led the vampire nation straight to her. Maybe she was right about her decision after all.

"That's kind of odd, don't you think?" I asked, trying to push thoughts of Sheila from my mind for the time being as I continued pushing through the crowd.

"Which part?"

"All of it. Usually, the Draculas are far too happy to throw me to the wolves." I stopped when I noticed that a young boy walking alongside me had looked up at my mention of the D word. "Errr...I'm talking about a movie I saw." I quickly hurried my pace to catch up to Sally. "Also, it sounded like James was pretty sure they'd be keen on icing this guy as quickly as possible. What happened to that?"

"That's what I thought too, but Colin wasn't overly forthcoming with information. It was pretty clear this was one of those disobey-at-your-own-risk-type things."

"It's not like you to..."

"I pick my fights. Making more enemies when we still haven't killed the old ones didn't seem like my idea of a smart strategy." She glanced out of the corner of her eye at me. "Don't worry. I have a feeling we'll be pulled back into the loop when they're good and ready to do so. For now, let's just enjoy the break."

At last, we reached the front of the terminal. Sally stopped and looked at me expectantly. Almost without realizing I was doing so, I opened the door for her and we stepped out into the warm night air.

"Not bad," she said. "Maybe you're not a lost cause after all, but we still have a lot of work to do if I'm gonna whip your ass into shape."

"What do you mean by that?"

She began walking again. After a moment, it became obvious her destination was a long black limo waiting at the curb. A tall man with thinning blonde hair held the door open for her. Just as she reached it, she turned to face me. "Welcome to Pandora Coven, Bill Ryder. Mind your manners."

"*My* manners?"

"Yes. I'd suggest you remember that from here on in, the game has changed."

"Oh?"

"For starters, I'm in charge. Don't worry - if you forget, I'll be sure to remind you."

Oh, crap. I had a sinking feeling I was better off letting Sheila disintegrate me.

7

ALL SETTLED IN

The flimsy plywood gave way as my body slammed through it. It wasn't the hardest I'd ever been hit, but it had been perfectly placed, catching me straight on the jaw. I probably could have either blocked it or stepped out of reach before it had connected, but alas, I'd been too busy enjoying the expression on Sally's face. What can I say? Some things just never stopped being funny.

Of course, humor was a relative concept when one found oneself in an uncontrolled thirty-foot freefall at the hands of a pissed off vampire. On the upside, at least I didn't have to worry about hurting anyone other than myself. The squatters had figured out weeks ago that the main stage was best left clear of people and possessions.

There was likewise no need to fret about interrupting any dancers in the middle of a set. Tragically, it had been over a month since the last pair of tits had been flashed on stage to the beat of trashy music. That's when the main power had gone out for good and the denizens of Vegas had been forced to stop pretending that everything was fine and dandy - that the weirdness of the outside world would just pass them by.

Three months had passed since Christy had teleported me here. At the time, one could have almost pretended that everything I'd seen in New York had just been my imagination. This city had seemed so normal at first, relatively speaking, of course. Now, those times were over and it was starting to look like a set piece from a Mad Max movie.

Those were thoughts for another time, though. The condition of the world as a whole wasn't my main concern right at that moment.

I landed hard on the formerly mirror-polished stage - now marred by scratches, scrapes, and a body-sized crater that marked the landing place of most who dared test Sally's wrath.

Oh well, at least the ballistic glass that once covered the window looking down upon the club hadn't been replaced. That shit kinda hurt to be flung through. Thankfully, custom, bulletproof, one-way mirrors were in short supply these days.

"You know she doesn't like to be called that."

I pulled myself to a sitting position and turned to find Kara's grinning face staring back at me. Tom's younger sister was cute in all the ways her brother wasn't. Unfortunately for her, he made up for that by still living in all the ways she was no longer capable of. She'd been turned into one of the undead at some point in the recent past, under circumstances that I still wasn't entirely clear on. Regardless, I sure as shit wasn't going to be the one to break it to my oldest friend that his sibling was now Sally's bloodsucking sorority sister.

I stretched and felt my vertebrae snap back into place - ouch. "I think you'll find that I have no problem calling our illustrious leader whatever the hell I please."

"Your funeral."

"Smart girl," Sally's voice carried down to us from the now open portal above. "Now get the fuck back to work."

Kara muttered something under her breath before scampering away. It was probably a petulant dig at being ordered about. She tended to do that a lot, but Sally mostly pretended not to hear her, oddly displaying an extra dollop of tolerance for her antics. Of course, maybe that was just relative to what she afforded me.

"Care to rephrase your earlier statement?" Sally grinned as she peered down from above. Oddly enough, clocking me usually seemed to help improve her mood. Go figure.

A momentary temptation to nod respectfully passed through my mind, but fuck that shit. Our roles might've been reversed from back in our Village Coven days, but all that meant to me was I could give her a dose of her own medicine - something that *always* improved my mood. "Yeah, I was thinking maybe we should just quit with the foreplay and move right on to the sex. Sound like a plan, *Lu*?"

Her eyes flashed black with annoyance. "How's this for an answer?" She ducked back in, and I heard the sound of wood scraping against wood. By the time I put two and two together, her desk was already crashing through the remainder of the plywood and headed my way.

I rolled to the right and fell off the stage just as it landed where I'd been sitting a moment earlier, shattering into pieces and greatly widening the crater in the middle.

Some people just had no sense of humor.

I was still dusting myself off when Sally came downstairs. While there was little doubt she'd put on a show for all the eyeballs present, I could also tell whatever real annoyance she'd felt had already burned itself out. Had she been serious about chewing me a new asshole, she'd have taken the express route from above - probably landing far more gracefully than I had. Instead, minutes had passed and I saw that she was taking the time to acknowledge some of the refugees as she walked by them.

As much as I wanted to make a douchey comment about that, I couldn't. Despite her iron-bitch exterior, she'd continually surprised me by showing what appeared to be genuine concern toward the welfare of most of the humans here.

Most being the operative word. It certainly didn't go unnoticed that some had just up and disappeared - there one day, gone the next. Usually, it was troublemakers - people that the others wouldn't be sad to see leave. I wasn't quite so naïve to believe they had conveniently moved on, though. At the end of the day, this was still a coven, and there were vampires that needed to be fed.

Sally sure as shit hadn't reformed to the point of becoming Mother Teresa. Even so, I found myself growing fond of seeing her human moments, although I wasn't about to admit it out loud.

She walked up to me and put her hands on her shapely hips. Despite the rapidly deteriorating state of the world, she somehow still managed to appear both kempt and fashionable - no doubt thanks to her personal stylist and fellow Village Coven refugee, Alfonso. Sally was only willing to go so far when it came to suffering for the cause. "Have I made my point?"

She'd asked her question loud enough to get the attention of the room. It wasn't surprising. Since joining her in Pandora Coven, she'd continually reinforced that showing any weakness wasn't an option for her. I could respect that, but it still didn't mean I cared to lie down and play dead at her whimsy.

No matter what title she held, she was still Sally to me. More so, lately I had a newfound appreciation for our time together. Our banter had always been like a game between us, but it was one that I took increasing comfort in - regardless of the often painful side effects. Who knows? Maybe it was my time spent alone in Alex's dungeon, or the impending end of the world, but I'd been making it a point to be more mindful of the good times as of late.

Even so, there was no way I was bending over and taking her shit. I opened my mouth to reply with something guaranteed to piss her off when we were saved by the proverbial bell.

"We have visitors," a voice called out. "They look official."

We both turned toward the source. Steve, her other lieutenant in the coven, had relayed the news. He was tall, thin, and pretty much all business - definitely a yes-man, but I couldn't deny he often got results. Needless to say, I had to listen to Sally constantly crowing about him. It would have become quickly grating had I not been certain that was exactly the reaction she was going for.

"Check them out," she instructed him.

He turned back toward the entrance of the club and disappeared, nary a comment made. There's always gotta be one kiss-ass in the crowd.

I raised an eyebrow. "Vamps?"

"Or shape-shifters," she replied tersely, our little spat apparently over for now.

In the weeks prior, the few visitors we'd had could mostly be compartmentalized into two camps: things trying to kill us and those seeking protection from the things trying to kill us. The former were usually not overly subtle, but there had been a couple of near disasters - enough to make everyone a bit paranoid.

The ugly rock monsters that inhabited the storm drains beneath the city - the Jahabich, or whatever the fuckers were called - made for pretty good doppelgangers when they wanted to. They'd tried more than once to gain entrance that way, but had failed mainly because we weren't complete fucking idiots. No matter how human something looked, if it smelled like a pile of shit-encrusted granite, chances were it was getting blasted to hell. Pretty simple rules to live by, all in all. Even so, the damned things kept trying, so it made sense to keep our shields raised at all times.

After a few minutes passed and we noticed no gunfire or other such pleasantries exchanged, we made our way to the entrance hall. Steve was reentering the building, followed by five others. Two were ours - guards. They stood flanking our guests. Even with so-called friendlies, one couldn't be too safe.

I didn't need to catch their scent to conclude the three newcomers were vamps. Most humans who came looking for sanctuary were in pretty dire straits, usually lugging the tattered remains of their belongings with them. Decked out in their black suits and trench coats, it almost seemed these guys hadn't noticed the world going to Hell around them. Judging by their bored expressions, they found Armageddon about as interesting as watching moths fly into a bug zapper.

We'd gotten official visits before. The Prefect of the West Coast, a vampire named Yvonne, was known to send her representatives every so often. Sometimes, they came with orders. Occasionally, they came to check on how we were holding up. Rarely did they come with supplies, though.

The two in the rear carried a large cargo container,

roughly seven feet long by about three feet wide and deep, between them.

"Is it Christmas time already?"

"Could be," Sally commented by my side.

The lead vamp, sporting an overdone mustache and goatee combo that made me wonder if he was going to start bartering for our souls, stepped forward. "Coven Master Sally, I presume."

"You presume correct," she replied.

His eyes strayed in my direction for a moment, looking as if he wanted to say something, but then turned back toward her. I seemed to get a lot of that lately.

"We have been ordered to provide safe passage to your newest charge."

"My newest charge?"

"Yes. We are delivering an assignee to your coven."

I glanced toward Sally and her eyes met mine. They asked the same question I was thinking: *What the fuck is this joker talking about?*

"I didn't realize Yvonne was in the habit of pre-stocking her covens," Sally said. "If I'd known, I'd have baked a cake."

"We are not from the Santa Clara complex."

"Oh?"

"Orders from the First Coven," he replied. "For security and safety reasons, the designee has been placed under your command."

"Security and safety?" I asked. "Whose?"

"They didn't elaborate." He produced a thick sheet of papers from his jacket and held them out. Ye gods, even in the middle of the freaking apocalypse, the rulers of the vampire world loved their goddamned paperwork.

Almost as if sensing my disdain, Sally took the bundle from our visitor and passed it over to me. "My assistant will see that these are properly filed."

I took hold and promptly tossed them over my shoulder. "Filed. Can we open our present now?"

The look on the other vamp's face was priceless. Typically, that sort of thing would mean an instant beating at the hands of an elder, but I had little doubt these clowns knew who I was. Maybe I wasn't the prophesized flavor of the month anymore, but I still had enough of a reputation that most vamps wouldn't start shit with me if they didn't have to.

Sally, for her part, was wearing an expression that was halfway between exasperation and amusement. She liked the official bullshit about as much as I did, but still had an image to maintain. Concealing the barest of grins, she addressed the lead vamp. "Do you have anything else for me?"

He shook his head.

"Okay, then. Steve, provide our guests with some refreshments and then show them the fuck out."

Needless to say, her skills as a hostess had been somewhat strained these past several weeks.

Steve, being a far better subordinate than I, nodded for our guests to follow him inside - most likely to the bar. There was no point in ticking off the Draculas over something as silly as failing to offer their lackeys a little hospitality.

The two holding the crate let go unceremoniously, and it landed with a heavy thud. A muffled curse sounded from within.

My eyebrows shot up at the seemingly familiar cadence. Nah, it couldn't be.

I held my tongue until the undead delivery boys left the room, leaving Sally and me alone with the package. "Did that sound like...?"

"Only one way to find out." She stepped up to the crate, extended her claws, and shoved them under the lid.

One quick heave later and the nails holding the top shut squealed against the wood as they gave way to her strength.

The cover clattered to the floor and we found a very familiar face staring angrily back at us from within.

"It's about fucking time. I couldn't breathe in this thing."

Smiling broadly, I offered a hand to help our newest *recruit* out. My eyes glanced toward Sally. "So what do you think? Return to sender?"

"Nah," she replied, a wicked grin forming on her face. "I think this one has possibilities."

8

THE NEWEST MEMBER OF THE TEAM

"I would never presume to speak for our voluptuous coven master," I said, earning a glare from Sally, "but I think it's safe to ask for both of us: what the *fuck* are you doing here?"

"You mean besides the fact that vampires are assholes?" Ed asked, looking none too pleased despite being out of the packing crate and having a nice stiff drink in hand.

I could sympathize, having traveled as a boxed lunch before. The shiner on the right side of his face further drove the point home. "Let me guess - they didn't ask nicely?"

"Oh, they did...once." He lifted the shot glass and drained its contents in one gulp.

"Need something for that?"

"Just a couple of aspirin and the names of the vamps who grabbed me." He reached across the bar for the bottle of Scotch, but Sally pulled it away before he could grab it.

"Sorry, shipments of single malt are a little behind these days. Besides, I don't recall opening a tab for you." Her voice was only semi-serious, although I knew there had been several thefts from the booze stockpile as of late -

mainly because I was the one doing most of the stealing. "Now, if you two are done stroking each other off, let's get down to business."

She got up and walked out, her meaning clear - follow. There were too many prying ears around, both human and vamp, and they'd probably heard too much already.

There would no doubt be questions as to his *recruitment* status. Ed's condition was...well, weird. Bitten by a former Templar turned vampire, he'd been saved, if just barely, by Sheila's healing touch. However, something had gone not so much wrong as *off* with the process. Ed had returned to the land of the living, but it would have been a lie to categorize him fully under the species *sapiens* of the genus *Homo*. His blood was now somehow infused with the power of faith, making it extremely lethal for the undead to partake of. At the same time, though, James had casually remarked that Ed still had some vampire taint - his words, not mine - upon him.

The problem was most of the vamps who'd been witness to Ed's power since then had either exploded, freaked out, or gone batshit insane with the desire to kill him. How that translated to him being here, though, I had no idea.

Sally closed the door to her office and sat in her chair, which now stood in the middle of a mostly empty room, her back against the formerly gaping portal overlooking the club. It had once again been hastily covered with plywood, at least until the next time I pissed her off. She ignored Ed's look of confusion and gestured toward a couple of other seats in the room.

"Don't ask," I mentioned to him as we sat.

"Smart of James to send you here," she said.

"James?" I asked. "How do you..."

"He's the only one who makes sense. Calibra is still a prisoner, Vehron wants him dead, and Colin wouldn't spare him two thoughts if he was the last blood-bag left on the planet."

"That doesn't really add up," Ed replied.

"Actually, it does," I said. "Remember that bullshit story he gave the HBC about you, how you were some sort of half-assed biological weapon?"

"Don't remind me. He was talking like I was some sort of fucking virus."

"Don't feel bad. To most vampires, humans pretty much are," Sally replied. "Tasty viruses, but that's beside the point. I don't pretend to know how James thinks, but I can probably surmise the rest. Bottom line is nobody knows what the hell you are. You might be just another human waiting to be squashed like a bug..."

"Thanks."

"Don't mention it. Or you could be useful. If you do have some vampire still in you, it would be utterly unprecedented."

"You'd be a daywalker," I said, grinning.

"Yep..."

"Or a gaywalker."

"Fuck you," he growled.

"See what I mean?"

Sally sighed. If she still had a desk, I had little doubt her fingers would be digging furrows into it at my asinine comment. She was so cute when she was annoyed beyond...

Purity is key for the First. He shall be your downfall.

Ed jumped at the outburst from Harry Decker's skull, now sitting on a bookshelf off to the side.

"Oh, hush up." Sally stood up and started looking for something amidst the clutter.

"Still holding on to that thing?" Ed asked.

"Of course."

"Well, I think the batteries must be going," I commented. "That made no fucking sense to me. Anyone have a clue?"

Harry Decker had been a wizard with a hard-on for killing me. Unfortunately for him, his obsession had ended badly. Sally had retrieved his skull as a gruesome souvenir, unaware that it still had some residual magic left in it. Every so often, it blurted out some prophetic bit of gloom and doom for us. More often than not, it would come to pass, but lately it had apparently been getting desperate. Its last warning - something about us being washed away in a sea of our own sins - had foretold nothing worse than the second floor toilet overflowing. Even in death, Decker was still a dick.

"Maybe we're out of hand sanitizer." Sally found a towel and tossed it over Decker's skull like it was some kind of fucking parakeet, then turned back to us. "Getting back to the point at hand, any way you look at things, it costs James nothing to take a few minor precautions to keep you alive until such time as we can figure out what role, if any, you play in this mess. Also..."

"Yeah?" I asked, when she didn't continue.

She leaned forward. "You don't repeat this or I make matching earrings from your scrotums. Got it?"

We both nodded.

"I think it might be James's way of thanking us for saving him."

"Then why didn't he just..."

"He can't. Technically, he should have died at Vehron's hands. We stepped in and stopped that, but knowing the Draculas' fucked up logic, he still had to publicly shit on our actions - like we soiled his honor or something. This way, he kills multiple birds with one stone - he saves face *and* helps us."

"He could have just said that," Ed complained. "Instead, he sent a trio of goons to stuff me into a box the second I stepped out of the apartment."

"Appearances are everything to the Dracs," I offered by way of explanation.

"Yeah, well, appearances are pretty big for me too...especially since I look like I just lost ten rounds in *Fight Club*."

"Aw, I think it looks kind of cute," Sally said flirtatiously. "Gives you some character."

"Really?"

"Yes, really," she replied, almost causing me to gag on my own bile. "Don't get your hopes up, though, big boy. All things considered, I don't foresee us swapping bodily fluids anytime soon."

Ed looked crestfallen for a moment, but then, much to my horror, he replied, "Never discount the magic of prophylactics."

Oh, Jesus Christ, they were *not* doing this with me in the room!

"Sorry, stud," she said, "but I've always been a bareback kinda girl."

"Okay, can we get back to non-disturbing topics, like vampires wanting to crush my roommate's skull in?" I fixed both of them with a glare of death. Goddamn, I really didn't need to be the meat in this sandwich - a continual reminder of my own lack of immediate prospects. "Speaking of roommates, is Tom okay?"

"Better than okay," Ed replied, thankfully dropping the subject of boning Sally. "The tenants in our old place have been moving out in droves. Most of Christy's coven took over their leases. I won't lie. Living in witch central does translate into a better night's sleep these days."

"Cool. Any of them single?" I asked half-heartedly.

"I hate to interrupt," Sally interrupted, "but it's time, Bill."

"What?" I looked at my watch. Fuck! "C'mon; can't we skip a day? I mean, it's practically a celebration here."

"Then you can celebrate downstairs. Now let's go." She stood and pointed to the exit.

"What's up?" Ed asked, confused.

"Only the most hilarious part of my day. You're welcome to come along if you want. There's nothing quite like watching Bill's combat training."

9

TRAINING DAY

I'd been pretty down in the dumps when I'd first joined Pandora Coven. It stung finding out that Sheila had moved on. The only thing keeping me from blubbering like a little baby had been the misconceptions I'd had about my new gig.

In between fights for survival in an increasingly hostile world, I figured I'd at least get some downtime surrounded by multitudes of T&A. That's only logical, right? You get a job at one of the premiere strip clubs in Vegas and you expect a few perks, like heavily discounted lap dances. Things like that can go a long way toward mending a broken heart.

Not so much with Sally as the proprietor. It didn't help that, unlike Village Coven, most of the vamps under Sally's rule were a by-the-book bunch. Sure, there was Kara, but Sally had read me the riot act before we'd even first stepped through the door - not that she needed to. I mean, jeez, she was Tom's baby sister. It's not like I would've thought...well, I would've *thought* about it, but I wouldn't have tried - much.

My next mistake was in thinking my various interactions with the other vamps would be the same. I'll admit to having run Village Coven fairly loosely. Usually, I'd show up on the weekends, grouse about how Sally was fucking things up, yell at anyone for being too...well...vampiric when it came to hunting humans, and occasionally sit around and watch the more attractive members jiggle for a little while. All in all, it wasn't a particularly demanding gig - minus the occasional assassination attempt, coven war, mage bombings, and the like.

I had been considered the coven master on paper, but Sally had been my partner all along, so I assumed our relationship would continue along that path. In that, I was likewise wrong. These days, if she said I needed an ass-kicking, my status as the formerly unique Freewill didn't mean shit.

I contemplated this as I slammed upside down into the solid concrete wall. Judo was quite the effective combat technique. Adding vampire strength to it made it utterly brutal - cool to watch, but a lot less fun to experience.

"Again."

I peeled myself off the perpetually damp floor. The subbasement wasn't technically a part of the sewer, but was connected to it. As a result, the humidity was always high and there was always an ever-so-slight background smell of ass. In short, it was gross. Painful, too, because Sally didn't believe in using mats.

I turned and faced the large vampire who'd tossed me. He was a big guy, about six-foot-four and a former bouncer, according to Sally. His name was Brock, but I always referred to him as John Holmes behind his back - mainly on account of the ridiculous porno-stache he wore. Jeez, one of these days I was gonna have to break it to this guy that the seventies were over. For now, though, I did as

Sally ordered and once again approached my larger, and much better trained, opponent.

It wasn't quite boot camp, but Sally insisted on a training regimen for all vampires under her leadership - especially me. Don't get me wrong - some of it was cool. I mean, watching Kara and the other girls train was great fun in a *Dolemite* or *Sin City* sort of way. The mental image of walking into a strip club, failing to tip one of the girls, and receiving a proper kung fu smack-down in return was an awesome one.

Where I was concerned, though, it mostly just hurt.

Brock and I began to circle each other in the dim torchlight of the subterranean enclosure. He was larger and more skilled, but he wasn't a very old vampire. Although the concept was somewhat laughable, I actually had a small leg up on him in terms of strength. He was also a petty goon, possessing far more brawn than brains. So, in theory, this was a fair fight.

In actual practice...

"Sweep the leg!"

I turned to where my roommate stood watching the sparring match, a smirk upon his face. "What the fuck are you...?" and found myself airborne again. Fucking dickhead. I was an idiot for having even acknowledged him - especially since he'd been doing the same goddamned thing nearly every day in the two weeks since he'd arrived.

Sally walked over to where I lay and looked down upon me. "Distraction is the enemy."

"So is being a smug bitch." I reached out, grabbed her ankle, and knocked her legs out from beneath her. It was petty as all hell, but I got a shit-ton of satisfaction watching her ass smack down on the dirty concrete.

Brock opened his mouth to laugh, but caught himself before it could escape. He might've been built like a moose, but I'd seen Sally take on bigger and badder foes.

Ed wasn't quite so discreet, and a quick huff of laughter escaped his throat. Normally, a glare from Sally would've silenced him. We'd all played that game, but before she could react, Brock was across the room and had slammed Ed against the far wall by way of his throat. Shit! Never underestimate a vampire to either puss out or look for an opportunity to suck up to a superior.

"Humans do not laugh at their betters," he snarled.

I'm sure Ed would've had something to say had his windpipe not been in the process of being constricted. I scrambled to my feet, ready to peel Brock off of my friend, but Sally beat me to the punch...figuratively, at least.

"Drop him," she said casually as she stood and dusted herself off.

"He dared to mock you," Brock replied, flashing his fangs at Ed.

My roommate turned a sickly shade of purple as way of response.

"Then he is mine to punish. Not yours."

"But this human..."

"Is a member of *my* coven," she interrupted, making no move toward him. She could've torn him apart, but I began to understand that some challenges were best won with words. Psychological scars could run much deeper than physical ones, especially for a species that healed as fast as we did. "I have decreed it, and so has the First Coven. Are you trying to tell me you disagree?"

Brock hesitated for a moment, uncertainty on his face. Heh. Vamps were suckers for name dropping. Finally, he let go of my roommate, who doubled over and sucked in a great gasp of air, the color returning to his face.

"Now get the fuck upstairs," she said in an even tone as she turned away dismissively. "And take the others with you." She walked over to the far corner to a small weapons locker, where she put in the key, then punched in a code to unlock it. She began rooting around inside of it as if nothing out of the ordinary had just occurred.

Brock glared at Ed, but that was the extent of his bravery. Rather than risk pissing off Sally any further, he nodded toward the two vampires standing guard at the massive metal gate that led to the tunnel connecting the subbasement with the sewers. Together, they climbed up to the club's storage room. A few moments later, the booming sound of the heavy trapdoor shutting rang out in the room.

Sally bent over the weapons locker for a moment longer, a distinct dirt stain showing on the ass of her jeans from when I'd knocked her down. Oh yeah, target sighted. When she stood up straight, she held three weapons in her hands. She walked over to Ed and handed him one. "Brock is going to give you shit again."

"So you want me to plug him with this?" he asked, hefting the Glock. "I prefer my shotgun."

"No, that's for target practice. We're doing that next."

"Oh. So, what, you want me to tell you if he tries anything?"

"Yeah," I added. "You could put him under that ninety-day protection thing, like James did for me."

Sally rolled her eyes, then turned back to him. "Do I look like your mommy?"

Ed appeared to contemplate a response, but then reason took over and he kept his mouth shut. Sally was, after all, now armed.

"Don't wait for it. I want you to start in with him first. Then, when he gets nice and pissed, let him bite you."

"What?!" Ed and I cried in unison.

"You heard me. The others aren't going to take your coven status seriously otherwise. They're either gonna think you're a thrall or my pet, regardless of what I say. I have little doubt that an example will need to be made.

That being said, I'm not willing to leave such a sacrifice to chance. Brock is, to put it bluntly, both an asshole and a coward. He won't be missed, and this way, he'll be doing the others a service in his passing."

"Damn, you are cold," I commented.

She tossed one of the handguns to me. "You have no idea," she said as she raised the one she still held and shot me in the kneecap.

The subbasement was pretty well insulated, so it made for both a perfect vampire sparring ring and makeshift firing range. Thus, it was no surprise at all that my screams didn't attract any undue attention from the club. I'm sure some of the squatters still living in the tunnels close by heard it, but by now, they were probably so used to odd noises coming from the direction of Pandora's Box that they took it in stride.

Thank goodness too. I so dislike bothering people when I'm experiencing the agony of a 9mm slug slamming into my leg. I'd hate to *inconvenience* anyone into doing anything silly, like racing to my side with a first-aid kit.

The pain finally abated a bit as my healing kicked in. The sight of the bullet being pushed out of my knee as the flesh and bone knitted itself back together almost distracted me from the agony. On the upside, at least it hadn't been a silver bullet. If that were the case, I would've spent the next several hours crying for my mother like a little kid on his first foray to sleepover camp.

"Overreacting just a little bit?" I growled when I could finally trust my tongue again.

"Not at all," Sally replied as she topped off the magazine on her handgun. "I was actually impressed by your counterattack. It tells me you've been paying attention."

"Then why..."

"The bullet was for doing it in front of Brock. Did you see that fucker's face?" She held up two fingers side by side. "He came *that close* to laughing at me. I don't need that shit from the newbs."

I glared at her, then eyed the gun she'd tossed my way before the screaming had begun.

"Not recommended," she chided. "Your fighting has gotten better, but you still shoot like shit. Speaking of which, get your ass up and let's go. I don't have all night. I want to be done before the next patrol gets back."

Sally had her patrols down to a science, or so she claimed. Every day, at varying times, a group of five would head down into the sewers - two mages and three vampires. Their mission was simple: hunt down and eliminate any Jahabich, or however you pronounced it, that they found. The random timing was in case our foes started to grow wise to the strategy.

The Jahabich were nasty fuckers; shape-shifters whose true forms were that of granite-bodied monstrosities with glowing orange eyes and obsidian teeth that made vampire fangs seem very inadequate by comparison. According to Sally, they'd first appeared in the tunnels beneath the city when those freaky storms had started, following our fuckery up in the Woods of Mourning - the place where we'd accidentally started a supernatural war. Their attacks had originally seemed to coincide with the storms.

After decimating the population of homeless that lived beneath the streets of Vegas, they'd eventually grown ballsy enough to target the casinos themselves. Around that time, Sally had somehow come into mastery of Pandora Coven through means she never really fully explained to me.

She'd somehow convinced the population of Magi that called Vegas home, mostly masquerading as stage magicians, to team up with her and begin fighting back.

Things now stood at a stalemate of sorts. The patrols had cleared most of the upper tunnels of the ugly dickheads. In fact, their presence seemed to be diminishing now that those supernatural storms were hitting with far less frequency. Sadly, the end of the storms, rather than signaling positive change, indicated that the two sides of the war were done flexing their muscles and were now ready for a good, old-fashioned, world-ending throwdown.

The only question now was: how much longer were we expected to sit here in exile of sorts? The power might be out, but we could still catch the occasional radio report to know how things were going. With towns disappearing left and right, swallowed by forest, I had to think the vampire nation would eventually want us to do something a bit more productive than sewer patrol.

"Sally has a point. You *do* still suck."

"What? I hit the target almost a dozen times."

"And missed it almost five dozen."

"You shouldn't talk," Sally said to Ed as she cleaned her weapon. "You were right; you should stick to a shotgun."

"Told ya."

A noise from off in the sewer tunnel caught our ears. Well, mine and Sally's anyway. "What time is it?" she asked.

I glanced down at my wristwatch - thank goodness I'd invested in a rugged sports model. "Almost ten."

She nodded. "Kristofer's team should be heading back

about now." She reached into her pocket and tossed her key ring to me, which I caught. "Want to go let them in?"

"Sure." I walked down the ramp that led to the tunnels beyond. Normally, it would be manned almost twenty-four seven. All of the vamps under Sally's banner got a turn at guard duty - well, all except for Sally herself. Bitch!

The only time guards weren't stationed at the post was typically when she and I trained. It would give us a chance to talk without the overly sensitive ears of other vamps listening in and hearing something that they shouldn't. The side benefit of this was twofold: there were no eyewitnesses for me to embarrass myself in front of, and it gave Sally and me some alone time - something that I'd been increasingly enjoying despite her often violent disposition. Of course, now Ed had started joining us during these sessions. There's always gotta be a third wheel.

Anyway, in the time I'd been here, the Jahabich had only made it to the tunnel once, and it had been short lived. A pair of the creatures was fried in their tracks before they'd gotten halfway through. Nowadays, the only ones who approached the gate were either returning patrols or the occasional homeless squatter.

That last part was a mindblower, I mused as I reached the gate and peered through it to the dark tunnel beyond. Thanks to Sally's patrols, the homeless had returned to Vegas's tunnel system, but they mostly stayed close. If there was an issue or any sightings of the rocky abominations, they knew to come tell us. In return, although she wouldn't have admitted it had Alexander himself compelled her, she would occasionally give any food rations we could spare to them.

Go figure. Sally helping humans - the same Sally who ran a fake suicide hotline back in New York to lure unsuspecting victims. Now she had somehow become their guardian angel. For perhaps the thousandth time, I wondered what the hell had transpired during the months I'd spent as a prisoner in the vampire stronghold of Switzerland.

Oh well, there would be time to bug her about that - *again* - later. Hell, I had all of eternity to weasel it out of her.

I hunkered next to the gate, looking down the tunnel beyond for any sign of our returning patrol. It wasn't an exact science, sadly. There was the possibility I'd be there for a while waiting, although hopefully not too long, as I kind of had to take a piss.

Sally and Ed wandered off to the far end of the room to talk, probably some pointless flirting on his part with a lot of eye-rolling and violent innuendo on hers. Talk about a pairing fated to end badly. They were a match made in Hell even before I'd gotten taken prisoner - or at least that's how it was for Ed. He was like a little mouse being toyed with by a crazy blonde cat. Now things were different. Ed's blood was a lethal cocktail to vamps. That didn't bode well for a relationship with a woman who admittedly liked to get bitey.

There was also the immortality factor. Though nobody, Ed included, knew the extent of the changes that had been wrought upon him, there was nothing I'd seen so far to indicate his lifespan was any different than it had been before. In all likelihood, he'd be dust in a grave while Sally was shaking her ass at the dabo tables of *Deep Space Nine*.

Hah, that was a good one. Was it really any different than my situation with Sheila had been? Goddamn, we must've all had rocks in our heads. At least she had been smart enough to hook up with a human, someone she could potentially grow old with. Ed would be wise to do the same. As for Sally, well, the life of an immortal was bound to be a lonely one. I mean, sure, if we all somehow survived the end of the world, I'd be there to annoy her for the rest of...

The thought caught in my head. Us together for centuries, maybe longer? Whereas once the concept would've made me cringe, now I found it oddly comforting. I mean, I sure as shit wasn't Harry Potter, and Sally definitely wasn't Hermione Granger by any stretch of the imagination. Should the opportunity ever arise to bang her, you wouldn't see me turning that down. Even so, I had never really considered the concept of...*us*.

I glanced back toward where she and my roommate continued to converse and was surprised to find some ugly emotions swimming in my head, ones I seemed to be experiencing with increasing frequency where their relationship was concerned. I finally recognized it for what it was...jealousy. I'd felt it before, but always assumed it had been little more than a case of him making inroads with a hot babe while I was still a single loser.

Nah, that was crazy talk. Sure, Sally was attractive beyond anything I aspired to ever date, but she was also a crazy dangerous bitch - a mass murderer. Even so, she was also one of the smartest people I knew, seemingly always several steps ahead of me. There was also the fact that she had a wicked sense of humor - *wicked* being the operative word.

I shook my head. What the fuck was I thinking? Ever since I'd first laid eyes on Sheila, I'd been in love with her. Nothing had changed in that regards...except that she was living with another guy, one she seemed to be pretty cozy with, while I'd spent the past few months learning to accept that and move on.

Wait...*move on?* Had I actually allowed myself the possibility of thinking there could be someone else in my life? I'd spent so much time pining for her that it didn't seem I'd ever...

Argh! I so didn't need this right now.

"Open the gate! They're coming!"

The frantic cry from down the tunnel dragged me back to the here and now. Someone rounded the corner from the sewers beyond and raced toward my position. Two more soon joined him. Despite still needing my glasses to focus, my eyes cut through the darkness and recognized them as the group we'd sent out - or at least part of them. There were three vampires, but none of the mages who'd gone out with them.

As they neared my location, more shapes entered the tunnel behind them - misshapen creatures with eyes of pure orange fury.

Oh, shit!

I scrambled to unlock the gate while screaming over my shoulder, "Sally, we have incoming!"

The loud boom of the trapdoor opening above indicated she had raced up the ladder to the club. Hopefully, she was hauling ass for reinforcements, because the creatures were gaining. Goddamn, for stupid rock monsters, they sure could move fast when they wanted to.

"Come on, come on," I muttered, simultaneously to our people and to myself while struggling with the heavy lock. I managed to swing open the gate just as the vamps reached it. Kristofer and his crew dove through, and I slammed it shut again, managing to lock it just as the group of angry Jahabich crashed into it. The entire structure shook, but it had been built to last - heavy steel, sunk deep into concrete.

"Close, but no cigar, fuckers!" I stepped back from the gate, not wanting to tempt fate. "You guys okay?" I asked over my shoulder a second before the mildewy smell of the creatures reached my nose.

"*Yes, we are more than okay now,*" a gravelly voice responded.

What the?

My blood turned even colder than usual as I spun to find Kristofer and the other two vamps standing there smiling. Sadly, gone were their normal white fangs and teeth. Black spears of obsidian jutted out in their place.

Oh, fuck!

10

A ROCK MONSTER AND A HARD
PLACE

For a moment, I just stood there, trying to absorb what had just happened. The faces the creatures wore seemed to melt away, reforming into their native shapes. Their heads tripled in size and their mouths grew to accommodate the stalagmites that passed as their teeth. Their eyes sank in until a strange orange glow, like a fire burning somewhere deep inside, replaced them. Perhaps worst of all was seeing their fingers thicken and consolidate until their arms ended in heavy, jagged clubs.

Yeah, this day had just taken a turn for the worse.

Why is it always on my watch?

Three on one sucked, but thankfully I'd locked the gate. I risked a glance over my shoulder...oh, fuck - it was much better than *a lot* against one.

How the hell had this happened? We'd seen these things assume the shape of people before, but never of anyone we knew.

Alas, any such answers weren't forthcoming as the nearest of the beasts swung its arm club. I sidestepped in the nick of time to watch it clank off the gate behind me, sending up a shower of sparks that I was surprised didn't catch my hair on fire.

"You're supposed to yell 'It's clobberin' time!' first."

"*You are the Freewill*," one of them said in that rock-salt gargling voice of theirs. "*We will enjoy you.*"

Enjoy me? Why did that sound like it had a sick sexual undertone to it? Well, fuck that shit. I wasn't into being pegged by giant talking dildos.

The creature came at me again and its buddies decided to join it this time. My only chance was to survive long enough for Sally to get back with reinforcements.

These things might've had twice the girth of linebackers, but fortunately, they weren't overly tall - barely Sally's height. That gave me at least something to work with.

I backed up a step to the gate. The creatures beyond bellowed with rage, but the openings in it were too narrow for them to reach their appendages through. They weren't too small for me to get a foothold on, though. I planted a sneaker and kicked off, using my awesome undead strength to propel myself up over the ugly heads of the monsters in the room. I doubted I'd score a perfect ten on the landing, but it would give me some breathing room to maneuver while...

...while I got properly fucked.

Three things happened nearly simultaneously. A gunshot sounded, the report deafening in the enclosed area. Sparks flew as something ricocheted off of the furthest creature's back, and then fire exploded in my gut as the bullet decided I'd make a much more impressive target - airborne as I was.

It wasn't heavy caliber - another of the 9mm weapons we'd been training with, but it certainly ruined any chance

I had of sticking the landing. I hit the slick concrete floor with a meaty thud as I clenched up into a ball to keep my innards from leaking out.

"Oh, fuck!" Ed cried. "I'm sorry, Bill."

"Don't mention it," I croaked, silently thanking several pantheons Sally didn't insist on practicing with anything bigger.

I would've said more, but one of the Jahabich brought its arm down onto my shoulder in a crushing blow, shattering my collar bone and decimating several square feet of skin from my body. Man, and I kinda liked this shirt too.

Risking a glance up, I saw the creature raise its arm again. Who'd a thunk it? After all the bullshit - after Jeff, Turd, Alex, Vehron, even Gan - a stupid pile of masonry was going to do me in. I was sure somewhere those blind seers that had made all those bullshit prophecies about me were laughing their eyeless asses off.

I braced myself, hoping the sensation of my skull caving in wouldn't hurt too much. Then, just as the creature brought down the massive club of an appendage, it shape-shifted again. It was only partial, but it morphed its hand back into that of a human. It reached down, dug into my pants pocket, got a wee bit too personal with my junk, then found what it was looking for and pulled back, its prize in hand: the key to the fucking gate.

I actually found myself rooting for them to finish me off because if Sally caught wind of this, I'd have to hear about it for a long time to come.

The thieving Jahabich smiled down at me, the meaning clear - it meant to open the gate and let its buddies in to have all sorts of smashy fun with my skull.

Just then, another shot sounded. Oh, shit! Was Ed trying to finish the job he'd started on me?

Instead, the bullet hit the monster right in one of its glowing orange eyes. The creature's head snapped back and it roared. Unfortunately, it was more of a cry of rage than an "I'm about to die like a good defeated foe" sound. It was hard to tell if any real damage had been done, but even so, Ed's bullet bouncing around in its skull had definitely pissed it off good and proper.

Sadly, the nearest projectile to hurl at my roommate just so happened to be me. The Jahabich delivered a massive kick to my midsection with its cinderblock of a foot, pretty much ensuring a liquid diet in my near future.

I flew across the room, causing Ed to dive out of the way lest I use him as a human air cushion to stop my flight. Once again, I found myself slamming into the wall, this time at a much greater velocity. I had the briefest glimpse of my blood splattering out in a Rorschach pattern before ending up face down on the ground.

My roommate was there in a split second. "Are you okay?"

"Nothing three months in a body cast won't cure," I mumbled as his hands grasped me under the shoulders and begin to haul me into a sitting position. Normally you're not supposed to move trauma victims until the EMTs arrive. However, I doubted any ambulances were on the way. Besides, those rules kind of went out the window where vampires were concerned. We could absorb a massive amount of punishment and still bounce back. The only problem was it all still hurt like a motherfucker.

As he propped me up against the wall, I happened to glance back toward our attackers.

Oh, shit!

The two other creatures who'd slipped by my defenses were headed our way. Guess they weren't taking any chances. Behind them, the first one, arm still human - and looking pretty fucking ridiculous sticking out of its nearly spherical stone body - was busy unlocking the Gate.

Double shit!

"Get out of here," I said to Ed, my voice stronger as my healing finally began to kick in. "They want me."

Instead of running like he should have, he turned and took aim with the inadequate weapon again.

"That won't work, stupid."

"You got a better idea?"

"He doesn't, but I do," a voice called down from the open trapdoor above us. It was Sally, and she wasn't alone. All right!

She jumped the distance to the floor, landing nimbly. In her hands she held a sledgehammer that looked massive next to her small frame.

The first creature reached her and she swung with everything she had, connecting with the side of its head and sending shards of rock flying everywhere. The beast staggered back and she turned to face the second one.

Figures began to descend the ladder. Judging by the mystical symbols on the robe one of them wore, we were finally bringing some real firepower to this fight. Sally wasn't trying to win, just keeping the opening clear for the big guns to make it down.

There wasn't much I could do yet to help her, but that didn't mean I couldn't provide assistance in my own way.

"Go, She-Thor!" I yelled. What? Cheerleading is a perfectly acceptable backup solution in a fight.

The mage made it to the bottom of the ladder, steadied himself, and shouted something that sounded like "*Magnos Ignise!*"

Sally immediately hit the floor as a wave of red hot energy lanced out from the wizard and struck the two monsters. One was hit head on and immediately fused into the world's ugliest sculpture. The other monster was somewhat luckier and managed to dodge enough so that only the right side of its body caught the full effect. Even so, it was obviously out of the fight; its legs melted to the floor and half its body cauterized solid.

Sadly, any victory we might have experienced was short lived as the last of the invaders managed to unlock the gate and swing it wide open.

One moment, it looked like we were about to win, and in the next, a tidal wave of living stone began rushing toward us.

11

WHAT MOTHER WANTS, MOTHER GETS

There was no doubt in my mind this was a planned offensive. In the months since I'd been with Pandora Coven, nearly all of our run-ins with the Jahabich had been in small numbers - never more than three at a time - which was good because three of them were difficult enough. No way was this just a random incursion.

It was hard to tell from where I sat, as all I saw was a wall of granite advancing on our position, but I was pretty sure at least ten more of them swarmed through the gate. It wasn't quite an army, but I suspected it was more than they needed to get the job done. Whatever happened next, I had a feeling the subbasement was now lost to us.

The mage managed to flash-fry another of the things before three more got past his defenses and were upon him - clubbing and biting. They shredded him almost instantly. It was a gruesome way to go. Sadly, there wasn't time for a proper eulogy. Hell, we'd all be next if we didn't get the fuck out of there fast.

Sally swung the sledgehammer in a violent arc. She

struck one of the monsters full on, knocking its teeth right the fuck out. Goddamn, she was hot.

Unfortunately, she was about to be flanked too. Screw that shit. No fucking way was that happening on *my* watch.

"Get up the ladder," I growled at Ed as I pushed myself to my feet. Thankfully, my healing had kicked in enough so that I didn't immediately fall back down on my ass.

One of the creatures swung, trying to coldcock Sally in the back. I threw myself at it in a dive tackle, taking it in the midsection with my shoulder.

It was like running into a brick wall, but thankfully, I had momentum on my side. I shredded more skin in the process, but managed to knock the creature off balance.

I put a hand on Sally's shoulder and she immediately spun, still on the attack. Fortunately, I saw it coming and ducked before she could crack my skull like a melon.

"Let's go," I said, trying to avoid letting on how close I was to shitting myself.

"We have to hold..."

"We can't defend like this. Up the ladder, *now!*" I'd completely disrespected her authority in front of whatever eyeballs happened to be looking down upon us, but I didn't give a single shit. She could always kick my ass later to save face if she needed to. For now, we had to move.

Multiple beams of red-hot magical fury rained down from the open trapdoor. Upon seeing their fellow mage fall beneath the rampaging Jahabich, the rest of Sally's reinforcements had hightailed it back upstairs - smartly so. Once there, they'd thankfully regrouped so as to give us cover fire, quite literally. In the past, I'd had some not-so-great dealings with wizards, but right then, I would have gladly kissed each and every one of them - and we're talking tongue too.

"Ed, up first!" I commanded.

"I'm not..."

"You're the squishiest one down here. Get upstairs or I'll club your ass myself."

He looked down at his gun for a nanosecond as if contemplating getting a few more shots off, but then thought better of it. Thank goodness! I wasn't keen on taking any more ricochets for the team.

He got to the ladder and began making his way up it. The wizards continued firing from above, but their death beams were more spaced out so as to not hit any of us in the crossfire.

Sadly, the Jahabich hadn't received the memo about the rules of war. When the enemy lays down cover fire, you're supposed to duck. Instead, they continued to push forward.

I punched one in the side of the head, probably doing more damage to my hand than anything, while Sally managed to club the shit out of another with her hammer. Just then, one swung a haymaker. I jumped back, the blow just missing taking my nose clean off, but Sally wasn't so lucky. The creature's club-like arm clonked her near the top of the head, nearly scalping her in the process. Blood flowed freely, and she went down hard.

Motherfucker!

"Goddamnit!" a voice cried from above.

"Don't..." But my warning came too late. Ed leapt off the ladder and landed beside me.

I love my roommates like brothers; they are truly the best. But Jesus Christ, what a pair of dumbasses they could be!

Oh well, there'd be time to bitch him out later. We knelt where Sally lay dazed and each grabbed an arm to haul her up.

Positioning her at the ladder, I said, "If you're in there,

Sally, get your sweet ass climbing." With that, I hauled back and gave her a hard slap on the rear to get her moving. I was gonna pay for that one, but it was worth it if we all lived. Also, damn, she really did have a tight little bottom.

She had just climbed high enough to let another person on when the horde of Jahabich broke through the blasts of fire raining down from above and bum-rushed us. I kicked out, driving one back, but it wasn't nearly enough to keep them from surrounding us.

They dragged Ed into their ranks and I was about to follow when a massive pain flared from the top of my head.

What the fuck?

"Stop fighting me, Bill."

I glanced up to find that Sally had mostly regained her composure - gotta love that vampire stamina. She was trying to save me. Unfortunately, her way of doing so was to yank me up the ladder by my hair. I didn't exactly mind the rough stuff, but the hair pulling was supposed to be a side dish for slightly more fun activities.

Oh, and there was also Ed to think about.

"Let me go!" I warned, struggling to free myself from her iron grip. "I have to..."

"What?" she asked, a hint of sorrow slipping past her iron façade. "Die too? We have to regroup."

Helpless, I watched as the creatures converged on my friend. He looked up at me and his eyes said it all. This was his swansong and he knew it.

I cried out as the monsters swarmed him while Sally continued to drag me up to safety against my will.

"*Wait.*"

The horde stopped almost instantly at the granite-like voice's command. *What the hell?*

Sally paused in her ascent, equally as confused, to watch as the beasts took a small step back - all except one.

In dragging him away from me, the invaders had all but beaten Ed to hell. Blood ran down both arms, his chest, and the side of his face, but he was still alive.

The creature who'd stopped the others leaned in and made an odd gesture with his head, almost like he was sniffing Ed - despite the lack of any visible nostrils.

My roommate, in return, showing that in a bad situation his ball-sack outweighed his brainpan, hauled off and punched the monster in the jaw. The brisk **crack** that followed, along with a string of curses that would have made Quentin Tarrantino blush, was testament to the fact that his knuckles were likely pulverized on impact. As for the creature, it didn't even budge. Ed might as well have smacked it with a damp noodle.

The brute reached out with one of its club arms and held it under my roommate's dripping face. Ed's blood sparked ever so slightly where it splashed onto the creature. Sadly, that was all it did. Whatever effect the faith-imbued plasma had on vampires, it obviously didn't do nearly the same to these fuckers.

"*This one is pure,*" the creature gurgled. "*The one Mother told us about.*"

An assembled acknowledgement of "*Mother*" rose up from the beasts, almost reverently so. The hell?

"*She will want him,*" it continued. "*We will bring him.*"

"The fuck you will!" I shouted from my place on the ladder.

Every single one of the creatures swiveled their heads in my direction, some of them a good one hundred and eighty degrees - talk about creepy. All at once, a dozen pairs of soulless, lantern-like eyes bored into me.

"*We still want this place,*" one of the others said. "*We want all of them.*"

The creature who'd sniffed Ed opened his mouth wide in the most gruesome of grins. "*Yes. We will have all we want and more.*"

That didn't sound promising.

I could see Ed's mind working a mile a minute, looking for some way to slip past his captors, but it was a short-lived effort. Almost as if sensing what he was going to try, Sniffy turned back toward my roommate and head-butted him, knocking him clean out. Another of the walking rock piles tossed him over its shoulder and the two made their way back to the tunnel entrance.

"Fuck this shit," I growled. "There's no way we're letting..."

"Uh, Bill," Sally said from above me. "You may want to pay attention to the big picture."

"What are you...?" The words died in my throat. Two of the creatures were leaving, but the rest now swarmed in our direction.

Well, this had gone to hell quickly. And the day had started out so nicely too.

12

PANIC AT THE STRIP CLUB

I was loath to abandon my friend, but Sally had a point. He was alive for some reason, but these monsters didn't seem to have a similar fate in mind for the rest of us.

Muttering several unkind words under my breath, I scrambled up the ladder after her, making it to the opening a split second before the creatures plowed into it. The only good part was that they might be vaguely humanoid in appearance, but the Jahabich were as heavy as their rocky appearance suggested. Each of them weighed in at close to half a ton, if I had to guesstimate based on the pummeling I'd just taken. There was also their lack of digits with which to grasp...

Oh yeah, they were shape-shifters too. Well, fuck that shit.

"Thinking the same thing I am?" I asked Sally as I pulled myself up through the trapdoor.

"Way ahead of you," she replied.

As a duo of wizards squeezed in with us, shooting straight down - cauterizing at least one of the beasts into place - Sally and I each grabbed one side of the heavy ladder and ripped it from its moorings. It tumbled down into the subbasement, clattering as it landed on a few of the monsters below.

"How do you like that, assholes?" she spat before addressing one of the assembled Magi. "Feel free to take some target practice."

"My pleasure," a middle-aged man, dressed in far more normal attire than the last mage, said.

He and two others crowded around the open portal while Sally turned to the rest and started barking out orders. "Get Steve in here. I want him to assemble a rescue..."

"Um...I think you'd better look at this," the mage said, backing up from the subbasement entrance.

"What are you...oh fuck me," Sally growled. "You have *got* to be kidding."

"What?" I pushed my way back in to see. The Jahabich couldn't fly - or so we hoped - and they weren't particularly suited to climbing ladders. However, they could make one fucking awesome inhuman pyramid.

Using the ones at the bottom who'd been fused solid as a base, the others climbed up, forming tiers upon which yet more stood. It didn't take a genius to realize they'd easily make it up to our level with that tactic.

Sally shoved me to the side and grabbed hold of the trapdoor. It was heavily armored against unwanted entrance, but it wouldn't be nearly enough should several of the creatures start pounding the shit out of it.

The look on her face said she suspected as much, but she slammed it shut with a heavy clang nevertheless, sliding an inch-thick deadbolt into place.

"What do we do?" I asked.

She addressed the crowd rather than me. "We gather every fucking vampire and wizard in the neighborhood and defend this place for as long as we can. Get ready; they're coming."

At first, we thought we had them contained. Though the creatures were able to reach the trapdoor in short order, it was a chokepoint. We'd set up a staggered defense around it - mage next to vampire. As the creatures pounded through, the mages would blast the fuck out of them. For any that managed to make it past that, it was the vamps' job to knock them back.

In the past few months, Sally had made it a point to stockpile anything that even remotely resembled a weapon. Guns, at least anything short of a bazooka, were mostly useless against the Jahabich, but where firearms failed, the garden department of Home Depot stood tall. Hammers, hatchets, pickaxes, and the like were the flavor of the day - as well as goggles all around. Flying chips of granite in the eye were painful as all fuck.

For an hour and a half, we managed to hold the line, but then I realized that the ones we'd blasted into statues numbered greater than the amount who'd originally burst through. They were still coming, and with the gate wide open, they could keep doing so. Who the hell knew how many of those things lived beneath the city? There could have been a couple dozen or it could have been an entire army.

Worse, our mages were starting to get tired. Wizards and witches were dangerous as all hell, but they were like double-barreled shotguns. They could do a lot of damage up front, but had limited ammo. Once they were out, they were basically just humans who liked to chant in Pig Latin and run around naked under the harvest moon.

Sally had sent runners to ask for more backup.

Although one could almost be fooled into thinking the streets of Vegas were almost normal during daylight hours, all of that changed after dark. The casinos rapidly became something akin to city-states once the sun went down. The various bosses ran them almost like kings, keeping them locked up tight and providing protection for the people under them - continually trying to fortify their defenses. God only knew what would happen once food began to run out.

Regarding those defenses, though, as it turns out, Vegas was also home to a sizable portion of Magi. Back before things had turned to shit, they'd naturally gravitated here as a place that was almost a Mecca of sorts for stage magicians - the perfect cover for a true practitioner. Over the years, some had become more ingrained in the system, augmenting the technological security systems some of the casinos used to catch cheats. Some card counters were damn clever, but I had to imagine the surprise on their faces when they were caught, never suspecting magic behind the scenes.

In the past month, Sally had been working hard to forge some mutual defense agreements. Some of the Magi were already on board with us, knowing that those fucking rock monsters were rapidly replacing roaches as this urban sprawl's number one pest. In other cases, the casino...oh, fuck it; let's be realistic here...the *mob* bosses would loan us out their magic users for our patrols. In return, we'd provide some vampire muscle for various jobs - some simple and others, I had little doubt, less savory.

The problem was, no backup came this day. Hell, most of Sally's messengers hadn't even returned. The few who did spoke of some grim shit indeed. Further down on the Strip, Mandalay Bay and the Mirage were both burning. Over at the MGM Grand, they were firing on everyone approaching - friend or foe - and that was just the tip of the iceberg.

The tidbits of news we got back all pointed to the same thing: the Jahabich had hit in force at multiple locations. We'd gotten complacent, thinking they were no better than a random monster encounter in D&D, when in reality they'd just been probing our defenses and waiting for the right moment.

As for why now was that time, I had no idea, nor was I given a chance to think it over. A few of the human refugees in the club happened to overhear what was going on and, before Sally could do anything, panic had broken out.

I'm no hero, but before running like a pussy, I try to form a plan. Doesn't always work out, but I at least try. Not so with others. Word spread like wildfire while the rest of us were still trying to keep those monsters from getting a foothold upstairs. The next thing we knew, Kara came running in to let us know a group of about thirty humans had rushed the doors from the inside and gone screaming off into the night.

Fucking idiots.

Between the Jahabich, the trigger-happy paranoia in the streets, and the nearby desert, there were a whole lot of ways for a person to meet a bad end if they ran off half-cocked. Hell, that didn't even count any other nasties that might be lurking nearby. Our ancient enemies, the Sasquatches, were mostly forest dwellers, but a brief trip to Mongolia about a year back had taught me they had no problem with desert terrain either.

Unfortunately, we couldn't fight this battle on two fronts and hope to win. Sally may have become a bit more user-friendly in the past few months, but that didn't mean she'd become soft. The only bleeding hearts in her nature were literal ones from those who pissed her off. Without hesitation, she ordered Steve and Kara to secure all ground-level exits. Anybody who approached who wasn't either a mage or coven member would receive exactly one warning shot before being turned into human - or otherwise - Swiss cheese.

I didn't like what she was doing but found myself unwilling to argue against it. Not too long ago, she'd read me the riot act, telling me that shit was about to get real and I needed to either man up or destiny would run me down. Little by little, I was beginning to see what she'd meant. I'd always favored neutral-good characters in my game campaigns, but I had a feeling that before everything was said and done, I'd find myself dallying with darker deeds.

Regardless of any of that bullshit, the Jahabich kept coming. Each time they made it up, they smashed at the stone around the trapdoor, widening it. More and more of them began to push against our defenses as our wizard friends started to blow their loads.

And then it just stopped.

One moment, I was trying to pry a pickaxe out of a rock monster eye socket in a desperate bid to counter another trying to flank me, and the next, a sound like some giant clearing its throat came from below. One by one, the Jahabich stopped to listen before opening their own mouths to repeat the noise until it became a massive chorus. I'd like to say I kept pounding away at the fuckers, using the distraction to my advantage, but nearly all of us backed up a step, wondering what the hell was happening. I can't speak for the others, but I've seen enough *Final Fantasy* battles to expect an enemy to pull a brand spanking new surprise attack out of their ass at any moment. For all I knew, we were about to be hit with some freaky rock monster sonic death beam attack.

Instead, almost as one, they stopped making the sound

and disengaged. There was no retreat, no sense of urgency. They just turned and left as if they'd suddenly grown bored.

Sally returned to us in time to see the last of them falling to the subbasement floor and walking away.

"Did we win?"

"I have no fucking idea," I replied.

One of the mages, having had a moment to catch her breath, stepped up to us and fired a burst of magical energy through the hole in the floor. It didn't have a lot of juice behind it, but it was enough to strike one of the beasts in the side, fusing its right arm to its body. It didn't even turn to acknowledge us. It just kept shambling along until it entered the tunnel leading away from Pandora's Box.

Within minutes, they were gone, almost as if they'd never been there - minus the smashed gate, the rampant destruction, and the multiple burnt Jahabich still standing around like particularly gruesome lawn jockeys.

Gone was the body of the wizard they'd killed, along with any sign of my roommate.

I couldn't do much to help the mage, but I very much intended to remedy that last problem.

DAMAGE CONTROL

A short while later, I surveyed the fallout. It wasn't pretty. In addition to the wizard who'd been overrun, we'd lost two vampires during the assault and a second mage was gravely injured, his survival looking unlikely.

I caught up with Sally, who was in a discussion with Steve near the main stage. I relayed to her this information.

"So that's nine more," she said, no doubt adding the members of our lost patrol to the total.

"Not going to tell me ten?" I asked, surprised. This was the part in most war movies where the commander gave the "He's gone, you need to accept that" speech.

"Not until I see a body...oh, don't look at me that way. It's just common sense. Those things could have stomped him into a greasy smear, but instead, they ran off with him like they were the Trojans stealing Helen."

"I hope they lube up first because otherwise...ouch," I muttered.

Sally smiled, but Steve just glared at me. That one was

all business. My utterly charming personality was lost entirely on him.

"I need..."

She held up a hand to stop me. "What you *need* to do is wait until I can assemble a search party to go with you."

"But..."

"*But*, I don't need your ass lost in the fucking sewers of Vegas," she snapped. "Besides, I might have a plan."

"A plan?"

"Something I've been toying around with in the back of my head, but you need to be patient. We're still calculating our losses."

I gritted my teeth at that, but knew deep down that she was right. "How bad?"

Sally nodded at Steve. He lifted a clipboard that he'd been holding and glanced at it. "At least three more vampire runners didn't return. Also, by last count, we've found sixteen fresh human bodies scattered about in the immediate area alone."

"Ours?"

"Hard to tell."

Oh, shit. That didn't sound promising.

"Put together an exsanguination party," Sally ordered him. "Bag up any that are still fresh and in relatively one piece."

"You've gotta be fucking kidding me," I said. "What are you gonna do, squeeze them like oranges?"

Sally's eyes flashed black. "Could you say that maybe a little louder? I don't think everyone in the fucking city heard you." She quickly glanced around, but thankfully, most of the remaining humans were either huddled with their friends and loved ones or scurrying about helping with the cleanup effort.

"Waste not, want not," Steve said dispassionately.

"You drowned kittens as a child, didn't you?"

"Knock it off," she said to me. "We don't have time for this shit. We got hit with our fucking pants down and lost a lot of resources as a result. We'll do what we need to. Is that clear?"

I was tempted to click my heels together and throw my right arm up in a Nazi salute, but I refrained. I could tell from the sound of her voice that she was stressed, and a stressed Sally tended to be a dangerous Sally...and not just to her enemies. Instead, I simply nodded.

"Good. What's it look like downstairs?"

I would have loved to lie and claim that the second those monsters took off, I was in hot pursuit - chasing after them until they lost me in the maze of tunnels beneath the city. In truth, it was several minutes before any of us dared venture down into the subbasement, long after the sound of the retreating creatures was lost to even my vampire hearing. When we finally did...let's just say we were a jumpy bunch.

It didn't help that the Jahabich we'd beaten were still standing in place. Though logic dictated they were fused into solid lumps of rock, they still looked like they could come back to life at any moment and wallop us good. Twice while trying to secure the ladder back up, I'd almost dropped it, certain I'd seen movement out of the corner of my eye. She didn't need to know that part, though. "At least a dozen statues."

"Any talkers?" The tone of her voice implied that she knew the answer. In the past, we'd attempted to take some of them as prisoners - cauterizing everything but their gruesome mugs. It had been a complete waste of effort. The things could seemingly off themselves at will, quite literally. One moment you'd be looking into those creepy orange eyes and the next, the lights would go out. You'd be stuck with just an overly ugly lump of rock. Apparently, these creatures weren't big on the whole name, rank, and serial number spiel.

The big question was whether they were capable of coming back to life at a later time - like the second you turned your back. Nobody knew the answer to that one, so we'd taken an approach that ensured we'd be better safe than sorry. "Nope," I replied. "And they won't be yapping anytime soon, unless someone heads downstairs with a lot of glue."

She nodded, a tight grin forming on her face. It wasn't much, but knowing that we'd taken down some of them offered a small bit of comfort.

I turned and left so they could continue figuring shit out. I had no doubt Sally would summon me soon to go over her ideas for a rescue mission. In the meantime, I tried to be as patient as possible.

Believe me, it wasn't easy by any sense of the imagination. I had to keep reminding myself that the situation was currently out of my hands. If Ed was alive, it was for a purpose. We needed to figure out what that purpose was and how we could twist it to our advantage so as to extract him. If he was dead, well, no amount of running off half-assed into the sewers would change that.

It was that last part that especially haunted me. Although I tried to busy myself, every second that passed felt like an eternity.

"Jesus Christ!"

"I take it you approve?" Sally asked, a dangerous grin upon her face.

Maybe an hour had gone by, perhaps two, since I'd left to help the others clean up the mess in the basement. Sadly, it was pretty much a lost cause until we could get an acetylene torch - and someone who knew how to use it - down there. Though they'd left quickly, the Jahabich hadn't done so stupidly. They'd taken enough time to smash the shit out of the gate on their way out. The heavy metal barrier was now little better than an over-sized pile of scrap. We'd need to secure things from up above for now or run the constant risk of another ambush.

I was just starting to lose myself in the work when Sally had sent for me. She was up on the second floor in what used to be a lounge reserved for private parties, repurposed as another storage room since things had gone to hell. Looking at the spread before me, it was probably the first time I didn't immediately rue the lack of ongoing lap dances.

"Where the fuck did you get this stuff?"

"Some of it is stolen, some bartered, and a few pieces were even provided by Yvonne."

"Really?" I arched an eyebrow. From what I'd heard, the West Coast Prefect seemed to have about zero interest in us as of late.

"She may be a cold hearted bitch, but she knows that James had a hand in me taking over here. Never discount a little name dropping. Besides, my laundry list was fairly reserved, nothing she'll miss. Oh, you might want to put that down before you kill us both. It's not a dud."

I'd been so wide-eyed at the weaponry before me, a small part of my mind refused to believe they were real. I mean, under normal circumstances, I typically wouldn't pick up a hand grenade and toss it around like a Nerf foot-ball. "Sorry."

"No problem," she said, a mad glitter in her eye. "I feel almost like a kid in a candy store myself."

Something about the look on her face set off some-thing primal in me. A mad image rose up in my mind of me tackling her and tearing her clothes off, taking her good and proper among the piles of ordinance.

O-kay...that was kinda weird.

"You all right, Bill?" she asked. "For a second there..."

"What?"

"Nothing." She quickly averted her gaze. Was it possible she had seen it in my eyes? Nah, couldn't be.

"Uh, yeah. Sorry. Just got distracted for a moment. You do realize I have no idea how to use any of this."

"What's there to know? Pull the pin and throw it before it blows your arm off. Just make sure you mean it."

"How so?"

"Need I remind you you're going to be deep underground?"

Oh yeah. Typically, one didn't want to start blowing shit up when there was hundreds of tons of rock above their heads. "So why..."

"In case it's needed."

She didn't say it, but her meaning was clear. We were planning a rescue mission, but I knew Sally. If things went bad, she was the type who would advise fucking everyone over rather than lose.

And yes, oddly enough, I *was* turned on by that. Go figure. There was something about guns, the threat of violence, and a hot blonde that combined into the perfect ingredients for a mega-boner.

"So what's the plan?" I asked nonchalantly.

"It's easy as pie...a small group goes down, just enough people to put up a fight if need be. You track down the monster's lair, find Ed, and get the fuck out of there as quickly as you can."

"Sounds easy on paper."

"Doesn't everything? Oh yeah, one last detail. Assuming it can be done without collapsing the entire city, blow the shit out of wherever these things are coming from and bury them for another thousand years."

Ah, there was the gotcha. Well, that was...okay, it was utterly insane.

You could always forget about Ed. Stay up here and enjoy the lack of competition.

What the fuck? Was that just some errant crazed thought from my subconscious or was that...?

No, he was still broken - *asleep* - as far as I knew. Ever since my imprisonment in Switzerland, that aspect of my powers hadn't functioned. Was it possible he was waking up again?

Hello, anybody home? Dr. Death, is that you? Is your angry douchebag ass back amongst the unliving again?

Mental silence greeted me - nothing but my own muddled thoughts. Weird.

"...Kara will be in charge of making sure the squatters stay safe while..."

"Huh?" I asked, noticing Sally had continued talking while I zoned out. Man, I really needed to invest in a personal voice recorder one of these days so I could play back all the important shit I ended up missing. Maybe when this was all said and done, I should put my ass on some ADD medication.

"I don't want her down there, end of story," she said, as if I were arguing the point. Perhaps realizing she was once again being overprotective of Tom's sister, she quickly added, "She isn't worth shit in a firefight and you know it."

"Uh, sure. So how am I supposed to find Ed again?"

Sally stopped and stared me in the eye, the top of her left brow twitching ever so slightly. "You haven't been paying attention to a single fucking thing I've been saying, have you?"

"Of course I have," I replied indignantly. If one was

going to bullshit, one might as well go all the way. "I just wanted you to repeat it...for clarity's sake."

"Repeat what I haven't said yet?"

Oh. "Well, maybe I missed a *few* seconds."

She glared at me, her eyes saying she'd gladly stuff one of those grenades down my throat if I said another word.

Finally, she took a deep breath, her lips silently counting to ten. "It's very simple. You're going to lead the strike team right to them."

14

BLOODY GOOD SMOOTHIES

"Oh, well that answers everything. This is sure to be a piece of cake now."

"Bill..."

"No, you're right, it's a *brilliant* plan. Why, I'll just turn on my magical Freewill rock monster tracking abilities and..."

"You're not tracking the Jahabich," she said patiently. "You're tracking Ed's scent."

"Sure, why not? That's so much bet...*oof!*"

Her fist shot out like lightning, pegging me right in the kisser. It wasn't her best shot, but it was more than enough to split my lip.

She put a hand to her ear. "What's that? Ah yes, the blessed fucking sound of *silence*. Now, if you will keep your goddamned mouth shut and actually pay the fuck attention for the next two minutes, maybe I'll actually get a chance to finish what I was saying."

"No need to get testy," I replied, wiping blood from my mouth. "Continue."

Judging by the look on her face, she was seriously contemplating setting off every explosive in the room right then and there. Thankfully, she thought better of that course of action, for she turned and walked to the far end of the room where multiple freezer chests stood. They were hooked directly into the backup generators of the building and run intermittently so as to conserve fuel, but they were most definitely a necessity. Spoiled blood would mean hungry vampires, a bad combo for the tens of thousands of humans still living in this city.

On top of one stood a blender, which Sally walked over to and plugged in.

"You making margaritas? Because now probably isn't the best time to get drunk and fool around. We can save that for the victory celebration."

"I'm actually tempted to agree to that."

"Really?!"

"Sure. The odds of us living through this are probably so slim, that's gotta be a safe bet if ever there was one."

Bitch!

"Watch and learn, oh halfwit subordinate of mine." She lifted the lid on the freezer next to her, rooted around for a second or two, and pulled out five bags of blood. She extended the claw on her right index finger and used it to slice the top of the first one open. I arched an eyebrow at that, wondering why she was making such ceremony out of taking a quick snack break. Instead, though, she poured some of the contents into the blender cup. She then repeated the act with the remaining blood packs.

"You really don't want to mix O positive with AB negative. Leaves a bit of an aftertaste."

She grinned, then proceeded to replace the top of the blender and turn it on. The blood mixed together, getting nice and frothy, for about ten seconds before she turned it off and removed the lid. "Come over here and have a sip."

"Is the war effort going so badly that you're stepping down and becoming a bartender?"

"No. Now, can you just do as I fucking ask before I rip your bottom jaw off and pour this shit down your throat?"

"You and your pillow talk," I quipped, walking over.

She handed the pitcher to me.

"Care to split it? I'm not that hungry," I said.

"I'll pass."

I lifted the container to my lips, but hesitated. "You're not trying to poison me, are you?"

She tapped her foot impatiently.

"Did you spit in this?"

She raised her hand in a fist and cocked it back.

"Okay, okay; jeez..." I took a sip. It tasted...much like any other blood, pretty damn good. I was actually kinda digging the extra body whipping it up had added. Blood smoothies. I'd have to remember..." *Urk!*"

I almost dropped the pitcher as what felt like a small nuclear explosion went off in my stomach. Heat spread through my body and my muscles tightened. The smells in the room grew bolder, and my ears tingled as I began to pick up conversations happening on the floor beneath us. No wonder she hadn't wanted a sip.

"So?" she asked.

I tilted my head, listening. "I think Brock is hitting on Kara."

"Is that so? Well, then he's definitely a part of this hunting party now. I meant the blood, by the way."

"This is vampire blood," I said.

"Give the man a cigar." She held out her hands expectantly and I took the clue, handing her back the pitcher.

"You're not going to drink that, right? Because you know what happens when..."

"I know." She turned and put it down on top of the freezer again. "I just didn't want any spilling."

"Why?"

"Because of this." She spun back toward me, eyes

blackened and fangs descended. With no hesitation whatsoever, she lunged, the claws on her fingers extending into wicked talons. I didn't know why she was doing it, but her target was painfully obvious.

She meant to tear out my throat.

I sidestepped at the last moment, her claws missing me by bare inches. She spun and threw a backhand, which I managed to parry.

"What the fuck, you crazy..."

She wasn't interested in talking, though. In the time it took for me to open my mouth, her foot was coming up - aimed squarely at the spot where a guy my age formed his happiest memories.

Shit!

I brought down an arm to block her and slammed it into her knee. I'd only meant to stop her from crushing my nuts, but the crack of bone told me I'd hit home harder than I was trying to. If I thought that was the end of it, though, I was mistaken.

Putting all of her weight on her good leg, she came at me again, throwing a right cross. I saw it coming a mile away. I realized the blood had amped me up by a decent amount, empowering me far beyond a vamp of her age and ability. She might as well have been coming at me in slow motion. I caught her by the wrist and spun her around, bringing her arm up behind her in a hammerlock. I brought my other arm around her, pinning her to me lest she try anything else.

"That's enough!" I growled. I didn't want to hurt her, but if she didn't regain control, I'd have no choice but to clonk some sense into her.

Almost at once, the fight went out of her and she

stopped struggling. In fact, her posture became almost relaxed. Maybe my voice had more authority in it than I realized.

"That was better than I expected." Her voice had a tone of admiration to it.

"Huh?"

"You can let go of me now."

"Not until you..."

"And can you *please* get your erection out of my ass?"

Oh, shit. It was only then that I realized I was still sporting wood. Not too surprising, now that I thought of it. Sally's tight body was pressed up against me and my left arm was around both of her breasts. This was how some pornos started. Even so... "That's...just a pen in my pocket."

"Mighty small pen."

"Fuck you," I said, releasing her. "It's perfectly average...um, never mind that. What the hell is up with you? Any reason why you chose to go completely psycho?"

Sally limped over to a chair and eased herself down. Straightening her hurt leg with a wince, she began to massage it. "Didn't expect you to crack my femur so easily."

I'd used the moment to readjust my pants. No point in being obvious about things. I pointed an accusing finger. "That doesn't answer my question."

"The blood." She nodded her head in the direction of the pitcher.

"What about it?"

"What did you think?"

"It's vampire blood. I've had it before."

"You've had it like that?"

"Well, yeah...I've had a lot stronger too. What was the donor - eighty, maybe a hundred years old?"

"Not even close. Oh and it's *donors*."

"What?"

"You heard me. That was a mixture of the blood of five coven vampires, all of them youngsters - none more than a few months old."

"That can't be right, I..."

"Kicked my ass?"

"Well, yeah."

"Thus proving my theory and giving us a shot in hell of actually getting back to the surface alive."

"Whoa, hold on a bit." I put up my hands. "Back up. I'm still not sure what you're talking about."

She sighed, her way of opining that her opinion of me was once more dropping a notch. "We know you can drink vampire blood, right?"

"Of course. It makes me stronger for a while."

"How so?"

"Duh. I gain the power of whatever vamp I happen to use as a sippy cup."

"*Gain* being the operational word there. I suspected it first way back when you took on Jeff. You managed to overpower him."

"He was bleeding pretty badly at the time."

"Doesn't matter. You were slightly stronger. You've even said it yourself in the past: you add their powers to yours. It gives you an edge, even if just a tiny one."

"So you were thinking..."

"Exactly. You've just never tried it before with multiple vampires."

"I'm usually lucky if I can get the bite on one."

"That's the point. Up until now, you've mostly used it as a defensive power."

That wasn't entirely true. I thought back to Sheila's boyfriend. What I did to him would probably be considered pretty damn offensive.

"But now," she continued, "with us in need of some

brute force with nary an ancient vamp in sight, I figured it wouldn't hurt to run an experiment. If you only got the strength from one of them or if maybe their blood canceled each other out..." She trailed off, then snapped her fingers. "But what you did back there says otherwise. I'm not ashamed to admit you took me out way too easily - even with all the training I've been putting your ass through. It worked. You currently have the power of five other vamps coursing through you. On their own, they're pretty pathetic...no real threat. Together, though, well, I'd say you probably have the power to take on a vampire twice my age."

I considered this, and it actually made sense. "So what you're telling me is that by drinking the blood of multiple vamps, basically they combine to form Voltron inside of me?"

"No, I'm really not saying that at all."

"Same general concept, though." Goddamn, why hadn't I thought to try that before? Well, the answer was pretty obvious - the lack of willing donors. As Sally had said, I'd used it more as a defensive weapon than anything. Back when I'd ruled over Village Coven, I'd never thought of asking the various assembled vamps to line up and let me bite them all in succession. Even if I had, chances were most of them would have told me to go take a flying fuck off the Statue of Liberty. "I get what you're saying, but I'd never really considered it. I mean, I've usually been happy just to be strong enough to beat off any bad guys who were kicking my ass."

She raised an eyebrow and smirked. "Beat off?"

"Poor choice of words."

"Methinks the lady doth protest too much."

"Bite me," I said, but with no real rancor. I was too busy considering the possibilities. Past a certain point, my body normally couldn't handle the power and it could trigger my change into Dr. Death. The thing was, he currently wasn't an issue. In theory, with the right slushie made from the blood of potent donors, there wasn't any limit to what I could do.

Sally stood up and placed some weight on her leg, grimacing. It obviously wasn't fully healed yet, but it was good enough to support her weight. She hobbled over. Almost as if reading my mind, she said, "It does open the door to possibilities, doesn't it?"

To my surprise, I found myself grinning at the prospect. "And then some."

15

GOING DOWN

Despite my earlier optimism, I realized Sally's plan had some potential snags. For starters, the blood may have had a cumulative effect on my powers, but as it turned out, it didn't do anything to extend the duration the boost offered. My body still seemed to metabolize it at the same rate. Thus, while it would be good for a fight or a quick escape, it still wasn't ideal for a prolonged operation. I could get the benefit from a small sip, but there was still only a finite amount I could carry with me on a journey that would last God knew how long.

There was also the fact that Pandora Coven was a relatively young group these days. I'd picked up hints from Sally that the previous master had a few centuries under her belt, but she was no longer amongst the present and accounted for. Sally was now the oldest vamp in the building. Steve and a few others had a couple of decades on their side as well, but there were none that could be considered even remotely ancient among our number.

In short, this was far from being a done deal. Even so, I could have kissed Sally for giving us as much hope as she had. A snowball's chance in Hell was better than none and, hey, we were in Vegas after all. Playing the odds was practically an unwritten law here.

Once our plan of action was confirmed, Sally and Steve set to work prepping things with brutal efficiency. Sally ordered mandatory blood donation from any vampires over two years in age, herself included. I was taken aback by the amount she drained from each not-so-warm body. Needless to say, if any sane blood drive had tried to do the same, they'd have been locked up for attempted murder.

To compensate, any vampire heading down with me received free access to our human blood reserves. After all, it wouldn't do to load up for battle only to have everyone around me get all woozy and faint.

While Sally went upstairs, presumably to mix up the blood cocktails, Steve took charge assembling the strike team. His original plan called for a six-man crew: me, three other vampires, and two mages. Unfortunately, we ran into a bit of a problem with that latter part. Being part of a vampire coven meant that the concept of volunteering was more or less a bad joke. The Magi weren't vampires, though. Technically, we could've tried compelling them, but I for one didn't want to be walking into danger and suddenly have a pissed off wizard come to their senses around us. They'd been helping us for the purpose of mutual defense, but it was entirely of their own free will.

Steve tried to use the logic about the best defense being a good offense to persuade them, but one of the mages who'd helped us defend Pandora's Box - a wizard by the ridiculous stage name of Fontaine the Astounding - pointed out there was a fair bit of difference between the patrols they helped out with and making a stab directly into the heart of the enemy.

I had to admit the risk-reward ratio on this one was kind of slim. I tried to use the argument that there must've been a reason the Jahabich kidnapped Ed rather than just biting his face off, but it was a dubious affair, as there was no guarantee the end would justify the means. The bottom line was this was a rescue mission because Ed was my friend. Painting it any other way was the equivalent of offering everyone a shit salad for lunch and asking them to close their eyes and dig in.

Much to my surprise, though, the truth was all we needed. We were just about to ixnay our plans for magical backup when a volunteer stepped forward - a witch by the name of Miranda. I didn't know her too well, but I'd heard that she and her husband had been performers at a small club off the Strip. The scuttlebutt around the club was they'd been active in the community, doing what they could to help Vegas's large population of homeless. Their generosity had proven their undoing. At some point in the weeks prior to my arrival in this city, they'd been handing out sandwiches when one of those freak supernatural storms had hit and a pair of the Jahabich in disguise had waylaid them. She'd gotten away, but he hadn't been so lucky. Ever since then, she'd been a mainstay in our patrol schedule.

I was still surprised to hear her volunteer. In my few brushes with her, I'd gotten the impression she didn't much like vampires. She wasn't overly hostile toward any of us, but I definitely got the vibe that she considered us lower life forms. We were simply the lesser of evils and a means for revenge against the monsters who'd killed her mate. I didn't figure her for the type to join us on what was probably a suicide mission. Maybe the possibility of getting some revenge in the Jahabich's main lair was too tempting. Either way, I wasn't about to look a gift horse in the mouth. The plan called for six, but we could deal with five.

It turned out Sally hadn't been joking earlier. Brock

was assigned to the team, although whether it was because of his martial skills or his desire to get into Kara's pants I didn't know - or ask. Speaking of Kara, she actually asked to join too. She knew Ed from our days of living in New York - when I'd still possessed a heartbeat - and had been on neutral terms with him. I think it was more out of loyalty to her big brother than anything else. Regardless, Steve vetoed that quickly, assigning Vlad - not his real name, obviously - to the team. He'd served as one of the club's bouncers back in the days when it was still entertaining clientele.

Steve put himself down as the final member of our little expedition, which made my opinion of him climb a notch. It also made me feel a bit better. I didn't necessarily like the guy much, but he was competent.

We'd need that trait down there as if our lives depended on it...probably because they did.

We suited up and armed ourselves. Hardened Kevlar and ceramic body armor was the dress of choice for this mission, as touching those fucking monsters was akin to running one's hand over broken glass. The downside? We would likely smell like a Sasquatch's ass before we traveled more than a mile. Each of the vamps got a pickaxe or hammer, a combat knife, a shotgun loaded with explosive shells, and other such accoutrements - in short, mostly stuff I really wasn't qualified to use.

Steve was just loading up a backpack with grenades when Sally reappeared. She was carrying four large canteens, the contents of which I could easily guess.

She put them down next to our supplies then turned toward us. "Strip."

"What?"

"Not you," she replied, pointing a finger at Steve. "Him. Take that stuff off and hand it over. You're staying."

"But..."

"I'm going with them. That's all you need to know."

Steve froze in place. "Coven Master Sally, as your lieutenant, I must inform you that doing so is ill-advised." I had to admire his courage. Most vamps had it beaten into their heads from an early age they shouldn't breathe incorrectly at their master if they wanted to keep living.

"And as coven master, I must inform you that I don't give a shit about your opinion."

Silence overcame the room. No doubt everyone wondered if they were about to see their second bloodbath of the day. Eventually, Sally said in a nice, even voice, "Clear the room. I need to have a word with my subordinates."

It's funny. When most people get all worked up, they usually start screaming at each other to sound intimidating, raising their voices to painful decibels. What they don't realize is that a quiet, steady voice can be a lot scarier. Not surprisingly, the room cleared out quickly. I'd have gone too, but I'd heard the plural in Sally's request. Also, she knew damn well I would jump at her commands about as well as she had during our Village Coven days.

Once we were alone, she said, "I'm leaving you in charge, Steve."

"But I'm not..."

"It's time to stop being a behind-the-scenes guy. Both the coven and the refugees respect you. They'll listen and do as they're told. That's key because if anything gets weird up here, I want you to relocate. Hell, it's probably a good idea regardless."

"But this building is defensible. We have supplies..."

"This building won't mean shit if we can't bury this problem. They've already proven that."

"They took us by surprise."

"Yeah, and who knows what tricks they'll use next time. We underestimated them. These things are obviously smarter than they're letting on. They didn't need to stop today. They could have overrun us. For some reason, they chose not to, but next time, they might not. We don't have enough vampires or wizards to fight them all. Also, you've seen what it's like out there. There are things watching us from out in the desert, things that aren't on our side. Eventually, they're going to try their luck. We can't fight a war on two fronts with what we've got."

"Reinforcements?" he asked.

"Good luck," I scoffed.

"Bill's right. Yvonne has about as much chance of helping us as I do of sprouting a penis."

"Chicks with di..."

She turned and glared at me. "Don't start. The Draculas won't do shit either. We're here to contain this problem, but Vegas isn't otherwise tactically important to them. They won't commit a sizable force if we get squashed."

"You could try calling James," I offered.

Sally's face fell. "I already did. He's not answering. He hasn't answered my calls since New York."

Steve closed his eyes and took a deep breath. "I still think this is a poor idea. I could do this job. The coven needs you."

"No, the coven needs a *leader*. Anyone competent enough can fill those shoes, and you're more than up to that task. Let Kara watch out for the humans. She's good with them, but keep an eye on her. She's young and occasionally her bloodlust gets the better of her."

"But where should we go?"

"If things go to shit or we're not back in a few days, try heading southwest. Find a quiet suburb to settle down in.

Nobody in this godforsaken war seems to give a shit about those."

Sally was right on that one. Last I'd checked, my parents were still nestled pretty cozily in mid-Jersey. There'd been a little bit of weird stuff, but the main nastiness so far seemed to focus on the heavily rural and urban areas - go figure, the main strongholds of the respective sides in this clusterfuck.

"When you get settled," she continued, "make contact with Christy on the East Coast. Let her know where you are and what happened."

Steve opened his mouth again. I thought he was going to protest, but he closed it and then started unbuckling his weapons belt. "I just have one question...why?"

Sally didn't answer right away. Instead, she turned her head toward me and smiled. It was similar to one she'd given me months back, when we'd first discovered that Sheila was the Icon. I'd been on the verge of a breakdown, but she'd surprised me by coming through and standing by my side when I needed her most.

"My partner needs me."

16

JOURNEY INTO DARKNESS

Though I'd have gladly taken a bullet than see any of my friends in harm's way, I felt better as I stepped from the tunnel into the sewer proper with Sally by my side. We didn't always win, but we always seemed to make it out of shit alive when we were together. I wasn't a great believer in luck, but at that moment, I'd have taken anything that offered a bit of hope. Now to see if our streak held up.

Sally handed one of the canteens to me as we stood at the intersection. "Time to juice up."

I took it from her overly pristine hand with its freshly polished nails.

She must've noticed my confused stare because she added, "While I was mixing up the blood, I had Alfonso give me a manicure."

"A manicure?"

"Yep."

"Why? You do realize we're heading into a sewer, not a nightclub, right?"

"Of course, and I also realize that the chances of us coming back out are slim. If I never make it to the surface again, at least my last memory aboveground will be a happy one."

All of a sudden, that lucky feeling felt more like a leaden weight around my throat. What the fuck had I been thinking? "If you're wearing five-inch heels when it's time to bug out, I'm leaving your ass."

"If I have an occasion to wear five-inch heels, then you'd better damn well leave me because I'm probably in a situation where I don't want us to be seen together."

"Are you two going to do this the entire trip?" Miranda asked, a high-powered headlamp shining from her forehead as the sole member of the search party without night vision.

"Probably," I commented, unscrewing the lid on the canteen. "Bottoms up."

Although we probably had about two gallons of vampire blood on us, I took only the barest of sips - maybe a shot glass's worth. "Ugh."

"Something wrong?" Sally asked.

"Weird aftertaste."

"Sorry. I mixed some anticoagulant in to keep it from turning into a clotted-up mess."

"Good idea, but next time, make sure it's cherry flavored, okay...whoa!" The mingled blood mixture hit my stomach and I immediately felt the effects. It was similar to drinking one vamp's blood, but a bit different neverthe-less now that I took a moment to experience it. Think of the difference between drinking flat versus carbonated soda - something like that. Gee, I really hoped the concoc-tion didn't give me gas, although considering where we were headed, it's not like people would notice.

"So, what's it like?" Brock asked.

"Kinda like this." I cocked back a fist and drove it into the wall. The damp masonry shattered like glass.

"Whoa! Need to get me some of that shit."

"Trust me, you don't want to try it," Sally said. "Vamp blood is an acquired taste that only Freewills can stomach."

"Jealous much?" I teased her. "I have some of you inside me. Maybe you want some of me..."

"Finish that thought and I'll finish you in my own special way." She patted the oversized holster that held her preferred weapon - a fifty caliber Desert Eagle. "So how much of a boost did it give you?"

"Not quite at James's level, but not too far off, either."

"It'll have to be enough. Now, make like a good little bloodhound and start sniffing."

Even a young vampire has senses far beyond that of normal humans. We can hear better, smell better, and see in the dark. The only downside of that last part is that I'm still stuck wearing glasses. With regards to smell, that's not always a good thing, either. Don't get me wrong; waking up just when the bakeries pulled their rolls from the oven was quite the joy, despite the fact that I preferred my muffins soaked in blood first. Reverse that, though, and a bad enough smell could feel like it punched you right in your soul. Sasquatches, for example, probably smell like rancid shit to a person, but to a vamp, it's enough to make us wish for a quick death. Oddly enough, it's not much different in sewers - go figure.

The problem with acquiring a scent and locking onto it is that first, you have to take in all the other smells, mentally analyze them, and then home in on the one you want. At my current power, I could pretty much visualize scents down to the user level - someone had the burrito squirts, another beer diarrhea, still another who apparently had a fondness for pickled herring - and so on. Had Ed not been one of my best buds, a guy who'd gone to bat for me more times than any sane person should, I'd have probably given up and declared, "Sorry, he's not down here," before racing back to the surface for a lungful of relatively clean air.

Finally, after what felt like hours of sifting through scents in my mind, a familiar smell stood out. I'd lived with the guy for years, I sure as hell knew what he smelled like - and yes, that sounded creepy to me too.

I opened my eyes and faced the others. "I've got him." Judging by their positions relative to when I'd started, I'd say it had taken me maybe three or four seconds to lock on.

I pointed down the tunnel toward my right. "He was carried that way. Still bleeding, but alive."

"How many..."

"I don't know," I replied. "Hard to say. They have a distinct odor for their species or whatever the fuck you'd call them, but they all kind of smell alike."

"I've noticed that too," Sally said. "And they smell enough like rock that sometimes it's hard to tell when you're surrounded by wall and when you're about to get your head caved in."

I nodded solemnly in the darkness. My nose could lead us to Ed, but it didn't offer much in the way of a tactical advantage.

In many ways, we were still up shit's creek without a paddle.

The first hour of our journey did nothing to lift our spirits. We passed more than one side tunnel, transformed as best as its occupants could into modest living quarters. A whole community called the Vegas underground home.

While some were addicts or drunks, many others had simply fallen on hard times and couldn't make ends meet up on the surface.

Even now, with the world falling to shit, things weren't much better for the downtrodden. The rich, influential, or physically powerful were given preference by the casino bosses. Smaller collectives had formed amongst those living in the more modest neighborhoods off of the strip, but they were cliquish and wary of outsiders. I almost had to laugh that seemingly the most open community in the City of Sin was the area in and around Pandora's Box, and it just so happened to be run by Sally.

Sadly, the laughter died in my throat. There was nothing funny about the dwellings we passed. Whatever minor joy the occupants might have been able to eke out of life had been silenced. Each and every one of the dwellings was empty, some abandoned mid-meal. The people had assumed themselves safe due to our patrols, but we'd gotten complacent and, in the end, had let them all down. As we walked, Miranda offered the idea that maybe some of them had joined Ed as prisoners. I let her keep that small bit of hope, but my nose told me otherwise. There may have still been people alive down in the tunnels, but right now, the dead far outnumbered them.

17

THE FELLOWSHIP OF THE MUCK

"So what does it taste like?" Miranda asked as I took another swig from the canteen to shore up my enhanced abilities.

"Huh?" We'd taken a short break, and I'd stepped away from the group to recharge and double check we were still on the right path. I hadn't realized she'd followed me.

"The blood. I know you need it to survive, but do you actually *like* it?"

It had been rare for anyone outside of my roommates to ask that, and they'd mostly just made fun of me for it. Dave had inquired on a few occasions, but it was more in a clinical sort of way - like I was a lab rat.

I smirked at the thought of him. Much to my dismay, he'd gotten firsthand experience as to what it was like. Unfortunately, ever since we'd zapped out of the Northeast, Dave had been off the grid - whereabouts unknown. That wasn't good, because my friend and former DM was high on ambition and low on human compassion. In truth, when those vamps had walked in with that crate, a part of me was certain he was in it, that someone had

133

finally noticed his uncovened ass and moved to rectify the situation.

"The truth is," I said, "it's hard to describe. Think of your favorite food."

"Oh, that's easy. There was this little roadside stand right outside of St. George that used to make these incredible fried brain sandwiches served with fresh okra. They were..."

"Seriously?"

"Yeah."

"You ate fried brains?"

"Whenever I could get out there."

"That's fucking disgusting," I said, horrified.

"You drink blood."

"I know, and I still find that vile."

"You don't know what you're missing."

"And for that I am thankful." Ugh. My stomach churned at the very thought. I had figured nobody outside of that crazy Andrew Zimmern dude would stuff shit like that down their gullet. Man, people were just fucking weird. "Anyway, imagine that every single one of your senses was now attuned to...brain, I suppose, especially your taste buds. Think of how that sandwich would taste magnified a hundred-fold. That's pretty much how it is with blood."

"But even something that tastes that good doesn't explain why."

"Why what?"

"Why some of you are such animals."

I chose to ignore the implied insult. "Actually, I think it does. If something is so insanely good, it's gonna be almost like a drug."

"So what you're saying is that you're all addicts?"

"I'm not ready to call myself a crackhead quite yet,

although I've gotta have some rocks in my head to be in this place."

"About that, why *are* you down here? I'd heard the official story upstairs, that it was a rescue mission, but there's gotta be more to it."

"No, not really."

"But this guy..."

"Ed."

"Fine, Ed. He's just a human," Miranda said skeptically.

I decided to hold my tongue on that *just a human* part. Ed was something else nowadays, something that had apparently not been seen before. Even so, at the end of the day, he was still my friend, and that was what counted. I voiced as much.

"That's it?"

I blinked for a moment. "What do you mean, 'that's it'? Isn't that enough?"

"I didn't mean it that way. It's just that..."

"Most vampires you've met wouldn't step across the street to help out a human?"

"Yeah."

"I know what you mean. Of the vamps I've met, I'd say the vast majority of them have been total assholes."

"But you're different?"

"No, he's still an asshole," Sally called from where she and the others were checking their ammo.

Goddamned vampire super hearing. "Will you stop fucking eavesdropping?" I lowered my voice to a bare whisper and added, "Bitch."

"I heard that."

"You were meant to," I snapped before turning back to Miranda. "Here's the deal. I've been a vamp for less than two years." Her eyes opened wide in surprise. "It's true. Before that...well, okay, during most of it too, Ed was my roommate. He and my other roommate, Tom, are my friends. I'd do anything for them."

"And they're not thralls?"

"Would I risk my ass to save a thrall?"

Miranda appeared to consider that. Finally, she nodded, satisfied with my answer. She glanced back toward the group where Sally was busy spray-painting a marker on the wall to note our passage, as she'd been doing every couple hundred yards since we'd started this journey. When it was time to bug out, chances were we wouldn't have the luxury of waiting for me to smell our way back to the surface. Finally, she stopped and put the can away in her pack.

It was time to move again.

Before we stepped to rejoin them, Miranda said, "Your friend is lucky to have you."

"Us," I corrected. "Sally didn't have to come along. This was her choice too."

"Are you and she..."

"In his dreams," Sally replied from her position a couple of yards away.

I sneered in her direction. "Only the ones that take place near a free clinic."

Sally had told me some tales of her battle with the Jahabich down in these tunnels during one of those freak storms - real nightmare shit. I still wasn't sure why she'd been down here - she'd always been vague on that point - but it was enough for me to thank my lucky stars it had been dry for the past couple of weeks. Ignoring the fact that it made tracking Ed's scent so much easier, I had no real desire to be submerged in ass-water for any part of this journey.

The problem was, dry as it might have been, this was still a sewer. The water had to go somewhere, and chances were it went in the direction we seemed to be heading - down.

We'd been at it for hours, following tunnel after tunnel. Part of the problem was that many of them interconnected. More than once, Ed's scent had seemed to come from one direction, only for us to find we'd been led in a circle. It was usually at these junctures that I stopped to top off my powers. Thankfully, the fresh swallows of vampire blood seemed to do the trick, giving my nose enough of a boost to right us again.

Even so, it was a fucking slog. At some points, the ground was solid and at others...well, let's not go there. Miranda, the lone mortal amongst us, was starting to get tired. All of us were filthy, and the two meatheads in our group were starting to get twitchy - occasionally opening fire at nothing more than shadows. All the while, we'd encountered nothing more than rats and cockroaches - along with the occasional freak-out as the sound of our voices seemed to continually echo back at us.

"Any idea where we are?"

"Do you mean..."

"Yes," I snapped. "Besides the fucking sewer."

I expected Sally to have some clue. I mean, she always seemed to know something that I didn't. Thus, I wasn't particularly pleased when she held up her hands in defeat and said, "No idea. I'm not familiar with the tunnels we've been in this past hour. We could be in the heart of the city or well on our way to Reno for all I know."

I turned a corner and stopped dead in my tracks. "Well, I'm pretty sure you're at least wrong on that last part. I don't know where we are, but I'm pretty fucking sure this ain't the Mustang Ranch."

The rest of the group joined me at the mouth of

the...whatever it was - cavern, central hub, giant fucking French drain...I don't know. The tunnel opened up in front of us to a space at least fifty feet across. Multiple other outlets along the sides and even the ceiling led away, but it was what sat in the middle of the room that was of interest to me - what appeared to be a massive sinkhole, at least fifteen feet in diameter, leading down into the pungent darkness.

"Ladies and gentlemen," I said, "I do believe from here on out, things are going to get interesting."

18

THE WELL OF ASSHOLES

ampires can see just fine in pitch darkness. Everything takes on a colorless grey hue, but the details are all there. Even so, it's not like a clear day where you can see all the way to the horizon. Needless to say, it was a bit disconcerting that even with my smoothied-up senses, I couldn't see the bottom of the pit. I doubted it went down too much farther than what my range of vision allowed. I mean, it's not like I could feel the heat of Hell rising from within its depths. Still, this was the point in most horror movies where you know that most of the group that's going in won't be checking back out again.

"Let me guess: down there, we all float," Sally joked, standing at the edge.

I raised an eyebrow at her.

"I do read, you know."

"I didn't realize *Cosmo* had a monthly horror feature."

She flipped me the finger in the oppressive darkness. "Just be warned, if there are any giant spiders waiting for us, I'm standing aside and letting you trade jokes with them."

139

Miranda chuckled at that. Brock and Vlad, well, I doubted they were readers of anything that didn't have either bimbos or "Guns and Ammo" printed on the cover, so the blank looks on their faces weren't exactly shocking.

"Did anyone bring rope?"

Sally's rolled her eyes in my direction. "When are you going to stop being such a newb?" She held up a hand and extended her claws.

Okay, I guess it was the Spider-Man route down. That made me ever so slightly nervous. I'd seen it done several times, so I knew it worked in theory, but I'd never tried using my claws as climbing tools for anything major before.

"I can levitate down," Miranda offered.

"No," Sally replied. "I want you fresh in case there's a welcome party waiting for us. Hold on to Bill's back."

Oh, great. So not only did I get a trial by fire for my climbing badge, but I had the added benefit of knowing that if I slipped and fell, I could take someone else down with me. No pressure there.

I took an extra pull from my canteen to bolster myself. It was starting to run low after all this time. I'd need to grab another from Sally soon. For now, though, I knelt down so Miranda could climb on piggyback style.

She was an average-sized woman, which would hopefully not unbalance me too much. When I stood up, though, I realized that was just my subconscious fucking with me. Amped up on the vampire blood, she could have been a silverback gorilla and I wouldn't have noticed the extra weight.

In a move that was surprisingly supportive, Sally started down, then looked back at me and said, "It's just like climbing a tree."

"I didn't climb trees as a kid. I didn't want to get bugs all over me."

She let out a sigh and addressed Miranda before continuing her descent. "You might want to keep that levitate spell handy after all."

Gotta love the confidence.

A small part of me had been sure my fingernails would rip right out and send us careening to a painful landing below. Much to my delight, though, they proved to be damn handy - strong and sharp enough to dig into the rock like it was Styrofoam. The only tricky part was figuring out how to brace my feet before shifting my grip. After a few dozen feet, and maybe one or two threats from Miranda regarding vaporizing me if we fell, I got the hang of it.

Honestly, I have no idea how far down we climbed. You always hear of people talking about descending X-thousands of feet, but when you're plastered against the wall - and not entirely sure of what you're doing - five feet can feel like fifty. All I can say for sure is we descended for a while before catching sight of the floor below.

I stopped descending for a moment and sniffed the air. Ed had definitely been brought this way. The singular scent of the Jahabich was strong as well, although whether from numbers or continuous passage, I wasn't certain. There were other scents too - a multitude of them. It must have been my mind playing tricks with me, or maybe I was confusing something new for something familiar, but I could have sworn I caught odors that couldn't have been down here.

"Are you okay?" Miranda asked, her legs around my waist and her arms clinging to my neck in a death grip.

"Yeah, I'm fine." I tried refocusing on Ed's smell. "Just making certain we were on the right track."

"Maybe you should have done that before we started down."

"Better late than never," I quipped before beginning my descent again.

Unsurprisingly, Sally and the others were all at the bottom already. Seeing that nothing had leapt out to eat their faces, I hurried down the last few feet to join them. I stepped off the wall, Miranda hopping off my back in the process, and noticed that the ground beneath us was spongy - almost like walking on a trampoline. Weird, but then I realized it was probably the compressed remains of whatever runoff that had fallen down here over the years. Regardless, I probably didn't want to trip and fall on whatever we were walking on.

"You didn't happen to bring any antibacterial wipes, did you?"

"Huh?" Sally asked, turning to face me.

"Never mind. What do you think of this place?"

"It's weird, it..."

"It smells like a fucking zoo," Brock said, spitting onto the ground - classy guy that he was.

Vlad grunted his agreement, being one of those men of few words and probably fewer thoughts.

"More or less," Sally replied, echoing my thoughts from earlier. "It's like there've been a lot of different things down here, and not just the things we're looking for."

One side of the pit wall was open, leading to a tunnel beyond. Being that it was the only exit that didn't involve going back the way we'd came, I waved the group on. "He was taken this way."

Sally stepped to my side and clapped me on the shoulder. "Good job, Captain Obvious."

The air, although still breathable - as indicated by Miranda's lack of dying - was thick, almost oppressive. I normally wasn't one for letting my mind play the obvious tricks on me, but it really felt like this was a place where we didn't belong. It gave me the heebie-jeebies.

"Check out the walls of this tunnel," Miranda said as we walked slowly down it.

"Looks like rock to me," Vlad replied, contempt practically oozing from him.

Sally pushed past him. "Like your head."

"This doesn't look like it's part of any sewer construction," Miranda continued, putting her hand upon it. I half expected her to pull back a stub, but nothing happened - other than maybe getting God-knows-what germs lived down here all over her. "It's not natural, though."

I had to agree. The walls of the tunnel were definitely not any modern masonry that I was aware of, albeit advanced stonework wasn't an elective offered at my college. Regardless, there was too much symmetry to it all. The tunnel was a little too perfectly round and the walls way too smooth.

"A lava tube?"

"Maybe, but it's a little too perfect even for that," Miranda said. "The wall feels almost like glass. Heat was definitely involved, but I get the impression it was quick. I don't think this was a gradual thing."

"Could magic have done this?" Sally asked, likewise reaching out to touch the sides.

"I don't know. Would have taken a lot of it, though."

"The dwarves dug too deep and too greedily," I paraphrased in my best wizard voice.

"Let's go," Sally said, the moment of wonder broken.

"You...shall...not...*oof!*"

She elbowed me in the gut and continued walking. Nobody has any respect for the classics these days.

The tunnel continued for several hundred yards, the same eerily smooth rock continuing to line the walls. The light from Miranda's headlamp bounced off the surface and made odd shadows that almost made me jump a few times. It made me wonder what it would have been like walking through this in dim torchlight and, for a just a moment, I forgot our purpose and laughed.

"Something funny, Bill?" Sally asked.

"Fear not, maiden." I turned and bowed to her. "For Kelvin Lightblade shall slay the orcs and recover the treasure of Kalinbac, the bejeweled city on the River Morrow."

The group as a whole stopped and stared at me for a moment.

"Did the air go bad down here?" Vlad asked.

"No, it's just Sir Dipshit vying for the sword of dorktitude," Sally scoffed.

"You people have no sense of adventure."

I turned back to continue leading the way, but not before I heard Brock mutter, "What a fucking weirdo." Huh! See if I invite him to game night.

I was tempted to continue with that line of thought. After all, if ever there was a time to lapse into dungeonspeak, now was it. Hell, it might've made the whole trip seem a bit less intimidating if I treated it as another D20 waiting to be rolled. Just then, though, I happened to look ahead. Dim light seemed to be visible - very faint, but in the darkness, it stood out like a beacon. It was uneven, however - broken up as if by...and that's when I saw the debris.

"Come on, guys." I raced forward, all pretense of roleplaying forgotten. Pity for that, because I forgot one of the main rules of dungeoneering - always check for traps.

Well, okay, traps might have been a bit overdramatic. I tripped over a stone I'd missed and went sprawling, landing amongst multiple sharp little rocks that led up to the destruction in front of us.

"I meant to do that," I said, clambering to my feet.

"Sure you did." I didn't need to turn to know Sally was smirking.

"What the hell happened here?" Miranda asked. It was a worthwhile question. Beyond, where the light was dimly glowing, the tunnel ended and opened up into a much larger cavern. In front of us, though, a field of jagged rocks and shattered stone stretched out over thirty feet.

"Cave-in, maybe?" Brock offered.

"No," Sally said. "Look at the rest of it. The tunnel is still relatively smooth up at top, just some minor scarring. If this had been a cave-in, it would be pitted to all hell."

"If not that, then what?" I asked.

"I think I know." She walked to my side and turned to face me. "When I first got here - to Vegas, that is - the tunnel from the subbasement, the one we gated, was sealed up. The previous coven master had ordered it closed up tight with a concrete plug."

"What happened to it?"

"We blew the shit out of it, that's what."

"We?"

She ignored my question and continued. "When the smoke cleared, what was left looked a bit like this, only a lot smaller in scale. I think the same thing might have happened here."

"Something was trying to get out?"

"No, something *did* get out." She took a deep breath and began to pick her way forward, but not before turning back to the group. "I think this is it - where those things call home. The problem is it might also be a former prison, and I have a feeling the inmates won't be too happy to see us."

19

TALE OF THE TERRORS

I took another swallow of blood and tossed the now empty canteen to the side, the hollow container bouncing loudly off the ground.

"Why not just ring the bell, Bill?" Sally asked in a hushed voice.

"Sorry."

My powers bolstered once again, I took the lead, easily climbing over the large rocks that lay in our path. Despite the danger we were no doubt heading into, a small part of me smiled inwardly. I realized this had been the longest I'd ever been juiced up on vampire blood. The power almost began to feel familiar. I'd definitely miss it once this was over and done with - assuming there was still a *me* left to miss anything. Never let it be said I didn't have an upbeat attitude.

I turned back to see how the others were faring. Brock and Vlad shuffled their own ape-like forms past the debris, but I was happy to see that Sally had hung back to give Miranda a hand. It was almost like a part of her had redis-covered some small sliver of humanity - not much, mind you, and most of it was in a Hannibal Lecter sort of way, but there was some. Maybe being around me and my roommates was rubbing off on her after all.

Or maybe it was just her ensuring our major source of firepower didn't fall and crack her skull right before we entered the mouth of madness. That kinda made sense too.

Finally, we were all past the rocks. I shared a quick glance with Sally. The look on her face matched mine and I had a feeling we were thinking the same thought: if things turned sour - which they were almost guaranteed to - that pile of debris was going to majorly slow us down.

"Don't worry," she said. "I've got this one covered."

She gestured Vlad over, and the two of them walked back toward the debris field. I was about to question what they were up to when I heard the other members of our party gasp in surprise.

I turned back toward them, afraid that maybe our luck had finally run out, but what I saw instead took my breath away. I'd been too busy clambering over rocks to really take in our new surroundings, but now that I was really looking at it for the first time, I had to admit that if this was a prison, it was a pretty fucking wild one.

I wouldn't have called this place well lit by any stretch of the imagination; more like standing outside on a clear night with a full moon. Even so, had a festering pit of evil monsters not lay somewhere before us, it would have made a surreally awesome make-out spot. The cave was huge, several hundred feet across at least, with the ceiling rising up a good fifty feet above us. The walls glittered in the massive cavern. I wasn't sure of the source, but from the faint glow, I wouldn't have ruled out bioluminescence - maybe moss or rock worms or some such.

Hopefully, Sally still had some spray paint left. Otherwise, we would have a hell of a time finding our way out. Multiple caves led away from this grand chamber. None of them seemed as perfectly symmetrical as the one we'd entered from, though. They were either naturally formed or the result of some cruder method of digging them out. Even so, assuming I could trace Ed's scent to the correct one, there was the problem of getting out again. In a pinch, running for our lives, I could see how easy it would be to head down the wrong one and find ourselves thoroughly ass-fucked. It would be a real...

"What's that?"

I turned to find Miranda staring up at a section of wall, her headlamp illuminating it.

Holy shit. I'd been too busy marveling at the size of the place to notice it, but now that she pointed it out, the massive pictograph seemed to stretch as far as the eye could see.

Even wilder, now that I could see the images and odd scratchings up on the wall, I noticed that some of that bioluminescence was woven into the pictures. Certain parts sparkled, seeming to highlight passages of whatever message or story it was trying to convey.

A low whistle of surprise sounded behind me and I turned to find Sally and Vlad had returned from their meanderings and had joined us in staring up at the wall.

"I agree," I said. "My ass *is* quite spectacular. Although I'd ask you to refrain from the wolf whistles. I'm not just a piece of meat, you know."

Sally chose to ignore me and instead dug into her pack for something. She produced a high-powered LED flashlight and used it to augment Miranda's lamp, showing us more of the pictograph above.

"What the hell?"

The very left-most image showed a figure standing with its arms outstretched. The shimmering crystals, or whatever, had been ingrained into the being's form - white flowing robes, it seemed - making it sparkle as if with power.

Waves of energy were drawn flowing out from it, over what were either rocks or a crudely drawn pile of shit. I assumed the former as the next series of pictures showed those rocks gradually taking on humanoid form.

"Is this what I think it is?" Miranda asked.

"What? Just a bunch of stick figures," Vlad offered.

"Go be useful and scout out the room," Sally ordered him and Brock. Once they had walked off, she shook her head disgustedly. "Morons. Anyway, yeah, I'd say so. If I were a betting woman..." She turned to me and held up a hand. "No comments from the peanut gallery. Anyway, if I had to bet, I'd say we're looking at the creation of those things."

"Yeah, I was thinking the same thing, but who is that?" I pointed to the glimmering figure who seemed to be giving them life. "If I didn't know better, with the white glow and all, I'd say that was..." I trailed off, not wanting to say it out loud.

Fortunately, Sally was there to give voice to all of my unpleasant thoughts. "An Icon?"

"Yeah, but that doesn't make any sense."

"I agree, but that's as close as I can come to making sense out of that picture. Miranda?"

"I don't know," she replied. "Could be a metaphor."

"Those fuckers sure as hell aren't metaphors."

"I know." There was frustration evident in her voice, as if she thought she should be of more help to us.

"There's more," I pointed out, nudging the hand Sally used to hold the flashlight further along the path of the pictograph.

Rather than slug me, which was the norm for her, she focused the beam on what appeared to be the next part of the story - unsurprisingly, a bloody battle. "Okay, now this really makes no fucking sense."

I couldn't disagree. Here, the crude rock monster drawings were dog-piling on a variety of other figures. Some of them were larger than the others, *much* larger. They stood on two legs and were colored a dull brown. "Are those Bigfeet?"

"Could be," Sally replied. "But if so, then why aren't we signing these assholes up to fight on our side?"

"Because I think the others being attacked are you," Miranda said. "See those scratches on their heads? Those could be fangs...and look." She focused her beam a bit higher where a moon clearly shone, hanging above the combatants.

"That's the best they could do?" Sally scoffed.

"I'm pretty sure the batwing motif is more of a modern conceit," I commented.

"Fuck that. I've never been much into impressionist art." She played the beam of the flashlight further on where the scene concluded. "Now *this* is where things get interesting."

"I didn't realize you were bored."

Sally glanced sidelong at me. "I'm a high maintenance kind of girl."

"So I've noticed."

Our banter done for the moment, we all took in the final part of the story before us. Another figure stood before the creatures. This one was also highlighted with the luminescent thingies, but colored differently. Also, this time, the sparkles were around the figure's outstretched hands. The Jahabich appeared as if they were being forced back toward a deep hole in the earth.

"I'm no archeologist, but I'd bet my left testicle that this shows these things being defeated with magic."

"You can't bet what you don't have and the house isn't

giving credit today," Sally countered, "but I agree. Look at the way that guy is depicted - like he's wearing a skull mask or maybe a headdress. Some kind of shaman maybe. Miranda?"

"Some of this looks vaguely familiar."

"The pictures?"

"No," she explained, trailing her headlamp lower on the wall below the retreating figures of the rock monsters. "See that stuff?" She pointed to several lines of symbols.

"Yeah. Are those hieroglyphics?"

"Maybe. I'm not sure, but look how it's spaced out."

Sally and I both stared at it for a moment. I turned to her and she shrugged, having no clue either. "Um, it's a haiku?"

"No, the cadence is...it's hard to tell, but I think it might be a spell. Kinda resembles some scrolls my master showed me years ago."

"Guess you should have studied harder," Sally commented.

"It's not even that. I was only in a coven for maybe two months."

"Really?" I asked, curious.

"Yeah. None of the mages in Vegas are covened, although a few are in unions."

"And nobody has a problem with this?"

"The Magi aren't like vampires. Covens aren't mandatory. They're more of a way to protect ourselves, to learn, to pass down the lessons of the past."

"Doesn't sound so bad."

"Believe me, it's not all wine and roses. You have some wizards who insist on making their covens more like harems than anything else. There're all sorts of abuses of power. Some even go crazy. Hell, I heard of this one witch from a coven out on the East coast that betrayed her brothers and sisters and got them all wiped out by..."

"By what?"

"Vampires," she spat.

Sally and I shared a sidelong glance at that, but wisely kept our mouths shut.

"And nobody has an issue with it if you leave?" I asked, steering away from the potential minefield that was Harry Decker's bunch.

"Well, my master wasn't happy about it, but that was it. I met my husband when I joined. Five weeks later, we made plans to elope. After that, we decided to make our own way."

"That's fascinating," Sally said, "but unfortunately, it doesn't help us much."

"Sorry. I was a lot more interested in being in love and using my powers to make a buck than I was in ancient history."

"Maybe we can still make some use of this." I pulled out my cell phone and checked the battery; still over half a charge. Thankfully, there wasn't much cause to check email while a mile underground. I turned on the camera app and hoped the flash was enough to get the job done as I started snapping pictures of the scene before us.

"Aren't camera flashes supposed to be bad for cave paintings?" Sally idly asked.

"During times like this, I have to ask myself whether Indiana Jones would give a shit. I'm thinking the answer is no, unless there was money to be had."

"Or Marion."

"I always favored Willie Scott myself," I said. "Bet she was a real screamer."

"Pig."

"You know it." I pocketed the camera and turned to Sally. "Another canteen, if you don't mind."

"Do I look like your serving wench?"

"Are you going to threaten to shoot me if I say yes?"

"Almost definitely."

"Then no, of *course* not."

She handed one over. I unscrewed the cap and took a quick swallow, keeping my motor humming along nicely on high-octane. As I capped it back up, she said, "Well, this has been fun, but I think the sightseeing is over." She inclined her head and I saw that Brock was approaching us from the far end of the cave. She waved him over.

"Anything?"

"All's quiet," he said, leaning his weapon over his shoulder.

"I'm beginning to wonder if that's a good thing."

"Me, too." Sally turned and scanned the cave. "Where's Vlad?"

Brock's face went blank. "We split up further down. He said he wanted to scout a few of the side caves."

Sally turned to me. "Bill?"

After a second, I picked up on her meaning. I took a deep sniff of the air. Ed's odor still lingered and the smell of the Jahabich was stronger than ever, but as for Vlad, there was no...oh, wait. "Here he comes," I said pointing off to a far corner.

I was half amazed. For a second there, I'd been sure he'd volunteered for duty as the obligatory red shirt of the team. Sure enough, though, his form resolved itself as he stepped out from behind some rocks.

And that's when the wall followed him, malevolent orange eyes opening a split second before the attack.

There was no chance to shout so much as a warning before the creature hit him square in the back. The sound of breaking bone reverberated around the cavern as Vlad's spine shattered like fine china.

A gargled scream escaped his throat as the creature bent him over backwards and bared its wicked teeth. The mouth of the Jahabich opened impossibly wide for a moment and then snapped shut, taking Vlad's head and a sizeable chunk of his chest cavity with it.

"We're gonna need a bigger boat," I gasped.

"Got one," Sally replied, chambering a round in her shotgun.

I expected it to charge us, but much to our surprise, the creature turned tail and ran - even as Vlad's remains sparked up and littered the ground with dust where he'd stood only moments before.

"Let's go, Bill. I don't want that asshole getting away and ratting us out. Brock, you stay and guard..."

"*Unnecessary*," a voice spoke from somewhere behind us.

I somehow managed not to entirely shit myself as we all spun to face another one of the monsters. Damn - for living rock gardens, they could sure be quiet when they wanted. Sadly, my enhanced nose was of absolutely no advantage with them, especially now that their earthy stench assaulted me from all sides.

"*We are aware of you,*" the creature said in its gravelly voice. Almost immediately, its features melted together and, within moments, it was gone, replaced by the form of Kristofer that it had used to trick me into opening the gate. "We...I know you, coven master." Its voice now eerily resembled that of our former coven-mate. The only telling sign was the black teeth, sharp as knives, which showed as he opened his mouth. "You show compassion for your people. We knew you would eventually come. We just thought it would be for the Freewill once we took him."

"I'm standing right here, you know."

It ignored my protest and continued on. "Imagine the surprise that it was a human that brought you to us...unless you know what he is."

"He's a pet, nothing more," Sally growled, stepping

forward. "I lost him and want him back, that's all. Thanks for finding him. Here's your reward, by the way."

The move would have made Sarah Connor weep for joy. In one fluid motion, Sally brought the shotgun up to hip level and fired. The shot rang true and the explosive round hit home, square in the Kristofer clone's face, erasing his smile and most of everything else.

Before the sound of the blast had subsided, the Jahabich had resumed its true form, with the exception of a foot-wide crater where its face used to be. An orange glow flickered inside the wound for a moment before going out for good. It fell backward and landed with a dull thud.

"Subtle," I said.

"I'm a get-to-the-point kind of girl." She turned and flashed me a smile full of fang. Goddamn, she was hot when she was like this.

Unfortunately, now was not the time to wonder whether it was too late in the day to be sporting morning wood. Unsurprisingly, Kristofer's funeral was going to be well attended as pairs of orange eyes appeared in the myriad tunnels around us - minus maybe the one we'd entered through.

I won't lie and say I wasn't tempted to bolt. I could have probably beaten them all to the cave and then raced up the wall. From there, it would just be a matter of heading up until I found a manhole cover and...

It was a nice fantasy, but it wasn't going to happen - at least not until all of us, including Ed, could make the journey together. Still, a small part of me wished I was a wee bit more of a coward. The number of Jahabich approaching our position easily equaled the force that had struck Pandora's Box, but down here, we didn't have the advantage of any choke points.

"Any thoughts?"

"Yeah," Sally said, chambering another round. "We blow holes in them until we get bored and then we celebrate the Fourth of July." Her hand reached back and unzipped her pack, no doubt for easy access to her stash of grenades. Oh boy, this was gonna get messy.

"Works for me," Miranda said. Her body began to glow a furious red, and I was forced to step away from her lest my eyebrows get singed. Sally did likewise, probably less for her body hair and more to keep from prematurely blowing us all into bite-sized chunks.

Oh well, when in Rome. I unshouldered my weapon and prepared to use it. The nice thing about shotguns and multiple enemies was that one didn't need to be a Navy SEAL sniper to be effective.

"Come on, assholes!" Sally leveled her gun and appeared to be deciding between targets. "I'm not afraid of you."

"Oh, Lucinda, you always were such a poor liar," a smooth voice said from behind the creatures, further back in the cave.

The sea of rock monsters parted to let the speaker through. A guy of about medium height and build strode toward us. He maybe had a few extra pounds around the middle, but he wore it well, dressed as he was in an expensive-looking suit. To say that he looked out of place down here was definitely stating the obvious.

"No way," Brock exclaimed as if he knew him.

"Is it me, or does that guy look a bit like you, minus the glasses?" Miranda asked me.

"I don't see the resemblance." I raised my gun. "But even if he does, he's going to look like me minus a head in a second."

To my surprise, though, Sally stepped in front of us, her own weapon lowered - her guard down.

"Mark?"

20

X MARKS THE SPOT

"Who the fuck is Mark?" I asked, breaking the momentary silence.

To say Sally's reaction was a mind-scramble was the understatement of the century. I'd never known her to react to, well, much of anything in a way that wasn't cool, calm, and psychotically detached. Needless to say, time stopped for a moment - at least for us - in quite possibly the worst situation in the world for a smoke break. Thankfully, the creatures surrounding us seemed to be waiting for some cue to smash our heads in. Ah, stand-offs - allowing people to trade awesome last words since time immemorial.

"I killed you," she said quietly.

"Another lie," he replied, raising a finger in a *tsk tsk* manner. "Technically, the Jahabich did the work...oh, and you *tried* to kill me. I believe that makes twice now that you've left me for dead. Sadly for you, all that seems to ever happen is I keep coming back better than before, lover."

Lover? "Who is this clown and, more importantly, why is he under the impression that you've banged him?" My question was purposely intended to get a rise out of her - as well as sate my morbid curiosity - but I might as well have been in an entirely different cavern full of deadly monsters for all the reaction it got.

She turned to me, but it wasn't out of anger. Instead, she had a sort of deer-in-the-headlights look to her. That wasn't particularly promising. It's never a good sign when the proverbial immoveable object suddenly loses its shit. "Bill, I..."

"Bill, is it?" Mark, claimant to knowledge of Sally's nether regions, asked. "You wouldn't happen to be that legendary Freewill we've all heard so much about?"

"Well, I don't like to brag. Legendary is such an egomaniacal word, even if it is true."

He shifted his gaze back to Sally. "I have to say I'm a bit disappointed that you traded down to this."

"Traded *down?*" I put a hand up to stay Miranda, who was about to start with the shooting again. "Look at you. Trust me, dude, a dork knows another dork when he sees one. The fanciest suit in the world can't change reality. Don't even try telling me you've never rolled a percentile die at the gaming table."

"That stuff was a bit after my time, I'm afraid...although I did read a lot of Asimov back when I was younger, if that helps."

"Really? I kinda dug the Foundation books, but his robot novels were a bit dry for me."

"I'd agree, but I preferred the Starr series over..."

"Oh, enough of this bullshit!" Sally cried, seemingly jolted out of her funk. She reached into her pouch and produced a grenade. My god, some people just couldn't handle a little geeking out.

Sadly, the Jahabich were more than ready for her. She'd just barely had time to remove the pin when the creatures were upon her. One closed its mouth over the hand holding the explosive, severing her fingers in the process. Before she could so much as scream, another clubbed her hard in the side, splattering the canteens of blood and sending her flying.

The creature who'd eaten the grenade clamped its mouth shut just as the explosive went off. All that was produced was a muffled boom of sound, followed by its eyes flickering out as it fell to the ground, dead. Whoa, talk about suffering for the cause.

Unfortunately, the time for talking was quite plainly finished and we held the short end of the stick. The creatures converged upon us. The last thing I saw before being swarmed was Mark's countenance melt away, only to be replaced with the soulless orange eyes of one of those monsters.

"Yes, we agree that it is enough. It is time for you to join us now."

Amazingly, I found myself still alive several minutes later. The Jahabich attack had been for the purpose of subduing us, not outright killing our asses. That was always a good thing. I, for one, would always take torture with the possibility of escape over my head stuck on a pike, but I've always been a glass-half-full kind of guy.

That didn't mean we were exactly in great shape. Not killed wasn't the same thing as ready to rumble. To put it mildly, they'd pretty much clubbed us into submission. Brock and I had gotten a generic pummeling; nothing our vampire healing couldn't fix. Miranda clearly had a broken nose, freely bleeding, as well as a matching set of black eyes. I had little doubt she was likewise missing a few teeth. Aside from that, though, she was mostly just bruised up.

Sally, on the other hand, had taken the brunt of it. Currently, all she had left on her right hand was a semi-intact thumb. Thankfully, the nubs that had been her fingers had scabbed over. Even so, by the way she was limping and holding her side, it was clear her insides had been scrambled too. Even more telling was the hungry way she kept eyeing Miranda. I had a feeling if I didn't keep Sally's mind off of things, our resident witch would soon be covered in bite marks in addition to her other injuries.

We were being marched forward together in a group, the Jahabich surrounding us at least three thick on every side. Our weapons had been removed and smashed to bits and the rest of our belongings discarded like a pile of rubbish. All that we had left were the clothes upon our backs as they led us down one of the myriad caves leading out of the massive cavern.

As casually as I could, I managed to step between Sally and Miranda to try to keep any casualties inflicted by our side limited to the bad guys.

"So tell me about your rock monster boyfriend," I asked idly.

Sally just glared at me.

"Seriously, now would be a good time to share." I lowered my voice to a bare whisper. "If there's anything you know that could help us here..."

She glanced around. I had the feeling she was looking for the monstrosity named Mark. What the fuck? Talk about anticlimactic. Back when we'd first encountered Vehron, we'd called him Chuck as kind of a goof so we didn't have to keep referring to him as that badass vamp who scared the shit out of us. His real name, however, ended with "the Destroyer." I could respect that. But this clown who'd just captured us...really? I sincerely hoped to find out later that maybe he was called something awesome like The Deathbringer or

The Harvester of Souls. For some rock monster nerd named Mark to take us down so easily was just embarrassing.

"Right before they fed me my own teeth," I said, "I saw your boy toy head out ahead of us. I'm pretty sure he's not in this crowd." I looked around, noticing that the Jahabich pretty much all looked alike in their rock forms. "Maybe."

"That's not Mark," Sally said at last.

"He seemed pretty sure he was."

"He can't be. I saw him die."

"Okay, that's a start, but let's back up a bit. Why did he call you *lover?*"

"Oh, Jesus Christ, it's because we dated a long time ago."

"Is this really necessary?" Miranda turned and asked, unaware of how close she was to becoming Sally's next chew toy.

"Mind your Ps and Qs, sister," I replied. "Inquiring minds want to know."

I turned back to Sally. "So was this an 'opposites attract' kind of thing? Two ships, or boulders, passing in the night?"

"No, stupid," Sally growled. "We were both human at the time...ugh!"

She stumbled, holding on to her side, which still freely dripped blood - although whether it was hers or the remains of our canteen stash, I wasn't sure. Regardless, I caught her before she could fall and let her support herself against me. Amazingly enough, she didn't put up a protest. I guess she was hurt worse than she let on.

"Okay, so you were both human...crazy kids in love." I looked around as I said this. They were leading us down a long, wide tunnel, dimly lit by whatever had given light to the cavern we'd come from. "So then you vamped out and what...he got bombarded by cosmic rays and became The Thing?"

"It wasn't like that," she gasped. "I was turned first, and then I killed him."

"On purpose?" For just a moment, the mask of bitchiness fell off of her face and I saw real pain; pain that had nothing to do with her injuries. I immediately felt bad about the question. "Sorry."

"It's okay. It's the same story as with any other of our kind. I couldn't control myself."

"Wait," I said, stopping. "So what you're saying..."

That was a mistake. The Jahabich apparently had no problem with us yammering amongst ourselves, but they definitely took issue with me slowing down the parade. One moment, I was coming to a conclusion of sorts, and the next I saw stars as I was clubbed rudely in the back of the head.

"You okay?" Miranda asked.

"Nothing four or five bottles of Advil wouldn't cure." Fuck that shit. No way was I letting a teeny tiny, head-erupting migraine interrupt this. I shook my head until the double tunnels before us merged back into one.

"I know what you're going to say, Bill," Sally said, having regained her own footing. She was walking a little more solidly now, her healing taking over. Even so, I knew it would cost her if she didn't get some fresh blood soon. "I turned him. I just didn't know it at the time."

"Into a vampire?"

"What the fuck *else* would I turn him into?"

I decided to bite my tongue and let her continue.

"But I didn't realize it. I thought I'd killed him. It was only recently that I learned otherwise."

"So what happened?"

"He tried to kill me in revenge, and then I fed him to those things."

"Oh, of course. So how'd he become one?"

"I have no fucking idea. You'll notice I was just as surprised as the rest of you when he appeared."

"More so," I commented. "I personally had no idea who the fuck he was."

"Well, now you do."

"And you two really dated?"

She nodded once.

"Well, look at you with a taste for the old nerd sausage after all."

Brock guffawed, but the Jahabich seemingly found his braying as annoying as I did because they smacked him upside the head for it. Oh well, dude had a stupid laugh anyway.

I expected Sally to try to disembowel me with her good hand, or at least glare daggers back at me for my dickish remark, but instead, she simply lowered her head and let her hair droop down, covering her face. Holy crap, this was really unlike her. I always envisioned Sally as a blonde tigress, toying with men like they were mice waiting to be swallowed. Now I was forced to wonder whether she and this guy had actually meant something to each other and now...

...and now she was living out her own version of the very prophecy I feared coming to pass. Though it now seemed I wasn't the Freewill the various prophecies spoke about, the thought that one day I'd have to face Sheila in a fight to the death had been a massive Sword of Damocles hanging over my head. I'd pretty much considered myself the unluckiest guy in the world; that I'd been born under a bad sign, and various other woe-is-me scenarios. In my self-centered conceit, I hadn't stopped to consider the plight of others. I'd been so ingrained in how other vampires acted in the here and now that I more or less assumed they'd always been that way. Perhaps the road to darkness wasn't a quick exit to Evil-ville. Perhaps it was a long, winding path.

Don't get me wrong; I wasn't about to go all sappy with most of them. Folks like Colin could go eat a fat dick long before I'd sit down and give them a shoulder to cry on, but maybe, just maybe, I could consider cutting Sally a bit of slack.

She suddenly raised her head, her eyes black and her fangs out. "This time, I'm gonna finish the fucking job if I have to kill each and every one of us," she muttered, more to herself than anyone else.

Okay, so maybe not *that* much slack.

21

A TRIP TO THE ZOO

I wasn't sure what would await us at the end of our forced march through the tunnels, but my imagination was happy to fill in all sorts of unpleasant scenarios. Conversation had lapsed after Sally decided to take a vacation to Crazy Town, and the Jahabich weren't particularly loquacious conversationalists in their ugly rock forms. I tried to make some sense of that. Speech was probably not the easiest thing when your mouth was a craterous maw, but it almost seemed as if the Jahabich had two distinct personalities at play, depending on what form they inhabited.

I could understand that a bit, what with a rampaging nutcase camping out somewhere inside of my cerebral cortex. At the same time, it didn't seem quite the same. I couldn't put my finger on it. Thoughts of Sally and her ex kept crawling back into my head, which didn't help either. She was so far out of that dude's league that I was having problems making sense of it all.

I thought back to the first time I'd met Sally. It was on a subway train in Manhattan. She'd approached me, we'd gotten to talking, and eventually she'd invited me to a party - a party I just so happened to get killed at. Following my rebirth as an undead horror, she and I had gotten along in a sense, but I never hesitated to remind her that she was at fault for my current condition as well as everything that followed - including the impending global apocalypse. "Oh yeah, well, it's your fault the world is being destroyed" is a pretty hard argument to come back against.

During that first meet-cute; she'd seemed somewhat hesitant - almost as if she'd had second thoughts. I'd always assumed it had been a bullshit act, her way of looking vulnerable so as to keep me focused on the dangled carrot in front of me. Now, though, I had to wonder. Jeff, the master that Sally had served under back then, often sent out his minions under compulsion. She'd told me as much long ago. Ultimately, she didn't have much choice in what she was doing.

But what if that small bit of hesitation had been real, her mind's way of rebelling against the edict of her master? Miranda had said Mark looked a bit like me. I didn't really see the resemblance, but whatever. Was it possible Sally saw it too back then, her memories causing a momentary hiccup in her resolve?

Gah! All of this was fascinating to think about, but ultimately useless in our current plight. This was a real life horror movie, not some chick flick in which we'd all realize everything had been a big mistake right before the climactic kiss at the end. Whoever this Mark guy was, I had the suspicion he wasn't trying to impress Sally in the hopes of winning her back. It would be in my best interest to envision him more as the Freddy Krueger of this story.

No, fuck that. He was the evil lich king and once more, I, Kelvin Lightblade, battlemage of the Silent Order, had been called forth to do battle with the forces of darkness. Hell, was this really any different than that time my party got captured by those daemon-phage-infected centaurs? I'd gotten out of that one by the skin of my teeth, but I'd walked away with a plus-three cloak of warding for my troubles. Damn, if only I'd remembered to pack my dice with me on this trip.

I was still considering these things when I realized it was getting brighter. We'd been traveling in the dim twilight that those glowing cave thingies afforded us, but up ahead, a much brighter light seemed to stream forth. Fortunately, most of the Jahabich were five foot nothing or shorter, so I could crane my neck to see what waited ahead.

The tunnel opened up once more to a wider space. A brilliant orange-hued light flowed forth from it - a shade not entirely dissimilar to that which glowed from these creatures' eyes. Whatever this was, I had a feeling answers awaited. But would those answers help us or screw us in our quest for survival?

"Holy shit."

"I don't think there's anything *holy* about this place," Miranda said.

She had a point.

I had been envisioning some throne room, a place where we'd be forced to kneel before some rock god - and not of the Ozzy Osbourne type. That, or maybe a grand cathedral where we'd be sacrificed for some stupid reason or other. Instead, this was...I don't know. Was it a prison, a torture chamber, some sort of giant smelting pot? Fuck, maybe it was all of the above.

All I knew for sure was we were no longer alone, minus our ever-effervescent Jahabich company, of course. The place was huge, easily as large as the cavern with the pictograph. This one was far from empty, though, and filled with what I had to assume were prisoners.

The first ones I saw were a group of humans. They all sat together, looking tired, hungry, and without anything remotely resembling hope upon their faces.

A group of vampires were next. They were unmistakable as their blackened eyes and fangs shone in the dull light. They were all scraped raw and bloody, but that didn't stop them from circling one another, hissing like animals and taking the occasional swipe at their fellows with their claws. All of them had a disturbingly gaunt look about them.

"Are they..."

"They're starving," Sally said bluntly.

Well, that at least answered one question I'd wondered about ever since being turned.

Some greasy monstrosity was next, looking like a two-headed condor that had been dipped in red tar. Its wings were spread, but speared to the floor with stalagmites. More groups of oddities followed, each weirder than the ones before them, but the last bunch especially caught my eye - Sasquatches. There were four of them, but they were far from the vicious brutes I'd squared off against - appearing mangy and beaten down as they sat in a circle. They looked more like they were planning to die than escape.

The assembled creatures all had one thing in common - the fences of living rock that walled them in. Dozens of Jahabich stood motionless, side by side, facing inward, their unblinking eyes staring at the prisoners within their enclosures. Amazingly enough, the first thing that popped to mind at the horrific sight was the lack of privacy. I mean, seriously, how could one be expected to drop a deuce in peace with all those creepy eyes watching you?

The holding cells weren't the only sights to be seen, though, not by a long shot.

At the far end of the cave, there was a depression in the ground containing a vast pool of some strange liquid - glowing a brilliant orange that was almost too bright to look at directly.

At first glance, I thought it might be lava, but if that were the case, we'd all be busy burning to a crisp. Hell, all of the prisoners in the room looked like shit, but heat stroke seemed to be the least of their worries. So if it wasn't lava, then what the hell was it?

Sadly, the lone occupant of that section of the cave didn't appear to be forthcoming with answers anytime soon. A statue over twelve feet tall stood directly behind the glowing pool of weirdness. It gleamed white - carved from marble would have been my guess - the glow of the pool seeming to enhance its presence in the room.

The interesting part was it didn't look like a giant Jahabich. It actually looked kinda human. Flowing robes covered its body and outstretched arms. Unfortunately, its facial features had eroded, either through time or calamity. It had a head, but beyond that, I couldn't tell any real details from it. I strained my eyes to see if I could pick out any other telling nuances, but our tour guides picked that moment to hustle us forward again.

I thought we'd be tossed in with the other vamps, a prospect that didn't really appeal to me. I had a feeling feral vampires would be as dangerous to sane ones as any of our other enemies. Instead, our entourage marched us up right next to the Sasquatch cage and spread out until they were side by side, essentially doubling as our holding pen.

"Not so fast," a voice said. I turned my head to see Mark striding into the cavern, back in his human...vamp...*whatever* guise. In his hands, he held a pair of rusty manacles.

Two of the Jahabich guarding us stepped to the side to let him through. He walked up to Miranda and said, "We'll make this nice and easy. No protests or hesitation. Just hold out your hands or I will have your arms torn out at the socket."

I was ready to intervene if he tried it, for all the good it would do us in our current situation, but thankfully, she wasn't in a mood to test the resolve of our captors. She lifted her hands and he slapped the restraints on her. They were old, barely holding together, but the symbols scratched into them were plain as day. My gamer senses immediately tingled.

"Anti-magic field...err, I mean cuffs?"

"Yes," he replied evenly, as if discussing a particularly dull news item. "Do I need to warn you about trying to tamper with them?"

"Let me guess - forceful removal of appendages?"

He smiled, a row of obsidian spears glaring back at me. "At the very least."

"Gotcha, sport," I replied, keeping my tone upbeat as if none of this was of any concern. A little psychological warfare might not help us out against these things, but I wasn't averse to playing the game. Also, I was still trying to wrap my head around the fact that Sally used to bone this guy. Fuck me, but I was half tempted to ask him what his secret was. Oh well, maybe I'd wait for our no doubt impending execution - as far as last requests went, that would at least be interesting.

He turned to leave, but not before fixing his human-looking eyes on my partner. "Don't be afraid, Lu. It's not the end. In fact, it's just beginning. This world could still be ours. These bodies we inhabit, all of us, they're more malleable than you'd ever imagine. It's the spirit that matters. That doesn't change. There are influences, of course, but you needn't concern yourself with that yet. You'll get used to it. Maybe in time, we can even set aside our differences and be like we were again."

I had no fucking idea what he meant by that *influences* part, and it didn't appear Mark was in the mood to enlighten us further. He turned to leave.

"Hey, boss," Brock spoke up.

"What?" Sally asked through gritted teeth.

"Not you, bitch," he spat. Uh oh, this didn't sound promising. He stepped toward Mark, his hands up, indicating he wasn't looking for a fight. "You know I was with you, right? After Marlene got iced, I was all for you dusting this whore and taking over."

"Did you just call me a..."

"Now now, Lucinda," Mark interrupted. "Men are talking. Mind your manners."

Either this guy had more balls than brains or he really didn't know Sally as well as he thought. Hell, even if I were hopped up on Alexander the Great's blood, I'd have thought twice before saying that.

Mark grinned broadly, his smile looking like the worst case of tooth rot in history. "I always liked you, Brock. You know how to take orders and are obviously smart enough to recognize the winning side when you see it. Consider your offer accepted."

Brock stepped forward to join him, but Mark held up a hand. "I'm afraid I need you to stay here for now. It's too early for the joining to begin, but I will make sure you are a part of it."

"Boss?"

Rather than reply, Mark's form dissolved back into that of one of the Jahabich. The Jack O' Lantern grin that seemed to be ever-present on the monsters' faces replaced his condescending smile. Overall, it was not an improvement. "*You stay. We must serve for now. Will come for you when it pleases us.*"

"But..." I could tell Brock didn't want to show any fear in front of us. So-called tough guys were like that. Sadly for him, the one area of the supernatural that was the great equalizer was not in his favor. For humans, size and strength could be the defining factors. For vamps, it was age, something Brock didn't have the upper hand with here.

Finally, our traitorous fellow decided to swallow his pride and just say it. "But they'll kill me."

The Mark-Jahabich walked out of our holding cell, and the living walls stepped together once more to block us in. He turned and laughed, a sound not unlike metal scraping against concrete.

"*No, they will not. But even if they try, it will not matter.*"

22

SMALL WORLD, ISN'T IT?

Brock kept his distance, never taking his eyes off of Sally. It was probably a smart idea on his part. It was also useless if Sally decided to get creative with a compulsion. She didn't, though, which was a bit of a shame. I, for one, was curious to learn what the very worst thing she could imagine doing to a person was. I had little doubt it would be a masterpiece of creative butchery. Normally, I wouldn't be particularly keen on such things, but the asshole had sold us down the river. There were times when even I was willing to make an exception to my general rule about holding on to my humanity.

All Sally did, though, was sit there. She appeared to be in deep thought, but it was possible she was in shock. There was also a chance she was just trying to keep herself in check. Over the next hour, I noticed her fingers had begun to grow back. The act of healing would most certainly continue to drain her reserves. I just had to hope Sally understood that chewing on our resident mage wouldn't help us in the short term.

Either way, this wasn't good. I could normally count

on her to come up with something we could use to even the odds. She was a far superior strategist compared to me.

Fortunately, I'd had an inkling that something like this might happen back when Mark had first shown his face. I didn't have anything solid yet as far as plans went, but a few potential ideas were beginning to form in my head.

Of course, none of those would be worth dick if we didn't accomplish what we'd set out to do. The whole point of coming down here had been to save Ed and, so far, we'd seen no trace of him. His scent had still been strong as we'd been marched through the tunnel to this prison, but now...it was hard to tell. The boost from the blood still seemed to be in my system, but it wouldn't last much longer. Regardless, there were enough powerful scents in this room to confuse even me, not the least of which were our next door neighbors.

I stood up and surveyed my surroundings, my eyes stopping first on the nearby Sasquatches. They weren't in their four-armed mega-squatch forms, but they didn't need to be to pound a vamp like me into paste. At an average of eight feet in height, they would also have been able to step right over the Jahabich and into our pen if they wanted to vent any frustrations. Despite my nervousness, however, they continued to sit in their circle, ignoring us and everyone else.

They did stink like shit, though, and that's what was fucking things up more than anything. Christ, trying to locate a single mostly-human scent through theirs was like trying to find a car after the parking garage had collapsed on top of it.

Rather than give myself a sinus headache trying, I busied myself with standing on my tiptoes to survey our surroundings and see if I could catch any sight of Ed.

It was pretty much a snipe-hunt. He wasn't with the other humans as far as I could see. That led to the hope that he'd maybe been labeled as *other* and put in his own pen. I mean, there were several lone monstrosities off in their own holding cells. Alas, that seemed to be a dead end as well.

Fuck this shit. Sometimes, the direct route was the best.

"Yo, Ed!" I shouted, cupping my hands around my mouth. "Are you here?!"

Throughout the cave, several pairs of eyeballs turned in my direction - some glowing orange, but most of varying hues and general grossness.

"What? I'm not talking to any of you fuckers."

"Oh god, we are *so* dead," Miranda muttered somewhere behind me. Such a lack of optimism.

Next time I got trapped in an unescapable situation, surrounded by insurmountable odds, I was gonna make sure I was accompanied by more positive people.

Another hour passed and I started to get antsy. It didn't help that I kinda needed to pee and didn't really relish the thought of unleashing Gorgo in front of the ladies. On the flipside, it would have been pretty fucking hilarious to use one of the Jahabich as my personal hydrant...right before it disemboweled me, of course.

Much longer and it would be worth it, though...hell, maybe I could try my luck at hitting one of them right in the eye socket. Even if they killed me, that particular Jahabich would never live that shit down if...

Whoa. A feeling of vertigo passed through me and I had to sit down. I was pretty sure my boost from the vampire blood had been on the wane, but out of nowhere, I felt like a truck had run me over. I wasn't injured and there wasn't any pain; just a feeling of being tired - like getting up too early in the morning and it all catching up to you around mid-afternoon. Sadly, I was in the worst place in the world to take a nap break. Even so, my eyelids seemed to grow heavier with each passing moment.

Just then, a howl of sorts rose up in the cave, completely derailing any sheep I'd started to count. It was as if a hurricane was blowing across a million open beer bottles, and it was getting louder.

Shaking my head, I managed to clear the cobwebs and get back to my feet. Whatever was going on, I had a feeling it would be unwise to snooze through it.

I turned toward the source of the sound. At the far end of the cave, the Jahabich forming the humans' holding pen had all lifted their heads up and opened their mouths wide. As they did, the next group followed suit in turn, then the next. As the odd behavior completed itself, the sound rose from each pair of stalagmite-laden jaws that joined. Within seconds, they were all doing it.

By the time it reached us, it was near deafening - like being stuck inside of the amps during a rock show sound check. Apparently, my group wasn't the only one with super-sensitive ears as cries of pain rose up in the room, although they were just barely audible over the rush of noise coming from our jailers.

It continued long enough that I was pretty sure I'd be driven insane, and then it suddenly stopped. One moment there was that sound, like being trapped in the world's largest leaf blower, and then it was gone. The Jahabich continued to stare skyward, though, as if something really interesting was happening on the ceiling.

I checked - there wasn't.

Then a voice poured forth from them, nearly as loud as the sound before it, and I realized it was all of them talking in unison.

"Long have we slept and dreamt of this time. Ages have passed and we are now worthy to return."

Return? Return *where*? Also, was it me, or was that howl more or less their way of asking, "Is this thing on?" So many questions and so little...

"The pure one is the key. We shall rise and enjoy the surface once more. But first, we must replenish those who were lost."

Gah! I had to raise my hands to my ears to stop their voices from reverberating in my head. Did nobody ever teach these assholes the concept of using their inside voice?

I waited a moment to see if there would be more, but the Jahabich present all lowered their heads and resumed their guard stances.

"Can somebody tell me what the *fuck* that was about?" I asked to nobody in particular.

"It simple, T'lunta," a coarse voice said from just a few yards away. I turned to find one of the Sasquatches had risen to its feet. It was an ugly fucker, a solid eight feet of muscle - some of its mottled skin exposed where the hair had either fallen or been torn out. It stepped forward and eyed us all. *"Are you prepared to die?"*

That didn't sound good. These guys had obviously been here longer than we had. Did they know something we didn't - like, maybe some kind of assholish ritual combat that was about to ensue? God, I hated that shit. Why couldn't people just talk through their issues?

I was about to open my mouth to tell this hairy shit-stain to go fuck himself, when, to my surprise, Sally stood up and addressed him.

"What did you have in mind, Grulg?"

23

HAIRY BEDFELLOWS

rulg?

"Very good, she-T'lunta. You remember. Grulg afraid you and Freewill T'lunta forget."

"Uh, y-yeah," I stammered. "I recognized you the moment they marched us in here." That was, of course, complete bullshit. Most of the Sasquatches looked pretty much the same to me. The only one I'd probably be able to pick out of a crowd was one named Turd, and that was only because he was bigger and a fuck-ton scarier than the rest. Sally had once mentioned that each of them had a unique odor, but I'd never bothered to try and figure that out. As far as I was concerned, they all smelled like sewage runoff on a hot sunny day.

"Then Freewill T'lunta remembers that Grulg is sworn to kill you under broken Accord."

Uh...

"Of course we remember, Grulg," Sally replied. "And as signatories of the Humbaba Accord, we must act accordingly. Would you not agree?"

"Grulg agree. Be ready to die."

Sally simply nodded in response.

Fully awake now, I assumed a defensive stance, thinking that shit was about to get real. The Jahabich outnumbered us by a good amount, but I knew how powerful the Sasquatches could be. If Grulg decided to charge us, I had little doubt he'd knock them aside like bowling pins before they could respond.

I was so intent on waiting for the attack that I nearly jumped out of my skin when a voice said, "It's time to join us."

Being surprised with a full bladder is never a good thing. Thankfully, I managed to keep from pissing myself as I spun to find Mark had returned - once more wearing his human guise.

"Come with us, Freewill. It is time for you to be enlightened."

Oh, crap.

"Hey!" Brock elbowed past me. "Remember me? I'm the one who volunteered to help you."

Mark seemed a little surprised, but then said, "So you did. I guess the first honor is yours, after all. The Freewill shall join us soon enough. So sorry, Lucinda, but we'll be saving you for last. I do apologize, but you may be in for quite a wait."

"Take your time, stud," she shot back, sounding like her old self.

Brock looked back at us, a smirk of triumph on his face. He stood next to Mark as the *gates* closed up again. Unsurprisingly, that look turned to one of confusion as Mark next gestured for the Jahabich holding the Sasquatches to open up.

Grulg gave a nod and one of the others stepped forward.

"Hey, Mark, what's this?" Brock asked. "I thought I was going to help you."

"You are. He will too, as will one of each of the

chattel."

"I don't understand."

"You will in short order."

Two Jahabich stepped to either side of the traitorous vamp, blocking any escape. The poor dipshit.

"Call off your goons, man. We're cool."

Mark raised an eyebrow. "They aren't my goons."

"Wait, aren't you in charge here?"

"Of course not, fool," Mark said with a laugh. "I am merely exerting my will because of this *special occasion*." He glanced back toward Sally with a leer. "Once that's over, I shall take my place back amongst the gathering."

"Gathering?"

"That you are about to join."

By now, even Brock was burning off enough brain cells to realize he'd stepped in shit. He made to move, but the Jahabich were quicker. They swung their club-like appendages and hit home with solid cracks of bone, breaking both of his arms in the process. None of the Jahabich, not even Mark, showed any emotion at his cries of anguish, albeit the Bigfoot that had been plucked from Grulg's group did sort of smile a bit.

Leading their prisoners onward, Mark made a similar withdrawal from most of the pens. Some came willingly, but most had to be dragged kicking and screaming. At the end, the only cells left untouched were those that held singular occupants. I wasn't exactly sure what that meant, but maybe...

"*The strongest saved for last*," Grulg growled, as if that explained anything. "*Greatest warriors for the final conflict. All the rest, just fodder.*"

I tried to process the meaning of this, but then a thought hit me. "Hey!" That asshole had told Sally she'd be last. Talk about insulting. Christ, being the vampire Freewill garnered absolutely no fucking respect these days.

"Oh, like you expected any different," she replied with an eye roll.

What the hell? Just a short while ago, she'd been Miss Catatonic. Now, she had that predatory gleam in her eye again.

I knew that look. It meant she was preparing to fuck someone over. Hopefully it wasn't me.

"Just do what you do best, Bill," she said. "Follow my lead."

All in all, they led off probably a dozen prisoners. Their destination seemed to be pretty obvious: they were herded in the direction of the glowing pool at the far end of the cave.

Before they got there, though, another commotion caught my eye. More of the Jahabich were marching in - a lot of them. It almost looked like a military procession, so perfectly in step they paraded. Side by side, multiple columns entered - dozens in all.

"*Soon they leave,*" Grulg slobbered.

"Where?"

"*Grulg not care. Grulg only know they leave.*"

"Well, that's fascinating, but how..."

"I don't think we can wait that long, Grulg," Sally interrupted. She pointed at something in the middle of the Jahabich procession. I'd missed it at first, lost amongst the sea of living stone, but now I saw what looked like a head of hair peeking up from their ranks.

The procession stopped on the opposite end of the pool from the statue, about ten paces back from the edge. Their movement ended abruptly with no warning and the figure in the middle stumbled forward for a moment, clonking his head on the Jahabich in front of him. As he stepped back, I caught a momentary glimpse of his face. "It's Ed."

"In the flesh," Sally said.

"*What is an Ed?*"

"He's the one who took a shit on Turd's tree. Remember?"

Grulg bared his teeth at that, but whether it was at my roommate or the mention of the Sasquatch chieftain, I wasn't sure. Hmm, maybe that wasn't the best scenario to jog his memory with.

"It's got to be now," Sally said.

"*We wait. They leave soon,*" Grulg countered.

"You asked if we were prepared to die. Well, we are, but we'll die at a time of our choosing, not yours. You can either accept that or go fuck yourself."

For a moment, I wondered if Sally had gone off the deep end after all, because she sure as hell seemed to have lost her mind. We were no longer under the protection the summit at the Woods of Mourning provided. Talking smack with a Sasquatch warrior was bound to result in them smacking back a lot harder.

Much to my surprise, though, Grulg actually grinned - I think. He turned to me. "*Grulg see your mate still have much fire. Grulg think you will have many fine cubs together.*"

"Uh...yeah." I turned to Sally, but she just mouthed "not a word" back at me. Probably a smart strategy, all in all.

The two remaining Sasquatches growled something at Grulg that I couldn't even begin to hope to understand, but he bared his teeth at them until they looked away. I didn't know what had gone down, but I would have bet it had been because Grulg hadn't immediately ripped Sally in half for mouthing off.

Finally, the ugly beast looked back at us. "*Grulg can see that you will die well. So be it.*"

Oh great, so that was two death sentences hanging over our heads. Seemed like we were collecting them like Pokémon cards as of late.

Screw that shit! My partner could trade threats with big hairy dirtballs all she wanted. All I knew was the target of our rescue mission was in sight. We would need to act fast, but how? We were surrounded, outnumbered, beaten, and bloody. There was little chance...

Hold on...bloody!

Glancing at Sally, I finally had an idea of how to hopefully get us out of this mess.

She'd had her brain scrambled by the reappearance of her boyfriend, but I had to trust that when I made my move, she would back me up. I turned to Miranda. "How are you holding up?"

"Pretty peachy. Thinking I might build a vacation home down here."

I sighed. Guess she'd been hanging out with Sally a little too long. "Just be ready."

"For?"

"Be ready," I repeated, not wanting to raise suspicions among the wall of Jahabich still staring at us. As it was, any chance we had would already be slim as all hell.

"Look," Sally said, pointing, "I think the show's about to start."

Sure enough, it seemed like that was the case. Mark and his goon squad had marched the prisoners, Brock at the forefront, to the glowing pool of muck - right in front of where the statue stood.

Mark stepped up to the towering effigy and bowed his head respectfully toward it, then began to speak - or at least I was pretty sure he was doing so. It was too low to hear, but I could see his jaw mov...

"*The eyes of the mother smile at the gifts we have brought her.*"

What the fuck? The voice erupted from everywhere around us as the Jahabich spoke in unison again like the world's freakiest public address system.

Grulg noticed me jump, his lips splitting back into a hideous grin. "*Funny T'lunta.*" Dickhead.

Mark continued talking, and so did the Jahabich. If I had to guess, I'd say they were mirroring his words, like they were all connected via the rock monster equivalent of wi-fi.

"*We welcome the newly risen. May they serve until they can serve no more.*"

"Any idea what's going on?" Miranda asked.

"No, but I get the feeling we're about to find out," Sally replied.

As Mark turned toward Brock, his body once more assumed the form of a Jahabich. Brock looked confused. His mouth opened as if to say something, but he was cut short as Mark savagely slammed his club arm into and through the vampire's chest. Ouch.

I had just a moment to register the shock on Brock's face before he combusted from the inside out. Mark immediately resumed his human guise - cupping his hands in the rapidly expanding shower of dust that had been my former sparring partner.

"What the fuck?"

With a handful of dead vamp in each fist, Mark turned and stepped toward the pool. He opened his hands and flung the ashes into the magma-looking suspension.

"What the fuck, indeed?" Sally asked, stepping up next to me. "Give me a boost. I want to watch."

"What? No...go away."

She ignored my protest and began to climb me like I was a human stepstool. She perched atop my shoulders like we were watching the fucking Macy's Thanksgiving Day Parade. So glad I could be her personal furniture. On the upside, there were far worse things to have pressing down on me than her firm ass.

"I always knew I'd eventually wind up with your legs wrapped around me."

"Shhhh!" She smacked the top of my head. "Something's happening."

Sure enough, the calm waters of the pool began to churn, bubbling as the surface took on an angry red color, bathing the cavern in its new, bloodlike hue. Neat special effect, but a little cliché - albeit it was still more sinister than, say, turning green or sky blue.

The bubbling started to concentrate in one area of the pool. It began to move, as if something swam underwater - crossing to the opposite end where the rank and file waited with Ed stuck in the middle.

A head broke the surface. At first, I couldn't see any details - it was far away and covered in red-orange goop - but then, the figure emerged more fully and the sludge began to drip away revealing...Brock?

"Okay, that's a little weird."

He was somehow whole again. As he stepped out of the pool, his flesh shimmered and the clothes he'd been wearing appeared on his body again.

"I thought when vamps died, they..."

"Shut up; I'm watching this," Sally growled, reaching down and twisting my ear.

"Ow!"

Brock turned and faced his killer on the opposite shore.

Mark smiled and called out, "How do you feel?"

"I feel fine," he replied. He reached down and touched his body, seemingly surprised to be alive. "Hell, in fact, I feel...argh!" Brock stumbled, losing his footing and going down to one knee. He reached up and grabbed hold of his head, opening his mouth as if to cry out.

"Don't fight it," Mark called back to him. "It's easier that way."

With that, Brock's form changed - losing cohesion as his body melted away. His clothes disappeared, seemingly absorbed back into him, and his skin hardened and turned grey as he shrunk in on himself until the form of a Jahabich stood in his place. Its orange lantern eyes burned brightly for a moment before settling down into the typical hue of the monsters.

"How do you feel *now*?" Mark asked, an obsidian smile on his face.

The thing that had been Brock chuckled. "*We feel good. We are ready to serve.*"

"Holy shit," I muttered.

"Oh my god," Sally gasped from her perch. "These things are just like us."

"What do you mean 'just like us'? I don't know about you, but I sure as shit am not made of rock."

"No," she explained. "It's like what we do, but worse. Vampires turn humans into other vampires. These monsters can do the same thing...but it's not just humans. Judging by the prisoners up there, these fuckers can make more of themselves out of just about anything."

"That's fucked up."

"It's worse than that. These things could infiltrate both sides of the war. They could destroy us from within and we'd never know until it was too late."

24

BREAK OUT

Sometimes I hate it when Sally's right. Mark next dragged some three-armed imp-looking thing from the crowd. Now that the prisoners knew what was in store for them, he didn't waste any time with ceremony. He simply snapped the creature's neck and tossed it into the orange slime. A few moments later, another Jahabich crawled from the other side, this one wearing the skin, and presumably containing the memories, of the creature it had somehow been born out of.

"That must have been what happened to Mark," Sally stated, seemingly more to herself than anyone else.

"Wait, I thought you said you killed him."

"I might have had a little help. If I'd known those things would have used his ashes, though..."

"Though what?"

"I'd have killed him and then maybe stuck around to finish those fuckers off too."

"There's something to be said for being thorough."

Speaking of thorough, I could either stand and watch this spectacle continue to play out - the Jahabich growing stronger with each victim - or I could do something about it. I doubted there would be a better time, and I sure as shit didn't want to wait around for whatever suicide pact Sally and Grulg seemed to have going on. "Sorry, doll, but it's time for Daddy to put you to bed."

"What are you yammering abo..."

I tossed her off my shoulders and to the ground. Under different circumstances, I would've told her my plan, but I didn't trust her current state of mind. She could always thank me later if this worked...and, knowing Sally, by "thank," I mostly meant cock-punch.

Before she could get up, I was upon her.

"What the hell?" Miranda cried, but I ignored it.

Using my superior leverage, I managed to pin Sally's arms above her head with one of my hands. There was no way I could hold her like that for long, so I couldn't afford to do this gently. Extending the claws of my free hand, I grasped hold of the ragged Kevlar she wore, as well as the shirt beneath it, and tore with everything I had.

The Sasquatches grunted in surprise as well as various other creatures. Apparently, my little attack hadn't gone unnoticed, but that was okay. If these fuckers were looking for a surprise, they were about to get one.

I ripped off a large swath of cloth from Sally's midsection, then scrambled backwards with my prize. The look on my partner's face was more one of shock than anything, even more so when I balled up the fabric, stuffed it into my mouth, and began sucking on it with everything I had.

Earlier, once it had become obvious the Jahabich had intended to capture us, I had purposely held back. Letting loose against these monsters needed to wait until we'd found Ed. Of course, it really hadn't helped when they'd casually tossed our possessions to the side like refuse, including my last canteen. Then I remembered that Sally had been quite literally splattered with the mixed blood when the creatures had swatted her like a bug. We'd been locked up long enough for it to have dried to a disgusting crust on her, but thankfully, the laundry facilities had been sparse. I just had to hope that, even dried, it still had some bang to it and that I could work up the saliva to free enough of it to have an effect.

I will say, for the record, it was vile work. We'd spent several hours trekking through a filthy sewer, not to mention walking, climbing, and fighting enough to work up a good sweat. As I sucked down whatever I could, I made a vow that if we got out of this mess alive, I was gonna subsist on a diet of nothing but Tic Tacs and Listerine for the next week.

Sadly for me, my actions were drawing attention. Now the wall of Jahabich around us slowly turned their heads toward me. I guess interrupting their ritual was considered a social faux pas. Either that or they were wise to escape attempts.

There was also the wee issue that Sally was back on her feet, a generous amount of underboob showing on her chest, and a look of pure murder upon her face.

If this didn't work, I'd either have my balls torn off or find myself taking a nice long dip in a bubbling orange bath. Somehow, I had a feeling my Freewill exemption to compulsion wouldn't survive my rebirth as a granite-covered shit pile. No fucking way did I want that.

I swallowed hard, feeling something go down. At first, a wave of nausea struck me as whatever gunk from the sewer hit my digestive tract, but then, finally, came that burst of heat from my innards that told me it was time to do some damage.

I sensed the two Jahabich closest behind me step

forward as volunteers for the crusted blood smoothie's true test.

I stood and spun, quick as lightning, to face the beasts. They advanced upon me, but they might as well have been moving in slow motion as far as I was concerned. I stepped up, grabbed hold of the opposite sides of their heads, and brought my hands back together with everything I had.

Their noggins collided with a sound not unlike a pile driver hitting asphalt. They shattered, drenching my hands in globs of orange goo as they crumbled against each other. Eww, rock monster brains. At least it didn't burn my arms off, proving my theory that the glowing goop inside wasn't lava.

Now I just had to fight off several dozen more of them, grab my friends, and get the fuck out of Dodge. Piece of cake.

Oh well, I'd figure out the details later. For now, I opened my mouth to voice my defiance, only to be completely drowned out by something much louder.

The fuck?

I turned to see Grulg with his head tilted back and screaming the most god-awful sound I think I'd ever heard. Even with my amped up powers, I was half certain I'd piss myself.

And that's when all Hell broke loose.

I wasn't sure whether Grulg was congratulating or condemning me with his horrific death cry, but interestingly enough, it turned out to be neither.

"*NO!*"

The cry rose up simultaneously from all the Jahabich

gathered. I swear these things were the fucking Fred Flintstone version of the Borg.

Just as suddenly, all of their heads turned toward the far corner of the cavern. I craned my neck and realized what Grulg had just done. It hadn't been a war cry; it had been a signal.

The Sasquatch they'd taken out for swimming lessons had broken free from his guards, knocking them to the side with its massive fists. Before Mark could intercept, it raced back behind the marble statue. There came a loud groan, although whether from it being torn loose from its moorings or from the collective Jahabich, I wasn't sure. Mark dove to the side, his survival instincts apparently trumping whatever radio control he was under. As he did, the statue tumbled over into the pool of orange nastiness.

It didn't take a genius to see this was not cool in our captors' book, but that was fine with me. I didn't need to watch to know the Sasquatch in question was doomed, but I sure as shit could make use of his sacrifice.

I stepped over to Miranda and shattered the chains on her wrists. "You ready to dole out some revenge?"

Confusion reigned on her face for a moment, but a predatory smile quickly replaced it as a red glow slowly emanated from her. "I was born ready."

"Good, Sal..." I stopped, though, when I saw that my partner was stepping toward where Grulg towered over his side of the wall.

"Grulg," she said. "Are you ready to die?"

"*By she-T'lunta's side, if great beasts so will it,*" he growled.

What the?

"*I offer truce per Humbaba Accord. You accept?*"

"I swear by the First," she replied.

Apparently, that was good enough for Grulg because

he grabbed two of the distracted Jahabich and threw them like they were made of balsa wood instead of stone.

I just stared for a moment, my mouth agape, but Sally turned and said, "What? Great minds think alike."

"This is what all that 'ready to die' shit was about?"

"Duh."

"Why didn't you say anything to me?"

"We needed to speak in code because the walls quite literally have ears. Besides, we're probably going to die anyway, so it really wasn't a lie. Now, do you want to get the fuck out of here or should we sit on our asses and debate this some more?"

I smiled back at her and simply said, "Chaos is the name of the game," knowing she'd almost certainly take the hint.

The two monsters whose heads I crushed had left a gap in the fence that the others, their attention still focused on the bath their beloved statue was taking, hadn't filled yet. I barreled out between them into the open, with Sally and Miranda following close behind. Grulg and the two Sasquatches with him continued to toss their jailers about. I was about to shout for them to follow us, but then saw their throws were purposeful, aiming Jahabich at Jahabich, knocking holes in the walls of the other pens.

I had no idea whether most of the creatures in this hell hole were friend or foe - probably the latter, knowing my luck - but I was willing to bet most of them would be more interested in either running for their lives or taking a chunk out of their tormenters than anything else.

It was a good strategy, so I decided to steal it as I barreled toward Ed's location. Every couple of steps, I would stop and coldcock a Jahabich from behind. Under normal circumstances, this would've done little more than break my fist. It still probably did, but my healing took over almost immediately and my blows had a lot more force behind them.

The Sasquatch that had knocked over the statue was leading our foes on a merry chase of hit and run. The other prisoners in his group, seeing what awaited them, were quick to revolt as well. Unfortunately for them, the column of rock monsters on the opposite shore began to march forward. Bad for them, good for us, though.

I almost whooped in joy when I saw they'd momentarily lost all interest in Ed, swarming past him to put down the uprising. It was their mistake to focus on the many while I had eyes for the one.

When whatever drove them took over, the Jahabich were nearly unbeatable, but with that attention diverted elsewhere, they were slow to respond - kind of like freakishly large ants made of stone.

By the time some of them had turned and began to notice the cavern proper again, anarchy was running full steam ahead.

25

THE BOOM BOOM ROOM

I began to understand what Grulg had meant about the last ones left being the strongest. Wherever there had been a singular occupant of a cage, now lay bits of Jahabich - crushed under foot and claw.

That disgusting flying thing I had seen earlier had taken to the air despite the massive puncture holes in its wings. I ducked as it spewed forth some horrid bile. Good thing too, as the Jahabich that received the brunt of the attack began to immediately dissolve. Nasty.

I refocused on the prize ahead, and what I saw gave me hope. Ed might've been a lot of things, but he wasn't stupid. The second the horde swarmed forward, he began to make his way to the side nearest us. I threw up a hand and he caught sight of me, waving back. Maybe we had a shot at this after all.

It was all going better than I could have hoped. Everything was fighting back against their captives and doing pretty well.

Oh, crap! Make that *nearly* everyone. The humans we'd spied earlier, being amongst the squishier things here, had mostly formed up into a defensive group - trying to stay out of the way. That would have been smart, except for their proximity to the feral vampires. One of the other former captives, a large creature resembling a mega-sized, multi-legged armadillo, smashed into their wall, sending the rock monsters tumbling away and freeing the crazed vamps.

I didn't know the mindset of most of the creatures here, nor did I have any plans to invite them to a sit-down lunch anytime soon, but at least they seemed sane enough to focus their wrath against their tormenters. Not so the starving vamps. With an angry screech, they descended upon the humans and began tearing them limb from limb. Fuck!

I didn't know these people from Jack Shit, but I couldn't just leave them to their fate. I might not have been human anymore, but no matter what I became, I tried to hold on to as much of my humanity as I could - even if it proved to be a massively stupid thing to do.

I quickly turned my head. There! Miranda had just finished melting a Jahabich who'd gotten too close. Sally was hot on her heels, tearing the creature's arm off and brandishing it as a makeshift club.

"Get Ed!" I yelled at them.

I didn't wait to see their reaction before I turned and put on a burst of speed. Sometimes, the enemy of my enemy isn't even close to being my friend.

I'd been hungry a few times as a vampire, really hungry. Mostly it was a result of grave injury and then coping with the extra energy required to heal. Once, while up in Canada, I had even seriously considered snacking on my friends for a moment or two before realizing what the hell I was doing. I'd thought that had been bad, but now saw it was nothing. The vampires before me couldn't be called human by any stretch of the imagination. Their skin was tight and pale, their fangs and claws fully extended, and worst of all, there wasn't a shred of rational thought showing in their black eyes.

All they cared about was biting and sucking, clawing and drinking. Even when I ran up behind the nearest one and put my fist straight through its back and out the front of its chest, the others barely paid me any heed. The vamp I impaled immediately incinerated around my arm...and let me tell you, *that* is one fucking weird-ass feeling.

Sadly, three of the humans were beyond help. Even if they survived, they'd probably turn. As much as I wanted to save them, we couldn't afford to carry unconscious bodies with us - especially ones that would soon wake up hungry for a meal of blood. Some of the others looked like they were debating still trying to help their fellows. That would have been a mistake.

"Run!" I extended my own fangs to hopefully drive the point home but didn't stop to see if they'd listen. I couldn't leave the vamps to their own devices - they'd just pursue the runners the second they were done with their current meal.

Fuck it all. I lowered my head and bull-rushed the lot. The tightly packed foursome fought over the pile of twitching flesh at their feet, so it didn't require a ton of strategy to hold out my arms and slam them all backwards.

My timing, amazingly enough, was perfect. A group of Jahabich had finally pried themselves away from the spectacle at the lakeside and were approaching us. I slammed the vamps into their line, letting their razor sharp skin do most of the job for me.

It worked. Mindlessly enraged and in pain, the

remaining vamps turned on the Jahabich and began attacking.

Oh yeah! Some days, I'm almost as awesome as people say I think I...*oof!*

While I was busy gawking, I caught a club to the side of my noggin, nearly scrambling my head like an egg. Had I not been hopped up on a meager amount of super blood, it would have surely been lights out for me...at least, until they carried my ashes to that pool and I woke up with a pair of road flares for eyeballs.

I rolled to my back to size up my attacker and saw one of the Jahabich standing over me, its arms raised to smash me to paste.

Or at least, they were until the massive Sasquatch rising above it ripped them out of their sockets.

"Thanks, Grulg," I muttered weakly - hoping against hope that the truce still held. The whole "I only saved you so I could kill you myself" cliché was overplayed anyway.

Before he could disappoint me with a negative answer, Sally appeared by his side. I was glad as hell to see her, and not just because the view up her shirt from this angle was spectacular.

She reached down, grabbed a hold of my body armor, and hauled me to my feet. "Let's go!" She gave me a forceful shove away from the fighting.

"But Ed..."

"Miranda and Drulk have him."

"Drulk?"

"One of Grulg's men. Now move!"

She didn't need to tell me twice.

By the time we reached one of the side tunnels leading away from Alcatraz's diabolical cousin, our tormentors had finished off the prisoners rioting near the orange goo. I risked a glance back to see them tossing the last of the dead bodies into the vile liquid, which immediately started bubbling.

All at once, I understood. The Jahabich used whatever unholy powers the orange diarrhea held to replenish their ranks. We'd been fighting a pointless fight, thinking we were winning, but it had just been a war of attrition - them renewing their ranks from the remains of whatever of our forces they managed to pick off. Fuck me. "We need to end this."

"If by 'end this,'" Sally said from my side, "you mean 'get the fuck out of here as fast as we can,' then I concur."

"No. They're going to keep coming. You don't..."

Sally grabbed my shirt and dragged me to a halt. Without any warning, she backhanded me across the face. Amped as I was, it didn't hurt much, but she still drew blood. "Get your fucking head on straight, Bill."

Once more, I could have sworn Dr. Death stirred from within. A small part of me, a dark presence in the back of my head, wanted to haul off and clock her - knock her fucking head right off.

No!

Go back to sleep, asshole. You're just having a wet dream.

I took a deep breath and shook my head. We were both right. These monsters needed to be stopped, their source of power destroyed, but Sally had a really good point - we couldn't do that and have any hope of surviving.

The horde of Jahabich were now fully engaged against the rioting prisoners, and the tide was quickly turning. As much as I didn't want to, I decided to heed Sally's wisdom. We'd need to fight this battle another day...preferably one in which we had the full forces of the Draculas behind us and maybe a couple of tactical nukes at our disposal. Never let it be said I didn't have a fertile imagination.

"Are we good?" Sally asked, staring me down.

"You know, I have some other parts that might be more fun to smack."

With a growl of annoyance, she turned and took off down the tunnel. I smiled at her rapidly retreating backside and raced to join her.

The trip back to the cavern with the cave paintings was shorter than I remembered. Amazing how things seem so different when you're running for your life as opposed to being force-marched to a prison camp.

I wasn't sure if it was my amped-up hearing, the echo of the caves, or if it was just that fucking loud, but sounds of battle poured out behind us. Shrieks, crashes, roars of anger - all of it pointed to one hell of a fight going on. But I had no delusions as to who would win. The Jahabich had their self-replenishing numbers to back them up, not to mention some kind of hive mind that could direct them all as one. Some of the entities back there were both angry and pretty badass, but the odds were heavily stacked against them.

"What took you so long?" Ed asked, panting next to Sally.

"I was gonna leave your ass, but I really didn't want to have to mail Tom your part of the rent check too every month. Sally pays me like shit as it is."

"Ass," he replied, clapping me on the shoulder.

"*Enough talk*," Grulg said, towering over us. When something that big said to shut up, you shut the fuck up with extreme prejudice.

He was right, though. We weren't even close to safe

yet, and I could have sworn the commotion behind us sounded closer.

I took quick stock of our group. Sally and Miranda were all that remained of my expedition. Grulg and one of his brutes, Drulk presumably, made it out too. Along with Ed, I was pleased to see that three humans - two women and a middle-aged man - had possessed enough sense to join our fleeing group.

Grulg likewise surveyed us. He opened his mouth and spit out a disgusting wad of phlegm - enough to make me back up a step to avoid the splash. Eww. *"You fight well, T'luntas. Truce now over."*

Oh, crap. "Wait, I..."

Right then, my vision doubled, and I went down to one knee. Fuck, not now! My strength was quickly ebbing, and even worse, my stomach was turning - probably a result of swallowing more sewer grime than dried blood.

Either way, if Grulg decided to settle shit between vamp and Sasquatch right this moment, I didn't like our chances one bit. I was forced to remember our alliance with the Magi was only in regards to keeping the Jahabich in check. They were still neutral when it came to the Humbaba Accord. Miranda would be perfectly in the right to stand back and let him twist our heads off like beer caps.

"Grulg wish you well. Perhaps one day Grulg will have honor to crush you on battlefield."

Huh? The other Bigfoot didn't seem too pleased to hear that, but he got a massive hand upside the head before he could so much as bare his teeth.

I'd almost forgotten that during our time up in Canada, Grulg had been the one Squatch with a sense of honor about him. Thank goodness for small favors. Had we been trapped down here with Turd, I had little doubt he'd be having himself a good ole time right about now rearranging our limbs like we were Mr. Potato Head dolls.

With that, Grulg turned and headed away from us - aiming for one of the other tunnels out of this cave - presumably one that would lead him up and away from here.

"Good luck!" Sally called after him.

"Think they'll be okay?" Ed asked.

"As long as they make it to the surface."

"Think we should have followed them?"

"Nope." She turned and offered me a hand. "The truce was over. Walking outside with them would have ended badly."

I gladly accepted her help, managing to stand up straight despite feeling like I was about to puke my guts out. I took a deep breath and looked around. "Where?"

"What?"

I quickly scanned the cavern walls, trying to make sense of where we'd come out. Finally, I saw some of those glowing rocks in the shape of a robe...the wall painting. That meant...

"Over there!" I pointed toward an area of the floor a ways off.

An echoing roar sounded behind us - more fear than rage. I turned to see the greasy flying thing from earlier, the one with the really bad acid reflux, come tearing out of the cave we'd run from.

It didn't stop to give our group a second glance. It landed awkwardly and raced into another of the caves leading out of here.

"Uh oh," Miranda said, but she needn't have bothered. Even with my rapidly diminishing powers, I could see an orange glow beginning to shine from the direction the prison lay.

Without a word, I turned and ran, hoping I was right.

One of the humans called out, "Hey, where are you going?" That's right, genius. Let them know exactly where we are.

A moment later, Sally caught up to me. She was breathing hard, the exertion and lack of fresh blood beginning to catch up to her. Before she could say anything, I pointed toward the small pile on the ground that I was heading toward.

"Holy shit, it's our stuff."

"Hopefully, still in one piece."

The firearms lay where they'd been discarded, broken beyond repair. I mean, we could've used them as clubs, but I didn't see much use there. The melee weapons, also known as gardening supplies in other circles, were likewise destroyed. Their handles had been snapped off, ensuring they wouldn't be caving in any Jahabich skulls anytime soon.

Thankfully, the rest of our gear was in much better shape. Sally grabbed one of the backpacks, while I found what I was looking for: the last remaining canteen of vampire blood.

Bonus! Next to it lay my cell phone, the screen only slightly cracked. Fuck it; I'd take what I could get - upgrade fees were a bitch anyway. Stuffing the phone into a pocket on my chest piece, I quickly unscrewed the cap of the canteen and lifted it to my lips. Thankfully, it hadn't leaked. Three cheers for military-grade equipment. I sucked down great big gulps of blood, my body gladly taking it in. Before I'd even put the cap back on, I could feel myself racing back toward the level of power afforded me by the mix of plasma.

Sally watched me, eyeing the canteen hungrily. Although I knew better than to say anything, I felt bad for her. The effort she put forth to keep her shit together must have been heroic indeed. "Sorry, but it'll do you more harm than..."

"I know," she replied. "I guess, for once, I have to live vicariously through you. Hell has finally frozen over."

It was then that the others finally caught up to us. Sadly, they weren't alone. A dozen sets of orange eyes gleamed in the darkness behind them - quickly closing the gap. Shit!

I turned to Sally. "Can you climb?"

"I'll fucking sprout wings if I need to."

"What about carrying anyone?"

That gave her pause. I knew she wanted to give me the tough girl answer, but the tired look in her eyes betrayed her. At last, she looked away. "One...maybe two."

Damn. With Ed, we had...

"I can handle that," Miranda said. "I have enough in me to take everyone. We can apparate to the top no problem."

"Wait a second," I said.

"What's the matter?"

"I thought it wasn't *called* apparating."

She looked at me like I had two heads. "What else would we call it?"

"Uh..."

"Hey, I have a crazy idea," Ed jumped in. "Why don't we worry about that *after* we get the fuck out of here?"

Every team needs a voice of reason, and I certainly wasn't going to argue.

I turned to the group, ready to lead them back toward the perfectly circular tunnel leading out of here. The three humans looked like they were on their last legs, fear and adrenaline being the only things holding them up. Sally wasn't much better off. Ed was beaten to hell, but only he and Miranda looked like they had any fight left in them. Damn it!

"Go," I said, turning to Sally. "Get them out of here. I'll be right behind you."

She took a look behind me and apparently decided to forgo any stupid heroics. She simply nodded. "Don't be too long. You really don't want to be on this side when it's time to open the little present Vlad and I planted earlier."

With that, she waved the group forward and started off toward the exit.

Ed hesitated for a moment too long, so I grabbed him by the shirt and gently helped him along - to the tune of ten feet through the air in the direction he needed to go. He managed to land without too much effort, but finally got the hint. "Asshole!"

"You'll thank me for this later." I turned, smiling, but the look vanished from my face as quickly as it had appeared.

The Jahabich were here, and a very angry-looking Mark was at their forefront.

Oh, great. Just what I was hoping to avoid: a heroic last stand.

26

WHEN THE WALLS FELL

I tossed the canteen strap over my neck and swung it around to my back. I wanted to keep it safe as long as possible in case I needed a quick recharge - which, from the look of things, seemed likely.

Oh well, there was no point in delaying the inevitable. I took a look around and spied one of the mallet heads lying on the spongey ground - just what the doctor ordered.

I picked it up and let fly, putting what felt like the strength of the entirety of Pandora Coven behind it.

Sadly, Mark was in his human form. I didn't know exactly how things worked with these fuckers, but they appeared to possess more of their former self-awareness in their non-rocky form. Almost as if confirming this, his eyes opened wide as I threw the projectile and he dove to the side, valiantly letting the Jahabich behind him take it full on in the face. Its head caved in from the impact. The creature wavered drunkenly to the side for a moment and then its form lost cohesion. It began to transform back and forth, out of control - one moment flesh, the next rock. Finally, it solidified long enough for me to catch a small glimpse of Brock's mangled features, just before keeling over.

"Serves you right, fuck face."

Unfortunately, that was the cleverest thing I had time to utter before ducking a swing from another of the monsters. The top of my scalp tore as its jagged skin rubbed against mine, but I ignored the pain and followed up with a blow of my own - putting a fist-sized dent in the side of its head before shoving it away.

Two more rushed forward, taking me low in the midsection. I went down, but managed to roll with the momentum, tossing them off before they could pin me to the ground.

I immediately threw a kick to the crotch of the next in line. Sadly, there were no rock nuts to be found and I had to be content when it flew back and smashed into another of its buddies.

I scrambled to my feet to avoid being caught in the prone position. Every gamer worth his salt knows it's an automatic plus to hit for the opposing side. Screw that shit. These monsters had enough of an armor class advantage as it was.

Another pair of them charged me and I couldn't sidestep in time. I kicked out, using my superior height and reach to my advantage, and caught one in the chest, but the other got inside of my defenses. It wrapped its arms around me and, with a quick chuckle of triumph, sunk the obsidian daggers that made up its teeth into my shoulder.

Fuck me!

Vampire nerve endings work pretty much the same way human ones do - meaning I got to experience the wonderful feeling of my flesh and tendons tearing as the ugly fucker sank in to the bone. Had I not been flying high on vamp juice, it would have surely severed my arm. As it was, the ugly heap of rock held on tight, a stonework bear trap on legs, while its friends moved in from behind it.

No fucking way was I going down like that. "That's not a bite," I said in a bad Australian accent. "*This* is a bite!" And with that, I sank my own fangs into the neckless juncture where its pumpkin-sized head met its body.

Any kid who's ever eaten dirt knows it's not the most wonderful of flavors. It tastes pretty much like its name suggests, with some extra grit thrown in for texture. This wasn't much different. At my current power level, my teeth chewed through its rock-hard carapace like it was made of sugar glass and kept on digging - hoping to find the candy surprise inside.

Apparently, it wasn't too pleased at my attempt to discover how many licks it took to get to the center. It let go of me and screeched a sound like tires squealing against pavement as a driver slams on the brakes to avoid a squirrel in the road.

There was a moment's pause as I considered the oddly specific metaphor running through my head, then I shoved the creature back with everything I had - sending it tumbling into three of its friends.

Now, if I could just repeat that a few more times, I'd be home free. Sadly, they had other plans as, just then, something slammed into the back of my head - erasing the scalp there and making me see stars.

Powerful stone arms reached around me and pinned my arms in a full nelson. Maybe I could've powered out of it, but not before severing my arms against the sharp rock-like hide of the creature. Out of the corner of my eye, I could see its massive head next to mine. If it bit down now, there was no fucking way I'd be able to do anything except die.

But it didn't. Its face shimmered and melted - quickly replaced by a familiar grinning countenance - Mark's. Oh, fuck me sideways with a wood lathe!

"You know, for the legendary savior of the vampire race, you sure are a fucking idiot." His breath smelled like dirt, moss, and mildew...gross.

"Works for me," I replied, struggling to free my body without literally disarming myself. "Everyone in the super-natural world is so busy patting themselves on the back for being super geniuses that when a moron comes along, they have no clue how to handle it."

I looked up. The scattered Jahabich, of which there were more than enough to mess up my day good and proper, were getting back to their feet and turning in my direction. I needed to think of something quickly.

"You have no idea how good you could have had it," Mark said. "I've seen the way you look at her. What man wouldn't? But are you aware of the backstabbing viper that lurks beneath that pretty face?"

"Trust me, well aware."

"We would have scraped that away, saving the good parts. She would have been beautiful forever, but much more compliant."

"Uh huh. Not the first time I've heard some guy make that claim."

"I would have shared her with you. We could have been brothers, and she our willing servant."

"I'm all for threesomes, dude, but not of the two-guy variety - sorry. I just don't see any appeal in us rubbing our rock junk together."

Oh shit, his friends were closing in and I was still held tight. *C'mon, think of something, stupid!*

"Cute," he replied. "I used to be like you, thinking a

clever joke would get me out of anything. But I learned the hard way life is not that easy. I had to pull myself up by my fingernails, suffering all the way, but I became better. No matter what happened to me...no matter what tried to kill me, I survived. I have had my back against the wall my entire life, been slammed into it repeatedly, but I've learned to push back." His face hardened once again, and his eyes opened wide until orange Hell light spewed forth from them. "*Now you will too.*"

Oh, crap...

Wait, what was that about being slammed into the wall? Holy shit, I am such a fucking moron.

"Well, consider this another life lesson." I bent and twisted my shoulder. For a second, I wasn't sure I had it right, but then Mark was flying over my shoulder in a spectacular - for me anyway - Judo throw. He slammed into the approaching monsters as if shot from a cannon, sending granite chips flying everywhere and knocking the whole group ass over teakettle.

Fucking-A! I almost wished I hadn't already killed Brock. He might've been proud to know I'd been sorta paying attention after all.

Oh well, now definitely wasn't the time to stand around waiting for applause. I flipped my middle finger to the bunch of them, mentally directing most of it at Mark, then took off like the devil was on my heels...mainly because, in a few seconds, he probably would be.

I was pleased to see my friends had mostly heeded common sense and made a run for it. I was less pleased to see Sally amongst the debris that littered the entrance leading to the long climb outta here.

She was on her knees, rummaging through the back-pack she'd managed to salvage.

"Don't tell me," I said, catching up to her, "you need to touch up your eye shadow before climbing back up to the sewers."

"Did you kill Mark?"

"Well...not really."

"Then here's an idea: why don't you shut the fuck up and not bother me?" Frustrated, she emptied the contents onto the ground - bandages, a flashlight, a tube of lipstick - Jesus fucking Christ - and various other items fell out. "Where is it?"

"What?"

"The fucking remote detonator!"

"What detonator?"

"The one I need to detonate these, genius." She pointed to several bundled items attached to the debris, the wall, and the ceiling.

Holy crap. "I see you and Vlad were busy."

"Well, we sure as shit didn't come back here to make out." She threw the pack to the side in disgust. "They must've recognized it."

"Maybe it just fell out back there." I hooked a thumb.

"Do you want to go and search?"

"Not really."

"Well then, how..."

"What's going on?" a voice called from further down in the tunnel. It was Miranda. She was approaching us with Ed by her side, a flashlight beam illuminating their way.

"Just fucking great," Sally snarled softly before raising her voice. "I thought you were going to teleport everyone up top."

"I thought you were going to just be a minute."

"What's wrong?" Ed asked as the two joined us.

I was tempted to reply with something appropriately pithy, but I took a quick glance behind me. Numerous angry orange eyes were closing in on us. "Sally rigged this cave to blow, but she can't find the detonator."

Insanely enough, Ed didn't even blink at this revelation. Guess he'd been hanging around with us too much as of late. "Can't we just shoot the explosives?"

"With what?" Sally's eyes turned black with frustration. "These fuckers broke all our noise makers."

"That's it, then," I said. "It was a good try, but we need to get moving. Hopefully, we can beat these fuckers back to Pandora's Box and get some reinforcem..."

"Wait," Miranda said. "Would enough heat set these off?"

Sally shook her head. "It's too stable. It needs more than that; an explosion to set off an explosion."

"I could do that. Fire magic is one of my specialties. Just tell me how far back to stand and..."

"All the way," Sally said. "We can't be in the cave when these things go off..."

"Uh, guys," I said, pointing.

"Even if the entire thing doesn't collapse, the shock-wave will tear apart anyone that's..."

"*Guys!*"

They stopped and turned toward me.

"We're out of time."

Sure enough, the Jahabich, with Mark in the lead, were converging on us. We had maybe thirty seconds and they'd be all over us like new suits.

If the tunnel had been narrower, it might've made a good choke point to fight them off. As it was, though, it was way too wide to give our small group a tactical advantage.

"Fuck!" Sally cried in frustration. I could see why. Mark was now close enough that we could see the predatory grin on his face. He might as well have had a graphic superimposed over him that read, "Game Over."

"We need to run." I grabbed hold of Sally's arm and began to drag her back toward...

"No," Miranda said, stepping past us. She raised her hands, screamed something incoherent, and a ball of green flame shot out from her. The Jahabich scrambled out of the way in time, but it bought us a few more seconds.

"Thanks," I said. "Now we really need to..."

"I said no. I'll hold them off while you run."

"But..."

"And then I'm going to give these assholes the biggest surprise of their lives. Just be sure to be out of the tunnel by then."

"Good luck," Sally said as she turned. Goddamn, what a heartless bitch.

"Wait, we can't just let her do this."

"Bill's right," Ed said. "We...ugh!"

He was cut off mid-agreement by Sally's fist. Before he could hit the floor, she'd scooped him up and tossed him over her shoulder. With a nod, she took off into the darkness.

It was a surprisingly effective way to end an argument. Heck, if it worked for Ed, I didn't see any reason why it wouldn't work for...

"Don't even think it, vampire," Miranda snarled. I turned back to find another orb of green flame dancing on her fingertips. Her stance said she hadn't quite decided which way to throw it.

"Miranda, this isn't the way to..."

"Just shut up and listen. The last few nights, I've had dreams...dreams of my husband."

"What?"

She smiled. It was sad, but tinged ever so slightly with

hope. "I think it was a vision, a sign. I think he was telling me that it was time for us to be together again."

"That's crazy!"

"Is it? I don't think so. I'm tired of all of this and I miss him. You have no idea how much."

I momentarily thought of Sheila and when I'd been convinced that she was dead. I had more of an idea than she knew.

Her grin widened. "Besides, I knew this was a one-way trip when I signed up for it. It's okay. I get to see Carl again and maybe even bring a bunch of these fuckers with me as an entourage."

A bellow of rage sounded at the mouth of the larger cavern. The Jahabich were here.

"Go!"

There was no time left to argue. Goddamn it all!

"Thank you," I said softly.

"Oh, and Bill," she said. "I can tell you're different from the rest. Don't ever forget your human friends - your humanity."

"I won't."

Miranda turned away from me and the glow intensified around her. This was definitely not the time for long goodbyes.

I turned and ran, putting every ounce of speed into my stride.

I was going to need it.

The spongey ground beneath my feet wasn't made for sprinting, so I found myself long jumping down the tunnel, using the give of the ground to my advantage...and trying my best to not clonk my head against the ceiling. That would've been a hell of a way to check out.

I saw the opening up ahead and the wall beyond that signaled the long climb up. There was no way I could leave this one to chance. Reaching around behind me, I grabbed hold of the canteen and unslung it from my shoulder. Ripping the cap off, I raised it to my lips just as the floor began to rumble.

I glanced back as the sound of the explosion reached me - nearly blowing out my overly sensitive eardrums. Green and red flames raced down the tunnel in my direction, their image distorted by the shock wave they rode.

I gulped down a swallow and put everything I had into my legs...only to stumble as the ground rippled in front of me. The ages-old layers of grime and shit began to give way.

It was all I could do to keep my footing. Just a little bit more...

A sinkhole opened before me, the quivering mass of floor collapsing in on itself, perhaps into an even deeper abyss below us.

My hair caught ablaze as the fire overtook me and then I jumped, using every bit of stolen strength at my disposal.

I slammed into the wall, the canteen knocked out of my grip as I desperately sank my claws into the rock and began to climb with everything I had.

And that's when the full brunt of the explosion overtook me.

27

ONWARD AND UPWARD

Had Sally not shared her brainstorm about mixing up blood cocktails, I have little doubt I would have been a goner. As it was, my body armor was still far more heat resistant than the rest of me.

As the shockwave slammed into me, pretty much crushing me against the wall like a bug, my skin blistered and burned. Within seconds, I turned into a human pyre.

But still I climbed, managing to stifle a cry if only because I didn't want to open my mouth and experience the wonderful sensation of my tongue melting.

All the while, I kept sinking my claws nearly knuckle deep in the wall as the entire thing shook as if God himself had come down from heaven and decided, "Enough of this shit."

I was surprised there wasn't more sound, but then again, I really couldn't hear much of anything at all. In short, I was in bad shape. I just had to hope the Jahabich were worse off. Miranda had done as she'd promised and then some. If there was any justice in this crazy universe, she'd received her reward for her effort and been reunited with her husband in whatever afterlife awaited mages.

Now, all I needed to do was make sure I didn't join them.

Finally, the shockwave passed. The air remained super-heated and I couldn't see shit with all the dust, but almost immediately, I began to feel less crispy. The healing power of half a dozen vampires was working its magic inside of me - knitting things back together at a pace I wouldn't see naturally for several hundred more years, assuming I was lucky enough to make it that far. Fuck it; the way things were going, I considered every new week as cause to celebrate.

Yeah, a party sounded nice right at that moment - one with strippers, good food, and lots to drink - preferably all of it ice cold.

I held that last image in my head as I continued to climb, my skin alternating between peeling off and growing back again. I just hoped my healing kept at it. Now would be a really fucking lousy time for it to up and burn out, like that time Magneto ripped Wolverine's adamantium skeleton out - not one of my favorite comic arcs, as each subsequent issue seemed to be about him either getting his ass kicked or whining about it.

At last, the heat began to subside. Little by little, my epidermis grew back and stayed that way. The rumbling continued, and I realized I could now hear the sound of rock caving in on itself from far below. Jesus Christ, how many fucking explosives had Sally set down there? Only one thing was certain - she sure as shit wanted to make sure those monsters stayed buried this time.

Sadly, I had a feeling that wasn't to be. Unless the entire cave network had crumbled, multiple exits led away from that place with the cave painting. There likewise might have been more egresses in the cavern with the orange pool of glowing death. It would have taken a tremendous amount of luck to have brought the entirety of their home down upon their heads. I felt pretty good about making it out, but didn't dare fool myself into believing the gods of fate smiled upon me in anything even approaching that capacity.

Oh well, their main path to the Vegas sewers was hopefully shut. If they managed to surface again, they'd have to find another coven to haunt.

Hah, the Vegas sewers. I had a moment to consider that and hope we hadn't collapsed the entire city with our antics. How embarrassing would that be?

I lifted my claws to grasp the next handhold and instead found I'd somehow reached the top.

Thank goodness too. The battle between my healing prowess and the fires of destruction had really taken everything out of me. I practically had to drag myself up over the edge.

I bent over for a moment, my hands on my knees - catching my breath in between trying to cough out any gunk in my lungs. The hard part was seemingly over. Now all I had to do was hope the others were still alive, find them in this rat maze of tunnels, and somehow not get lost down here for all of eternity.

Yeah, sounded easy as pie.

Holy crap, my head was spinning. Had the explosion taken that much out of me? I mean, normally, when my body healed, it was a done deal, but it seemed that down here, whenever the vampire blood began to wear off...

Oh, crap. Was that the cause? I'd been so psyched at the success of Sally's little experiment I hadn't stopped to consider any side effects. What if it was poisoning me somehow? What if I...

Oof! I tripped and fell over something. The smoke

from the explosion had started to thin out, but it was still hard as hell to see anything. Vampire eyes might be awesome for night vision, but they were about as useful as a bag of dicks for seeing through dust and debris.

I felt along the floor and found what I'd fallen over. It was covered in hot ash, but it didn't take me long to determine the humanoid shape. Oh no.

It wasn't a vampire; that much was easy to figure out. There was an actual body beneath the dirt and grime. Had it been a vamp, there'd have been nothing but floor under it, but I definitely felt at least an arm and a torso. Dusting it off further, I could feel that it was pretty badly burnt up - no doubt from the explosion. From the size and shape - and by that I mean boobs - I could tell it was female. One of the humans we'd saved, maybe?

But why was she so close to ground zero? Did that mean Sally hadn't gotten them away in time? Fuck!

I began feeling along the floor, panic rising in me. What if it had all been for nothing? What if we'd escaped only for our desperate gambit to consume everyone but me? "No!"

Aside from whatever had been caused by Miranda's explosive exit from this mortal coil, there wasn't any breeze to clear things out. Fortunately, though, that meant stuff started to settle quickly in the still air.

Sadly, it still wasn't enough yet to give me more than a few inches of visibility. It also didn't help that I was so dizzy at this point I probably couldn't even stand back up if I tried. I started feeling blindly along the floor for anyone else. Unfortunately, it rapidly became an exercise in futility as I'd check one section and then realize I was doing so again in the same spot just a second later.

Thinking was becoming a chore and I couldn't be entirely certain I wasn't going to puke.

Darkness began to play at the edges of my vision, and

it had nothing to do with the debris in the air. Despite a ton of adrenaline coursing through me, all I really wanted to do was take a nice long nap.

And that's when a hand reached out of the darkness and dragged me to my feet.

Oh shit! Had Mark or some of those other freaks gotten out? If so, there was no way I could...

I reached out to shove my attacker away and felt rough fabric, but beneath it lay firm yet supple mounds of flesh.

"What the fuck are you doing, Bill?"

"Sally?"

"Yeah, now get your hands off of my ti..."

I pressed my lips against hers in the dusty confines of the cave, cutting off her protest. I grabbed hold and held her tight as I did so - all caution thrown to the wind in my joy at finding her alive. At first, she stiffened in surprise, but then I could have sworn she relaxed a bit and began to return it.

Unfortunately, that last part could have just been wishful thinking, as I picked that exact moment to pass out.

"Ow, I think you dislodged a tooth."

"Stop whining. It was for your own good."

"You didn't need to hit me."

"Yes, I did. Are you going to tell me you were just about to run like you'd been told to?"

"Well..."

"Exactly. You seem to share that stupid trait with Bill. You both pick the absolute worst times to be chivalrous. Must be something in your shithole apartment's water."

"You don't find that cute?"

"I find it annoying."

"Come on, not the slightest bit..."

"Uhhh," I groaned as I tried, and failed, to open my eyes. The voices had started filtering into my subconscious right around the time I became aware of various sensations - a wetness against my back, coupled with the sense of movement.

As the moan escaped my lips, the movement stopped and there came the *wonderful* feeling of a dull impact on the back of my head. "Ouch."

"Oops," a female voice replied. "You finally awake?"

"I think so. Not sure I want to be, though." I pried my eyes open and winced as my head throbbed from the effort. It had been a while, well over a year - basically ever since I'd been turned into a vampire - but I distinctly remembered how it felt to be hung over. This wasn't all that different. However, it didn't help that someone was shining a flashlight in my eyes.

"Get that fucking thing out of my face."

"Sorry," a familiar male voice responded.

I took a look around, but didn't see much of anything at first. Panic set in until I reached up and realized my glasses were just coated in thick dust from the explosion. They were filthy but intact. Thank goodness I had splurged for titanium frames with shatterproof lenses.

Using my fingers to wipe the worst of the gunk away, I was finally able to see further than the tip of my nose again, making out the forms standing above me - Sally, Ed, and...and that was it. Nothing else came into view save the dark walls of the sewer tunnel.

I reached up a hand and Ed grabbed hold. Bracing myself for the unpleasant feeling of being vertical again, I let him drag me to my feet. Then I immediately stepped to the wall for a little added support. "What happened?"

"You fainted," Sally replied with a smirk.

"I'm pretty sure I passed out."

"Same thing."

I looked around the tunnel we were standing in and saw marks on the floor leading off into one direction. I put two and two together, then reached around to confirm my backside was coated in muck. "You dragged me?"

"Yep."

"Couldn't have made a litter or something?"

"Look around, Ranger Rick. Do you see a forest here? What was I supposed to do, make one out of rocks?"

"You could have carried me."

"Could have, but didn't."

Bitch!

"You okay?" Ed asked, concern in his voice.

"Not sure." I moved away from the wall, still woozy but gaining some semblance of equilibrium back. "What was in that blood, Sally?"

"Nothing but blood."

Seeing Ed's confused look, I explained Sally's plan to him and how it had worked out better than I'd hoped - leading us to him and then saving our asses big time. The only downside seemed to be what I felt now, which was worrisome. I'd already suffered from one power burning out - in a sense of the phrase. What if this was a chain reaction? Maybe soon, I'd find myself crawling on my knees, a slave to some other vampire's compulsion. Wow, wouldn't that suck big hairy Sasquatch balls? I voiced my concern of such.

Sally raised an eyebrow, seemingly thinking this through. To my surprise, though, Ed just laughed.

"Did I miss the punchline?"

"Only every time you look in a mirror."

"Eat me."

"Seriously," he said, his voice even, "it seems pretty obvious to me - you crashed."

"*Crashed?*"

"Yeah, remember that time about two years back when you finally swore to God you were gonna ask Sheila out?"

"Um..."

"We were all sitting around doing shots, but you were sucking down Red Bulls, too."

"Oh, yeah," I replied sheepishly.

"So what happened?" Sally asked, her grin widening.

"The usual," Ed replied. "We were at it all night. Bill must've downed at least a six-pack. Come the next day, I had to cover for him in three meetings - wouldn't have been able to wake him up if he was on fire."

"And what about her?"

"Do you need to ask?"

Assholes, both of them. "You know, considering your boyfriend back there wanted to pass you around like a blow-up doll to all his stone-dicked buddies, you may wish to refrain from commenting on the love lives of others."

"Boyfriend?" Ed asked.

"Yeah. Sally used to date one of those rock monsters."

He turned to her, the obvious question on his face, but she just held up a hand. "Drop it."

"But..."

"Or I'll *drop* you again."

And that was pretty much the end of *that* conversation.

28

THE ENEMY OF MY ENEMY IS STILL A DICKHEAD

It took me a few minutes to regain my equilibrium, and even then, I was still shaky. What Ed had said made sense now that I took some time to think it over. The truth was, every time in the past that I'd ever powered up on vamp blood, it had been a singular event. I'd bite some asshole vampire, go all Super Saiyan, then power down a short while later - hopefully after winning whatever fight I'd been in.

This was the first time I'd ever held a constant vampire *buzz*, if you will, for so long of a stretch. The truth was, I'd been so psyched at the discovery, I never bothered to consider whether there might be any consequences. Now I realized it had been a stupid, desperate gambit - relying on something that was entirely untested.

Thankfully, we'd gotten lucky, although now I was paying the price. My stomach rumbled, partially answering the question of why I felt like crap. Oddly enough, I was hungry; starving, actually.

"This makes no sense," I said after voicing those thoughts to my two friends in the dark tunnel. "I've been sucking down blood for..."

"Vampire blood," Sally corrected.

"I know that."

"Yeah, but what if that's the cause?"

"Not following you."

"It's simple," she said. "We know vamp blood is different than human blood, right? Otherwise it wouldn't be toxic to other vamps."

"True, except for me."

"Yeah, but what if that difference is also partially detrimental to you?"

"Now you've lost me too," Ed said.

"It's okay. I'll explain slowly since you're both men." She walked over to the wall where I was leaning and took a spot next to me. "What if you don't actually get a lot of nutrition out of vampire blood?"

"Kind of like with normal food?" I asked, curious to see where she was going with this.

"More or less."

"But what about that time you saved me up in Canada? I was bleeding out like a pig, but you managed to get me back on my feet."

"I'm thinking that was more the extra kick to your healing, and also, with the amount you lost, anything was better than nothing. Maybe you get something out of it, just not enough to really sustain you in the long run."

"Empty calories, but with a wicked rush," Ed surmised. "Kind of like downing a bucketful of espressos?"

"I think I get where you're going with this," I said. "You have, say, a soda in the middle of the day and it's not going to matter since you're probably not too far away from your last meal, or the next one, for that matter."

"Which kind of fits how it's worked for you in the past."

"Yeah, but if you go on a bender - trying to survive on nothing but that..."

"You're gonna feel like an absolute piece of shit when it's over and done with because you forgot to take your Flintstone Chewables."

I considered this. I remembered the first time I'd sucked down another vamp's blood. It had been against some goons from the Howard Beach Coven of Queens. The next morning, I'd felt similar, if not so intensely bad, to how I felt now until drinking my morning cup of blood. I'd nearly forgotten because it hadn't happened since then, but perhaps that had just been my body acclimating to it.

Shit, if I ever got my ass back east, I'd need to find Dave. After kicking his ass for running off, I wouldn't mind him running some tests to confirm all this. Maybe next time I'd need to mix my vintages - put a little human blood into the pitcher to fortify it as part of this nutritious breakfast. That way, I might not end up feeling like shit.

Speaking of feeling like a piece of crap, though... "How are you still upright?" I asked Sally.

"Huh?"

"Back there, between the beating and having your fingers chopped off..." I noticed they had grown back and looked the same as before - minus the nail polish she'd been wearing before that Jahabich had decided to go all Pac-Man on her hand. "...I saw the look in your eyes. You would have gladly chewed Miranda's head off if given half a..."

Oh crap.

"There were three people who escaped with us."

"Oh, yeah," Ed said. "I almost forgot about them after I got decked."

Sally just shrugged. "I did what I had to do. It was either that or collapse. After climbing up the pit, I couldn't carry Ed and get out of the blast radius otherwise."

"All three?"

She held up her hands. "Just the guy. The girls freaked out and took off running. I don't know what happened to them."

I remembered the body I'd found while feeling my way around in the burning fallout from Miranda's explosion. Sometimes, I forgot that despite our friendship and her newfound caring of the people living in Pandora, a bloodthirsty predator lurked just below Sally's surface - she was a complex individual that way.

"Fuck," I muttered softly.

It wasn't so much that I was mad at her. It was more that we'd won by only the barest of margins, and even that remained questionable. There'd been other tunnels leading out of that one cave. Unless we'd gotten extremely lucky, all we'd done was cut off one of the Jahabich's routes to the surface.

Then there was Mark to consider. I'd like to think he'd been crushed under a hundred tons of falling rock, but without having seen it myself, I didn't want to hope for the best. That wasn't good. The guy had seemed ever so slightly around the bend where the subject of Sally was concerned. I'd read enough real-life horror stories online to know that the operative word with crazy exes was the *crazy* part. That particular subset of society didn't know how to take a hint.

The worst of it all, though, was knowing that had any of the humans survived, I'd probably have attacked them myself.

We could fool ourselves all we wanted, take in as many refugees as we could fit, but at the end of the day, we were still monsters. Maybe Sheila was right after all. I could pretend to tread along a righteous path, but that was crap. No matter what any of us did, there was a good chance this world would eventually become a place with no real heroes - just the lesser of many evils.

Over the course of the next several hours, Sally offered me some of her blood a few times. I declined, fearful of another crash once it wore off. Besides, anything I took would eventually weaken her. On the off chance we ran into more of those goddamned walking rock piles, one of us needed to be close to the top of their game.

Thankfully, I was able to make a go of it on my own. I didn't feel great, but after I'd gotten my balance again, I had enough strength to go on. At the very least, I wasn't anywhere near the condition those feral vamps down below had been in. Who knew how long they'd been denied sustenance? If things got that bad, I'd certainly take Sally up on her offer, but I had the feeling it would be days - hopefully - before that happened, and if we were down here that long, we'd be so lost as to be thoroughly fucked.

On the upside, at least Ed didn't have anything to worry about from the present company - his blood now the equivalent of downing a gallon of rocket fuel and chasing it with a lit blowtorch. Besides, he had his own issues - like being pretty much one big walking bruise.

The trip back to the surface took a long time. Go figure; heading up was more of a chore than going down, especially when you've been through the ringer. One bit of luck held for us through it all, though - we didn't get lost.

Sally's spray-painted markers turned out to be easy enough to find, thank goodness. I could have kissed her for having the foresight to leave those. Speaking of which, I had a vague memory of doing just that right before keeling over from my blood crash. Had that been real or a sick dream? Sally certainly didn't bring it up on our long walk back. Likewise, she hadn't bounced me off of any walls, threatening me with worse should I ever do so again. At the same time, the memory was pretty solid. It sure as hell had felt real, especially near the end when it seemed like she was getting into it.

What did that mean?

Of course, it might have meant nothing. It was always hard to tell with Sally. It might have been because we now had Ed with us and that could have made for some decisively awkward conversation. "Hey, man, glad to see you're still alive. By the way, before I forget to mention it, I just tried ramming my tongue down your wannabe girlfriend's throat." Yeah...rock monsters grown from a pool of orange jizz was one thing, but talking about relationships was a whole different level of weird.

At the same time, Sally wasn't one to shy away from making anyone feel uncomfortable and she hadn't said shit.

Thankfully, I was soon distracted by these thoughts - and my own spinning head - when I realized we were finally back in a section of the sewer that was familiar. Hah, what a concept. A few years ago, you couldn't have drunken dared me to wander down a drainpipe. Now, I actually had familiarity with various tunnels and routes. I swear, never again will I laugh if someone tells me, "In the next year you shall..." followed by some outlandish proclamation. I'd seen far too much strangeness to keep a closed mind.

At long last, we reached the tunnel leading to the subbasement of Pandora's Box. Sally was still going strong thanks to her snack break down in the depths, but Ed and I were both on our last legs. It would be a quick stop for me at the fridge to grab a couple pints of blood and then a nice long session of passing the fuck out. The others could keep guard for a while. Let Steve take an extra shift since he'd missed out on all the fun.

The subbasement looked just as we'd left it. The gate

was still smashed to all hell and the place littered with broken pieces of the fused Jahabich we'd smashed to shit.

"You know, when this whole apocalypse thing is over and done with, we might want to consider seeing if there's a market for these things. I mean, shit, people pay for garden gnomes and they're no less creepy."

My two companions chuckled as we got to the ladder. Looking up, I could see the blocked opening above us. The Jahabich had trashed the trapdoor during their earlier assault, but it looked like it'd been sealed with some heavy crates for now.

"You go first, Bill," Sally said as we stepped to the ladder. "In case they open fire without bothering to check that it's us."

That stopped me in my tracks. "Fuck that shit, *coven master*. Kindly lead us lowly minions by example."

"Wimp," she replied, starting up. Even joking as she'd been, about halfway up, she yelled out, "It's us! We're back. Don't fucking shoot!"

Gotta love vampire tact, but then again, being the master of a coven of monsters typically meant one didn't need to apologize for having a poor bedside manner.

They apparently heard her because a scraping sound came from above and we saw the crates being moved aside, opening the way. Thank goodness. I could practically taste the cold Bloody Mary - made with real blood, of course - that I would treat myself to in a few short minutes.

Of course, that's the problem with wishful thinking...it's a good way to ensure you're going to be fucked in the ass nice and thorough.

Sally went up, followed by Ed, and then me taking up the rear.

I had just about reached the top, when Ed asked with some uncertainty, "Uh, Sally?"

I popped my head up through the opening a scant

second later to find a full house waiting for us. Now that's what I'm talking about. It's about fucking time I got a hero's welcome for putting my ass on the line. I mean, as far as vampires go I might as well be shitting in my diapers, yet it seemed I kept getting thrown into the fucking meat grinder. One of these days, probably right after I've gone irrevocably insane, I swear I'm gonna march into the Draculas' meeting chamber and tell them to fix their own goddamned messes for a change.

I smiled as I got to my feet, looking around at the masses waiting for us, when I noticed I was the only one looking jovial.

That's when two things hit me. First, all of the beings in the room, minus Ed of course, were vampires. Second, I had no idea who any of them were. They were all dressed in the typical garb of what I'd come to expect of emissaries of Prefectures or higher - basically, all looking like fashion rejects from *The Matrix*. Didn't anyone ever tell these fuckers that look went out of style around the time the second movie came out?

Then I remembered. Hadn't Sally said something about calling Yvonne for reinforcements before we left, but that she hadn't held out much luck for anything more than a "too bad, so sad" response? Guess she was wrong after all. I found myself wishing I'd bet her ten bucks on that before we headed down into the mines of Moria.

"You guys are a little late," I said. "We already kicked their asses back to the Stone Age, but you're welcome to..."

"Are you William Anderson Ryder?" one of them interrupted. He seemed to be of mixed Asian descent with some kind of tribal tattoo running down his neck to under his shirt, but otherwise, he wore similar clothes to the rest. I guess these guys all shopped at the same store in the mall.

"That's what's on my driver's license," I answered flippantly.

"You are the Freewill," he continued in a monotone voice, "also known as..." He lifted a tablet computer in his hand and stared at it for a moment, his expression one of slight disbelief.

Oh, for Christ's sake. "Yes, also known as Doctor Death."

The man stared at me for a moment as if sizing me up. I didn't feel the need to elaborate that my old Village Coven moniker had resulted from nothing more than being put on the spot. What can I say? It had sounded good at the time.

After giving me one last sour glance, he turned toward my friends. "You are Sally Sunset, former Coven Master of Pandora Coven..."

Wait, *former?*

"Also known as Lu..."

"Sally will do just fine," she snapped. "Now what the fuck do you mean by..."

"And you," he continued, addressing Ed, "are Edward Peyton Vesser?"

"*Peyton?*" Sally and I asked in unison.

"What? Mom liked that old movie," he replied.

I snickered. "Okay, *Peyton.*"

"Go fuck yourself."

If our banter perturbed the vampire who'd been addressing us, he didn't show it. Sally, on the other hand, didn't seem to be overly pleased. Oh yeah, that whole *former coven master* thing might have had just a wee bit to do with it.

"Explain yourself," she said. "As master of this coven and a representative of the West Coast Prefecture under Yvonne, I demand..."

The vamp cut her off with a backhanded slap across the mouth. *Whoa.* What the fuck was going on here?

"You will demand *nothing*," he spat.

I stepped up into his face, putting myself between them. It was partially out of chivalry, but more so to keep her from launching herself at his throat and turning this into a full-on brawl. This was not how a victory celebration was supposed to start. "Listen, asshole, we just put the hurt on a whole shitload of rock monsters, and if you don't want us adding a few new casualties to that list, I'd suggest you start apologizing real quick."

Hmm, that had sounded a whole lot less inflammatory in my head.

Before I could backpedal to something a wee bit less threatening, the entire ensemble around us produced silver stakes. Oh shit.

Thankfully, their leader held up a hand before they could converge upon us in a manner that would probably end up hurting quite a bit. However, his smug grin as he turned back to Sally stopped me short of offering up my thanks.

"By the order of Yvonne, honored Prefect for the Western United States and Northern Mexico, you are hereby stripped of your station..."

Whoa, harsh. Didn't realize Sally had been pissing her off that badly.

"...at the bequest of the almighty First Coven..."

Oh, *those* fuckers. But why were they going after Sally? I mean, usually I was the one in their crosshairs.

"...Furthermore, the three of you, on order of the esteemed First Coven..."

Jesus Christ, could this dick stain fit more ass-kissing adjectives into his sentence if he tried?

"...are to be placed under arrest for your crimes against the vampire nation."

Wait, *what?* Arrest?

The group of armed vamps converged on me and my friends, restraining us before we could even give voice to our protests.

This was bullshit, plain and simple. I said as much, not that it made any difference. A vampire closed in, holding heavily reinforced cuffs out before him. I might have taken a little more offense to that than I should have. Rather than go quietly like a good little prisoner, I instead lunged at him - my teeth bared. What can I say? I tend to get cranky when I'm hungry.

Sadly, they were obviously well versed in who I was and what I could do. Multiple arms grabbed me from behind right before several fists, all reinforced with the silver stakes they held, slammed into my face.

It was too much punishment and I was too fatigued to fight it. The lights went out and, for a time, I knew no more.

The vampire cops might not have respected my Miranda Rights, but they definitely made sure my right to remain silent was in full effect.

PART II

29

THE LONG DRIVE

For the second time in a day, I found myself clawing my way rather unwillingly back toward consciousness. I would've loved to have stayed in that nice, warm place in my mind where the only company was my partner in crime and a certain Icon - both of them wearing bikinis and wrestling in a tub of pudding over which of them would get to serve my needs first. Talk about just desserts.

Unfortunately, another part of me felt terrified at staying put. I knew what lurked deep in my subconscious, and although it had been mostly quiet ever since my adventures in Switzerland some months back, I didn't want to tiptoe past its bedroom more times than necessary out of fear of waking it back up.

The only reason I was me again was because it had let me go. I'd given up, handed over the reins, so to speak, and had been thrust into a prison in the nether reaches of my mind. Thankfully, however, the monster hidden inside of me got bored of the day-to-day bullshit being a prisoner entailed.

Wait, prisoner? *Shit!*

That snapped me out of it. The nice dream of Sheila, Sally, and their nickname for me - "Lord Thor" - faded into nothingness. Jostling and a sense of movement replaced the fantasy. Goddamn it! I'd better not be in the sewers again, being dragged around like a sack of fucking potatoes. Then came the rumble of an engine and I realized that wasn't the case.

I opened my eyes, but thankfully, the vertigo from before had receded. I was still hungry, famished even, but whatever plasma crash I'd suffered from earlier had apparently evened itself out with regards to my undead body chemistry. Of course, my head still hurt, but I figured having it pounded in while my friends looked on might have caused that.

Crap!

That shook the final cobwebs from my mind and I sat up in a near panic...or tried to. My arms were restrained behind my back and I was on a seemingly short tether.

"Welcome back, Bill," Sally said from off to the side.

"Shut up, bitch," another voice barked.

"Make me."

I looked around. Metal walls surrounded me on all sides. I sat on the floor and was pretty sure my hands were cuffed. Sally sat on my left, similarly bound. Ed was on my other side. His hands lay in his lap, bound with plastic zip ties. He could have gotten to his feet, but it looked like doing so would have just gotten him pummeled.

Across from us, on a bench that ran the length of the room - a trailer, if the bouncing and road noise were any indication - sat seven of the vamps who'd been waiting for us upon our ascent at Pandora's Box. I quickly took in their faces - nobody familiar. At least their leader wasn't in sight. These fuckers had apparently pulled guard duty with all the discomforts afforded that station.

One of our minders, a youngish-looking vamp - not

that appearance meant shit in the supernatural world - stood up and brandished a silver stake. He awkwardly spun it around, almost dropping it in the process, so that the flat end faced out as he brandished it menacingly. "I'm gonna warn you one last time."

"Go fuck yourself, junior," Sally said. "And if you even think of touching me with that thing, you're gonna be compelled to pull out your own fucking eyeballs and eat them."

His hesitation was slight, nearly unnoticeable, but it was there. I'd seen it before on vampires a lot older than this punk.

"Go ahead and try it," he replied in a tough guy voice. "We've been insulated against you."

"I actually wasn't going to do jack shit." She stopped to blow a piece of hair that had fallen in her face. "But he might." She nodded toward me.

"Him?"

Oh crap. Sally had a nasty habit of writing checks with her mouth that my body couldn't cash, and she seemed to never tire of doing it.

"No, the human over there. Of course him, numbnuts. That's the fucking Freewill sitting next to me."

"He's no threat to us."

"Really? You're gonna tell me you haven't heard the stories? What he did to the king of the Sasquatches up in Canada?"

The guard hesitated.

"What he did to the Icon in New York?"

Uncertainty shone nakedly on his face and those of his colleagues as well.

"How he escaped from Switzerland?"

Confusion replaced the hesitant looks, but the gleam in Sally's eye told me that's exactly what she'd been hoping for.

"Oh come on. Your bosses didn't tell you how he escaped from the clutches of Alexander himself? That the entire fucking First Coven couldn't hold him?"

The assembled masses turned a collective shade paler. I inclined my head toward my roommate and his expression said it all. Sally was a master chef when it came to making bullshit stew.

"I thought so," she continued. "That's the problem with your bosses - they keep their secrets and you're the ones left holding the bag. Now, why don't you back off like a good lackey and we can spend the rest of this trip in relative peace without anyone wrenching off their own limbs?"

Much to my amazement, the guard lowered his weapon and sat back. He refused to meet the eyes of his fellows, but while some of them held smirks on their faces, I could tell it was a ruse. You could practically feel the unease running through them.

Funny enough, none of them seemed to have the brainpan to put two and two together. If I was the threat Sally made me out to be, then why had such an obviously green group been put in charge of my transport? If I had nearly the power that she suggested, then her ruse would never have worked because the guards sitting across from us would be far too seasoned for that shit.

"Well, if he's so tough, then how come he went down so easily back there?" a dude with freckles and ginger hair asked. Hmm, maybe not all of them were as dumb as I thought.

"It's pretty fucking simple, Opie," I croaked, my throat bone dry. "I'd just fought and won a war about a mile underground. You assholes got lucky and caught me by surprise when I was tired. But I'm a lot better rested now." I sat up straight and made as if to flex my muscles. The chains holding me were solid as fuck. I'd have needed a hacksaw, a blowtorch, and a gallon of Sally's blood cocktail to break free, but I let out a laugh anyway as if I could shed them with but a shrug. "I'll tell you what. I'm a little parched. You give me a drink and I'll sit here and let you bring me in like a good doggie playing fetch. You'll get to live - hell, maybe even get a commendation - while I see what trumped-up bullshit this is all about."

Unsurprisingly, there was hesitation amongst them at my request.

"Or we could do this the hard way."

The number one rule of the vampire world is never blink first. Vampire culture is almost entirely fear-based. The older and stronger vamps control the younger ones like cattle, and that gets paid forward to each subsequent generation. Typically, it was easy to tell who was top dog. If another vamp could compel you, then that meant they were in charge and you were a piece of shit.

The problem was, I was the exception to that rule. I couldn't be compelled, and that threw a monkey wrench into most vampires' worldly outlooks. I may not like a lot of things about being undead, but I sure as shit loved fucking with the system.

The redheaded guy who'd tried to sass me seemed to have his act together a bit better than the rest, but just barely. If I had to guess, he was a corporal to their buck privates. The others looked at him questioningly and he shrugged.

The vampiric Ron Weasley reached into his trench coat and produced a flask. He unscrewed it and held it out to me, hand shaking slightly as if afraid I might try to bite him. Had I not been solidly chained to the ground, I might've given it a thought, but as it was, the concept of having my head kicked in again didn't sound particularly favorable at the moment.

"Don't try anything funny," he said. "You won't get nothing out of this anyway. It's just human blood."

Fuck yeah! That's what I'd been hoping to hear. For once, the power-up didn't matter to me. From the look of this crowd, it wouldn't have been worth shit anyway. I didn't let him know that, though. I just glared until he held the flask to my mouth and tipped it.

Oh, sweet mother of God, how good it tasted going down. Ooh, and an added bonus - Junior here had spiked it. Apparently, his victim had been named Johnnie Walker. I sucked down a huge swallow and bared my lips in a snarl when he tried to pull it back.

I quickly drained the contents, wishing there'd been more, but feeling a thousand times better nevertheless. My head cleared and lost the numbness that had been weighing it down since I'd awakened following Miranda's sacrifice.

"Well, *that* was useful," Sally groused.

"Hey, I'm a simple guy. 'One problem at a time' is my motto."

"I thought it was 'bang anything with two legs, then make excuses four seconds later.'"

Ed chuckled - what a dick - but then, so did a few of the guards.

"They're my friends - *they're* allowed to laugh. Everyone else..." I let the threat hang in the air. Fuck it, as long as I was playing alpha dog, I might as well have some fun with it.

It had the desired effect of sobering up this crew. Right about now, I imagined they all thought back to any of a hundred movies in which a group of hapless guards were transporting a dangerous-as-fuck prisoner you just knew would escape before the first act was over.

The truck jolted, making me think we'd either hit a massive pothole or just run over something big. Considering the state of the world, at least what I knew of it, I didn't care to speculate which. For all I knew, we were currently living out a Mad Max style car chase in a sparse desert populated by masked weirdos.

"Yo, Ayatollah of Rock and Rolla," I said to the guy who seemed to be in charge. He raised his eyebrows questioningly at that and I blew out a sigh. Was nobody in the undead world into pop culture? What a sad group of deprived assholes. Oh well. "I didn't get a chance to ask politely back at Pandora, but what are the charges?"

"Excuse me?"

"What are we being arrested for?"

"That's none of your business," he replied back after a moment. "And the name is Farley."

Farley?

"He doesn't know," Ed surmised.

The look on the vamp's face took on a decisively unfriendly countenance. "I would hold my tongue, human, before I tear..."

"That *human* happens to be my friend," I interrupted. "We have a nice easy truce going on here, Farley. Would be a shame to break it and force things to get all messy." I stared him down, not unlike this one time my D&D character was in a standoff against a pissed off frost giant who didn't like us trespassing on his mountain. I'd rolled an eighteen on my bluff check and Dave had been forced to act it out rather than drop an avalanche on our heads like he wanted to.

"The First didn't tell them," Sally said at last. I couldn't help but notice her usage of their proper title. No doubt she realized what thin ice we stood on. If forced to choose who they were more afraid of - our ruling council or a bunch of schmucks chained to the floor of a truck - I had little doubt we'd wind up with the short end of that stick.

"Okay," I said. "Fair enough. But can you at least tell us where we're going? I mean, I'd like to know if we're almost there or if I should be asking what the schedule is for piss breaks."

"It is not for any of us to question the First," Farley replied, toeing the party line like a good sycophant.

"Of course not," Sally replied. "All glory to their wisdom." Amazingly enough, she managed to keep from rolling her eyes as she said that, but I could tell what she was doing - reassuring them we were all on the same side, that this was one big misunderstanding...whatever the fuck it was about.

That was one giant steaming load of bullshit, of course. I'd done a shitload to piss off vampires much higher ranked than me. Hell, barely a day went by when I wasn't forced to consider that had I been anything other than the Freewill, I'd have had my ass staked to dust long ago - probably deservedly so.

That my sins were finally catching up to me wasn't a surprise. I just had no idea which one I was destined to fry for.

30

THE MEN UNDER THE MOUNTAIN

I wasn't sure how long I'd been unconscious after those goons had kicked my ass back at Pandora's Box. It probably wasn't too long - vampire physiology being what it is. Regardless, we seemed to be in for the long haul in our own personal cargo truck of doom. The vehicle kept going for what felt like hours. The seating arrangements were uncomfortable enough as it was, but after a while, the continual bouncing and swaying of the trailer made it near torturous - and that was just me. I could only imagine how numb Ed's mostly human ass felt.

Proving they weren't complete monsters, or perhaps they just weren't keen on riding in an unventilated box that reeked of piss, we at least were granted one quick bathroom break. Sadly, nothing could be gleaned from it. They tossed hoods over our heads once the truck had stopped and we were dragged out to do our business - or try to. Hell, I have piss anxiety as it is whenever a guy is standing at the urinal next to mine in a public bathroom. Trying to drain the mega-shark while blindfolded and surrounded by armed guards was a nerve-racking experience at best. At least they cuffed my hands in front, saving me the trouble of having to rely on someone else to shake it off.

Oh well, based on the protests she'd voiced on the trip back to our temporary metal prison, it was probably worse for Sally. All things considered, I decided to spare her any assholish remarks once we were underway again. Our situation was bad enough as it was. Also, I didn't relish her kicking me in the nuts the second she had a chance.

Finally, after more hours on the road, I got the impression we were nearing our destination. The truck stopped several times before moving on again for a short distance. Each time, my sensitive vampire ears could make out voices beyond the walls.

"Security checkpoints?" I offered.

"That or a lot of red lights," Ed replied.

A few minutes later, the sound of heavy machinery accompanied our next stop. A dull booming seemed to echo in the trailer.

When next we began to move, our mobile prison had a decisively forward slant to it. The implication was obvious; we were heading down. Judging from the slow speed, I guessed us to be in a parking garage or similar such structure - someplace where they could unload their *cargo* without being seen.

As to what would happen to us next, that was anyone's guess. I managed to keep my demeanor calm and collected for the benefit of our guards, but inwardly, I was close to crying like a pussy.

According to our captors, their orders had come down from on high, from the Draculas themselves. To me, this meant only one thing. We faced a possible confrontation with one of the few vampires I had no problem admitting scared me shitless: Alexander.

As the truck shifted into reverse and began slowly backing up - probably toward whatever final destination awaited us - I had a few moments to consider the implications.

I'd inadvertently unleashed Vehron the Destroyer back upon the world after fourteen hundred years. At the time, it had seemed like a good idea. I had figured maybe he had some intelligence he could share with us - stuff that could be useful in stopping our war with the Feet. I also had no idea at the time of his liberation that his surname was "The Destroyer." Had I known that, I might've stuffed his decapitated cranium into Alex's toilet instead and taken my chances.

That was the kicker right there. I'd found Vehron's remains not in a vampire prison, but in a locked display case in Alex's private quarters. He hadn't been alone, either. Rows upon rows of preserved vampire heads had stared back at me from that space. That in itself wasn't so much the problem, other than speaking to some fucking weird fetishes on his part.

No, the real problem had been the odd feeling I'd gotten in my gut upon viewing them...as if there was something different, almost familiar, about all the faces looking back at me. I learned too late Vehron was another Freewill just like me, except infinitely more powerful, twisted, and muscular. I mean, seriously, once that dude's body had grown back, I sure as shit didn't want to compete against him at a nightclub.

Ignoring him for the moment, the implications of it all had eventually become clear to me. The Freewills were the legendary warriors of the vampire race: generals, conquerors, and overall badasses. They were the guys the Draculas turned loose on their enemies when shit got real. The thing is, they all disappeared hundreds of years ago. Some thought they were killed. Others thought they'd just up and vanished into thin air. In truth, they'd all *retired* and taken up jobs as bookends in Alex's boudoir.

Now, at least as far as Alex was probably concerned, I was the only other vampire to know this secret. I had a disturbing feeling he had a vested interest in making sure I kept my mouth shut permanently.

At last, we stopped and someone unlocked the truck's back gate from the outside. Our captors unchained us from the floor but didn't bother blindfolding us this time. I was still debating whether or not that was a good thing when the back doors swung open and a greasily familiar voice wafted in.

"Well done, trainees."

Trainees?

"I will be sure to note your success on this mission in my report. The First will be pleased to learn you have proven your loyalty. Perhaps next time they will assign your squad to a mission in which the quarry is actually somewhat dangerous."

Farley and his men all stood at attention before the pale thin man in the overly crisp suit. Had my hands not been shackled behind my back, I'd have given him a nice one-fingered salute instead. "Hi, Colin."

We marched out of the trailer to an industrial-sized loading dock. I took a quick look around, squinting in the overly bright artificial light filtering down from far above. If this was a parking garage, it was like no other I'd ever seen. The place was fucking huge and every surface appeared to be made of concrete reinforced with heavy steel.

Unfortunately, the décor wasn't my main concern right then. Colin stood before us. A column of vampires that looked a lot more seasoned than the grunts we'd been forced to drive with flanked him on either side. I noticed our friend, the Asian commando who'd backhanded Sally, among them. He nodded to the men who'd been tasked with guarding us and they fell in line behind him.

We stood together, facing Colin. I spared a glance at my friends on either side of me. Ed's face was impassive, probably waiting to see what the fuck was up. Raw annoyance showed on Sally's mug. I could understand that. Colin was ten gallons of cheap prick stuffed into five gallons of expensive Armani suit.

He strolled over, his gait slow - obviously enjoying himself.

Finally, he stopped in front of us, albeit, I noted, right outside of the range where one of us could've punted his balls through the roof.

"I would correct you on my proper title, Freewill," he replied, the smarm so thick I could've planted daisies in it, "but that would be holding you to a standard that you are incapable of achieving. *This,* on the other hand," he gestured toward our shackles, "is far more in line with what I expect of you and your compatriots."

He turned his head ever so slightly. "As for you, dear Sally..." He backed up a step, eyeing the ripped up combat shirt she still wore. A sly smirk crossed his face. "Well, there is that saying about lying down with pigs."

"Oh, one day, I am *so* gonna enjoy..."

He put his hand to his ear and leaned in. "What was that, my dear? Speak louder, please. If you're going to throw out idle threats, you might as well make sure you have ample witnesses that can testify against you."

Sally gritted her teeth, but kept quiet. Considering the circumstances, I was pretty certain anything she said would be held against her with extreme prejudice.

"So what happened?" I asked. "Did you get demoted

again? Let me guess. You're now the esteemed prison warden of the First Coven?"

"Hardly, Freewill. I maintain my current position serving the Wanderer and the collective will of the First."

I raised an eyebrow at his mention of James, but said nothing. I had to wonder whether this was yet another ploy of Alexander's that he'd neglected to tell his younger coven brother.

"I just came down here to welcome you and your friends," Colin continued. "And enjoy the view of you in chains, of course. Speaking of which..."

He backed up a step, producing a high-end cell phone in a jewel-studded case - prissy douchebag. "They say a picture is worth a thousand words, and I tend to agree." He touched the screen and it made the digitized noise of a camera shutter clicking.

With that, he turned, obvious glee on his face, and walked away toward a thick steel door leading further into the complex.

Without further ado, the guards converged and began marching us forward. I had no idea what awaited us inside, but I had a feeling that Colin posting an embarrassing pic to Facebook would be the least of our worries.

31

THE GATHERING

I had no idea where the hell we were, but it was as heavily fortified on the inside as it had been out at the loading dock - maybe more so. Reinforced concrete made up every arching hallway. Every door we passed looked to be, at minimum, several inches thick, with some making my old cell back at Chillon Castle look like a country club prison in comparison.

We walked in silence. General Cockslapper was every bit the asshole here as he'd been back at Pandora's Box. The first time I'd opened my mouth, a fist filled it. I hated to admit it, but I was missing Farley and his snot-nosed commandos already. What the fuck had that been about, anyway? Something about proving their loyalty. As if the Draculas really needed to worry about that. Fuck, they could have just compelled the assholes to dance Swan Lake and that bunch would have been powerless to do anything other than pirouette.

I had no idea where Colin had gone. He'd turned a corner and disappeared soon after we'd been escorted in. After that, we'd seen nary a soul outside of our gracious hosts, and they didn't seem up to the task of explaining the history of every room we passed.

In fact, the place felt almost desolate. I was just starting to note the hollow echo of our footsteps in the wide hallways when I heard a snuffling sound by my side. I turned to see Sally, her nostrils working overtime. I haven't been a vampire all that long, but I'd been around the block long enough to know she probably wasn't just trying to clear out any nose nuggets.

Mirroring her, I took a long sniff of the air. Vampires...yeah that much was obvious, but then once you got past all of that, there was more - a *lot* more. Multiple scents, dozens of them, registered in my overly sensitive nostrils. Hell, I got the impression I was just scratching the surface too. Had I been hopped up on Sally's jungle juice again, I'm sure my brain would have enjoyed a veritable smorgasbord of smells.

Even so, a memory stirred within me. Some of these scents were vaguely familiar, but it was the wide variety that really triggered my neurons. The last time I'd sensed such a diverse array of beings had been up in Canada, during the failed peace conference in the Sasquatch-infested forest known as the Woods of Mourning.

"Holy shit," I muttered, stopping in my tracks.

So caught up was I in the thought that I barely felt the guard's fist connect with my midsection - barely.

I couldn't understand where all these smells had originated from. They seemed recent, but as far as I could tell, this place was barren as a tomb. As if to accentuate the silence, I once more made note of how loud all of our footsteps sounded as we walked.

Eventually, the hallway ended in front of us at another

armored door. After a few moments, it was opened from the other side and we marched in to...whoa.

This room was massive, reminiscent of the caverns down in Jahabich central - except a fuckload more high tech. Inside were many more vampire soldiers dressed in combat armor of a seemingly better grade than even Sally had been able to procure. However, the sight of them wasn't what caused my breath to catch.

I gaped at what stood opposite us on the far end, a massive portal sealed with what looked like the mother of all bank vaults. Jesus Christ, what did they keep on the other side, solid gold dinosaurs?

Ed, apparently forgetting for a moment we were in the middle of a group of slap-happy vamps, asked, "Is it too much to hope we're in Fort Knox and that this whole thing is a ruse so they can scream, 'Congratulations, take whatever you can carry?'"

I waited for a moment, but no beat-down came, although from the look on the commander's face, he definitely wanted to. Must have been the presence of others in the room. Maybe his penchant for smacking us around had only been at Colin's urging.

Apparently sensing this too, Sally said, "It's not a vault."

"No?"

"It's a blast door. If I'm not mistaken, this is some sort of bunker - a big one, by the looks of it."

So much for dreams of running off with an armload of gold bars. If she was right, this place was built for one purpose - to withstand an attack.

The only question now was...against what?

The massive portal was opened in front of us, giving a true sense of how thick it was. Damn, I could have probably sucked down every single member of the Draculas and still not been able to put a dent in that fucking thing.

It wasn't the only surprise this place held, either.

An antechamber of sorts - maybe a security checkpoint - awaited us, capped off by yet another massive blast door on the far end. We're talking uber-paranoia here. I'm pretty sure one could have ridden out Judgment Day, a zombie apocalypse, and the rise of an army of talking apes without batting an eye in there.

I was beginning to wonder whether this was gonna be one big joke...each door leading to another until we were back outside, but then they opened the second door for us and I realized we weren't destined to get that lucky.

I'd been wondering about the myriad scents that had filled the halls, considering maybe I'd missed one hell of a party. I saw now, though, that wasn't the case. Scents, sounds, and other emanations poured forth from within - nearly overwhelming in their breadth.

"Smells like a zoo," Ed commented, "if it was located in the fucking Twilight Zone."

"Tell me about it."

I remembered back to the Woods of Mourning. There had been a similar reveal back then, stepping through a magical force field of sorts that kept all the crazy contained within. The vampire nation apparently had similar thoughts, but dealt with them in a more pragmatic way - more than making up for the lack of magic with enough concrete to avoid detection from anything unwise enough to try spying on them.

That image was further reinforced as we were marched in. Almost immediately, the talking, cackling, hissing, and other vocalizations stopped as Sally, Ed, and I breached the inner chamber. Talk about déjà vu. Though the accoutrements couldn't have been more different - high end chairs, massive monitors lining the walls, a dome ceiling rising far above, and guards armed with some nasty looking firepower - the rest of the layout remained eerily similar. All of that and more rose above and around us in a stadium - or arena - layout.

The area before us looked as if it might have once been intended for a speaker to address the crowd, but now it was cleared - minus the multitude of armed guards.

As I walked forward, a small wave of air pressed against my back. I glanced over my shoulder and saw the blast door being shut behind us. It moved nearly silently, apparently kept in very good care - making only a hollow *thunk* sound as the locks were engaged. It didn't take a genius to figure out that was one escape route that would take a damn miracle to traverse.

I scanned the quieted crowd, all eyes - and other things - staring at us as we marched forward. I still had no names for many of them, but I could see several familiar creatures - if not the same, then related - I'd seen up in Canada. There were also several new monstrosities present including...

"Oh fuck!"

The oath sounded far too loud in the near silence. Always a wonderful thing to draw the crowd's attention when I least wanted to. I couldn't help it, though. Off to the far right, surrounded by far meaner and less human-looking versions of the zombies I was familiar with, stood a massive reptilian horror. It was like someone cloned a dinosaur and then decided to keep fucking with the DNA, throwing random parts into a blender just to see what came out the other end. It was Druaga, god of the dead.

That in itself should have been enough to send me screaming out of the room. That I'd sorta fucked him over, no doubt pissing him off massively in the process, when

I'd escaped from Switzerland was just icing on the bloody cake of entrails that I'd probably soon top.

"You got that right," Sally whispered.

I turned to her questioningly. As far as I was aware, she wasn't associated with any death gods. Of course, as far as I'd known, she hadn't dated any rock monsters either and that had been proven pretty damn wrong. Before I could ask whether he was another old squeeze, though, I saw her gaze was directed elsewhere.

I followed it and immediately wished I hadn't.

At the far end of the massive room, a section was set aside. Rather than the general seating the rest of the guests used, chairs of pure black onyx - more like thrones - were lined up in a row. I didn't need to count them, but I did just to make myself feel even worse. As I suspected, there were thirteen in all.

Upon them sat figures that looked human, but I knew weren't. I didn't recognize the majority of them, but some of the faces were more than familiar. Of them, only James brought any feeling other than dread and that was easily overwhelmed by who sat in the very middle: Alexander the Great.

The Draculas - more properly known as the First Coven - the thirteen most powerful vampires on the planet were present, and their eyes were all focused directly on us.

32

BRING OUT YOUR DEAD

"Are those..."

"Yep," I replied to Ed's unfinished question.

"Are we..."

"Fucked beyond all possible measure of the fuckery scale? I'd say so."

The crowd began to murmur amongst itself, no doubt commenting on our obvious discomfort. I couldn't bring myself to turn my head away from the Draculas, but I picked up bits and pieces of it anyway thanks to my superb vampire hearing.

"See how guilty they look?"

"Betrayers."

"Five bars of gold says they kill the abomination first."

"They should strip the blonde one. She is one fine slice of gorvu."

I was tempted to scan the crowd for the owner of that last one. There's always gotta be at least one perv among the bunch. Asshole. That was *my* job.

Before I could turn my head away, though, Alex's mismatched eyes met mine. I expected to find fury radiating from them, enough to scorch me where I stood.

Instead, he grinned and inclined his head ever so slightly. That motherfucker was one seriously weird dude.

I tore my gaze away and looked over the rest of the bunch. Each of them was dressed in regal finery, obviously befitting their station, but wearing fashions and colors which I assumed to be of their own respective preference. To Alex's immediate left and right sat Theodora and Yehoshua, respectively. I recognized them, and not just because Thea was probably the hottie the wicked stepmother in every fairytale was modeled after.

They'd been the ones who ultimately had let me go back in Europe, confiding in me that they weren't all that pleased with either Alexander's rule or his plans for decimating the world. Yehoshua wore a neutral expression. He might as well have been sitting down to watch a particularly dull game of golf. Theodora was far less collected. The look on her face was one of utter loathing. At first, I thought it might have been toward the crowd in general, but every so often, her eyes would flicker in Alex's direction.

With the exception of James, the rest of the Dracs were all new to me. I counted three other women amongst their number and six men, all of various lineages. Interestingly enough, none of them seemed to fit any stereotypes of what I might have imagined a vampire ruling counsel to be. There were no obvious Mayan high priests, Spanish conquistadors, or Roman consuls sitting there, looking like they'd stepped out of a time warp. Hell, most of them looked like you could pass them on the street without giving a second glance.

I wasn't fooled, however. Each and every one of them possessed several times the power needed to pulverize a vampire newb like me into a puddle of Bill-flavored goo.

For all I knew, the only one who lacked the inclination to do so was James and he was...what the fuck?

He sat at the last chair to Alex's right, dressed as regally as the others, but there was something very much off about him. Normally, James was bright-eyed and very full of life for a man who was over six hundred years in age. It wasn't unusual to find a wry grin upon his face. Not so today. The best I could say was he looked haunted. Sadly, I couldn't glean any further insight as he refused to look my way.

"What happened to his arm?" Sally whispered under her breath. She was just barely audible to me, but I didn't fool myself into believing that some of the others present hadn't picked it up too.

Regardless, I had no answer for her. His left hand rested upon his knee, but the right sleeve of his suit jacket was pinned to his side. It was the same arm he'd lost in battle to Vehron. That made no sense, though. It had already started growing back when last we'd seen him. It should have been fully regrown by the time he'd reached whatever destination Colin had spirited him off to after the fight.

Whatever was going on, it wasn't good. James was typically our lifeline; a guy strong, smart, and influential enough to pull our asses out of whatever shithole we'd gotten ourselves stuck in. Things seemed to be different now. For all of his rank, he had the look of low man on the totem pole with this bunch. What the fuck had happened since he'd left us?

Sadly, I got the feeling we wouldn't get an answer to that anytime soon. One of the vampires guarding the inner circle in which we stood turned and stepped toward the Draculas. Judging from the way he carried himself and the crispness of his dress, it wasn't hard to guess he had some position of authority here - maybe a vampire general or something.

Words were exchanged, but thanks to the continued

yammering of the crowd, they were lost upon me. The only thing I got out of it was the guard asking what sounded like a question.

Alex gave a single shake of his head, then inclined his gaze toward another door leading out. Who knows? Maybe he was having second thoughts and was gonna let us go.

Never let it be said I'm not an optimist at heart.

The vampire who'd approached Alex quickly turned and gestured toward some of the minions near that exit. He made a single "come forth" gesture with his hands before returning to his station.

Oh, fuck. I really hoped they didn't have a trial by combat in mind because I knew my luck. Whatever came through that door to kick my ass would probably be big, ugly, and mean enough to...

To be my other roommate?

"Tom?" Ed asked, giving rise to my question.

Sure enough, two vampire guards entered. Between them stood my oldest friend. For his part, he looked unharmed, if a bit bewildered. He turned toward one of the vamps leading him in and said something. I didn't catch it, but judging by the look on the vamp's face, it was a typical bit of Tom's stupidity. The vampire grabbed his shirt by the shoulder and shoved him forward.

My friend stumbled and went down to his knees. He looked up, saw us, and quickly got back to his feet. I was a little irked to see he wasn't shackled like the rest of us, but then realized it wasn't a surprise. Tom didn't appear to be wearing his magical amulet, the one that channeled the insane faith he felt for the toys he collected - especially a vintage Optimus Prime figure he'd once gotten cheap at a flea market. Without it, he wasn't much threat to anyone, outside of talking their ear off.

"Hey, Bill," he said casually. "What's up, Ed? Looking good, Sal…"

"Oh, shut up," she replied with an eye roll.

"I see they got you guys too," he continued, unperturbed.

"Are you okay?" I asked.

"I'm fine. They offered me a deal - don't try to escape and I wouldn't get my face torn off. Seemed pretty fair to me."

I sighed in relief. Tom could be an idiot when he wanted to be, but he'd been exposed to enough of the supernatural world to know when it was best to fight and when it was best just to do as told.

"What'd you tell the Gestapo over there?" Ed asked.

"Oh, just that Bill was gonna fuck his mother's corpse when this was all done."

"Thanks," I replied through gritted teeth, glancing over and noticing the sour look the guard threw my way. One could always count on Tom to make the situation *better*.

Although I was glad to see my friend, even under the current circumstances, I found myself curious as to why he was here. Of the four of us, his run-ins with the paranormal world had been the least severe, at least with regards to being on the Draculas' radar. I mean, the only time he'd really been exposed to it outside of New York had been…

Oh shit. Tom, Sally, and Ed all had one very important thing in common: they'd been my advisors up in Canada when it had all gone to hell. Was *that* what this was about? Some sort of after-the-fact reckoning? A way for Alex to place blame for the war he'd manipulated us into starting? Was it going so badly he felt the need to finger us as scapegoats?

If so, that wasn't good. I had a feeling that pointing

fingers back his way was a good way to get them cut off permanently. Likewise, this didn't look like the type of bunch who would accept a plea of stupidity as way of excuse.

We were alone, without many allies, and escape was only possible if we somehow learned to teleport...

Christy! I remembered what Ed had told me, how her new coven had taken up residence in our building back in Brooklyn. Shortly after his arrival in Pandora, we'd called them up to let them know he was safe and sound. They'd immediately stood down on any scrying incantations they'd been working on to find him. But if Tom was now on the missing list too, then that would be an entirely different story. There was no way Christy would let someone take him without magically looking under every single rock on the planet. With any luck, she was even now homing in on...

"Bring her in."

What?

Though the voice giving the command wasn't overly loud, one could hear the authority practically dripping out of it. Alexander spoke as one who was born to be king and knew it. It was a far cry from the practically mewling orders of middle management at my old job, where they pretty much could only hope you did as you were told. Alex's tone indicated he knew there was no doubt his orders would be carried out.

And they were. The guards at the perimeter practically tripped over themselves running for yet another egress off on the other side. I couldn't help but notice this door was considerably better armored than the one Tom had been brought through. It looked like they'd been holding him in a sitting chamber or side office. No real surprise there. What was he going to do other than mouth off to them?

The prisoner they brought in next, though, was considerably more lethal when she wanted to be.

Under different circumstances, I would have been happy to see her. Now, her hands were manacled in front of her with chains similar to those Mark had used on Miranda, if considerably newer looking. Happy was definitely not one of the emotions I felt at the sight of her entrance.

All hope seemed to slip from between our fingers as Christy was marched in to join us.

What the fuck was going on?

33

WIZARD DUEL

Christy was...a wee bit larger than when last I'd seen her. Part of it was no doubt her being about six months pregnant. The rest, well, let's just say I got a clear mental image of cravings for ice cream at three AM, followed by Tom's ass running out to grab a gallon of mint chocolate chip.

The smirk that arose on my face was only on the surface, though. Inwardly, my hopes had been dashed against the blast door we'd marched in through. In this chamber were the people I considered the bulk of my allies - the vast majority of them standing in the same rapidly deepening pool of shit as me. I got the distinct feeling no last-minute save was in the cards this time.

The only question was *why*?

Upon seeing Tom, Christy bolted toward us. The guards tensed as she did so and, for a moment, I was afraid of what they'd do. Thankfully, they held off on any action. Either they were under orders not to harm her or it was painfully obvious we were in no position to cause much chaos.

Christy threw her manacled arms around Tom.

"Thank the Mother you're all right!" She sobbed into his shoulder.

"Hey, babe," he replied casually, as if he'd just gotten back from the store. Yes, they made for quite the interesting couple.

Christy pulled back from the embrace, wiping a few tears from her eyes once it became obvious her boyfriend was okay. She glanced around and saw us there too. Confusion reigned on her face for a moment as she took it all in. Then her gaze landed on mine and, within seconds, anger replaced confusion.

Oh, shit, what did I do now?

Red-hot power gathered behind her eyes, but it went no further than that, no doubt due to the magic-restraining bonds shackling her. To my surprise and relief, though, Christy gritted her teeth and spun toward where the Draculas sat.

"What is the meaning of this?" she spat in their direction. "I am of the Magi, afforded neutrality under the provisions set forth in the Humbaba Accord. I have no quarrel with vampire-kind, nor do I answer to your laws. I demand to know why I and my fiancé have been detained in this manner."

"Fiancé?" Tom and I both uttered.

Christy spun and directed a glare at him that would have melted steel. Needless to say, he shut the fuck up quick. She then turned to me and her gaze softened. She mouthed, "Sorry" before turning back to face the First.

Her meaning was clear enough to me. She wasn't beholden to vampire law, but Sally and I were. Hell, Ed probably was now too, thanks to whoever had signed him up for Pandora Coven. That was fine. I trusted Christy and had little doubt she'd do what she could to help us out once she was clear of this mess.

As for the rest, I'll admit I took some amusement in seeing the looks on the faces of the guards surrounding us. Hell, *I* wouldn't have had the balls to talk to the Draculas like that aloud and I was known for pissing them off. Best yet, I could see that reaction reflected in the eyes of at least some of the fuckers sitting up there in judgment of us. They weren't used to being talked to in such a manner.

Sadly, whatever shock the other Draculas might have felt didn't register with Alex. "Well said, Christine Angelique Fenton - Magi of the Eastern Seaboard," he replied. "However, I might question your comment regarding no quarrel with our kind. Did not your master wage war against Village Coven of New York?"

I opened my mouth with the intent of protesting. Christy had been the only member of her coven who hadn't actively tried to fuck me over by way of disintegrating the pack of assholes who had once been my coven. Thankfully, Sally planted an elbow in my side before I could say anything that might make our situation worse.

It seemed that my help was unnecessary anyway, as Christy remained unfazed by the challenge. "My master, gods watch over his soul, had quarrel with the Freewill, as I believe the esteemed First Coven is aware, Alexander of Macedon."

Alex raised an eyebrow, but then grinned, apparently pleased she knew who he was. That made sense. From what I'd seen of him, both in person and in that movie where Angelina Jolie played his MILF of a mom, he was far more likely to give quarter to those who surprised him by being clever or unorthodox rather than lackeys.

"Have a care, sorceress," Theodora growled. "Neutral or not, your tone is insol..."

"That will be enough," Alex cut her off. Theodora

didn't appear to appreciate that one bit. She opened her mouth, but he started talking again, pretty much dismissing her. Dick. "I apologize for any rudeness on the part of my people or *my* coven."

Maybe it was me, but I could have sworn a lot of First Coven fur was bristled by that remark. Only Yehoshua and James appeared to be stoic in the face of it.

"You are, of course, correct," Alex continued. "The Magi are not subject to our laws, and the potential act of war perpetrated by your master was offset by the circumstances."

I had to bite my tongue. *Circumstances?* He was talking about Harry Decker going batshit about the Icon. The news of her emergence had sent shockwaves throughout the supernatural community, but before full-on panic could descend, the vamps had joined forces with the mages to hunt her down and obliterate her. As far as they were concerned, it had been a successful mission. As far as *I* was concerned, though, it had only resulted in the deaths of a lot of assholes who'd deserved it - Decker and his followers included.

Alex stood and held his hands open in a gesture suggesting supplication. "I would thus apologize and ask the guards to free you and your companion, begging your forgiveness for the slight." He nodded his head toward Christy and she appeared to relax.

She stepped forward, but Alex held up a hand. "I *would* do all of these things were you still protected by virtue of your association with the Magi." He turned toward the crowd and scanned for someone or something. Finally, he asked, "What say you, esteemed Grand Mentor?"

All eyes turned to follow his gaze.

"What?" Christy gasped.

A white bearded man stood up at the far edge of the crowd.

"Who let Saruman in?" Ed whispered to me.

I had to nod. The guy in question was, for all intents and purposes, your stereotypical-looking Hollywood wizard. He could have passed as Merlin, Dumbledore, or any of a dozen wizened mages from pop culture. Long, flowing robes covered his body and he leaned on a staff to round out the look. Christ, he was either the real deal or had been kidnapped from the local Comic Con.

"I say nay. I name this child as a heretic to our ways." Scratch that last part. When he spoke, it reverberated throughout the room - the barest glow surrounding his body.

Christy's eyes narrowed. "I acknowledge thee, Mentor of the Great Plains, but say you have no authority over me. By what right and cause do you name me heretic?"

Whoa, this shit was starting to get Shakespearean. It reminded me of the bullshit ceremony Sally had to oversee for Village Coven after we ganked Night Razor, the asshole who turned me into a vamp. What was it with mystical creatures and their fucking ritualistic bullshit, especially when most of them didn't normally speak as if they'd just stepped out of a comic book?

"By what right?" the old man boomed, tapping his staff to the floor and causing a crack of thunder to reverberate around the room. Under normal circumstances, I'm sure it would have been impressive, but the gathered creatures, imps, and other assorted weirdos barely batted an eye. "I called Master Decker brother of the mystic arts."

Brother? I assumed it was figurative, but either way, any brother of Decker's was automatically an asshole in my book. I normally didn't let my thoughts stray toward things murderous, but a small part of me wouldn't have minded seeing this guy's skull as a matching bookend on Sally's desk.

"My cause is justice itself, justice for the betrayed!" Mysterio waved his staff in a circle and the air next to him began to shimmer. Sparks danced for a moment as a shape began to take form, gradually becoming clearer. When the veil, or whatever it was, had finished decloaking, a young woman stood by his side.

Who the hell...

"No," Christy gasped.

"Oh, shit," Sally added.

I turned and looked again. For a moment, I had no clue what they were talking about, but then I realized the woman looked ever so slightly familiar. Nah, it couldn't be.

"Sister," Christy said sadly. "Forgive me."

"Forgive you?" the witch asked contemptuously. "You who sided with these beasts? You who betrayed our master? You who would be the harbinger of our doom?!" With each question, she got a little more frantic, unhinged. It was the harbinger of doom line that finally clued me in. The Magi had a prophecy about that, one which had ultimately been Harry Decker's downfall.

I leaned over and whispered to Sally, "I'm gonna go out on a limb here and assume one got away."

I really should learn sign language. Even the barest whisper of an insult in a room full of beings with supernatural abilities tended to get a bit of an overreaction. The old mage immediately waved his arms, a beam of red hot energy forming around him.

As fast as he was, though, James was faster.

"***NO!!***" The compulsion rang out in his voice just as

the wizard unleashed his death ray at me. Before I had a chance to even kiss my ass goodbye, one of the vampire guards dove in front of it, taking the brunt. He glowed for a moment before exploding in a shower of sparks and dust.

Note to self: remember not to piss off wizards.

With that, the crowd went nuts, losing whatever semblance of decorum a bunch of disgusting monsters might have. Cups, rolled up paper, and even a broken off piece of wooden bannister came flying in our direction. Cries of outrage followed, most of them seemingly directed at what an insensitive asshole I was for not dying when I was supposed to.

The guards formed ranks around us, blocking the worst of it. This continued for several minutes before a compulsion loud enough to make my head spin reverberated throughout the room. *"ENOUGH!!"*

Though it didn't appear to affect many of the creatures present, an equal number were bowled right over by the sheer force. I turned and saw Ed and Christy trying to get Tom to his feet, blood dripping from both of his ears.

It had the desired result, though. The crowd immediately settled down...those who were still standing, anyway.

"Thank you," Alex said evenly, once the worst had passed. He turned toward the far end, where James had resumed his morose grousing. "My appreciation, Wanderer." He nodded before addressing the crowd again. "I would kindly ask that allies and guests alike please refrain from summary executions until such time as judgment is passed."

He waited a beat to see if there would be further interruption. When there wasn't any, he turned back toward where the old wizard still stood. "As you were saying, Mentor?"

The old guy flashed me the stink eye for a moment

before taking a breath and composing himself. "This *child* with me is witness to the betrayal. The Magi are beholden to few rules, but those we have we hold dearly. To turn one's back on one's brothers and sisters is to spit upon the face of Kala the White herself, our blessed law giver, and all she has taught us. I say this woman sided with the enemy of us all, the beast that shall be our downfall."

"You don't know..." Christy started.

"I say you are Magi no more! I name thee heretic, little more than a vampire's thrall - beholden to their laws and punishment as they see fit."

A hush fell over the crowd as his booming voice finished. To add insult to injury, he and the witch beside him turned their backs upon us. Ooh, a shunning...harsh.

"Call it whatever you want, old man!" Christy fired back, breaking the silence and all pretense of ceremony. "You can call it betrayal all you want. I call it standing up for what's right...standing by my friends."

She looked to say more, but the sound of slow clapping interrupted us. It was Alex, looking smugger than ever as he brought his hands together in the most condescending golf clap I'd ever seen. "Truly a noble sentiment," he said, almost convincing me that he meant it. "I applaud you for it. Alas, the Grand Mentor represents the interests of the Magi in this gathering and he has spoken. I am afraid you shall have to stand with the others."

Christy visibly deflated, having been soundly outmaneuvered by the more experienced player. She drew in a great hitching breath that told me she wanted to cry, but wasn't about to in front of this crowd.

Tom, proving that he wasn't a complete dumbass, moved to her side and put a comforting hand on her shoulder. She leaned in to him, taking what support he could give. Of course, then he had to go and open his idiot mouth. "It was a nice try."

A sigh escaped from Sally's throat as Ed turned to me. "We're completely fucked, aren't we?"

"Yep, pretty much." I stepped forward. Christy had possessed balls enough to face down this crowd without blinking. Could I do any less? Also, it was kind of embarrassing for a heavily pregnant woman to completely show me up. The only solace I could take was that apparently my friends were just as big of pussies as I was.

It was time to man up - at least a little bit. "Okay, enough with the dog and pony show," I said, putting every bit of machismo I had into my voice. As expected, the assembled vamps all acted as if I'd personally shit in their mother's teacup. If you gotta go, then you might as well go big. "You've got us here. Now I want to know why."

If I didn't have the attention of the Draculas before, I sure as shit did now. Their expressions ranged from bemusement - Alex - to outrage - eleven others - to outright horror. That last one was James, who I saw mouth the word "no" to me. A little too late for that advice, I might say.

I gave the barest of shrugs. We were already in the lion's den. Fuck that, we were standing in the lion's mouth and it was only a matter of time before it decided to start chewing.

34

UNHOLY ROLLERS

Alex stood once more. Through a combination of his experience, rank, and location, he looked down upon me. I tried to put on a brave front as his eyes bored holes through me, but I half expected to be sentenced to death right then and there.

Instead, he simply said, "You look well, Freewill. Your time away from our hospitality has been kind, I see."

Hospitality? So I was right. This whole fucking thing was about my escape. I'd embarrassed the leader of the Draculas and, worse, threw a spanner into the negotiations he'd been conducting with Druaga. Maybe this was his way of setting things right with the oversized gecko. That would explain the death god's presence. Maybe if they sacrificed me, they could get their fucking treaty back on track. Well, fuck that.

I glanced around at the packed auditorium. If he wanted to play hardball, I had a stick of my own to use - my knowledge of his closet full of Freewill heads. I might not get out of this one alive, but I could certainly take him down a peg in the process.

I considered this. Alex was a smart guy. He no doubt

knew the ammunition I had to use. So maybe there was a way to use it to my advantage. "My friends had nothing to do with this. Let them go and I'll cooperate."

"Cooperate? I think you are mistaken, child." A murmur of laughter rose up from the crowd. Supernatural cocksuckers. "This is not a negotiation. This is a trial."

"I kind of figured that." I couldn't help but notice that while Alex didn't seem to have a problem with my attitude, the other Draculas bristled at it. Hell, Theodora was completely against him, and yet right about then she looked like she'd gladly snap my neck without a second thought. What an arrogant bunch of pricks.

Okay, maybe I needed to ramp down the attitude *just* a bit. I took a deep breath and tried again. "Regardless, my friends are innocent. Let them go and you can try me to your heart's content."

"Innocent, are they? So are you here to tell me that none of them were present, despite the report your colleague here gave to the contrary, during the incident with the Icon?"

"What? *That's* what this is about?" Oh, shit. I should have guessed by what had just happened with Christy.

Even so, I definitely needed to keep my shit together now. There'd been no survivors from the other side, as far as I knew, at least none that had been present for the final battle and subsequent aftermath.

I glanced at my friends and Sally nodded. It said it all. As long as we kept to our story, we had a shot at getting out of this.

I turned back toward Alex and swallowed every "fuck you" that wanted to escape my lips. "My apologies, Lord Alexander. I did not realize that situation was the one in question."

"Oh, you have other transgressions, perhaps, you wish to confess?"

I would have loved to have removed the wry smile from his face with a baseball bat, but I once more held back my true feelings. There were other lives at stake here, two of whom were only a few months away from the joys of changing diapers and three AM feedings. "No. It's just been a long week."

Okay, *that* was fucking lame.

"What I meant to ask was why are we all here? I believe Sally, coven master of Pandora, gave a full accounting of..."

"*Former* coven master," one of the other Draculas spat, a gaunt, dark-skinned man who looked to be reaching the end of his patience.

"Thank you, Vargas," Alex said offhandedly, keeping his attention focused on me like I was a bug under a microscope.

"Yes, that's what I meant," I replied, not daring to turn back and see how badly Sally was probably killing me with her gaze. "Anyway, I believe she gave a full accounting of what happened."

"She did. However, you did not."

The asshole knew damn well why I hadn't, but was twisting the screw - maybe hoping I'd contradict Sally's well-crafted bullshit. Fuck that. I may not be a master strategist who once conquered the known world, but I was smart enough to have my stories straight. "I was...indisposed following the battle."

"Indisposed?"

"Yes. After I..." *It's only a story*, I reminded myself. "After I killed the Icon, my Freewill nature got the better of me. I was lost to the bloodlust for a time."

"So you stand before us the conquering hero?"

Okay, not sure where this was going, but I had a feeling it was a trap I didn't want to walk into. "I'm no hero. I just did what needed to be done."

"Very well." He sat back down in his chair, his mismatched eyes continuing to stare through me. It was starting to get a bit creepy. Finally, he nodded toward one of the guards who stood at attention before us.

The guard saluted and said, "William Ryder, Freewill and former master of Village Coven, you and your associates are called forth before the glorious First Coven. You are hereby charged with treason against the First and the laws they have set. All glory to their wisdom!"

Oh, Jesus Christ. It was all I could do not to gag at the ass-kissing on display.

"How do you plead?"

"Plead?" I cried. "Those are some pretty fucking vague charges, asshole." Oh crap, did I say that aloud? Shit! So much for decorum.

"You tell 'em, Bill," Tom urged me on.

I heard a smacking sound behind me - probably Sally delivering some justice of her own upside his head, rightfully so.

"What I meant to say," I began, trying to rein things back in, "is that I don't understand the charges."

"Allow me to elaborate," Alex replied. "We have reason to believe the accounts given to us were falsified - that not only did you fail to slay the Icon yourself, but you actively sought to aid her."

Oh, fuck. Had someone blabbed, or were they just fishing? I had to assume the latter because throwing myself on the non-existent mercy of the court wouldn't do dick to help us. All that would do was get us dusted and start another Icon hunt, one I wouldn't be able to stop this time.

"The Icon is dead. I killed her," I said, keeping my voice steady.

"And her body?"

My mind momentarily wandered back to Sheila

standing there in a towel. Yep, quite the body indeed. Okay, that was definitely not helping. "No idea. Maybe the NYPD got it? Maybe I ate it. Who knows? As I said, I was a bit crazed with the need for carnage after destroying the foul abomination. All I wanted was more of our enemies to slay."

Nice one. I glanced to either side and saw some discussion amongst the crowd. Score a point for the Freewill.

I turned back to Alex, smiling. "That's a not guilty, in case you were wondering."

"Insolence to the First is also punishable by death," another of the Draculas commented - a woman with brown skin and Asian features. Hawaiian or Filipino, I'd say. Of course, her lineage was fairly unimportant right then. It was more her statement that was worrisome. I didn't know how much of an actual law it was, but there was no doubt those who sassed the Dracs tended to end up lining the insides of dustbins. An outcome like that could render any defense we put forth a bit moot.

Thankfully, Alex stepped in for the save - much to even my surprise. "I think we can dispense with protocol just this once. Let it be known that the First Coven believes in justice above our own gratification."

Somehow that didn't exactly make me feel better. The upside, though, was it definitely didn't endear him to the other Draculas, based on their reactions. It did, however, seem to mollify the crowd - which I got the feeling was probably the point.

"Are you certain of your plea, Freewill?"

"Not guilty," I repeated slowly, turning to get my message across as well. Alex wasn't the only one capable of playing to an audience. "The Icon is dead by my hand and I certainly didn't do anything to aid my ancient and hated enemy."

"So be it." Alex nodded to someone at the far end of the room.

The guards around us converged on our location. At first, I thought they were attacking, but they began herding us toward one end - closer to where the Dracs sat. I wasn't sure what they were getting at, but then the massive blast door began to open again - once more moving silently as if whatever oversized hinges held it up were kept well oiled. Aside from seeing it happen, the only notion of its movement was the slight change in airflow as the titanic steel portal swung.

More guards lay beyond - a lot more than had escorted us inside. These were different, however. Gone were the trench coats and silver daggers, replaced by full combat armor, helmets, and riot shields.

I saw a dull glint of metal from near their center and realized the ones closest to the middle were holding blades of some kind - swords or maybe spears. They had a weird sheen to them that I couldn't quite place, almost as if they were absorbing the light rather than reflecting it.

The gamer inside of me immediately wondered at their plus to hit, but before I could get a clearer look, I caught a glimpse of something else near the center that caused my cold dead heart to leap into my throat. It was a head of blonde hair, in itself not all that unique, but beneath it shone a set of eyes - silver in its purest form, making the stakes our guards held seem like dull aluminum sticks by comparison.

Holy motherfucking shit!

Sally moved to my side, standing on her tiptoes. "What's going on?"

"Oh, just us being completely and utterly assfucked. The usual." The flippant remark was just a defense mechanism. Deep down, I could feel myself freaking the fuck out as Sheila was marched in.

How the hell could they have captured her?

How were all of the vamps around her walking instead of turning to dust?

Of course, there was one question I should have asked myself above all, but didn't because the answer was painfully obvious. I'd visited her a few months back, tried to convince her to fight by our side. I had thought us clever - that we'd taken adequate precautions. Seeing her now, though, it was painfully obvious my self-assessment of that situation couldn't have been more wrong.

She was their prisoner and it was all my fault.

As the blast door swung shut again, gasps rose up from the crowd as some of the assembled creatures no doubt started putting two and two together.

I craned my neck to catch a better view, but the vamps surrounding her were big fuckers - most of them well over six feet. The closer they got, the harder it was to see if she was all right.

Go figure. I'd opened my mouth in front of some of the most powerful beings in the supernatural world and then proceeded to shove my foot straight down it - yet my own well-being was now secondary, as far as I was concerned.

If they'd hurt her...

The procession stopped and there was movement near the center. A flash of white light flared up and the dull blades immediately descended toward the cause.

Fuck that!

"Leave her alone!"

Although my own arms were still shackled, I couldn't have cared less. I shoulder-blocked my way past the vamps guarding us, their attention diverted like everyone else in the room.

Someone screamed something and I registered move-ment on all sides, but I paid it no heed. Tensing my legs, I prepared to leap, planning to dive into the fray and start biting whoever was closest. I had little doubt this new group was made up of seasoned warriors. Colin hadn't considered me a threat, but even he wouldn't have been stupid enough to make the same mistake with her.

If I could sink my teeth into just a few of them, maybe we could fight our way out of this mess.

Or not.

As far as plans went, it was about as half-assed as they came. The multiple hands that grabbed hold of me before my feet could leave the ground attested to that.

I was hauled backward and my legs kicked out from under me as they threw me to the ground at my friends' feet. As several sets of angry fanged faces converged upon us - their stakes raised as batons - Sally's voice managed to stand out from the chaos around us.

"Good job, Bill. That ought to help our case."

35

THE DEFENSE RESTS

I wasn't too worried about myself. Don't get me wrong, I'm not crazy enough to ever look forward to a good old-fashioned pummeling. Even so, I have a few tricks up my sleeve, not the least of which was knowing that my healing would patch me up pretty quickly. Some of my friends weren't so lucky, though, and one of them just happened to be heavy with child.

Fortunately, the angry vamps seemed mostly interested in me. After all, I'd just tried to bull-rush my way through their ranks. I was likewise the only one who'd lost their mind and attempted to come to the aid of the sworn enemy of the vampire race. There was also the part about me being their legendary savior turned epic disappointment. Don't forget the war I began while up in Canada. Oh yeah, there was bringing about the downfall of Boston, embarrassing one of the Draculas, and unleashing a foe who now threatened the stability of our entire way of existence.

All things considered, if I were on the other side, I'd be kicking my ass too.

Pandemonium reigned for the next several minutes. I

didn't think my friends were being beaten to a pulp as I was, but several compulsions passed over the crowd as an attempt was made to restore order. Heh, there was one major flaw with compulsions, though. Add in enough strong emotions and a vampire could potentially break free or resist it for a time. Both rage and fear were two very strong survival instincts designed to override our rational minds. Love was a tremendous feeling too, but I had the feeling there weren't too many folks in the room overcome with it at the moment. Go figure. If I had to guess, the Draculas purposefully forgot to invite any of the hippie covens to their little war council.

Oh well, none of that was particularly important at the moment. I was too busy *enjoying* the sensation of my arm snapping, a rib puncturing a lung, my nose breaking, and several other pesky contusions right before a size twelve boot came crashing down into my face, sending me into blissful darkness.

"Come on... **WAKE UP!!**"

Compulsions don't do dick when it comes to controlling me, but they sure as shit still feel like a claw hammer to the skull. At some point, my subconscious mind had started to emerge from the total nothingness that being knocked out produced, plunging me into another weird-ass dream in which Dr. Death and I were fighting over Sheila. Don't get me wrong; it wasn't some perverted threesome S&M thing. Well, okay, there might have been some nudity involved, but you can't fault a guy for...

"You're doing it wrong. Let me try."

A hard smack across my face sent the imagery fleeing toward the far recesses of my mind, hopefully to stay locked up there.

"You call that a slap, pussy? This is how..."

"Okay, okay, I'm fucking awake," I growled, not wanting to become a punching bag again. Christ, what the fuck was wrong with people?

I cracked my eyes open and squinted in the florescent light that streamed in from overhead. Two shapes stood over me, but I couldn't quite make them out.

"Here, these will help," Tom's voice said. "I managed to grab them before they got smashed to hell."

The familiar shape of a pair of glasses was pressed into my hands and I gladly slid them back on. The frames were a bit bent, but it was a shitload better than having cracked lenses.

Immediately, the room swam into focus, including the forms of my roommate and Sally - her presence explaining the compulsion.

"What happened?" I reached up and she grabbed my hand to haul me to my feet. At least we weren't shackled anymore. The room spun for a moment as I stood, but my equilibrium quickly righted itself.

"You mean before or after the worst rescue attempt in recorded history?"

"After." I was pleased to find my vampire healing had taken care of the worst of the damage. I still felt a little tender in places, but that would hopefully be short lived.

Unfortunately, the rumbling in my stomach quickly reminded me that the only blood I'd had in quite some time had been a mere flask's worth when transported here. I tried to push that thought away as Sally spoke, but in the back of my head, I became acutely aware of Tom's presence. Shit! I tried desperately to concentrate on her voice rather than the tempting treat standing just a few feet away.

"The whole place pretty much went batshit. The Draculas were forced to call a recess until everyone could calm the fuck down. Nobody was overly happy with that. Hell, I even heard a few of the guards actually mouthing off about it within earshot of Alex - dipshits. Methinks the industrial vacuums will be running overtime tonight."

"Cry me a river."

"Tell me about it. A few less assholes in the world. What a shame."

Sally's comment caused me to take a quick look around and notice the lack of anyone else in the room. Panic immediately set in. "Where..."

"We don't know," Tom said. "The guards dragged Ed and Christy off in another direction. They grabbed both of you, then tossed me in here too, like some sort of fucking afterthought."

"Do you think they're okay?"

"Relax," Sally replied, sounding unconcerned. "I'm pretty sure you pissed off everyone in there the worst of us all. If we're fine, they're probably okay too. Besides, I got the feeling Alex was enjoying things a little too much to just go and start executing everyone before the festivities even got started."

"But why separate us?"

"It makes sense with Christy. No matter how many wards they placed outside, if we got those manacles off of her - which we would - she could cause some trouble. She's also a Magi. No matter what that old geezer said, I have little doubt they're going to tread lightly with her. Politics are a motherfucker." She turned to Tom. "That means she'll be treated well so they can avoid any cross-cultural incidents...at least until they sentence us all to death."

"That's good," he replied. "Don't tell her I said this, but I'm kind of glad they stuck me in here with you guys. She looked pissed and...she gets a bit scary when she's like that."

"Pussy," Sally commented with a snort of laughter.

"What about Ed and Sheila?" I asked, forcing myself to remain calm on that latter front.

"Don't doubt that your girlfriend is in whatever passes for maximum security at this place."

The slightest bit of scorn hung on her use of the G-word, but maybe that was just my imagination. I forced it aside for now. Of all the things to worry about in our current predicament, relationship statuses were easily at the bottom of the list. Even so, it did give me cause to wonder whether...no! Now was not the time. "And Ed?"

"He's still an unknown, an X-factor. As far as they're concerned, that makes him dangerous and, thus, he'll get his own quarters where they can keep a close eye on him."

"So basically what you're saying," Tom surmised, "is they're keeping the threats under lock and key by themselves and tossing the rest of us in here together?"

I turned toward him, eyebrow raised. "Now that you mention it, that is sort of insulting."

"You're telling me," Sally groused.

"Seriously. I'm the legendary Freewill."

"*Were* the legendary Freewill. I'm pretty sure our buddy up in Boston is enjoying that title right now. Probably got it tattooed across that muscular chest of his."

"You should have taken a picture while you had the chance."

"Don't think I didn't consider it."

I shook my head in frustration. "Regardless of him being Mr. Muscles, I have the same powers. Hell, I could bite you right now and power up."

"And that's going to do *what* exactly against the small army stationed here?"

She had a point there. Sally's mind was as sharp as they came, but her blood was still only about half a century old. As far as the Draculas were concerned, she was practically still in training pants. James was the youngest of that bunch and he still had over ten times her number of years under his belt.

I considered all of this as I took in our surroundings. It was basically just an empty room about twenty feet square. There were no windows, no places to sit, not even a fucking toilet - which could become worrisome, depending on how long they expected us to stay here. A single door marked the only exit, and I could tell by the look of it that busting out was probably not going to be in our cards.

Just to be safe, though, I walked up to it and tapped with my knuckles - solid steel, by the sound of it.

"Already tried that," Sally commented.

I backed up a step and noticed there was a very slight depression in the metal, fist shaped, if I had to guess.

"Anyone answer when you tried knocking?"

"Nope. Fortified and most likely soundproof, although I have little doubt they can hear us - probably see us too."

I immediately got what she was hinting at. The vampire nation was in some ways a walking, talking contradiction. They were steeped in tradition, relying on prophecy to guide them. At the same time, they could be surprisingly modern when necessary. Alex had once told me of how the Draculas used radioactive tracers to track their troop movements. Likewise, Calibra, the last prefect of the Northeast, had informed us of some of the technical capabilities of the Boston complex - including a transatlantic gigabit connection. Considering the facilities around us, this room was likely bugged to the point where one would need a lot more than a can of Raid to clean it out.

Thoughts of Boston brought with it memories of our last disastrous trip there. Calibra was now a prisoner to Vehron, assuming he'd kept her alive. Oddly enough, that outcome wasn't considered the preferable option, considering how much she knew. Vehron had practically been a caveman when I'd accidentally freed him. Now, though, if he was anything less than a total muscle-headed buffoon, he'd probably spent the last few months forcing her to bring him up to speed.

It could have been far worse, though. James had been up there with us and had proven himself no match for the monster. Had he been captured, who knows the extent of the intelligence that could have been gained. He hadn't been, however. We'd saved him and...

I stopped mid-thought and considered this, rubbing my jaw with my hand.

"What is it?" Sally asked.

"James."

"I noticed," she replied, her voice dropping all hint of her usual attitude.

"Remember what he said before Colin took him away...something about atoning?"

"Yeah. I don't know what they did to him, but out there, he looked...broken."

Silence descended as that sank in.

"No fucking way," Tom said. "Dude's too tough. We've all seen him. So he got his ass kicked once. Happens to the best of us."

I eyed him skeptically. As if he would know anything about that.

"He's still a member of the Draculas, right?" he asked. "It's not like they voted him off the island."

"We don't know anything about that," Sally replied in a neutral tone. That she didn't immediately throw out a casual threat toward him spoke a lot about how much this subject bothered her. For not the first time, I wondered what, if any, history she shared with James before I'd come onto the scene. "The First Coven are a complete mystery. They rule us, but they're a closed circle. You don't get close to them unless they let you, and you don't say shit about it afterwards because you're probably compelled up to your eyeballs."

"Or don't want to die horribly," I added.

"That too. Bottom line, we have no insight into how things work with them."

"Other than Alex is the big dog," I corrected, then almost had to laugh. I'd been in their nerve center. Hell, they held me prisoner there for nearly a quarter of a year.

I was also afforded, by way of my status as Freewill, a small glimpse into how Alex thought and how some of the others saw him. "They present themselves as a coven of equals, and that may have once been true, but I get the feeling that's not the case anymore. I spoke to two of them, Theodora and Yehoshua, and they were definitely not happy with..."

"Weird name," Tom commented.

"Says you," Sally replied. "I doubt there were too many Dipshit McAsshats walking around in ancient times either."

"My name isn't..."

I opened my mouth to shush their bickering, but then clammed up. Like Sally said, this place was probably bugged, and even now, prying ears could be listening. I had been about to spill the secret that members of the Draculas, two of the top three, judging by their seating arrangements, were basically traitors to the cause - or at least Alex's cause.

What a fucking idiot I was. While they'd done little more to foil Alex's plans than help me escape, they were both still potential thorns in his side. Alex may have presented the Draculas as a team, but what few people realize about teams is there might not be an "I" in it, but there is most certainly an "M" and an "E" in the word.

Even if it all went to hell for us right now, resulting in

our painful executions - a scenario I preferred to avoid - they might continue to work from the shadows, manipulating events so the world didn't end up crowning Alexander of Macedon emperor for the second time in its history.

That concept was a mind-blower right there. I'm pretty self-involved. In my day-to-day life, I preferred to watch out for number one. That means no stupidly heroic self-sacrifices if I can help it. I've never had any intention of being a martyr - still don't. Regardless, for perhaps the first time, I thought of the big picture. Even if I wasn't around to see it, Alex failing in his mad quest for world domination remained our top goal.

Talk about humbling.

Was this how it started for history's crazed revolutionaries? One moment of clarity that led to a lifetime - usually fairly short - of resistance against the powers that be?

Goddamnit, how the hell did I end up here? I mean, the Freewill was supposed to be the harbinger of doom, the so-called Night Spawn, as the Templar put it. Wasn't I supposed to be out razing the countryside and carrying off wenches for my own nefarious purposes? Hell, I'd played out that scenario dozens of times at the gaming table and I can tell you one thing - it's kinda fun. Shit, wasn't it Sheila's job to do all the heroics?

Yeah, it was. And hadn't I promised myself I'd do everything in my power to both save her from this mess and try to put the world back together? Ah, the things I do to impress a girl.

Okay, that was bullshit. I'd do the same thing regardless. As awesome as the fantasy of being Dr. Doom or Lex Luthor might be, at the end of the day, I'd probably always choose to be the underdog hero fighting to stop them.

Goddamn, I must be out of my fucking mind.

I burst out laughing at all the irony, all the idiocy, everything that seemed to drive me forward toward what were no doubt impossible goals.

"Something funny, Bill?" Sally asked, dropping Tom - whom she'd been holding aloft by the shirt collar, presumably with the intent to clock him.

Tom coughed for a moment, catching his breath. "Think maybe he's finally lost his mind?"

Before either of them could answer, the heavy door to our holding cell opened from the outside. A man standing in the doorway blocked the concrete walls beyond. Scratch that - he wasn't just a *man*. Of average height, but strongly built, his mismatched eyes took us all in as he strode forward.

"The Freewill's mind has always been far afield, as far as I am concerned, human," Alexander said. "It is one of the traits about him I most admire."

36

DROPPING A MONOLOGUE

I immediately regretted the lack of bathroom facilities because the smell in this place was gonna get *real* funky if I ended up pissing myself out of fear - something I was seriously considering. Back during my *vacation* in Switzerland, Alex had attempted to coax my Dr. Death persona to the surface. That coaxing had resulted in me being beaten and broken with near surgical precision - all while he maintained the coolly detached attitude of someone reading a particularly unengaging book.

I sincerely doubted most sociopaths could have kept as straight of a face.

Now, here I was again in a similar situation, except this time I had my friends around to either watch him do so...or for him to torture while I looked on.

Oh, crap, what if that last part was his plan? Maybe Alex thought he couldn't break me - which was complete bullshit. I would have confessed to kidnapping the Lindbergh baby with fairly minimal persuasion. The tough-guy routine wasn't my shtick. I was more of the class clown type.

There was little chance of me stopping him from

hurting my friends, but I realized one thing as he stepped forward...

I would die trying.

Tom, in a fit of apparent insanity, approached Alex and said, "Dude, bringing in that old guy to piss off my girlfriend was *not* cool. Do you know how much shit I'm gonna have to listen to..."

"***SLEEP!!***" Alex barely whispered the compulsion, but my friend dropped like a bag of rocks.

I started forward, but Sally put a hand on my arm. Her meaning was crystal clear: Alex could have done *a lot* worse if he'd wanted to.

"Much better," he said. "My apologies, but your friend here seems to have a singular talent for inane chatter. I was even told that two of the sentries tasked with his retrieval had to be physically restrained from killing him - against my direct orders. They, of course, have since been relieved of their duties."

I glanced sideways at Sally. I had a sneaking suspicion their *relieving* was less a reassignment and more of a permanent retirement.

"Regardless, it is for the best," Alex continued. "Human ears are not fitting audience for any discourse we might share."

"Then why'd you lock him up with us?" I asked.

A wry smile played across his lips. "I was curious to see if either of you would drain him for nourishment."

Well, that was ever so slightly sick as all fuck.

"Interesting." He looked down upon my blissfully snoring roommate. "I can see the hunger in your eyes, Freewill, yet you resist without any obvious temptation. You too," he said, turning to Sally. "Even more so, since I am well aware of the carnage you caused prior to replacing Marlene."

I glanced in her direction, but if there was something to what Alex said, she wasn't in a confessing mood.

"The meatsack grows on you after a while," she replied, her voice steady and showing no sign of the terror I felt in my gut. "Besides, I'm kind of afraid to bite him. You never know when stupid will become contagious."

He appeared to consider this and his grin widened. "Indeed. A pleasure to make your acquaintance again, my dear."

She nodded respectfully.

Alex reached into his pocket and produced something like a remote control. He pressed a button on it and then put it away again. "Alas, human ears might not be a worthy audience, but I prefer our conversation be a private one from all others as well."

"Let me guess. There's going to be a section of the videotape that's mysteriously missing?"

"White noise and static, actually. Regardless, what is said here stays here."

He didn't even need to ask if that was clear or not. His word was law and he knew it. Of course, what we did when he wasn't around to crush our skulls into paste was a whole different story, but I decided against saying as much.

"So are you here to gloat?" I asked.

"Gloat? Quite the contrary. I have come to apologize."

A part of me wondered if maybe the Jahabich had knocked a screw or two loose in my head during our little underground misadventure. Hadn't we just been marched in, accused, and utterly humiliated - all at his bequest?

"Come again?"

"I wished to apologize for all that has transpired and what is yet to come. It was not my intention to inconvenience you with such pointless spectacle."

"You seemed to be having a pretty damned good time doing it, though," I pointed out, a small part of me realizing that I was mouthing off to the worst person on the planet to do so against.

"One must play the part one is given. Shakespeare was quite astute when he penned that all the world's a stage. Alas, when it became public knowledge that the Icon had survived, I had no choice but to take action. Sadly, your involvement in that affair was too well-known to overlook."

"Public?"

"Yes," he replied. "I, of course, surmised her survival almost immediately following the incident in question."

"Wait a second," I said. "You *knew* she was alive?"

"I was not aware of the details, but yes. Between the inconsistencies of the fiction presented to us as fact and being well aware of the Wanderer's lack of providing the necessary equipment for his strike team, it was quite obvious."

"So why didn't you..." Sally started.

"But how did you know I had feelings for her?" Her question was probably more relevant to our plight, but fuck it. I needed to satisfy my curiosity first.

"I did not," he replied with a smile. "That was merely conjecture on my part, a bit of window dressing to make the proceedings appear more dramatic. Imagine my surprise, though."

"Once again, good job, Bill," Sally said, clapping me on the shoulder. "But that still doesn't answer why you didn't immediately continue on with the witch hunt."

"It is simple. The Icon is inconsequential."

"What?" Sally and I both asked in unison.

"What do you mean 'inconsequential'? From what I've heard, covens up and down the Eastern seaboard were shitting bricks and then using them to seal up their doors."

"Quite the interesting imagery you paint there, Freewill."

"Yeah, the world lost a great philosopher when we brought Bill into the fold."

I shot Sally the stink eye. "Don't you have some dollars in your g-string you could be counting?"

"You assume I'm wearing underwear."

Wait, what?

A slight sigh escaped Alex's lips. "As I was saying, the Shining Ones have been present since the dawn of time. They even fought alongside us in the first great war with the Grendel."

"Makes sense," I said. "I imagine every person was one back then, worshipping the moon spirits or whatever the fuck."

"It does not, nor has it ever worked that way, child. That anyone of strong enough faith can become an Icon is nothing more than myth - used as a way of inspiring soldiers that they, too, could become legendary heroes if they fought hard enough for king and country."

"No?"

"Of course not," he replied dismissively. "As you said: otherwise, every priest, zealot, or self-proclaimed prophet in history would have become so empowered. It is no different, I suppose, than with Freewills. One is either born with the gift or one is not."

"Gift?"

"Magic, genetics, call it what you will. Had current events not played out, in a couple of decades I suppose science would have advanced to the point where we could have foretold from birth who held such a destiny - and taken appropriate measures."

He shook his head as if to say "What ya gonna do?" before continuing on. "But that is of no consequence. My point is that Icons have existed all throughout history, and yet, we are still here. They are to be feared and respected upon the battlefield, but that is all. One lone Icon will no more destroy our way of life than one lone Freewill."

"And yet people seem to think otherwise," I pointed out, pretty certain that Alex wasn't talking about me.

He clasped his hands behind his back and chuckled. "I suppose I am partially to blame for that."

"How so?"

"He's talking about the disappearance of the Freewills," Sally said.

Alex raised an eyebrow. "I thought you might eventually figure that out. You are a clever girl. Despite your age, together you both make for a surprisingly formidable team."

"Technically, I'm the one who figured it…"

"So," Sally interrupted, apparently happy to take credit for my brainstorm, "if I'm reading this correctly, what you're saying is it's simply a matter of vampires not being used to them anymore?"

Alex clapped his hands together. "Precisely. That was an unexpected, albeit not entirely unwelcome, result of culling Freewills from the world. Fewer and fewer Icons were born until such time as centuries passed before the world had seen either. Unfortunately, many of our kind suffer from the same weaknesses as mortals…they talk amongst themselves, spreading rumors. These rumors eventually become myth, and myth becomes legend. Barely an eon goes by before what were once merely considered warriors of note become the so-called destroyers of our race."

"Wait, but what about the prophecies?"

"What of them? Magic exists, and so does the ability to peer through the mists of time. But what of it? One can either sit idly and wait for events to play out, or one can manipulate them so that they come to pass at a time of one's choosing. Fools drop to their knees in worshipful reverence when lightning flashes in the sky. True visionaries see it for what it is and use it to guide the masses in the direction they so dictate."

Sally and I once again shared a glance. Holy crap. The only thing scarier than a nutcase was a nutcase with a dangerously high IQ and the charisma to put it to use.

With Alex at the helm, the Earth and everyone on it was headed toward a world of hurt.

37

TWO SHIPS PASSING IN THE NIGHT

"So all of it..."

"Careful planning, a little luck, and the ability to improvise," Alex proclaimed proudly. "I was originally unsure how you would play your part. Unlike how our official history reads, there have been others of your kind over the past few centuries."

"Others? But where..." I paused as realization set in. "You killed them."

"And all witnesses to their power."

My mind reeled. Alex had basically told us nearly everything I'd had shoved down my throat over the past year was bullshit. Don't get me wrong - I never quite fully embraced these so-called prophecies, but enough weird crap had gone down that I'd begun to wonder. Now, though, it seemed a puppet master had been behind the scenes, manipulating the marionettes since the very start.

"But why me?"

"Do not get me wrong. In all likelihood you would have shared the same fate as the others." Alex began to pace as he spoke. "Sadly, news of your birth was slow to reach my ears. By the time it did, many were already talking about you as the harbinger of our destiny. A sign of the times and the technology at our disposal, I suppose."

I felt something brush against the back of my hand. Sally was attempting to tell me something, but I wasn't sure what. I was still trying to make sense of Alex's revelation. It made no sense. James had been present the night of my death and subsequent *rebirth*. He'd even proclaimed me a Freewill then and there - right after I'd gotten my ass handed to me by Night Razor.

He'd been the Boston Prefect back in those days. It had been his job to...

Wait. Was it possible? James, Mr. Rulebook himself who seemed to eat, breathe, and drink protocol - and espressos; let's not forget those. Was that what Sally was trying to tell me? Assuming, that is, she wasn't letting me know she wanted to hold hands. That would have been cool too.

"I still might have had you slain," Alex continued, discussing my death as casually as if an annoying gnat had gotten into his house, "but then François's silly little gambit came into play - his petty revenge against the Khan. It was then I decided that perhaps the time had come to move forward with my goals. The rest is history...or soon shall be."

"Except for the parts that I fucked up," I countered. It wasn't much, but I was starting to feel mighty pissed. What was I, some fucking pawn in a chess match? Hell, I didn't even like chess. I couldn't physically hurt him, but maybe he needed a reminder I was still a potential fly in his ointment.

"Oh?"

"Yeah. Like how I messed up your plans with Druaga. You talk of petty revenge, but you can't tell me some of this shit here isn't the same thing."

I half expected to find myself buried in the wall at that

remark, getting a nice up close and personal demonstration of how thick the concrete of this place was.

Instead, Alex once more smiled. "What exactly did you *mess up*, as you so put it? Did you not see Lord Druaga amongst our guests out there? Our alliance has been sealed in blood. Even as we speak, his forces are engaging the enemy upon the field of battle."

"How? I thought..."

"You played your part perfectly, Freewill, as I assumed you would. Simply absorbing my strength would not have sufficiently impressed him. The bold move of attacking us both in your bid to escape ensured our alliance right then. The sheer audacity on display told Druaga all he needed to know - that our great nation was stalwart enough to march forward against any foe."

"Way to go..."

"Yeah, yeah, I know, *way to fucking go, Bill*," I snapped, redirecting my anger at Sally. The bitch didn't have to rub it in.

Oh, crap! If that whole thing had been by design...did that mean he knew about Theodora and Yehoshua? Worst of all, had he also planned that I would... "So Vehron, too?"

At that, a momentary pained expression crossed Alex's face. It was only there for a second, but it said a lot. For all his brilliance, he couldn't control everything. There was still chance to contend with, still - dare I say it - *free will.*

"I will admit that was unexpected," he confirmed. "An anomaly I hadn't counted on."

"Then why did you stop us?" Sally asked. "We went after that guy once. You had to know..."

"Of course." He waved his hand dismissively. "One does not need the counsel of the elder seers to have foreseen that." Once more, his voice assumed its normal arrogant undertone. "As I have already said, I did not achieve my position without learning the value of improvisation. The truth is, Vehron, though appearing as an agent of a long-dead foe, is in actuality doing *my* bidding."

"What?!" Talk about your fucking bombshells.

"Not purposely, of course, but despite his military prowess, the lout was always a bit one-dimensional in his thinking."

"Not following."

"Vehron has proven useful. The forests of the Northeastern United States are a Grendel stronghold, but a containable one. However, if they are allowed to press north, they could potentially catch our Canadian offensive in a phalanx."

"What a shame that would be."

"Mind your elders, child," Alex reprimanded. "François may be a shortsighted imbecile, but he is one that shall be disposed of at a time of my choosing, not our enemy's."

"When we tracked him up to Boston," Sally said, dragging us back on topic, "we came across a group of Feet. There were a few survivors, but the majority had been slaughtered."

"Exactly," he confirmed. "And that was only those who got in his way. He is a brutally efficient warrior. In his attempt to fortify his stronghold, he and those foolish enough to follow his banner have undertaken a scorched-earth policy - cleansing a rapidly expanding radius of all supernatural entities unfriendly to their cause."

"And how is that good for us?"

"It was a simple matter to inform our troops and allies to stay clear and let him conduct his work."

I had to admit it was a good idea in the short term -

introducing a hostile new species into an area to clean out the pests. But the problem with such strategies was in the long haul when they didn't play nice and die out when they were supposed to.

"Worry not, Freewill," Alex said as if reading my mind. "The enemy of my enemy is my friend, but only until such time as they outlive their usefulness. The Cult of Ib was crushed eons ago. Vehron is a fanatic to their cause; powerful and a ruthless battlefield commander, but he is a man out of his time, embracing long-dead ideals. He is a weapon of war, but lacks the finesse to lead as ruler. The ancient magicks once used by their priesthood are lost to all save our archives, and I have taken the liberty of having those sealed."

"I'm sure that'll piss off Colin."

"Excuse me?"

"Nothing. Inside joke." I waved a hand dismissively - not so subtly mocking him and just barely resisting the urge to smile. "But what about the possibility of vampires flocking to him? I mean, I was led to believe that might be a problem."

"And indeed it has been," he replied, seemingly no more worried than if I told him it might rain the day after he washed his car. "Some have abandoned their posts, hoping the ways of old might prove more to their liking. Still more have proclaimed him the true Freewill of legend - reborn to lead us into darkness."

"And that doesn't bother you?" Sally asked.

"Quite the contrary. In times of war, one must always be wary of traitors. The disloyal have done me the service of outing themselves. Once their usefulness comes to an end, so shall they. As for the deluded, they will see the error of their ways. Some have already returned, having found their new *savior* not to their liking."

Returned? I threw a worried glance Sally's way. We'd both been witness to what this psycho had been able to accomplish with seemingly little effort - planting orders in those who weren't even turned yet and being able to somehow undo the multiple safeguards compelled into the Boston staff.

"I assure you, I am well aware of Vehron's age and power. Those who have come back to the fold are thoroughly sanitized of his potential influence."

That didn't sound good. "Sanitized?"

"Indeed. It has been some time since so many of our people have been exposed to the glory of the First Coven. It has given us a chance to...reconnect, so to speak."

"Insulation," Sally muttered.

"Yes, and then they are put into service to test their loyalty."

Older vampires were capable of undoing the compulsions of those younger than them, even protecting their minions from the control of others. According to what I'd been told, it was likewise possible for multiple vamps to pool their powers - weaving a tapestry of defenses greater than the sum of its parts. The mass compulsion that had been used on the Boston crew hadn't been powerful enough, but that only meant the vamps doing the compelling hadn't been up to the task. Apparently, they'd never anticipated a foe of Vehron's might. But if the Draculas themselves were involved now, that was a whole other ball of wax right there. The combined power of even a few of them would be nigh unbeatable. If the majority of them...

That thought trailed off as the rest of what he'd said registered in my brain. "Wait. Did you say 'test of loyalty'?"

"Yes."

Hadn't Colin said something about that regarding the douche patrol that had guarded us? "Hold on. So those doofuses we rode in with..."

"I would not quite refer to them as that. They did prove themselves, after all, but yes, they were amongst a group recently liberated."

Maybe it was the hunger or the righteous anger or simply that Alex was a cock-meat sandwich with a side of twat, but I momentarily forgot whom I was speaking to. "So let me get this straight. You handcuffed us in the back of a locked truck with a bunch of inexperienced morons who might or might not have been compromised by a vampire who I did a really good job of pissing off just a few months back? Does that sound about right?!"

Silence descended upon the room for what seemed an eternity.

"Nice knowing you, Bill," Sally muttered as she backed up a couple of steps. So great to know she had my back when the chips were down.

Fortunately, Alex didn't seem to be in the mood to kill me horribly. No doubt he wanted to save that part for the crowd. It would probably make for a memorable after-dinner show. "Your way with words never fails to amuse me, Freewill. I thank you. So many, my colleagues included, often prove disappointing when it comes to verbal discourse. To answer your question, though, you survived, did you not?"

"Well, yeah."

"I calculated the risk to be low. Had they attempted to free you, I sincerely doubt you would have marched willingly into the Destroyer's camp. Had they attempted to kill you, I had little doubt you would have found a way past their meager defenses. In either scenario, they would have been exposed and we would have known their true intentions."

"Why can't you just compel the truth out of them?"

"We do. The test of loyalty is merely an extra precaution."

Right. Translation: we never miss out on a chance to fuck with Bill Ryder.

"The others feel it isn't necessary, but I have no intention of jeopardizing the war effort by relying on the fickleness of chance or the arrogant assumptions of others."

He certainly had enough of that latter part to go around. "So you had faith in our ability to survive long enough to arrive safely and be sentenced to death?"

"You wound me, Freewill. I would not have invested so much effort in you just to toss it away like dust in the wind. Had I wished, I would have ended your life without pomp and circumstance. I still could. None would question me."

In my periphery, Sally took yet another step back. That chick's a real confidence booster, I tell ya.

"The truth is, your death serves us ill. There are many who still believe in you, and I would not see that faith dashed to pieces. No matter the outcome, your survival this day is assured."

Alex inclined his head, then turned and stepped toward the door.

Well, that was a load off my shoulders. So this whole thing was just a fucking dog and pony show? I should have known. Probably an excuse for them to stick me with some other insane mission as a form of penance. Assholes. I could only imagine what fuckery they'd send me and my friends on next.

Hold on; he hadn't said anything about them. I glanced over at Sally and she gave me a quick "go on" gesture.

"Wait. My friends?"

Alex turned slowly back toward me, a predatory grin

upon his face. Suddenly, I had the feeling I'd just stepped right into a trap that had been laid out in front of me all along. "That can be arranged."

"All of them?"

"A distinct possibility, although that really is up to you."

And there it was, plain as day. "What do I need to do?"

"Nothing really. However, I believe it was you who admitted, right after your marvelous performance in the Woods of Mourning, that you have a singular aptitude for...how did you put it?"

"Fucking things up?" Sally offered.

"Thank you, my dear. That is it exactly. This day shall prove to be a grand morale booster for our people, as well as cementing their continued belief in me. I shall see that nothing interferes with that."

He had me between a rock and a hard place. Most vamps would have saved themselves at the expense of fucking over everyone they possibly could - friends included - but not me, and Alex knew it. "Fine," I said softly.

"So be it. Although, I must admit, a small part of me was curious to further examine the human."

I glanced over at Tom quizzically.

"The other human - the anomaly," he clarified. "That one..." He pointed down at my slumbering roommate, "I leave for you to do as you so wish."

"You're too...wait. You said *all* of my friends. Sheila, too?"

"Do you consider her to be just a friend?"

Silence stretched out between us for several seconds.

Amazingly enough, the arrogant grin disappeared from Alex's face and he looked thoughtful. Hell, for one short moment, he almost looked human. "Tell me, have you ever heard the story of the doomed lovers, Vara and Edgar?"

"Who?"

"I thought not. Their tale is buried deep in our archives, an embarrassment of sorts. However, I thought there might be a slight chance the Wanderer had perhaps mentioned it to you. He seems to have developed a fondness toward your plight."

I decided it was probably in my and James's best interests to not elaborate on that. "Never heard of them."

"Edgar was the son of a former soldier turned farmer. He lived during the tenth century in a village south of Normandy. One day, a band of raiders invaded. Edgar took up his father's sword and joined in with the defense, but it was all for naught. After a brutal fight against them, he found himself the last man standing, the only one left to protect the widows and children waiting to be raped and sold into slavery. He was ordered to surrender, but refused, vowing to protect his home no matter what."

"So let me guess. One of the women was a vampire and..."

"Hardly. Edgar's resolute vow awakened the dormant power within him. He became an Icon. Shining with the fires of faith, he proceeded to decimate the invaders. But Edgar wasn't a conqueror. He had no interest in adventure or glory. He stayed to help his people rebuild and eventually became their sworn protector. Some years later, word of his existence reached the ears of Vara. She was a Freewill, as beautiful as she was deadly. Having just cleansed a broad swath of Germania of trolls, she was eager for a new challenge - eager to kill one of the Shining Ones."

"Doesn't sound like much of a love story to me."

"You obviously haven't watched too many chick flicks," Sally replied.

"The two mortal enemies met in the fields outside Edgar's hamlet at dusk," Alex continued, ignoring us. "They battled throughout the night, neither able to gain an advantage over the other. Finally, both of them bloodied and tired, the sun began to rise. Shelter was too far away and Vara too spent to make it to safety in time. She would certainly have been doomed, but then Edgar, not wishing for such an ignoble end to a worthy foe, stepped in and raised his shield above her, blocking the deadly rays. For the entire day he protected her, refusing to let her burn. By the time evening came, they were no longer enemies and much more than friends."

"That's...pretty hot, actually," Sally said.

Give me a break. Chicks were such suckers for this bullshit. "So what happened?"

"For a time, they were happy. Vara renounced her ways to be with her love. By day, he would stand guard and, by night, she would keep their enemies at bay. Alas, eventually the men under Vara's command began to wonder why she had not returned. Thinking their commander slain, they ambushed Edgar at dusk, before Vara had risen. Using weapons consecrated in the blood of Baal, they slew him."

"So what did Vara do? Get her revenge?"

"Quite the opposite," he said. "Discovering the bloody corpse of her lover, she stayed with him until dawn - cradling him close as the sun rose. It is said that as her body caught aflame, so too was his form consumed by the heat of her love for him."

"That's so beautiful," Sally said, sounding almost choked up.

Uh, yeah. "I don't get it."

Alex looked pained for a moment, and I had a

feeling it had nothing to do with the story. "The moral of the tale is that you two never had a chance, I'm afraid." As he turned to leave, the full implication of this sank in.

Oh God!

"Please, I..."

"It is out of my hands, Freewill." He knocked once on the door and it was cracked open from the outside. "I would caution, however, that you think of your friends before trying anything foolish."

I bared my teeth, but said nothing.

"To that end, I am truly sorry."

"You already said that."

"I do not mean the trial this time. As I have already mentioned, I will not leave anything to chance at this juncture. I meant what I said about you two. You are a formidable team."

He turned to Sally. "I was truthful in Canada. I foresee a great future for you."

"Thanks, but..."

"But not at the Freewill's side."

I sensed a tingling in the back of my skull as the psychic energies built up inside of him.

"***YOU WILL FORGET YOUR ASSOCIATION AND PAST WITH THE FREEWILL AND HIS FRIENDS!!***"

"No!"

The compulsion, even targeted at her as it was, knocked me backwards from the sheer force of it. The effect on Sally was even more dramatic. She flew off her feet and slammed into the far wall, leaving a smear of blood as she slid to the ground.

Panic coursed through me, and I shook off the effect quickly and raced to where she lay. I cradled her head and took stock of her injuries. Thankfully, it seemed to look worse than it was - a solid clonk to the head, but nothing a vampire couldn't shake off.

"M...Mark?" she asked groggily, opening her eyes.

"No, Sally, it's me. I..."

"Who the fuck are you?"

"I'm Bill. You know me."

She glanced down at herself, no doubt noticing how close I held her to me...and probably noting her ripped shirt from our battle with the Jahabich.

Her eyes immediately turned black and she powered out of my grasp, elbowing me a good one in the solar plexus. *Oof!*

"Hands off, perv. What, a dickless loser like you can't get any unless you attack a girl when she's asleep?"

"It's...not..."

She backed up, hands on her hips, until she nearly stumbled over Tom's still sleeping form. She glanced down and her fangs descended. "Ooh, a threesome, is it? Well, I'd be rude to turn down the refreshments." Her claws began to extend and she bent down toward where he lay.

"Don't you..."

"Kindly leave him, my dear," Alex said from the doorway.

"Says who?"

"I am a friend," he replied. "A friend of the Wanderer...James."

Sally looked skeptical. "Ozymandias is here?" For a moment, a look of confusion crossed her face. "Wait...Night Razor too?"

"No."

"He's..." Her head cocked to the side as if she was struggling to remember. "Wait. He's dead, isn't he?"

"For some time now."

"But how?"

"Come with me. I will explain it all. You need not

bother with this rabble any further. They are inconsequential to you and your new life."

Sally hesitated for a moment. The compulsion had obviously scrambled her brain nice and thorough. Even so, it didn't take a genius to see which way she was leaning. On the one hand, you had a well-groomed, eloquently speaking gentleman standing at the door leading out. On the other, there was me - dirty, covered in dried blood, and wearing half-melted body armor - not to mention the groping.

Appealing to her wouldn't do dick. Compulsions could be overcome with sheer force of emotion, but he wasn't asking her to do anything other than walk with him. There was also the fact that he was insanely powerful. A compulsion from him could have torn through nearly anyone's mental defenses like tissue paper.

That didn't mean I couldn't try, though. Unfortunately, Alex was a step ahead - quite literally. I opened my mouth to say something and he was there in front of me, moving faster than I could believe.

"No, you will not manipulate her again, Freewill." With that, he grabbed my arms and made a show as if to restrain me. He appeared to be putting in a lot more effort than he was. We both knew he could have flattened me with a wave of his pinkie, but you'd have sworn he was struggling. Fucking asshole.

"Freewill?" she asked.

"Yes, it was my mistake to send you here. I didn't realize the danger you were in. Now go, while I still have him."

"Wait," I said, "that's not what..." But I was too late.

Confusion still reigned on her face, but Alex's performance had been good enough. She stepped through the door and out into the hallway beyond.

Alex resumed a casual stance in front of me.

"Remember that of which we spoke, Freewill." He glanced toward Tom, his meaning clear - I had more friends.

Before I could say a word, he had crossed the room again. He smiled triumphantly and swung the door shut behind him.

It latched with a hollow boom and then they were gone - leaving me alone in my misery.

38

RAVENOUS

I will perhaps admit to losing my shit ever so slightly. I don't know how long I pounded on the door in a fruitless attempt to batter it down, but by the time I heard the voice behind me, my fists had been beaten into bloody pulps against the unyielding metal.

"Ugh, what's going on, Bill?"

The self-inflicted damage only served to exacerbate my earlier hunger. I'd been able to ignore it temporarily during Alex's interlude with us, but now it was back with a vengeance - blotting out all other thoughts with its need.

I turned toward the voice and my fangs descended as my nostrils picked up the scent of blood flowing through human veins. As expected, it was right there, sitting on the floor like the good prey it was. This would be too easy.

"Dude, what the fuck did you do to your hands?" The pathetic thing got to its feet, perhaps thinking it would make a fight of it. That was good. I'd enjoy that greatly.

I looked down at my hands, seeing my nails extend into talons. The blood that dripped freely from them would soon be joined.

I took a step forward.

"And where the fuck did Sally go? Did they let her out for a bathroom break, because if so, I'm next. Gotta piss like a racehorse."

Sally?

I paused, conflicted, as rational thought tried to break through the haze. I didn't really want it to, though. This current feeling, while not exactly pleasant, was clean - uncomplicated. Kill, eat, and do it again - pretty simple rules to live by. I mean, it seemed to suit other vampires just fine.

But I wasn't other vampires, was I?

Fighting against every instinct I had, I raised my hand and slapped myself across the face...make that *slashed*. Kinda forgot my claws were still out.

"Holy fuck, man!"

"Stay back," I warned, cradling my torn cheek. Another injury was most certainly not going to ease the situation.

"Why? Let me help..."

"Because I'm trying to eat you!"

Tom...the mists in my mind cleared enough to fill in his name. It was my roommate and oldest friend, Tom, stuck here in this cell with me.

A look of confusion stood on his face. "I'm gonna assume there's an implied 'no homo' after that statement."

"Are you a fucking moron?" I pointed to my fangs, which I couldn't seem to retract no matter how much I tried. Taking a deep breath, I tried to calm down, desperately holding on to the memories of our past playing in my head - except for maybe fourth grade. That was best forgotten. "I've been running on fumes ever since these assholes picked us up and, unfortunately, you happen to be the only blood-filled snack machine in the room."

That seemed to get through to that small reserve of

common sense hiding in the back of his addled brain. "Yeah...I'm thinking maybe you don't want to do that."

"No shit."

He seemed to mull it over for a moment, then he rolled up his shirt sleeve and held out his arm. "You could take a little if you wanted, y'know, just because you're a bro. Don't tell Ed, though. I don't want to get shit about it."

I forced a fang-filled smile. I didn't have a lot of friends in this world, but I would've gladly died for the ones I had - if I really had to. However, I would have never wished the same for them. "Don't. It's too dangerous."

"C'mon, a little won't hurt me...well, except the biting and tearing part."

"I don't know if I'll be able to stop."

"If you don't, I'll just cock-punch you."

That would probably do it. There was one other complication, though. "I don't know if I can control it."

"What, eating?"

"No, not turning you. There's supposed to be some way to stop that, but honestly, I haven't chewed on enough living people to figure it out. I could take a single sip and the next thing you know, you and Christy will be forced to have a moonlight wedding."

"Technically speaking, we only talked about that - nothing official. There hasn't been too much chance to go ring shopping - I mean, with the end of the world and all that shit. Plus, what's with that stupid rule about spending three month's salary on a fucking ring?"

"If she hears you say that..."

"I know. I'll be wishing for the world to end."

We shared a laugh. It was cathartic in more ways than one, serving to further push down the desperate need growing in the pit of my stomach. I just hoped it would last.

The images of those feral vamps down in the tunnels kept flashing through my head. They were more like animals than anything else. How long had they been able to keep things in check before going mad: hours, days, weeks?

I really hoped I didn't have to find out.

"That was a serious dick move."

"Are you kidding? That was a fucking Long Dong Silver dick-sized move," I replied.

I'd brought Tom up to speed on what Alex had told me and what he'd done to Sally at the end of it. I hadn't seen Alex flip back on whatever surveillance he'd suppressed upon entering, but that didn't mean anything. Fuck it; hopefully, some other vamps were listening in even now and this was poisoning them toward what a multilayer cooze cake their leader was.

I had no idea how much time had passed since we'd started talking. Tom was the undisputed master of steering conversations down pointless side streets. Fortunately, though, the banter mostly served to keep my mind off the fact that he'd started to smell mighty tasty.

"So what did he do with her?"

"That's the million-dollar question."

"Think he's fucking her?"

I raised an eyebrow at my roommate's sense of priority, but then realized there might be some validity to that. "I probably would be."

"She'd tear you apart."

"But what a way to go."

Tom chuckled. "So, did you ever think about it?"

"Fucking Sally?"

"Yes, but not that. I mean, actually going out with

her? Don't tell him I said this, but I'm not sure Ed and her are compatible now that he makes vampires explode. Also, Christy said she thinks you two have chemistry."

"She did?"

"Yeah, although there's a slight chance that might just be because Sally isn't fated to destroy all of the witches in the world. I mean, Christy is cool with Sheila and all, but that still might make things a bit awkward on double dates."

Fuck me - was it happening *again?* For over three years, I'd worked for Hopskotchgames, pining for Sheila every day. I'd thought I'd been sly about it, but apparently, it had been a running joke in the office, at least according to Harry Decker. Great; would I have to relive all of that in the supernatural community as well? Those fuckers had slightly longer memories than most cube-mates.

I let out a humorless chuckle at the thought of being reminded for the next thousand or so years of what a gutless loser I was.

"What?"

"It's just that, right now, my social life is probably the least of my worries and definitely the least of theirs. Sally's been mind-wiped and Sheila...well, if we don't do something..." She'd been building a life for herself and, once again, I had to go and fuck it up. Maybe Alex was right about that. Maybe a Freewill and Icon pairing was more of a curse than anything else.

Even so, regardless if she was destined to marry that accountant of hers and have ten kids in the process - hating me every day that went by for the monster I'd become - there still was no way I could let her die.

Unfortunately, that was the extent of my brainstorm. "Fuck!"

"Doesn't sound good, does it?"

"It's about as far from good as it gets. We're

surrounded by enemies a shitload more powerful than us. Alex has one of our friends enthralled and has pretty much threatened the rest of you unless I play nice. Hell, I don't even know where the fuck we are even if we were to somehow escape."

"NORAD," Tom replied.

"What?"

"I got bored when they were bringing me in, so I started chatting with my guards."

"And they didn't threaten to kill you if you didn't shut up?"

"Hell yeah, they did that about a dozen times, but I wore them down."

"Fate truly does smile upon you, does it not?"

"Only if nobody is playing with my stuff while I'm stuck here."

"So what did you mean by NORAD?"

"Oh, that. One of the vamps got to yapping. Apparently, this is part of the whole bunker system that used to house it. According to them, this place is so fucking massive there are parts of it even the US government doesn't remember."

Wonderful. So not only were we in some sort of bunker, but it was a nuclear bunker as well. That didn't exactly help our odds of escape. "I don't suppose they happened to give you any key codes or such for the doors."

"No such luck. I did ask, though."

Of that, I had no doubt.

Try as I might, I couldn't get my vampire side to quiet down. My fangs and claws were still out, and I was pretty sure my eyes looked more like a shark's than anything resembling a human's. Sadly, the more Tom talked, the less

I found myself listening. The beating of his heart began to drown out his voice in my ears.

I even started to formulate a little fantasy in my mind. I'd bite him, taking just enough to clear my head. Then, if he started to turn, maybe I could get Sheila to lay her hands upon him and...

Yeah, I was sure the assembled masses would love to see that.

Oh God, what was I gonna do?

Just as I began to succumb to the idea that at some point I'd start chewing on my roommate, the door to our cell opened. I was on my feet in a second. If Alex was coming back to rub it in some more, I would go directly for his throat. I'd never make it, but being put out of my misery was preferable to killing my best friend.

Multiple figures stood in the doorway, but I pounced anyway. Something must have gone wrong with my trajectory, though, because somehow I landed on Tom.

"What the fuck, man?"

Likewise, I'm not really sure what I was thinking, but "Don't worry; it'll only hurt for a second," slipped out of my mouth as I tried to force his head to the side.

A couple of powerful hands grabbed hold of me and began to drag me off.

"No harm to any of the prisoners," a familiar voice growled. Hey, it was my pal from Pandora's Box - the guy who'd helpfully beaten the snot out of me and loaded us into a truck.

Maybe he wanted to share. "It's okay; you can have whatever's left."

"Restrain him."

"Sorry about this, sir," another voice said. I turned and saw the face of my old buddy Farley.

"Yo, Farl, maybe you're up for a bite of sweet human..."

I didn't get a chance to finish. Farley's reply to my kind offer was to stick the end of a cattle prod into my side and hit the trigger.

Bright blue light arced in my vision as I fell to the floor twitching. Okay, so maybe they didn't want to share.

39

THE TRIAL OF THE CENTURY

A good jolt of electricity could do wonders to take one's mind off their stomach. Should I ever get seasick. I shall have to remember that...assuming I'm not drenched in salt water at the time.

Anyway, once the uncontrollable twitching stopped, I was able to get my feet beneath me and walk rather than being dragged. That was good because, by this point, I needed every little bit of dignity I could muster.

Tom and I were marched back in through the huge blast door. As we entered, I noticed that, if anything, the auditorium looked even fuller than before. Maybe word had spread, or perhaps some had just decided to skip the arraignment for the main event. More vampires milled about, as well as some four-armed flying things, something that looked like a miniature dragon on two legs, a couple of living slime molds, and...huh, that was interesting.

A couple of older suited gentlemen sat off to one side. At first, I thought they were vamps too, but then I noticed their guards wore military dress and held M16s as opposed to silver stakes. Holy fuck, they'd even invited some humans to this? No doubt these were some of the crème de la crème - people in power who knew about us and signed off on the so-called treaties I had heard about.

Or they might have just been thralls, brought here as a buffet. I, for one, could dig that concept.

Oh great, and now I was drooling too. Between still wearing my burnt clothing, smelling of the sewer, and not having had a shower in the past couple of days I...

Oh, fuck me with a rusty cheese grater.

Tom shook my shoulder and pointed at the same time I noticed the asshole sitting just a few seats away from the Draculas' dais as if he was trying to be as close to that bunch as possible, despite being a two-time loser.

"Is that François?"

"Unfortunately."

Speaking of unfortunate, the walking twatsicle apparently heard my comment as just then he turned to face us. His expression was mixed, as if he wasn't sure whether to enjoy our predicament or just outright loathe us. What can I say? I inspire complex feelings in others.

Either way, all of a sudden, I was really glad for our guards. I had little doubt that had François come to visit us in our cell, the walls would now be stained a bright crimson - probably my and Tom's blood.

Once again, we were marched to the center of the massive auditorium where our guards spread out, this time leaving us unattended and unshackled - the meaning was clear. With all the firepower in this room and a ridiculous amount of concrete between us and freedom, there was little to no chance of escape.

I glanced once more toward François, then turned away, not liking the way that his eyes were boring into mine. I needed to take my mind off of him and keep occupied with other, more important things, like those succulent humans sitting over there...or maybe my friends now being escorted into the room.

Yeah, paying attention to how they were doing would probably be the decent thing to do.

Ed and Christy looked okay - tired, but okay. I didn't see any signs of visible scarring or beating, though, which was good. Ed walked freely, but once more, Christy's hands were bound with those magic-stifling manacles. I wanted to rip the damn things off and strangle someone with them, but I had a feeling our current company might frown upon that.

As they reached us, I stepped forward. "You guys okay?"

"Peachy," Ed replied. He took a look around and furrowed his brow. "Where's Sally?"

But I had already moved on from him, giving Christy my full attention. "And how are you?"

"I'm fine."

"Are you sure?"

I'm not quite certain what she replied with, for all I could hear was the rush of blood through her veins and the beating of two hearts in her body - her own and the rapid flutter of her unborn child's. Hadn't Gan once told me the blood of pregnant cows was the richest of them all? I wasn't sure what a witch's blood would taste like, but surely it was compatible with...

"...and then the fucker took her."

"He did?"

Huh? I looked up to find Tom and Ed staring at me, as if expecting some sort of response.

I turned back and found a mixture of pity and horror etched on Christy's face. Her hands instinctively went to her stomach, but she held her ground. "What did they do to you?"

Tears welled up in my eyes. Had I really just contemplated the unthinkable? Was this what happened to monsters like me the moment they skipped a meal - or several? "It's..." My voice cracked. "It's been a long couple of days."

Thankfully, I was spared from openly weeping in front of the crowd. Voices began to murmur in the packed courtroom, for surely that was what this now was. I immediately saw why. The blast door still stood open and another contingent of guards approached. It was that same column as before, with their black-bladed weapons pointing inward.

Sheila was joining us. For better or worse, although in my gut I knew it was worse, things were about to get started.

The assembled masses were all fixated on Sheila's entrance and I knew that as soon as I caught sight of her, I would be too, so I quickly turned back to Christy and said in a low voice, "I'm not a monster."

"I know that."

"Let me finish. If things go bad...if I lose control, don't hesitate to kill me."

"Oh, don't worry, I won't."

"Could you maybe sound a little less chipper about it?"

She smiled. "Sorry, but your answer tells me I won't need to."

I was going to say more, but the contingent of heavy infantry reached our position. They parted into two columns, revealing a girl who, even now - after dying, coming back to life, and dumping my ass for an accountant - took my breath away, as cliché as it might have sounded.

Sheila wore slacks, a t-shirt, and a light sweater. She might have looked like she was just running to the store had it not been for the scorch marks and rips that were indicative of a struggle. Her hands and ankles were bound in shackles made with that same oddly colored metal as the weapons her guards carried. Her hair was disheveled and hung down in her face, but it still wasn't enough to conceal the bright silver gleam of her eyes. She may have been bound and beaten, but the look in them said she was still unbroken.

Even restrained as she was, her guards were still not quite brave enough to physically touch her - probably smart of them. Behind her, one spun his weapon around and used the hilt to nudge her forward toward our merry bunch of prisoners.

For a moment, she looked ready to turn and fight, but then she stepped forward to join us. I was right there to greet her, momentarily forgetting the hunger as well as the hundreds of eyes glaring down upon us. She met my gaze and raised one side of her mouth in a lopsided grin. Whoa. Had Alex passed judgment right at that moment, I'd have died a happy vamp, gladly letting her be the last sight I saw in this world.

We stood there staring at each other for a couple of seconds before we both burst into chuckles. We had a habit of meeting up in the damnedest of situations.

"Aren't we a pair?"

"Are we?" she asked, the grin growing ever slyer. Damn, was it getting hot in here or was it just me?

Thankfully, some *helpful* multi-tentacled thing in the audience spared me from saying anything overly stupid. "Behold! The Freewill proves his guilt!"

Almost at once, the crowd started to chant, "Guilty!"

I spun in a circle, raising my voice and trying to

address them all. "Oh, go fuck yourselves!" As far as last words went, I could've done worse.

Sheila broke eye contact with me and moved on to the rest of the group. She nodded at Tom, exchanged pleasantries with Ed - as well as a joking threat that her company had better be okay, then she turned to Christy.

For a moment, I wasn't sure how that would go. Christy's eyes widened, almost as if uncertain whether Sheila would bite - a prospect I personally wouldn't have minded at all - then finally, she relaxed and smiled. "How have you been?"

Sheila looked down at her manacles. "I've been better. Boy or girl?"

"We're letting it be a surprise, but I'm thinking it's a boy by the way he's kicking the crap out of me."

"Don't be so sure. My mom said the same thing when she was carrying me."

"I guess we'll see soon enough. Can I ask you a question?"

"Now's as good a time as we're probably going to get," Sheila replied.

"Why is it only the girls are handcuffed?"

Sheila let out a musical laugh, her eyes flashing. "I guess they're smart enough to know who the real threats are here."

The comradery amongst our group might have just been gallows humor, but it definitely didn't endear us to the crowd. More jeers were thrown, some for all of us - except maybe Tom. He alone seemed to be spared their bile, almost as if they didn't know what to make of him.

"Go figure," he said to me. "No love for the token human."

"Don't worry. Maybe after they hang the rest of us, you'll get to be the main course."

"That works. I was gonna tell these fuckers to eat me anyway."

I was about to continue our banter when a hush fell over the crowd. The majority of the beings in the audience rose to their feet. Some, mostly of the nastier variety like Druaga, just looked bored. Death gods, can't live with them...

The reason for the hush soon became obvious: the Draculas had arrived.

Alex led the way through one of the other entrances. Every vampire he passed bowed his or her head reverently - mostly. François lowered his gaze, but I could still see murder painted in his eyes, especially for James, who brought up the rear.

James, for his part, looked the same as before - almost resembling a child who'd been hoping for that one special toy on Christmas, but hadn't gotten it. He didn't even spare a glance in our direction as he walked.

Once the Draculas reached their seats, Alex proclaimed, "You may seal us in."

Vampire sentries took up spots at each of the exits to the room. A slight movement of air told me the main blast door was being swung shut as well. I happened to glance in that direction and saw several of the vamps who'd been my personal escorts, Farley included, performing the task. Good for them. They'd been reassigned to door duty. Never let it be said being a vampire was a dead end job.

Each of the First Coven took their respective seats except for Theodora. She glanced at us, a look of confusion upon her face.

"Wait!" she said in a voice loud enough to gain the attention of the entire crowd. "I count only five." She looked down and pointed toward one of the guards. "Where is the other..."

"That will be enough, Theodora," Alex replied in a bored tone. "You needn't worry about her."

That got James's attention. For the first time since entering, he looked up at us. His eyes locked with mine, but there wasn't much more I could do than shrug. I mean, it wasn't like I could pantomime a message to him without everyone in the entire fucking room noticing.

"Needn't worry?" Thea questioned. "She is one of the accused, an ally of the traitors."

"In that, you are incorrect," Alex said. "I have personally pardoned her."

"*You* pardoned her? Without consulting with..."

"Yes, without consulting with any save my own counsel. I spoke with her and determined her loyal to our cause." He turned his head and nodded toward one of the soldiers standing guard at a side entrance. "If you will."

A sheen of sweat immediately broke out on the poor vamp's face. Being addressed by the man in charge, one who could order you flayed without a second thought, was a wee bit intimidating.

"Sir, we have already sealed..."

Alex did nothing as way of response. His expression didn't change. He didn't blink. He didn't compel the guard to rip out his own intestines and hang himself with them. All he did was continue looking at the vamp he'd addressed.

It took less than two seconds for the guard's nerve to break. "Yes, sir!" He quickly unlocked the door, opened it, and stepped through. A few more seconds passed and he reemerged with Sally in tow. She'd obviously been given a chance to clean up and had made good use of it. Her freshly washed hair shined. She wore light makeup, but needed no more to stand out in a crowd. She strode confidently toward where the Draculas sat, wearing a red dress that made even Theodora look like a frump in comparison. All of that would have been fabulous except for the fact that she didn't give our group a second glance upon entering.

Sheila stepped to my side. "Did something happen to your friend?"

"Not now," I warned. I would have loved to have spilled my guts, but there was no way to do so without being overheard. Besides, Alex had made it plainly clear what he expected of me if I wanted my friends to live to see tomorrow.

At least I wasn't the only one dismayed by this. James's face wore a mildly perplexed look, but I knew it was just a mask. Behind it, his mind no doubt was racing a mile a minute.

Sally stopped at his chair, then leaned down to give him a soft peck on the cheek - the look on her face ever so slightly more intense than that of someone greeting an old buddy. Okay, that was interesting. How badly had Alex scrambled her brains anyway?

James opened his mouth to say something, but right on cue, Alex interrupted him.

"My dear, if you will." He indicated a spot behind them where an empty chair seemed almost to materialize as the current occupant quickly vacated. "There will be time enough for pleasantries later."

Theodora, for her part, looked incensed. On the far side of Alex, Yehoshua stared at her, his expression calm - almost as if he were trying to impart his demeanor to her through empathy. If so, she wasn't having any of it.

"This is unacceptable," she said, apparently forgetting all pretense of presenting a united front. "I demand to know what has transpired. This matter was to be judged by the First and therefore..."

"And therefore, it shall be." Alex's tone was enough to cause the temperature in the room to plummet. "The accused stand before us. We shall try them and cast judgment as we will, but I say she is not one of them. *Now sit down.*"

And just like that, the gauntlet was thrown. Theodora looked to her fellow Draculas, but nearly all of them turned away, none of them willing to stand against Alex. Even Yehoshua acquiesced, making a gesture that she should take her seat.

With a growl, she spun and sat. Her eyes faced forward and momentarily met mine and let me just say this was one chick who was fucking pissed.

I would have almost felt bad for her had it not been for the fact that she was up there while we were down here on trial for our lives. Yeah, her pride could go fuck itself with a rusty meat hook.

Alex waited a beat, then stood, a hush falling over the crowd as he did so.

I couldn't help but notice that, whether subconsciously or not, my friends had all gathered closer around me. A shimmering white glow appeared in my periphery and the skin on my cheek sizzled.

"Ouch."

"Sorry," Sheila said, backing up a step.

I turned my head and smiled to let her know it was all right. In a stressful situation like this, one couldn't be blamed for letting their power flare up a bit. I remembered that she'd done the same earlier too, when they'd first marched her in. Whatever the manacles she wore were made of, they apparently served a different purpose than Christy's. If she still had access to her protective aura, then maybe...

"Allies, friends, and children," Alex started.

Oh great, it was going to be one of *those* speeches.

"You all know of the hardships we have faced and shall continue to face in our struggle against our enemies. They are strong, well supplied, and resolute. Yet we have met them on the field of battle time and time again, unyielding in our resolve. Now, though, we face dark days indeed. An enemy from the past has awoken, threatening our stability from within..."

Tom glanced over and gave me a pained look. I couldn't disagree. I hoped they planned to hand out snow shovels to all the guests because the shit was getting deep now.

"...enemies at our gates..."

Ed stepped over to us, trying desperately not to crack a smile at the pomposity on display.

"...destroy our way of life and derail our destiny..."

Christy let out a sigh, which I had a feeling was directed at us.

"...betrayed by those who we once counted as our most trusted..."

Finally, I turned to Sheila and the smile on my face died as I immediately felt like an ass. Our eyes met and, in hers, I saw the same strength and determination I'd seen during prior times, but now there was some sadness as well. Where my roommates and I were determined to flip off the powers that be until the very end, she took this with deadly seriousness, taking stock of our situation and finding it pretty damn grim.

The reality of what Alex had said finally hit me. I had a shot here, and so did my friends if I played ball. But they weren't about to let her walk out of here alive and she knew it.

"How do you plead, Freewill?"

Huh? Realization hit that the question had been directed my way. A part of me, an overwhelming part, wanted to make some comment suggesting what he could do with my dick, but I couldn't - not without my friends paying the price.

Almost as if reading my mind, Alex shifted ever so slightly to his right, revealing Sally seated behind him. She was actually filing her nails...the bitch. Amazingly enough, though, the sight brought a smile to my face and I knew I had no choice in the matter.

"Guilty."

40

THE PEANUT GALLERY

Apparently, Tom, who I'd had a chance to bring up to speed, and Alex - AKA the douche holding my balls to the fire - were the only two unsurprised with my plea.

As for the rest of the crowd, I might as well have told them I'd just taken a shit on the buffet table right before a blind taste test. Shock was plainly visible on several faces, including a few of the Draculas - albeit not James's or Theodora's. I knew James was a smart fellow. I'd have been surprised to all hell if he hadn't surmised that Sally wasn't acting on her own accord. Theodora, well, she'd either figured it out too or just didn't give a shit. It was always hard to tell with women.

"What are you doing?" Sheila hissed.

"Standing with you." It was the truth too. Even had Alex not been pulling my strings, there was no way I was letting her go down by herself.

"I was going to say not guilty."

"You can claim to be Napoleon if you want, but I don't think this bunch is going to buy that either."

"Good point."

The crowd began to get rowdy and drowned out any further discourse we may have had amongst ourselves.

"Traitor!"

"We believed in you."

"Death to the false savior!"

Oh, for Christ's sake. Was nearly everyone here a fucking moron?

I looked up and met Alex's gaze. Smug satisfaction practically oozed out of every pore. He knew he had me in his back pocket. Even if he let my friends go, there was still Sally. No matter how badly he'd scrambled her memory, making her forget everything about me, he knew I wouldn't jeopardize her. It was the price I paid for not becoming like the rest of them - for not becoming a monster.

That didn't even take into account Sheila yet.

I'd been trying my damnedest to get over her ever since my run-in with Robert and subsequent transfer to Pandora Coven - trying to accept that she and I were a fantasy that could never be.

In the here and now, though, she stood right beside me and I could only barely concentrate on the very real danger around us, despite knowing I really needed to.

In short, I was living out my own twisted version of *Sophie's Choice*. I could choose my friends and let Sheila die. The very thought made me want to vomit. The problem was, I could choose her and then we'd *all* die. The world would probably soon follow, although at that point, I'm sure none of us would give two shits.

Fuck!

There had to be something I could do, but what? Becoming Alex's fall guy while allowing him to execute Sheila would be damning myself to the darkness I fought so hard against. Letting my friends die because I was a lovesick loser wasn't any better. Either way you looked at it, I was...

"Stop!"

My head spun toward Sheila as the noise in the room immediately ground to a halt. "What are you..."

She raised a finger to my lips, the glow around her momentarily dying down to nothing. "Promise me you'll find a way to stop this," she whispered.

"This? But..."

"All of this," she clarified before turning away.

I immediately understood that she wasn't talking about the trial, but the world and what was happening to it.

"Wait..." But she was already speaking, drowning out my pathetic protest.

"The Freewill you have all put your faith in is a fool."

Huh? I was?

"I manipulated him, enticed him, made him my plaything..."

She had?

"All for the purpose of undermining *you*, the enemies of mankind."

What the fuck?

Now the crowd was getting riled up again. Angry murmurs rose up amongst them.

"I duped him and his friends into thinking we were allies - as if I could ever care for them - all so I could survive to kill each and every one of you."

Oh, the hell with this shit.

"Okay, enough of this." I stepped forward and put my hand on her shoulder.

She made sure I immediately regretted it.

White hot fire erupted from her body. It wasn't as intense as she was capable of, perhaps a side effect of the bonds that held her, but that was all elementary because it felt as if I'd just touched a live wire.

There came a flash, the sensation of heat, and I found myself airborne - my hand sizzling to a crisp as I flew backward and slammed into a line of guards.

A half dozen helping hands immediately came my way in the shape of fists, and I found myself beaten to the ground as if I'd just attempted a jail break. Jeez, touchy fuckers, weren't they?

I rolled away from them, noticed my friends closing in, and quickly waved them off. This wasn't a fight we could win in our current shape. I also didn't want either Tom or Christy getting too close to me. I was already on shaky ground from the hunger, and whatever damage my healing was going to need to take care of things was only going to make it worse.

My head throbbed and the smell of their blood filled my nostrils from where they stood.

No. I needed to keep it together.

"I could never have feelings for a monstrosity such as him," a voice cried. It was Sheila, continuing on in her insane rant. Goddamn it! What the fuck was she trying to do?

Then it hit home. She was trying to save me. Did she not realize I wasn't the one in danger here? She was going to goad them into killing her, but why?

Why?

Just then, one of the elite guards tasked with bringing Sheila in stepped forward with his black blade. She turned, too late, but her protective aura flared around her regardless.

I smiled, expecting to see a toasted vamp, but instead, he thrust forward with his weapon and the impossible happened. The blackened metal cut through her defenses like butter, burying itself in her shoulder.

She screamed in anguish as the blade sank to the bone. The crowd joined her, the difference being their cries were ones of triumph.

That did it. I scrambled to my feet, intent on one thing and one thing only: killing the vampire who had just hurt the woman I loved.

Before I could even stand, multiple whistling sounds filled the air. I looked up and saw nearly half a dozen silver stakes buried in the back of the vamp who'd attacked Sheila. A moment later, they clattered to the floor as he turned to ash.

"That will be quite enough," Alex calmly proclaimed from where he still stood. From the expression he wore, you'd have thought nothing noteworthy had just transpired.

I stood up, fangs bared.

"You as well, Freewill," he said with the barest nod of his head.

I followed his gaze and saw several more vampire guards, all with stakes at the ready, seemingly more than happy to mete out any more impromptu justice.

"The prisoners are not to be harmed...until such time as I say so."

None of the vamps in the room replied, but they didn't need to. His order was crystal clear and the results of what would happen to anyone stupid enough to disobey were currently settling to the floor.

I turned my head to check on...oh shit, Sheila! She was down on one knee, the weapon still buried in her. It wasn't a fatal wound, or so I hoped, but I had little doubt it hurt like shit.

Hoping that what I was about to do wasn't misinterpreted as a hostile act, I stepped forward and grabbed the handle. "Sorry about this," I said under my breath as I pulled. The blade offered some resistance, no doubt stuck in bone, but then slid out.

A weak gasp of pain escaped her lips, breaking my heart into little pieces, as she raised a hand to the spurting wound. Ignoring the faith magic still surrounding her, I made as if to step to her aid, but she stumbled back out of my reach - once more saving me from my own stupidity.

Her hand, red from her own blood, flashed a bright white - powerful enough that I could feel my nose hairs start to smoke. When it finally cleared, she was breathing hard, but the flow of blood had stopped. She'd managed to heal herself once the blackened metal had been removed.

I looked down at the weapon - a long wooden shaft with a nasty straight blade on the end, some kind of mini halberd. What the fuck was it made of to have cut through her defenses so easily? Sadly, I had a feeling no answers would be forthcoming, so I tossed it back to the guards before they got any ideas. We might all be doomed, but I had no interest in meeting my maker any sooner than I was scheduled to. "Are you okay?"

"Get away from me," she hissed. "I told you, you're nothing but..."

She trailed off and I followed her gaze, glancing over my shoulder to find the rest of our merry little group - Tom, Ed, and Christy - joining us.

Tom and Ed both stepped to either side of her, neither of them in any danger from her power.

"I mean it," Sheila protested weakly - tears in her eyes. "I fooled you all just so I could..."

"Oh, shut up," Christy said softly as my roommates helped Sheila to her feet.

Although both of them were shackled, Christy still threw her arms around Sheila and hugged her tight. She then looked over her shoulder at me. "You too."

"What?"

"Enough with the self-sacrificing crap. Do we look stupid?"

"What self-sacrificing crap?" Tom asked.

"Well, maybe not *all* of you," I replied, wanting to step in and join them, but not quite daring to. I'd already gotten enough taste of the Icon's power for one day. My hand was still blistered from where I'd touched her. I settled for being with them in slightly displaced spirit.

"This is all fascinating," a smug voice replied. It was Alex, reminding us that our little group hug-fest was maybe not happening at the most opportune time. "But your guilty plea still stands, Freewill."

What followed next, after order was restored, was a retelling of history. I'm normally cool with learning about all the badass exploits of the past. Hell, I used to sit for hours as a kid and watch those lousy Italian Hercules movies. What wasn't to love? You had a big musclebound hero killing monsters and getting the girl...or oftentimes, multiple girls. I won't lie and pretend my previously weekly D&D sessions weren't a way to relive those adventures in my mind, this time with me as the hero...at least when Dave wasn't busy smiting us.

Sadly, the problem with stories is they're only as good as the storyteller. Somehow, Colin had gotten himself assigned as the official blatherer of tall tales for these proceedings - probably because he'd had access to those archives under James. However, it wasn't hard to deduce a secondary reasoning behind his appointment: Colin was a grade-A toady. Alex could feel secure that he'd recount history in a way that didn't leave anything open for interpretation of an anti-Draculas nature.

The smarmy prick rattled off a litany of Icons from days past and their crimes against both vampires and the other supernatural races. Had James been doing the telling, I'm sure it would have made for a fascinating afternoon. Under Colin's ever tedious voice, though, it was more like listening to someone recite the assembly instructions for an IKEA entertainment center.

There was Zebbeh the Mad, a crazed Icon who lived thousands of years ago. He'd decided to cleanse the earth of vampire-kind following the conclusion of our first war with the Feet - credited with at least nine hundred confirmed kills.

Then he told of Lucius Severus, an Icon who lived during the reign of Augustus Caesar. Quite the nice guy, that one. When he wasn't busy crucifying early Christians, he amused himself by burning down whole colonies of the Aflar, which, judging by the pained response from a group off in a far corner of the room, were grey-skinned, elf-like creatures.

And let us not forget Tomas Cordoba, a 14th century Icon who was one of the Spanish Inquisition's nastier secret weapons. Seems he was directly responsible for nearly wiping out the Magi in Europe. Bet they didn't expect that.

I had little doubt there were exaggerations thrown into the mix. After all, Alex himself had admitted to being as worried about Sheila as he was of getting too much starch in his togas. Still, I had to wonder. Faith magic, as far as I could tell, had nothing to do with being good or righteous. I mean, fuck, Tom had somehow empowered an

Optimus Prime action figure just by sheer virtue of believing it to be worth a fortune - not exactly the most altruistic of motives. It wasn't hard to imagine that some who were born with the gift of...Iconhood, I guess...might turn out instead to be nutball zealots. Still, Colin's list was definitely a one-sided affair, obviously meant to stir the crowd.

Regardless, I couldn't help but notice the lack of Freewills in his stories. I guess when someone performs wholesale slaughter for your side that gives them a free pass from being reviled. The history books are funny that way.

I had to give it to both Sheila and Christy. They both stood defiantly as account after account was read.

Wish I could have been as attentive, but at least I was in good company. Tom was picking his teeth with his fingernails - gross. Ed busied himself looking through the crowd, maybe counting the number of tentacles present or something. Fuck me, even Sally - brainwashed as she was - had zoned out. The bitch had somehow procured a tablet and was busy tapping the screen. Saving her was at the top of my priority list, but if I found out she was busy checking Instagram while we were down here being sentenced to death, I probably would have to deck her in the mouth.

As for me, after a while, I tuned out Colin to the best of my ability and studied the reactions of the Draculas, trying to do so out of the corner of my eye so as to not be immediately stared down by Alex's self-satisfied grin.

James, seemingly lost in his thoughts, didn't appear to be paying attention to any one thing. Glancing at his missing arm, I once more found myself wondering what the hell had happened since last we'd seen him. He toed the party line as far as I'd been aware, with the exception of his quirk of being an actual pleasurable person to hang out with. Sure, he'd lost one fight to a superior foe, but had the penalties for such truly been that harsh?

Of the rest, I counted five as unreadable - apparently paying attention to Colin's greasy voice and taking the entire thing at face value. The remainder of the First were just playing at it, though. The thing about poker faces is even the best players will have a hard time keeping them completely up in the presence of someone they absolutely loathe. A neutral demeanor was best - something that James was usually a master at. Other vamps weren't like him, though. Arrogance tended to reign supreme as their number one vice. Someone utterly full of their self would bristle at anyone who held power over them.

Theodora was the most naked of them with regards to her feelings - sadly, just a figurative term. Every glance she stole at Alex was an openly hostile one. Those present could probably write it off as being miffed at his shoot down from earlier, but I knew she and her partner in crime were openly against Alex's plans for one plain and simple reason: self-preservation.

Alexander the Great had nearly conquered the world over two millennia ago. There hadn't been any bullshit triumvirate or senate either. He'd set out to make himself undisputed ruler, first amongst any - for there would be no equal to him. Time could change some people, but not all. It didn't take a Ph.D. candidate in Ancient History to surmise Alex stood in that latter camp. If he won the war, it would only be a matter of time before he pulled a Senator Palpatine and abolished the First - or simply killed them off.

Sidelong glances and other such gestures outed others of their number. All in all, I would have bet the majority of the First Coven weren't entirely on peachy terms with their leader. The problem was, with regards to vampires, a simple majority didn't mean dick. One vamp of sufficient strength could mow down an army of newbs. As long as Alex had a few allies on the board of directors, and I had no reason to doubt he did - he'd been playing this game and playing it well for a long time - he could potentially hold the others in checkmate. Once they were dealt with, it would only be a matter of removing his allies, something I sure as shit wouldn't do. Then again, I wasn't a complete and utter slice of dingleberry pizza.

Yeah, all of it made sense - or at least I thought it did. I couldn't help but feel a bit like James looked right now. Alex had struck a blow to more than just our friendship when he'd stolen Sally away from me. He'd said we were a formidable pair, and I sensed he wasn't one to idly hand out compliments to low-ranking rabble. She was my partner, in many ways my better half. Everything I'd just deduced, probably burning off ten million brain cells in the process, she'd have figured out almost instantly.

I loved my roommates like brothers, but I'd succeeded against the odds without them. Christy was terrifyingly awesome, but was a relatively late comer to our Scooby gang. Sheila was...well, she was a lot of things. I would have given anything to spend eternity by her side, in either war or peace. At the same time, I had to admit our few outings together hadn't ended spectacularly.

Sally was different, though. She was a constant in my universe, by my side for every major victory I'd somehow managed to walk away from. Hell, if she hadn't returned from Vegas when she had, I had little doubt I'd be lining an ash tray in Vehron's throne room.

The truth was simplicity itself: even if I somehow managed to get out of this mess, I didn't really believe I could win without her by my side.

At last, Colin ended his rambling tale of Iconic disasters. Jeez, talk about sucking up. If even half the shit he'd said was real, the world would have been reduced to a cleansed cinder long ago. As it was, the supernatural realm seemed surprisingly robust despite centuries of Icon-related slaughter. Bunch of negative Nancys, the whole lot of them.

"Most disturbing," Alex said when he was finished, false gravitas weighing upon his voice. "What say you to this evidence, Shining One?"

Sheila opened her mouth to reply, but then glanced toward me. I got the distinct sense she was going to try disassociating herself from us again, so I gave my head a quick shake. She let out a sigh and mouthed, "All right," before addressing Alex's question. "I do not know, nor have I ever met, any of the people you've just mentioned. I'm my own person and have no quarrel with anyone who respects the peace."

"The peace? An interesting choice of words in these dark times."

"I meant I have no problem with anyone except those who prey on the innocent."

"Is that so?"

"It is."

"So you deny being a student of the Templar? The same Templar who have hounded us for centuries - ineffectually, of course." His dig caused a chuckle to ripple throughout the room.

I couldn't entirely disagree with that. The Templar were warriors of faith, albeit more like crazed Bible thumpers from what I'd seen. This made the true believers among them formidable against the supernatural, but the problem with faith is that it's apparently pretty darn easy to fool oneself into thinking you have it when, in reality, you ain't got dick. About half the Templar I'd fought in my bid to rescue Sheila had been the real deal, possessing crosses glowing with the protective magic that true faith imbued. The rest might as well have been fighting with Nerf weapons.

"The Templar were the first who found me after I learned about my powers," she replied with neither fear nor threat in her voice. Smart, keeping things neutral. "I stayed with them for a time and trained amongst them."

"Being indoctrinated into their small-minded dogma?"

"They tried. However, I have since come to appreciate that the world is not so black and white."

"So you allied yourself with the Freewill, the lone vampire to...?"

"And his friend," Theodora said. "Let us not forget her."

The barest of shadows passed over Alex's face. For all of his patience, I had the feeling he was beginning to lose his temper with her. "That shall be stricken from the record," he replied, gazing icily at her. "We have already discussed this."

"Are we to strike from history that she was present during the encounter in question - that she helped aid in the destruction of a respected commander and his team?"

"History, as I am sure you are aware, is written by the victors," he replied with a tone that would have surely terrified lesser vamps. "Your objection is noted." Before she could say more, he turned back toward Sheila. "The fact remains, child, that you allied yourself with the Freewill and his friends. Against the wishes of the First, he led you on the offensive against Commander Remington and the Magi Harry Decker."

"They were holding Bill's friends hostage."

"Humans," he scoffed, looking at me. "Betraying the wishes of the First for an Icon and now humans? What is next, Freewill? Do you care to declare yourself an agent of the Grendel?"

"Fuck no!" I shouted.

Alex smirked ever so slightly at that. Apparently, my insolence amused him to no end - how wonderful. "It was a rhetorical question."

"Oh, sorry."

He turned back to Sheila. "You claim this was merely a rescue mission. Yet somehow you, the Freewill, a lone witch, and a few humans decimated an elite strike team and a coven of experienced Magi."

Sheila glanced toward me, but I was already turning away to scan the crowd for Christy's accusers. The thing about the battle with Remington was that we'd just barely won, but it hadn't been alone. Other forces had been present, information that the Draculas were apparently not privy to. I preferred to keep it that way. The fewer who had to suffer for my actions, the better. Considering the way my luck had been going, I fully expected the witch who'd spilled the beans on Christy to do the same regarding that little tidbit.

Or not. Neither the witch, the grand mentor of awesome beardedness, nor any of the other mages from their group were anywhere to be seen. Oh well, maybe they'd said their piece and then hauled ass. That would've been a welcome bit of news. It was bad enough two of the women in my life were in danger. I preferred there not be a third, especially since I didn't want her around making creepy little doe eyes at me. Talk about skin-crawling distractions.

While this was going on, Sheila had replied with some bullshit about Remington not giving us a choice. That was true in of itself, although letting any of them escape hadn't really been an option either, as everything happening now would have been exposed that much sooner.

Alex smiled grimly at her response. "So you still claim you are an agent of peace, a protector of the weak?"

"I do."

He lifted his hand and gestured off to one side. A vampire ran up, holding something in his hands. It was a long box, like something one would keep a guitar in. Maybe he was going to entertain us with a kickass solo of "Stairway to Heaven."

As the guard held it up, Alex unsnapped the locks and opened it. Whatever was inside definitely wasn't a guitar.

Most musical instruments didn't glow with a white light.

Sheila's eyes widened and the white fires of faith erupted around her, causing me to jump back a step as Alex lifted the sword from its protective case.

He hissed as his skin sizzled from merely touching it, but he powered through it, sucking up the obvious pain. Smoke rose from his hand as he held aloft the weapon. "Behold the sword of Jeanne d'Arc, Icon of Orleans. Despite what the human histories might claim to the contrary, this weapon was used to decimate nearly every coven that existed in Northern France during her day."

"It's mine now."

"And you deny having used it against Remington's forces?"

Sheila was silent.

"No? How about more recently against the coven formerly of Brighton, New York?" With flames now openly escaping between his fingers, Alex turned the sword blade down and drove it into the floor before his chair - sinking it several inches deep before releasing the hilt. "I thought not."

He stepped around it and addressed the crowd. "I believe we have heard enough, but it is tradition that the First be just and merciful before casting judgment."

A snort of laughter escaped my closed lips. I couldn't help myself - probably the hunger shorting out my common sense. Tom found it amusing, but he seemed to be my lone supporter in that. I half expected to be pummeled into silence, but Alex ignored me, as if expecting no better.

"I hereby suspend the protocols of rank set forth by this body. Any who wish to speak out, either for or against the Icon, may do so now without fear of reprisal."

He barely waited a beat before opening his mouth again, smugly sure that whatever his declaration, nobody, especially the vampires in the room, were insane enough to say shit against him.

In that he was wrong, for just then, a small voice spoke out from the back of the auditorium.

"You are a fool, Alexander."

41

THE CHINESE CONNECTION

The voice had a disturbingly familiar youthful cadence to it that belied the underlying confidence it carried forth. I only needed a single sentence to place it, but it was enough to make me wish I'd been executed up front.

I couldn't have spun faster had I been tazed in the ass. Ed was nearly as quick, his first meeting with the voice's owner having left quite the impression.

Gan stood on her chair at the far end of the auditorium to compensate for her diminutive size. That must have been how I'd missed her in my scans of the audience. When one was concentrating on all the big bad things in the room, it could be a fatal mistake to overlook the small *worse* things lurking about.

She wasn't alone either. Scattered throughout the crowd, vampires wearing traditional Mongolian assassin attire stood as she did. I didn't know if she was expecting trouble, but she'd come prepared for it anyway - no matter how badly outnumbered her people might be.

I will give her credit, though. Everything else I'd been feeling - hunger, despair, worry for my friends - it all shriveled up and receded deep inside of me, or maybe that was just my nutsack. Oh, crap. No matter which way you spun it, I couldn't see any way that her presence here wouldn't make our situation even worse.

"Looks like your fiancée is here, Bill," Tom said, stepping up alongside me. Oh, how I could have killed him for that remark alone. "Hey, why isn't she down here with..."

"Shut up," I hissed, elbowing him in the ribs - probably harder than warranted.

He had a point, though. Gan had been instrumental in our surviving Remington's team. Hell, she'd even been the one who'd personally dispatched Harry Decker. She likewise had ordered Christy's former coven to be hunted down and disposed of - succeeding *nearly* to the last witch.

She'd obviously done a better job of covering her tracks than we had. The only ones who knew of her involvement were us, Sally, and the witch from earlier. Sally was brain-fucked right now, and the witch had conveniently taken an unexpected smoke break. So that left those of us standing around as prisoners, and I sure as shit wasn't ratting her out. Rationally, that made sense. After all, having a powerful ally on the outside could be helpful. In reality, I just didn't want her down here, pawing at me like some crazed miniature octopus.

All of this introspection took place within seconds. A good chunk of the crowd seemed to be doing likewise - craning their necks to see who had enough of a death-wish to challenge the First. The funny thing was, they were right to think that. Gan had confided in me her two ultimate ambitions: marrying me and bumping off the Draculas. Considering the first one, I found myself wondering if it was too late to throw myself on the mercy of the court.

"Gansetseg," Alex began, seemingly unperturbed by her insolence, "Prefect of the Manchurian Steppe and daughter of the Khan, our late lamented brother. You are acknowledged. I believe you were telling the assembled what a fool I was."

Yeah, this was definitely going to be interesting.

"Indeed," Gan replied. "You yourself lowered protocol. If you wish to reinstate it, I shall begin again in a more formal manner."

"Unnecessary," Alex countered. "I believe your prefecture recently reported a significant victory in the Altai Mountains over a combined army of the Grendel and the Children of Erlik. Is that not so?"

"So it was. The heads of the alma adorn pikes leading out a full kilometer from my ger-tereg."

"My compliments, Prefect. I believe the First would be happy to indulge you in whatever you feel you need to add to these proceedings."

I had no idea what any of that meant, other than reinforcing that Gan was batshit crazy. Regardless, she apparently had the résumé to back up her words.

"Thank you, Lord Alexander," she replied in a respectful tone that I was pretty sure wasn't. "Likewise, my compliments to the glorious First Coven. My father was humbled to be among your number. One day, I hope to honor his memory by ascending to your ranks."

A loud, derisive sound interrupted from just to the left of where the First sat.

"Did you have something to add, François?" I couldn't help but notice Alex conveniently *forgot* to add his title to the question.

"Sorry, my lord," François replied with barely concealed contempt. "I was just clearing my throat."

"Then kindly do so quietly. You do not have the floor."

The tone of Alex's voice implied he probably wouldn't ever have it either. "Continue, Gansetseg."

Gan nodded to him, a neutral smile upon her face. It turned to something a lot less neutral for a moment when she looked down and locked eyes with me. Oh shit. I quickly eyed the guards at our periphery - the ones who'd brought Sheila in. With any luck, I could leap onto their drawn weapons and turn to dust before anyone noticed.

A hand fell on my shoulder and I nearly jumped out of my skin.

"Relax," Sheila said softly, repressing her faith power so as to not fry me. "You look like you're about to have a heart attack."

I almost had to laugh. Of all of us, she was in the most danger, yet she was offering *me* some comfort. For just a moment, I looked into her magnificent eyes and it was like the world ceased to exist. Then Gan started talking.

"It saddens me to see how far we have strayed from the path laid down for us by the elder seers," she said, throwing me a wink. Gah! "Have not their prophecies guided us through the ages?"

"So they have, but their time wanes. The seers, honored though they may be, have brought us this far, but they can see no further. The mists of the future are obscured to them in these regards. The time for strategy and guile is upon us. Considering your ancestry, I would think you would draw the same conclusions."

Ooh, nice dig by Alexander.

"Nonsense," Gan replied dismissively. "My grandfather, the great Temüjin, carried his mystics with him through all his journeys. He continually mixed their insight with his own strategic genius. That is why his empire eventually became greater than that of any other conqueror before or since."

Whoa, even bigger smack in the face by Gan. Not

only was that a burn, but she poured salt in the wound too.

"Regardless," she continued, "the outcome foreseen by the seers may be uncertain, but the steps leading up to it are not. The Shining One shall stand as the cattle's last shepherd..."

"Cattle?" a voice behind me asked.

"I think she means people," I whispered back to Sheila.

"...in the final days of the war, my beloved..."

"Will you knock it off already?!" Did I say that out loud? Oh, how I do love losing my shit and then finding dozens of unfriendly eyeballs turning my way.

Tom and Ed tried, unsuccessfully, to repress snickers - pair of cocks. Christy and Sheila at least seemed to offer me some sympathy in their glances.

"Freewill," Alex said, his voice stern, "know that I will give you even less quarter for interruption than our guests. My offer for input does not extend to you or your cohorts."

"Um, sorry."

"It is good to see you too, beloved," Gan said, completely ignoring what I just screamed. Oh God, she was infuriating.

"Can you please clarify your previous statement for the benefit of the assembled?" Alex asked.

For a moment, Gan looked perplexed. Apparently, in her mind, the word "beloved" had been officially substituted for "Freewill" in the prophecies she was quoting. What a complete nutball. "My apologies. In the final days of the war, the Shining One shall meet the Freewill upon the battlefield. Their actions shall determine the course the world will take."

"I believe most of us are aware of that. Your point?"

"And yet most chose to foolishly believe the Icon dead

when even a simpleton could have predicted her survival. Even the First themselves seemed to put stock in this folly."

That sent up a murmur of discussion amongst the crowd.

"Know that my indulgence is limited," Alex replied coldly. "I would urge caution, *child*."

Gan bristled visibly at the remark, but managed to keep her composure. "It was not my intention to offend, great Alexander. Yet the fact remains it came to pass. For centuries, we have waited. Finally, when Dr. Death was revealed to us, that long wait was justified. Yet now, we casually brush aside that wisdom because of something so base as fear?"

"What would you have us do?"

"My own mystics have been studying the portents. The time of this final confrontation is rapidly approaching, but it is not upon us yet. The Freewill and the Shining One should be allowed to forge their own paths, knowing that whatever roads they take will eventually lead them back to one another."

This was interesting, although I had a feeling it was a pointless argument. It was like putting someone on trial for murder, having them dead to rights, but then acquitting them based on the word of some psychic. Of course, that was in the normal world. Here, where creatures could burst into flame, fly, or poof out of existence with just a thought, things were a bit different.

Even so, the person in charge - the judge, jury, and probably executioner - was firmly in the camp of believing such things were bullshit. I tended to agree with Alex, knowing that it had been his personal interference, not fate, that had sparked the current war. If anything, Alex was using the prophecies not as a guiding hand, but as a way to further his own agenda.

A small breeze fluttered against my skin. It would have otherwise been unnoticeable except for the still air of the room. As Gan and Alex continued to argue metaphysics versus real world, I glanced over and noticed the blast door opening. Maybe some new dignitaries had arrived, or better yet, maybe it was time to adjourn for the day. Hopefully, it was a dinner break - one in which they actually fed their fucking prisoners some goddamned dinner.

"You would have us release the great enemy of our people? How many more must fall by her hand to satisfy your mystics?"

"As many as are fated," Gan replied coldly. Damn, she was the queen of the evil munchkins.

"She may have a point..."

"Not now, Theodora," Alex said dismissively. "Perhaps, instead, a compromise. The Freewill and Icon are both here in front of us. Why not make them fight to the death right this moment?"

"The time is not right, and I think we are all aware of it," Gan replied.

Judging by the continued discussion in the crowd, she wasn't being dismissed out of hand. Vampires couldn't harness the power of faith like humans, but many still needed something to believe in. Take away that belief and the results could be catastrophic. What Alex proposed was the vampire equivalent of the pope gathering the masses in the Vatican to announce he was jump-starting Armageddon to prove there was no God. Shit would undoubtedly get real at that juncture.

"What would the outcome serve, other than for our amusement?" she asked. "Would the Shining One's victory save humanity? Would Dr. Death's assure darkness? No. I say fate has decreed that the Icon and my beloved shall meet when..."

"*NO!!*"

All eyes immediately turned to the source of the compulsion. There wasn't a lot of firepower behind it, but it didn't need much to get the point across. Even a relatively weak vampire could use one as the equivalent of a psychic bullhorn.

I stood on tiptoes to see Farley standing in the now open portal that led out of here. What the fuck?

"What are you..." Alex started, as if speaking to a stupid child.

"No more!" Farley shouted out as the rest of his group took up positions on either side of the opening. "You have all followed the false Freewill for too long. I say he is nothing, an abomination to all we should hold dear. Drop to your knees and give praise to Vehron, the true Freewill of legend!"

O-kay. I hadn't pegged Farley as either this crazy or stupid. Besides, hadn't he and the others been mind-scrubbed?

"*ENOUGH!!*" Alex commanded. "*YOU WILL CEASE YOUR INSOLENCE THIS INSTANT!! APPROACH SO I MAY DECIDE YOUR PUNISHMENT!!*"

The compulsion rang out like thunder in the enclosed space. The entire room seemed to rumble with the power of it. Great, that's all we needed now - to be buried alive under tons of rubble because Alex lost his temper.

Still, as badly screwed as Sheila and I might be, Farley was completely fucked because...

Except he wasn't.

He stood his ground, looking as surprised as everyone else for a moment, but then he started to laugh. "Behold the impotence of your so-called leaders and know that the time of the First has ended."

As confusion took hold of the crowd, most of them

stunned that Alex's compulsion had, impossibly enough, failed, shapes beyond Farley converged upon his location.

The blast doors that shielded this place were massive - built to withstand a nuclear attack. But open to the outside, they would offer us no protection against the horror about to descend upon us.

Farley glanced over his shoulder and turned back smiling - his fangs gleaming white, a stark contrast to the dark sea of living rock behind him.

"All hail Vehron! All hail Ib!"

42

DEMILITARIZED ZONE

"What the hell are those?" Sheila asked as the first of the invaders reached the door.

By then, it was too late to stop their advance. A couple of the creatures threw themselves into the massive hinges, acting as living doorstops. Any chance we had of sealing ourselves in against the onslaught was immediately lost.

"It's the Jahabich," I managed to say through my shock.

"What are..."

Whatever answer I may have had was immediately drowned out in the chaos. Dozens, maybe hundreds, of the rock monsters swarmed inside - cutting down the first few measures of resistance they met.

They separated into three columns as they advanced. Two branched out into the crowd on either side, while a third group charged straight forward.

The forces guarding us were slow to respond. Over a dozen were turned to dust in those first few seconds alone, their backs still to the threat.

It was only then I realized the foolishness on display.

358

They'd been compelled to keep their eyes on us, believing us to be the primary threat. Even now, as the heavy club-arms of the Jahabich crushed the skulls of their comrades, they were finding it hard to break free of their orders and defend the room. Such was the arrogance of the First.

They'd undoubtedly thought no one would dare to attack them in one of their many strongholds. They'd assumed themselves safe from the Feet. They'd been right in that regard, but in doing so had completely underestimated another enemy - one apparently far more powerful than any of us would have guessed.

"Let's go!" I cried. If my friends and I continued standing where we were, they'd mow us down. We needed to get to the far side of the room and figure out how to get the fuck out of this death trap.

I pushed Tom toward Christy. I'm sure he figured it was so he could watch out for her, although it was more the other way around. Ed, no dummy, followed them.

I grabbed Sheila's arm to pull her along, risking a third degree burn if she misunderstood my actions. She took a step, then stumbled. Fuck! I'd forgotten her legs were shackled too. She'd no more be able to run than perform a *Karate Kid* crane kick.

"Sorry about this...please don't kill me." I bent down, put my arm around her midsection, and hauled her onto my shoulder - momentarily enjoying the sensation of grabbing her around the ass. Hey, when faced with certain death, one needs to take stock of the finer things in life.

Oof! She was heavier than she looked. Wait...no, that wasn't right. I was actually weaker than I should have been. I hadn't realized it standing there while the legion of assholes judged me, but I was apparently running on a fraction of my normal strength thanks to my prolonged unplanned fast. Talk about irony. In the midst of a full-on ambush, I was actually feeling like my old, non-vampire self.

Oh well, this was no time to cry over spilled milk

"Whatever you do, do not flare up!" I shouted, then took off after my friends, trying to weave my way past the guards, who were finally starting to realize there was a greater enemy in the room.

"*STAND YOUR GROUND AND FIGHT*!!"

The command immediately knocked me right back to nearly where I'd started, almost causing me to drop Sheila in the process. Fucking compulsions!

At least Alex was now in the game. Strangely, I found that somewhat comforting. The asshole had been trying to fuck me over since day one, but let's be realistic - having one of history's greatest generals on your side against an invading army was not a prospect one refused.

"You really want to keep moving," Sheila cried out from her vantage point, facing our rear.

Trust is important in relationships on a lot of different levels, not the least of which is when a loved one says, "Duck!" you do it without asking.

Suffice it to say, she didn't need to tell me twice.

Tom, Ed, and Christy were waiting at the far end of the auditorium floor, directly below where the Draculas had been sitting. Knowing on which end their bread was buttered, both my roommates were frantically working to free Christy from her bonds - for all the good that did. Even rusty old metal was a deterrent for normal folk...but maybe not me.

I put Sheila down, copping another quick feel in the process - figuring I might never get another chance.

Thankfully, she didn't say anything or vaporize me, for that matter.

Her cuffs looked fairly new despite their odd coloring. At my current weakened level, I had no shot with them. Christy's, though, were nice and weathered - apparently mage shackles were a vintage thing. I didn't have a lot left in me, but hopefully I didn't need much.

I pushed my roommates aside and grabbed hold of one of the manacles - putting everything I had left into it. Ugh! I was pretty sure I was about to pop something in my back, but finally the lock gave.

Bent over and breathing hard, I said, "I hope one is enough because I don't think I can get the other."

"Watch me," she said with a smile. Darkness enveloped her free hand and she reached down to touch the intact cuff with it. A moment later, it fell to dust.

"Bill..."

The warning was unnecessary, though, as right then a guard yelled, "The prisoners are escaping!" *Gah!* What fucking idiots. Did they not see the bloodbath happening on the other end of the room? What? Did they think we were going to help those fucking rock monstrosities?

Hmm, actually, that probably *was* what they thought. Silly me.

"Her next." I pointed toward Sheila. I wasn't too proud to admit that our best bet for survival lay in the hands of our fairer-sexed friends. Unfortunately, I didn't have the luxury of hiding behind them as guards were even now heading our way. "Tom, stay with Christy. Ed, any chance of you bleeding on them?"

"If they hit me enough times."

"Good, go with that." I might not be an ancient conqueror, but I could improvise with the best of them - sorta.

Fortunately, at least a few of the guards seemed to have

brains in their heads. They stopped short - brandishing their weapons, but more or less just trying to make sure we didn't escape.

Sadly, one yahoo was more overzealous than the rest. He charged in, silver stake raised. He was on me in a second, overpowering me with no problem whatsoever. I found myself on my back, both arms struggling to keep him from bringing the weapon down into my chest.

"Traitor," he hissed.

"The fuck? There hasn't been any verdict yet."

"You pled guilty."

Okay, he had me there. Sadly, I didn't appear to have time to discuss how I was coerced into that situation. The tip of the stake inched ever closer to my chest.

And then he was gone - grabbed by the scruff of his neck and tossed backward like so much refuse. In his place stared down one of the few faces in the room I could honestly say I was glad to see.

"Dr. Death," James greeted cordially before addressing the other guards. "The sanctuary of your leaders has been breached. Secure it at all costs."

The troops didn't waste any time questioning his orders. Rather than risk his wrath, they took off to engage the Jahabich. James watched them go, then offered me a hand.

"Um, thanks." I took it and let him drag me to my feet since I wasn't entirely sure I could make it up on my own.

As he pulled me up, his jacket swung open and I noticed the rather nasty looking knife - more a machete than anything - hanging from a sheath on his belt. He'd apparently upgraded since the fight in Boston. "I think you're going to need that."

"Sadly, such a weapon is not intended for the throats of our enemies."

"Why not?"

"It is a ceremonial athame, meant for *other* purposes." As if in answer to what was going to be my next question, his eyes traveled down to his missing arm.

Oh crap. Was he serious? My eyes opened wide at the implication. "What happened to you? I mean, are you all right?"

"I would think to ask that of you. Nevertheless, I am afraid our current circumstance does not allow for such pleasantries." Without further ado, his fangs descended and he tore into the wrist of his intact arm with them, ripping open a vein. He then held the gushing appendage toward me. "Please feel free to indulge yourself."

"Whoa, hold on..."

"Enough." His tone was calm, but firm. "There are two things obvious to me in this chaos. The first is you are nearly out of your mind from hunger. The second is that we shall require all the help we can get."

I was tempted to argue, but flashes of light in my periphery - more vampires biting the big one - told me I needed to save the arguments for another time. Hoping Sheila wasn't watching, I grabbed hold of his wrist and brought it to my mouth. Talk about heavenly. Empty calories or not, vampire blood still tasted damn good to me. I dreaded the crash that would happen once it wore off, but for now, it did the trick.

The second the blood hit my stomach, my head cleared. Better yet, I could feel my body charging up to my normal levels and far beyond. Within seconds, I felt like a million bucks as my body's healing amped up and fixed any residual injuries I might have had.

"Are you quite finished? We appear to be on a timetable here if we wish to survive."

Oh crap. The problem with blood is that it's sometimes easy to lose oneself in it. "Sorry, I'm good, thanks."

"Excellent." He stepped back, the wound on his wrist already starting to stitch itself closed. "Be mindful of yourself and your friends. This is dangerous ground."

Before I could even voice my thanks, he was gone, leaping into the fray and sending fragments of rock flying wherever his fists landed. His warning was not lost upon me, though. There were so many potential knives that could be stuck in our backs from so many different sides that we would need eyes in the backs of our heads to survive even sixty seconds in this mess.

"Watch those hands, mister!"

I turned back to find Sheila, finally unshackled, scrambling up the stadium seating to the next level. Tom was helping give her a boost. I smiled, noting she hadn't given me the same warning.

I didn't need to question her objective. It was painfully obvious. Her sword still stood where Alex had sunk it into the floor.

Christy covered them, her body glowing an angry red and her eyes scanning for any enemies getting too close. Ed stood behind her, pointing out any spots where it looked like the Jahabich were getting ready to punch through.

"You got this?" I asked.

She nodded grimly. Judging by her mood, she was more than ready to dispense with some magical justice upon whoever was stupid enough to challenge her. Okay then, as long as it wasn't me.

I looked up to see that Sheila had made it to the next level. Fortunately, the Draculas appeared to have vacated the premises, presumably to join in the fight, so ten thousand years' worth of angry vamp didn't immediately dogpile her.

What happened next, though, was nothing short of amazing. Sheila grabbed the hilt of her sword and heaved. At first, it stuck fast. For all I knew, the underlayment was solid concrete like everything else. Then, slowly, the glow of her power spread across her body and down to the weapon itself. She gave one last heave and it pulled free, her body and the blade both igniting in an explosion of white light as she held it aloft.

Tom said it best. "By the power of Grayskull, mother-fuckers!"

Indeed. All that was missing was her transformation into that hot mini dress She-Ra used to wear. Oh well, it's not like my mind couldn't fill in *that* blank.

So spectacular was it that it seemed the fighting paused for the barest of moments for all to watch.

I opened my mouth to cheer her on, but as my eyes opened wide, the words wouldn't come.

"I'm afraid I can't let you keep that," Alex said, stepping from the chaos of the crowd and facing her. He'd somehow procured a sword of his own at some point. The distinctive grey mottling of the blade glinted in the harsh fluorescent lighting.

Oh crap.

The whole point of becoming an Icon was an undying faith in oneself, or so the legends say. The truth was, if Sheila was afraid of Alex, she didn't show it, leveling her sword in his direction. Unfortunately, as much as I wanted to believe in her too, I had tasted Alex's power. It was immense, unlike almost anything else I could imagine - a real life Marvel superhero, or villain, as was the case. Add to that his experience and the disdain he'd expressed earlier regarding the threat Sheila represented, and I knew what I had to do.

Tensing my legs, I leapt - clearing the next level easily. I took a moment, but no more than that, to savor how awesome being an elder vampire must be. Sheila, thankfully, glanced over her shoulder rather than swinging wildly and cleaving me in two. She nodded, then turned back to face Alex, assuming a battle stance.

Unfortunately, she'd misjudged my motivation. I hadn't joined her to fight Alex. James was powerful, but that would have been little more than suicide on my part. Instead, I racked my mind, trying to remember what Sally and Grulg had said.

Alex stood there confidently. He waved Sheila forward with his free hand - his own sword at the ready.

White fire gleaming from her eyes, she opened her mouth to elicit a battle cry.

"I offer a truce as per the Humbaba Accord!"

Both combatants stopped in their tracks to turn toward my direction.

"Excuse me?" Alex asked.

"As per the Humbaba Accord," I repeated, having no real clue whether what I was saying made any sort of fucking sense. I mean, it's not like I'd read the damn thing. "Warring parties can enact a temporary truce, can they not?"

"Are you suggesting..."

"Yes. Right now, we have a bigger problem than all of this bullshit."

Alex narrowed his eyes, but I held my ground, not wanting to puss out while the girl of my dreams was watching. The things I sometimes endured a beating for.

"I've fought these things before. They're tough, act with one mind, and will turn any of us they capture into their slaves. They need to be stopped. When this is over, we'll surrender happily."

"We will?" Sheila asked.

"Well, okay, we can discuss that part. For now, though, what do you say, Alexander of the First?"

He took a long moment to consider it, glancing off into the battle beyond. The Jahabich continued to pour into the room, replenishing any of their numbers we managed to take down. Considering the force on display, I had to assume that once we'd escaped their clutches down below, they'd just said fuck it and dumped all remaining prisoners into the goo.

"Well played, Freewill. Your truce is granted," he said at last. "I swear on my honor."

Sheila once more glanced back at me, as if to ask if his honor was worth the toilet paper it was written on. I held my tongue for a second to avoid jeopardizing our situation and simply replied, "Thank you."

"Keep in mind," he warned, "should you try to escape, or any of our people fall by her blade, then it shall immediately be dissolved."

"Those are your terms?"

"They are."

Good enough for me, and probably the best I was going to get. "So be it."

With that, the three of us turned our attention to the fight at hand: the Freewill, the Icon, and the greatest military mind the world had ever seen.

Go figure. There's never someone around with a fucking camera when you need it.

43

THE WAR OF THE THREE FACTIONS

Things didn't look particularly promising. The room had been full of beings of considerable power, beings that should have been able to decimate the ranks of the Jahabich like bugs. The problem? They didn't appear to want to stick around for the fun.

I jumped into the mix, using James's stolen power to good effect. I'd just grabbed a pair of Jahabich by the arms and swung them hard enough into each other to embed their broken forms together when I spotted Druaga. The ugly fucker was standing off in a corner, looking bored. One of the rock monsters approached and he casually swatted it, sending its head and the orange goo inside flying. Then, just like that, he was gone - the air around him imploding in a pop of noise.

All around the room, others were doing the same. Those four-winged imps vanished in little balls of fire. A pair of ugly blobs of multi-eyed pus seemed to melt into the floor. Some*thing* that looked like the Grim Reaper's hairier cousin turned translucent and walked to the door, passing through everything in its path.

Sadly, that left the rest of us in a bad way. Most of

those elves I'd seen earlier got pounded into elven paste before anyone could reach them. A human arm, still holding an M16, went flying past me at one point. Vampires were turning to dust left and right. In short, it wasn't looking all too promising.

I ducked a swing from one of the attackers and dove for the floor as a red-hot beam of force cauterized it in place. Rolling to my feet as gracefully as I could, I made my way over to where Christy stood. "How are you doing?"

"I'll live." Sweat stood out on her face from the strain, but she appeared to be holding her own. "Find the others so we can get out of here."

"Um, there's a little problem with that."

"Don't worry. I've been saving enough in reserve to get us all to safety."

"Yeah, I kind of sort of promised Alex we wouldn't do that."

She stopped firing for a moment to turn toward me, the red glow around her never fading. To tell the truth, it sort of unnerved me a bit. "You *what?*"

"He was going to kill Sheila. I offered him a truce, but the terms were we couldn't run."

"Could you have made a *worse* deal?"

"Well, I also promised that she wouldn't kill any vamps during the fight." I grabbed a Jahabich trying to flank her, spun, and threw it into the wall.

"Anything else I should know?" she growled.

"You look great. Pregnancy really works for you."

Before she could blast me, I took a look around. "There!" I pointed out Tom and Ed.

The Jahabich were closing in on them. I had no idea if it was because they looked soft and squishy or if they still wanted Ed for their personal trophy case, but it didn't matter. "Get them out of here," I said, clearing a path toward my friends. I tossed the creatures left and right, not really caring who they flew into but hoping they slammed into someone I didn't like.

"But you said..."

"Don't leave the complex. Just get them to another room, preferably someplace with a really sturdy door. Shouldn't be hard to find in this madhouse."

A beam of heat flashed disturbingly close to my head. Were it not for James's power currently in my blood, I had a feeling I'd be missing an ear or worse. "What about you?" she asked.

"Don't worry about me. I've pissed off far too many people in this room for them to let these monsters have the fun of killing me." I only wished that was a joke. Oh well, better reaction than indifference, I say.

"I don't know much about..."

"Concentrate on your cell," I suggested. "It's better than nothing."

"There're mystical sigils in it. No sending in or out."

"What about right outside the door?"

She appeared to consider that, then nodded.

I glanced off to my left toward a bright flash of white light. Sheila was engaging the enemy. I had no doubt she'd fulfill her end of the bargain, but it wasn't clear yet if Alex was man enough of honor to live up to his. If not, I'd almost certainly live to regret it.

We reached my roommates just in time. One of the Jahabich had closed in and was about to cave in Tom's skull - something that might've hindered even his ability to carry on a conversation.

Before it could connect, I grabbed it from behind - my claws digging into its rocky skin like it was made of putty. I dragged it back, lifted it - enjoying how much lighter these things felt when my muscles were powered up - and brought it down upon my knee, shattering its spine, or whatever bodily structure kept it upright. "Go!"

Tom and Ed looked confused, but Christy didn't hesitate. She stepped up, placed a hand on each of their shoulders, and mouthed "Good luck" just as she winked out of existence in a flash of light.

Their quarry gone, the Jahabich who'd been closing in on Ed all turned their focus on me.

"Alright, assholes, who wants some?"

Turns out far too many of them did.

James's speed and strength kept me on my feet and my defenses mostly intact. Unfortunately, the problem with a half dozen clubs all swinging at you at once is that some of them are going to get through. Considering the composition of our foe's bodies, that meant it was going to hurt a lot - which it did.

That being said, a hundred Saturday afternoon kung-fu movies had taught me that in a fight like this, it's key to never let your opponent knock you off your feet. You stay upright and maybe you can find a way out or a wall to put your back to. You end up on your ass and you're fucked, just not in the good way.

Needless to say, one club to the side of my leg later and I was fucked. I looked up to see a circle of empty orange eyes glaring down. I had just enough time to think how pissed everyone would be at me for getting killed at hands other than their own when a screech of rage rent the air, as if someone had just run over an angry alley cat with a lawnmower.

I knew that sound. Hell, I heard it in my nightmares more often than not. A small, cowardly part of me wanted to shout, "Well, c'mon, kill me already!" but I was too late.

A dainty hand reached over the top of one of the monsters, grabbed hold of an eye socket and yanked back, ripping its head in half at the jawline. Faster than the beasts could register one of their own biting the big one, a small foot caught another in the side of the head with a vicious spin kick that sent it and its two closest buddies flying.

Even with James's power backing me up, I wasn't quite sure I could have moved as fast. Within moments, the glowing orange malevolence was gone, replaced by a set of bright green eyes that sparkled with their own nefarious intent.

"Thanks, Gan."

She smiled broadly, her slightly mussed hair the only sign she'd just kicked the ass of a bunch of rock monsters. Otherwise, she could have just walked home from school, the playground, or the various torture dungeons I had little doubt she kept. Her dress was regal, sparkling jade in color with gold highlights throughout it. The only oddity...well, visible oddity...were the smiling pair of SpongeBob faces that dangled from her ears. Oh god, what a weirdo.

She reached a hand down to help me up. "Is this not romantic, beloved - us fighting to the death against insurmountable odds?"

"Oh yeah, sure as shit beats dinner and a movie."

"Should we survive, I accept your invitation."

"Wait, that wasn't an...whoa!"

Before I could finish, Gan had grabbed me by the sleeve and dragged me once more into the fray. Though lacking my strength, she more than made up for it with speed and the precision of her blows. Judging by the look on her face, she considered this to be a grand ole time hanging with her *beloved*. Me, I wouldn't have minded being smashed in the head real good at that moment.

Alas, that didn't seem to be in the cards, so I followed along, punching the shit out of any Jahabich Gan happened to miss. Sloppy seconds, go figure.

The exertion was starting to cost me, though. Running on empty as I was, I could sense the boost from James's blood wouldn't last as long as it might otherwise. Already my steps slowed and my hands started to hurt whenever I'd smash one of those fucking monster's teeth out.

We reached a line of vampire guards and did what we could to bolster them, but it was like trying to fight off a living avalanche. The Jahabich appeared single-minded in their assault, not looking particularly worried when any of their number fell to our counterattacks.

I was just starting to breathe hard when a vamp, one of Sheila's former guards, bought it next to me. I caught a mouthful of dust when he exploded and found myself bent over, trying to cough him out of me. Just for the record, powdered vamp doesn't taste nearly as good as fresh.

Looking down, I saw he'd dropped his weapon - one of those black-bladed thingees. Fuck it, maybe I could put this one to good use. My D&D characters were normally swordsmen or magic users. I was never much of a pole-arm fighter, but that didn't mean I couldn't start to appreciate them.

Up close, I could see the blade wasn't naturally that color. Flecks of the normal sheen of steel shone through here and there. It was some kind of coating. I examined it closer, catching a familiar coppery scent as I did so. What the? The weapon seemed to be coated in blood of some kind.

Sadly, that was all the examination I could make. One of our enemies rushed me and I brought the weapon to bear, looking to spear the fucker like a mackerel. Spinning it toward him, and proud I didn't decapitate myself in the process, I thrust forward as it opened its ugly mouth in a wide grin.

"No, Dr. Death, I would not..."

Much to both my surprise and dismay, the blade shattered like glass against the Jahabich's obsidian smile. Since hammering a hunk of living rock with a stick seemed to be equally pointless, I quickly dropped the shaft so as to defend myself, but I was a little too late. I brought my right arm up in time to do nothing more than give it something to chomp down on.

Holy fuck! Being bitten by another vampire was bad enough, but nothing like the jagged daggers now impaling my arm from both ends. The pain felt unbearable and I was fairly sure that if I didn't shake it off soon, I'd get to experience the joyful sensation of waiting for one of my limbs to grow back. Our attackers wouldn't likely be quite so accommodating as to let me do that.

Trying my best to ignore the pain, I lashed out with my free arm - smashing my fist into the creature's face. Chips of granite went flying, but not nearly as much as should have. In the meantime, blood continued to pour out of my punctured arm in rivers as I rapidly ran out of steam.

Worse, that fuzziness in my head started to come back. Crap! The last thing in the world I needed right then was to pass out. If I did, the next time I woke up - if at all - I'd look like something dug out of a coal mine.

Thank goodness for Gan - and believe me, I hoped that was the last time I had to consider that concept - but she stepped to my side and launched a kick straight up. It hit the creature's upper jaw, forcing its head back and its mouth open. She yanked me backward before I could react, more or less tearing my arm off of its teeth.

And, oh yes, it hurt even worse than the thing's initial bite.

Reduced as I was to a sniveling ball of pain, I was only vaguely aware of Gan dispatching the monster and then dragging me along as she cleared a path to a corner of the room. As for me, my arm was healing at a much slower rate than I'd have preferred, telling me that James's power was all but gone and that soon I'd be coming down hard.

Almost as if in answer to that, my stomach grumbled, demanding to be refueled. I had to shake my head to keep focus, watching the blood continue to trail out behind us.

We reached a group that had formed a defensive perimeter near one wall. Vampires, along with a group of armed humans and some slimy reptilian-looking things that appeared to maybe be related to Druaga - on the lower end of whatever gene pool he spawned from - were working together to try to fend off their attackers. Gan bashed a few rock heads together, helping to lighten their load, and they parted to allow us in.

My head was swimming by the time she leaned me against a wall next to some of the other wounded. I didn't see any other vamps - not too surprising - but there were other species present, including a grey-haired human in uniform who sat holding his injured leg.

The man turned to me, a look of fear upon his face. "Damn these things. This place was supposed to be secure. Heads are gonna roll when I..."

If he said anything else of importance, it was lost to me. As I leaned over to listen to him complain, I found myself continuing forward with the action - sniffing the air and finding an intriguing scent upon it.

I believe the old soldier asked a question, something urgent in nature, but then his tone became high pitched until it eventually dissolved into a pained gurgle as I sank my teeth into his throat.

44

GENERAL TSO TASTES LIKE
CHICKEN

For a time, the world seemed to recede. Only delicious, juicy redness remained. It was kinda nice.

All good things must come to an end, though, and, eventually, my surroundings started to register upon my senses again. I didn't feel particularly great. My arm still hurt like nobody's business, but I felt *better*.

As I shook my head, like waking up after a long nap, I became aware of shouting around me - threats perhaps, but they were silenced following what sounded like twigs being snapped. I opened my eyes, blinked, and found a familiar face staring down at me. "Theodora?"

"Freewill," she replied, sounding annoyed. She was a bit disheveled. Her dress was torn and covered in slime that I suspected was originally orange in color.

Oh crap.

"The Jahabich!"

"Yes," she spat. "We are still dealing with them. Now, if you are quite finished making a scene, we should get back to driving the invaders off."

"Scene?"

"Yes. I dare say, feeding upon one of this country's Joint Chiefs of Staff has rendered it necessary to kill his bodyguards before they could shoot you - further depleting our already strained resources, I might add."

"Wait, I killed someone?"

"I do not think he is quite dead yet, but..."

I followed her gaze to the torn uniform, the General's stars scattered about it, and the unblinking eyes staring up from the pale skin of his face. "Oh my God!"

"Fret not, child, the humans were not overly effective to begin with. Their weapons were mostly useless against our foe."

She was completely missing the point - what a surprise. While I'd bitten people before, it had never been out of mindless hunger. Well, okay, I was pretty sure I'd killed a bunch of folks when I'd been vamped out as Dr. Death, but I was sort of out of my mind during those times - not that it made it right. Now, however, I'd crossed a line. I'd gotten hungry and hadn't even considered the consequences. Hell, what if that had been Tom?

Of course, if it had been Tom, that would have been horrible. He was my best friend and I would have never forgiven myself. On the flip side, if that were the case, I also wouldn't shortly be appearing on every Secret Service Agent's most wanted list. Just what I needed, a federal manhunt to add to all the other shit in my life.

I shook my head. No, that was being a selfish dick. What if this guy had a family, kids? I needed to get my head out of my ass and stop thinking about only myself.

"Are you quite done yet? Because if not, then I shall happily drag you along in a manner most uncomfortable."

Okay, maybe I could save the tortured soliloquys for later. Theodora wasn't a chick to mess with, and she didn't seem like a particularly happy camper at that moment.

"Relax, we're both on the same side," I said, pulling

my eyes away from my victim and forcing myself to stand. I wasn't powered up anymore, but I was happy to find myself at my normal levels with no debilitating hunger pangs. Considering how the day was going, I'd happily take breaking even.

"Are we? I am no longer certain of anything," she snapped, her eyes flashing black. "Know, though, if you are still true to your mission, you had best have a good reason for causing me such public humiliation."

"Me?"

"Yes. I assume all of this has been part of your scheme to bring down Al..." she hesitated for a moment, probably to avoid using Alex's name in a room full of beings with preternatural hearing. "Our mutual foe. Are you telling me it has not?"

Oh shit. "Um, nope. Everything is going smoothly. Just like clockwork. Could set your watch to it."

"Good, then I hope you have a suitable conclusion in mind to satisfy that requirement before this farce goes on for much longer. Perhaps the Icon..."

"Wouldn't want to ruin the surprise," I lied, looking about and immediately wishing I hadn't.

The remaining combatants on our side had formed themselves into tightly knit units to fight off the Jahabich. As for our enemies, there was one bright spot: so many had been killed that their bodies were forming unnatural barriers for the rest. This caused their attacks to lose focus, allowing the various beings that still stood against them to hold their own. Even so, it was obviously a bloodbath. Piles of ash littered the floor. Blood of multiple different hues coated every other surface. Bodies lay...actually, there weren't many bodies at all. That wasn't good. It meant the Jahabich were harvesting.

Oh well, there wasn't much that could be done about

that. We needed to worry about surviving and finding a way to drive them back.

Speaking of surviving. "Yeah!" I shouted triumphantly, spotting Sally amongst one of the groups of combatants. She was pretty battered and, once more, her clothing was ripped in ways that showed far more skin than she probably wanted to.

Sadly, she wasn't in the best of company. I saw her fighting with Alexander and Yehoshua nearby. Their strength was keeping the enemy at bay, but I couldn't exactly say I entrusted her life to them. At least she didn't look to be in immediate danger. Even with her memories wiped, I still had faith in her as a survivor.

That was one. Now where was...there! Sheila likewise stood her ground across the way from us. The Jahabich didn't seem as bothered by her faith aura as some other beings were, but whatever properties her powers had, one of them seemed to be bolstering her sword enough to slice and dice those creatures a good one. Sadly, she fought alone...no vampires wishing to dirty themselves by allying with her. Assholes.

That was about to change, though. Weapons lay strewn about from the fallen. I was tempted to grab another blade, but then remembered how useless they were against these monsters. It was weird how brittle it had been. Oh well, there were plenty of silver stakes lying around, as well as a severed Jahabich arm nearby. Not a bad combo, all in all.

"This way." I started forward, using the piles of dead or cauterized Jahabich as cover. No point in dying before I could be my lady's knight in not-so-shining armor. Sadly, stealth worked a lot better when you didn't have an ancient Elvira-wannabe jiggling alongside you. Of course, if I were her age and respective rank, I might be a bit less subtle, too.

As I played ninja, Theodora strode through the battle-field like it was a mall trip. A few of the monsters saw her and apparently thought she'd make for an easy mark. A couple of seconds later, I was dusting rock chips off of myself.

"You know, this would be a lot easier if you wouldn't mind sharing..."

She turned and fixed me with a glare. "If you even suggest putting your fangs upon my person, I shall rip them from your mouth in..."

"A manner most unpleasant?"

"Exactly."

"Wouldn't dream of it."

We reached Sheila's location not a moment too soon, as just then, the Jahabich surged forward again in force.

She swung her sword, still crackling with white fire, and two of the monsters were cleaved clean in half. The orange spooge that seemed to make up their lifeblood sprayed out in an arc. I tackled a third that was about to flank her. It was like ramming my shoulder into a concrete piling, but I managed to knock it down long enough to ram a silver stake into its eye-socket. Using both hands, I shoved the weapon in as deep as I could, the metal grating against stone, making a sound like nails on a chalkboard. Thankfully, it was enough. After a few moments, the crea-ture stopped squirming.

I looked up to find Theodora had likewise joined the battle, quite literally cracking skulls.

A hand appeared in my periphery. It was Sheila, the glow around her dying down to levels where I wouldn't immediately regret it. Oh, who was I kidding? I would have taken her hand even if it was covered in wasps.

"Thanks," she said, helping me up.

"Looked like you could use a hand."

"I'm doing okay, but yeah. Glad to have it."

"If either of you think I am doing this alone so as to allow you some quality time, you are sadly mistaken," Theodora growled over her shoulder. "Fight with me so we might dispatch these creatures or..." She let the threat hang in the air.

"Yep," I replied, rolling my eyes at her backside. "Wouldn't want to hold up our sentencing any longer than we have to."

A lopsided grin appeared on Sheila's face as once more she hefted her sword. "I'd certainly hate to inconvenience anyone." She stepped forward and struck a glancing blow against one of the monsters, her sword sending up sparks as it rebounded off of the creature's arm.

Theodora stopped her onslaught just long enough to turn and glare. "Make no mistake, Icon, I am not your friend. However, the Freewill has assured me that you will be instrumental in helping our common cause. For that reason alone, I tolerate your continued survival."

"Common cause?"

"It's...complicated," I said, still having no fucking clue as to what I was doing past surviving this bloodbath.

Thankfully, in a cosmic sort of way, the fresh tide of Jahabich chose that moment to hit us hard. Sheila kept her aura reined in, mindful of those of us nearby who might otherwise be a bit scorched by its power, but it still shone like a beacon through her sword - a weapon that had felt the touch, and seemingly channeled the power of, two Icons.

She sliced and diced, cutting through their rocky hide, maybe not quite like butter, but definitely like crusty bread. A few managed to breach her defenses, hitting glancing blows that drew blood, but each time she managed to parry and drive them back. It was quite awesome to behold.

Thea wasn't chopped liver either. Hers was a brutal

style, matching a vamp of extreme age who'd learned to use physical strength to their advantage. She sliced open gashes and tore out chunks from her foes as if trying to cause them as much pain as possible. Unfortunately, I wasn't sure if the Jahabich were incapable of feeling pain or just didn't give a fuck. Either way, they tended to die quietly only for the next one in line to step up and take its place.

That left me as the odd man out, trying to fight off a pair of them and just barely keeping myself from getting my head caved in. Fucking bitch. All Theodora had to do was let me take one fucking sip from her. Hell, I would've even pretended not to like it much, but no. Some chicks were just squirrelly about hickeys, I guess.

Fortunately, I'd been in enough scrapes to know a thing or two about ducking - my fighting style characteristic of the phrase "not in the face!" Luckily for me, the Jahabich weren't the most graceful of fighters in their rock-man forms. Whatever knowledge or skills they possessed in their former lives appeared to be suppressed in favor of brute force. That was a plus in my book. A half ton of granite-covered ninja would have been a major bitch to deal with singularly - much less an army of them.

Positioning myself carefully, I waited for the perfect moment. The first of the creatures swung wildly for my head as the second stepped in. I threw myself to the ground, letting the blow pass harmlessly over me and straight into the waiting jaw of its friend. The stricken one went down, and I used the distraction to grab hold of the foot of the first and heave with everything I had, sending it tumbling down the incline of the stadium seating upon which we stood.

"A crude but effective strategy," a smooth voice intoned. I turned, expecting the worst, but found Yehoshua's smiling form looking down upon me. Sheila glanced at him over her shoulder, but seeing him offer me a hand up apparently convinced her that she needed to keep her focus on the enemies we were fighting off.

Theodora seemed slightly more than pleased to see him. "Joshua. I had wondered where you had gotten off to."

"I have been surviving, dearest Theodora, surviving and sending these devils back to the Hell from whence they no doubt came." He stepped in and started kicking ass, allowing me a moment to breathe. "I have to admit I find it somewhat interesting you fighting side by side with faith's warrior."

"Must we discuss this now?"

"I just find it mildly fascinating being that you were the one most vehement in bringing the Icon to justice."

"Oh?" Sheila asked, performing a nice spin with her sword that took off a Jahabich's legs in the backswing.

"Yes, Shining One," Yehoshua replied, inclining his head toward her, "but please take no offense. I believe this stands as an excellent example of how one's role in life can be ever fleeting. Enemies may become allies, and allies may be at one another's throats with but a change in the wind."

I doubted Sheila had any idea of what he was talking about, but I had a sneaking suspicion that was his way - far more subtle than his girlfriend's - of reminding me that he and Thea would be more than happy to see Alex's plans end up in a big stinking pile of shit.

"Though it is obvious treachery has brought us to this point today," he continued, "I can see the benefit that might be reaped from it."

"Benefit, Joshua?" his Morticia Addams lookalike girlfriend replied, caving in the chest of a Jahabich with a single kick. "I do not see much benefit to be gained here unless one counts the potential for exercise."

"Have faith, my dearest," he replied. Sheila glanced at him and he smiled warmly. "Yes, child, I know a thing or two about faith myself. Once upon a time, I even counted one of your number as a friend."

"Must we?" Thea protested.

"But alas," he said, nodding deferentially to his gal pal, "such matters are ancient history."

Unfortunately, all of this banter served to distract Sheila. She turned her head at an inopportune moment and one of our enemies stepped in swinging. I moved to react, but the creature was faster - connecting with a bone-jarring hit to her left arm. Her aura flared to life at the last second, protecting her from the worst, but it still slammed home with sufficient force to make her cry out in pain, dropping her weapon in the process.

As powerful as Sheila was, she apparently had her Kryptonite. First those black blades, and now these monsters' ability to at least partially resist her abilities.

Well, fuck that. These things got one good hit in. There was no way I would let them get another.

The monster pressed forward with its attack, raising its arms above its head to deliver forth a crippling blow, but this time I shoulder tackled Sheila aside, her aura flaring to life again - thankfully, a moment too late to hurt me. Then, bracing myself for the fucks to come, I bent and grabbed her sword.

Yeah, I was right...FUCK!

My hands instantly ignited, a sensation I was hesitant to proclaim as pleasant even at my most masochistic. Not wanting to waste any unnecessary time holding the flaming death stick, I pointed it and jabbed - sending the tip of the blade into the Jahabich's mouth and out the top of its fucking head. I let go and tried to douse the fire by jamming both hands into my armpits - pretty much just spreading the flames to other parts of my anatomy. I made a quick mental note to not grab my junk next.

The monster I'd impaled stood with a blank expression upon its face for a moment and then keeled over backward, the hilt of the weapon still sticking out of its mouth. *Oh yeah, fucker! I bet that hurt you more than it hurt me…if only barely.*

Tears streamed freely down my face by the time the flames died down, leaving my hands blackened and blistered. Fortunately, Sheila was back on her feet by then. Her hand lay upon her bruised arm and it glowed, no doubt mending the injury. Neat trick. I wished it worked on me.

I dropped to my knees, waiting for my own enhanced healing to kick in and knit the two charred lumps of flesh at the end of my arms back into some semblance of working hands. Sheila stepped toward me, concern in her eyes. She reached out, letting her aura die down, and I would have liked nothing better in the world than to have let her finish that action. Alas, now was perhaps not the best time to share a moment.

I shook my head and gestured in the direction of her sword. Whatever she wanted to do or say could wait until she was properly armed again. I didn't want to see a repeat of what had just occurred.

She grabbed the weapon by the hilt and placed one foot upon the dead monster's chest to give herself leverage to yank it out. While she did that, I glanced over to see how our two resident Draculas were faring - pretty good, by the look of it. A crunch of rock came with every swing they took, filling the air and sounding as if they were busy digging out a mine instead.

So loud was it that I didn't notice the danger standing behind my kneeling form until it was too late.

"You are a great hero, my love, and deserve a hero's reward."

My eyes opened wide as a petite hand grabbed me by the hair and yanked my head back. Gan's crazy green eyes met mine and I saw she held a gleaming silver knife in her other hand.

I barely had time to scream as she raised the weapon.

I wasn't sure what the fuck was going on, other than Gan had finally lost it and was now looking to finish the job her father had started when he'd sent his assassins to behead me. Apparently, she'd had enough of my roaming eyes and had decided that if she couldn't have me, no one could.

Unfortunately, I had no leverage and my hands were still too damaged to do much more than flail uselessly. It wouldn't have mattered anyway. Gan possessed several times my strength. In such a position, there wasn't much I could do except hope she was joking.

"Listen, you don't want to do this."

"But I do, beloved."

With that, she stuck her tongue out playfully and sliced the blade across it in one quick motion.

"Gan, what the fu...ugh!"

Her juvenile mouth pressed against mine, suppressing the scream that really wanted to escape with every fiber of my being. She held my head fast, preventing escape as her lips locked onto mine and she shoved her tongue into my mouth before I could slam my teeth shut.

Holy shit! I was being mouth-raped by a three-hundred-year-old psycho in a twelve-year-old body, and there was nothing I could do about it. First, I'd fucking killed a senior official in the current government's administration, and now I would almost certainly end up on some sexual predator list for sure. Yeah, I was definitely having one of those days.

Still trying to protest, my mouth filled up with the blood from her sliced tongue. Gagging, I had no choice but to swallow and...and her power transferred into me. My muscles tensed as they strengthened, and feeling rushed back into my hands as the curious sensation of skin knitting itself back together took hold.

Reaching up, I grabbed hold of the side of her head...seemingly encouraging the little she-bitch even more so...and then used her own strength to try and pry her off of me.

Gah, it was like trying to disengage a stuck leech. In my short time upon this Earth, I will admit that the only kisses I have ever tried to escape were during the holidays - especially when Aunt Gertrude and her nicotine breath would visit. I never thought I'd be so eager to escape the affections of a non-related female.

Finally, I grabbed hold of her hair and managed to yank her away.

"Oh, my love, that was heavenly, unlike anything I..."

Perhaps it wasn't the most sporting thing I'd ever done, but in that moment, I gave in to whatever dark instincts I had and decked the little creep with every ounce of power in me, sending her flying into a cluster of nearby chairs.

Footsteps sounded in my periphery and I turned to find Sheila standing there, sword in hand. For a moment, I wasn't sure what she'd do, but she simply lowered the blade and chuckled. "You two have a really interesting relationship."

"Don't start with me," I glowered, trying to wipe the taste of crazy off of my lips as I hopped nimbly back to my feet. I was forced to admit that, despite her methods, Gan had most certainly helped me. I was back to fighting strength and then some. Of course, that realization brought with it guilt. I mean, what kind of man sucker punches a preteen girl...even a psychotically insane one?

Gan was already back on her feet, wiping a small smear of blood from the side of her mouth. I wasn't sure if it was from her cut or my punch, but it made me feel even worse.

I threw Sheila a glance and sighed before turning back to the little hellion. "Listen, Gan, I'm sorr..."

"Experiencing the fire inside of you makes my blood boil, beloved."

And there went the guilt, replaced instead by the wish that I'd clubbed her twice as hard.

"If you are done canoodling with your paramours, I would be most appreciative if you would carry your weight in this battle," Theodora said over her shoulder. Next to her, Yehoshua backhanded one of the Jahabich. It appeared as little more than a casual move, a slap of dismissal, but the rock monster's head spun around nearly one hundred and eighty degrees from the force of it.

"Believe me, I'd like nothing better than to..."

A mass compulsion swept over us and drowned out the rest, nearly driving me back to my knees from its force. "*TO ME, MY ALLIES!! IT IS TIME TO END THIS FARCE!!*"

One of the greatest military minds of all time was summoning us. I could only hope it was for good cause.

45

FIVE AGAINST THE WORLD

I may not be a tactical genius, but even I understood the painful reality of our situation. Fighting as we were, in small batches of survivors, we couldn't hold out indefinitely. This was a major offensive on the Jahabich's part. I took little comfort in how many of them we were taking down because I knew, judging from the lack of non-rocky bodies in the room, their fallen would be replenished if given enough time.

Alex's group was fighting their way back toward one of the smaller exits. That seemed to make sense. At worst, it would give them a defensive position with a chance for a tactical retreat.

The other fighting groups were taking his lead and doing the same, joining up with each other to form a greater defense against the tide of enemies still pouring in through the open blast doors.

I looked up and saw our foes weren't alone either. Fucking Farley and his traitorous friends stood there smiling as the rock monsters filed past. Those assholes needed to die, but there was a greater need beyond that - learning how they'd managed to pull it off. Everything about Farley screamed newb. That much even I could tell. Was he that good of an actor? Impossible. Alex had said they'd all been mass compelled to...

"Freewill!" Speak of the Devil. Alex called out to me from the vanguard of defenders.

My group was still a ways off from where the rest gathered and formed into lines. I wasn't even sure what our place there would be as I had a feeling the surviving vamps wouldn't be all too keen on fighting side by side with Sheila. If so, fuck them. I knew where my friends and I would stand.

Well, most of them anyway.

A glimpse of blonde hair from within the main group reminded me that Sally was still enthralled by Alex. Fuck me, but I had a feeling whatever he was beckoning me to do was going to be unpleasant. Whatever the case, I was in no position to decline.

"I'm here," I called back, taking a moment to grab one of the rock monsters and toss it into two of its oncoming friends.

We finally made it to where Alex's people were. The remaining guards all lined up and formed a phalanx in front of the group. Several members of the Draculas, James included, stood in the center to meet the foes funneled down to them.

Sheila stood a little ways back, no doubt wary of any potential trickery. Probably a smart idea around this deck of many assholes. Gan, of course, was practically plastered to my side. Her hand brushed against mine, and I immediately jerked it back as if I'd just touched a spider.

I'm sure Alex noticed, but in a rare moment of tact, he apparently thought better of mentioning it. "This room is a poor defensive choice," he said in a low voice to me without any preamble. "Reinforcements have been summoned. We will join up with them beyond this exit and utilize the tunnels of this complex to bottleneck our enemies and drive them out."

"Sounds good to..."

"However, we cannot allow ourselves to be flanked. I will personally lead the effort to destroy the remaining filth in this room, but we need the main bunker door sealed so more cannot take their place."

Oh crap. There it was: a suicide mission with my name written all over it. Hell, he couldn't have planned this better had he let the Jahabich in himself. Hmm, a small part of me wondered about that. Was it possible...?

"I charge you with this undertaking, Freewill," he said in a slightly louder voice so those around us could hear. "Do so and I will grant you clemency."

What a crock. He had me by the shorthairs and knew it. This was just pomp and circumstance for the masses.

I glanced back toward the open door on the far end of the auditorium and suppressed a shudder. "Sure. It should be a piece of cake." There was no way I would give him or the rest of these assholes the pleasure of knowing I was this close to soiling my already none-too-clean pants.

Even so, I was a bit surprised. I had thought Alex wanted to keep me around for some purpose, so why send me on what was quite likely a one-way trip? If I failed, it wouldn't exactly help his cause.

"I'll go too," Sheila said. "Someone has to keep you alive for our final battle." There was enough sarcasm in that last part to bring a smile to my face, even under these circumstances, but regardless, it seemed to go over at least one person's head.

"That is wise, Shining One," Gan replied. "I, too, shall accompany you."

"Afraid we're going to run off together?" Sheila asked abruptly. Thank goodness I wasn't drinking anything, for surely I'd have done a spit-take at that.

Gan's response was matter of fact in tone, with no trace she'd caught the playful note in Sheila's voice. "Not at all. Dr. Death and I are fated to be wed following your demise."

Suddenly, the thought of a suicide mission wasn't all that scary.

"Theodora, kindly go with them."

I spun back toward Alex so quickly, I'm surprised I didn't give myself whiplash.

"We're not gonna try to escape," Sheila said.

"I would hope not with the halls beyond full of an invading force," Alex replied curtly. "If you did so, it would mean you were either foolish or in league with them."

"Then I fail to see what purpose..."

Alex was ready for Theodora's protest, though. "I wish you there as witness, dear Theodora. As one of the First, your accounting of what happens shall be key once we resume our proceedings. Your opinion is, after all, beyond reproach." His tone suggested anything but that. However, I wasn't about to open my mouth and suddenly find my mission made any tougher. "If you fear for your life against these creatures, though..."

"I fear nothing of the sort. I have proudly stood against far worse in my day."

And there it was. Alex had told me earlier that his rule came down to careful planning and innovation when it mattered. He was clearly doing some of the latter right now. The only question was whether he was just sending Thea as a slap on the wrist for mouthing off earlier or if he knew she'd turned against him.

"I'll go too," James said, stepping up to us. "I am familiar with these..."

"The Jahabich. Yes, I know," Alex replied. "That is why I want you leading the offensive until such time as I am able to clear this room, Wanderer. That will go a long way toward your atonement."

Whatever Alex meant by that - although I'd have bet my left testicle he was referring to James's defeat up in Boston - it had the desired effect. James dropped his eyes and nodded respectfully, not putting up any more fight. Goddamn, what had this bunch done to him?

"Very well then," Alex proclaimed. "A small contingent led by me will remain behind until this room is secured. The rest will evacuate and join up with our reinforcements to begin the purge." He turned and raised his voice to compulsion level. "***THERE IS NOTHING IMPOSSIBLE TO HIM WHO WILL TRY!! VICTORY TO THE STRONGEST!!***"

A cheer rang up amongst the assembled and our fate was thus sealed.

"Hey," a familiar voice said to me as I was trying to figure out the best way to not die.

"Sally?" I spun back, to find her standing there.

"I just wanted to say good luck."

"Are you okay?"

"Yeah, I'm..."

"Do you remember anything? Anything at all?"

"Okay, weirdo," she said, backing up, "I just wanted to wish you good luck. That wasn't a fucking invitation for anything else."

Shit! Before she could turn completely away, though, I said, "Be careful."

"Always am," she replied, walking toward the rear exit.

Silently swearing I'd find a way to fix her, I turned and almost let out a scream. Gan stood creepily close to me, well inside my personal space.

"I believe your whore has been compelled."

"I know."

"We must undo it when this battle is completed."

I was touched. For all the crazy going through her, I hadn't assumed she would have cared at all for Sally. That she did meant a lot to me.

"I wish to have words with her over the death of Monkhbat and her lying about the witch's survival."

Or maybe not. "You mean Christy?"

"If that is her name."

"She's a friend."

"She is not my friend."

"Maybe, but you have to admit she's useful in a fight. Hell, I wish those other mages hadn't taken off."

"Oh, you mean the one called Grand Mentor?"

"Yeah."

"They did not leave."

"Really? Then where..."

"The witch who named your friend traitor caused my personal assassins much shame by escaping. It was an affront in need of rectification. I deemed it necessary to kill her colleagues as well, as I have neither the time nor inclination to deal with official protests."

"What?!"

"Yes. I will ask my retinue where their bodies are hidden if you wish to desecrate them."

I opened my mouth to point out that her little murder spree was quite convenient, as now there was nobody left to point fingers at her, but just as quickly closed it again. From what little I'd seen, the Grand Mentor had been a total ass not unlike Harry Decker. Hopefully with that loose end cleaned up they wouldn't bring any further grief to Christy. I just had to make sure Gan didn't try anything stupid against her if we happened to survive this.

I glanced over and saw Alex looking my way from

where he directed the offensive. I didn't need to understand ancient Greek to know he was mentally asking if I needed an engraved invitation. Also, it wasn't like Gan's power would stay with me indefinitely.

It was time to go.

Being in charge of anything wasn't really my cup of tea. I'd never considered myself management material. During my career, I'd been content to sit behind my screen, do as I was told, and then mock those in charge for their incompetence - all while doing little to change the status quo. What can I say? I like my routines.

Now, I found myself leading the charge with a group of folks all better suited to the task than me.

Hell, the first thing Thea said as we set off along the periphery of the auditorium was, "Dare to give me an order, child, and you will regret it."

I likewise doubted Gan would follow any command from my lips other than "Marry me!" and there was no way Hell had frozen over that much yet.

As for Sheila, the only thing I wanted her to do was stay safe - not exactly a job the legendary Icon was cut out for.

Most of the Jahabich were single-minded in going after the main defense awaiting them on the auditorium floor. With the battle condensed into two main factions, they seemed to sense victory. Thus, few appeared to pay us much mind. Thank goodness for a hive mentality.

The handful that did spot us were dispatched quickly as three of our party possessed speed enough to move out, kill them, and then get back before drawing much attention.

That was going to be the key to our living through

this, at least from what I could see. Forget any of the elaborate traps or schemes my D&D characters had invested in over the years - most of those had failed spectacularly anyway. This needed to be quick and uncomplicated.

We reached a corner of the room where the wall had partially collapsed, allowing us a vantage point from the rubble. The blast door was just a few dozen yards away, a straight run if there weren't still enemies marching through, not to mention Farley and his douche-corps guarding it.

The tide had lessened somewhat since their initial assault. Either this was the bulk of their force or their attention was now turned toward scouring the complex for Ed...

No! I couldn't let that weigh me down right now. Any indecision in this insane quest could potentially get me, Sheila, or Gan killed. Well, okay; I was mostly worried about those first two.

I turned to my strike team, hoping Theodora didn't tear my tongue out for speaking impertinently. "Let's keep this nice and clean. We clear the doorway and the space beyond long enough for one of us to start closing things up. The rest then run like hell before we get locked out with a bunch of angry monsters."

"That is your *great* plan, Freewill?" Theodora quipped. "I begin to wonder if perhaps the prophecies actually do reference Vehron the Destroyer."

"I think it is brilliant," Gan countered. "Simple and direct, much like my beloved."

"Wait a second..."

"Relax, Bill," Sheila said. "She's right...about the plan being simple, that is. I'll fight them back while you swing the door shut."

"No," I replied. "No offense, but you're not nearly fast enough. I'll hold them off while you take the door."

"I shall fight them by your side, Dr. Death," Gan added like a love-struck puppy. God, I so wanted to puke.

"That door is huge," Sheila protested. "There's no way I'll be able to..."

"Yes you can, child," Thea said dismissively. "It may be large, but it is perfectly balanced. A fly landing upon it could swing it shut. Once closed, the locks will engage automatically. There is one issue with this strategy, though. Before I offer my services, I need you to explain why I should willingly turn my back upon you."

"It is simple," Yehoshua said, stepping from the shadows and joining us. "She is not our enemy."

"What are you doing here, Joshua?" Theodora asked. "Alexander decreed..."

"I am of the First," he replied. "I need not ask permission for anything. Besides, it is very simple. If one of us is beyond reproach in our testimony, then two shall no doubt be absolutely unquestionable."

"What do you mean?"

"I ask you to reconsider your position. Who better to further our agenda than one of the few who has a chance of felling our foe?"

One didn't need to be a genius to figure out he wanted to use Sheila to kill Alexander. Oddly enough, I could dig that - minus the danger of attempting such an insane move, of course.

"How?"

"Now is not the time for such speculation. For the moment, it shall suffice to perform our duties and cut off our enemies. If we then speak to the Shining One's honor in upholding her word, we can ensure her survival. Even Alexander cannot deny that if enough of our brethren can be swayed. From there, opportunity will present itself." Before I could mention just how vague that sounded, he finished with, "We shall make certain of it."

"And Sheila?" I asked.

"The Shining One herself testified to not being our enemy. We may be able to forge an alliance of sorts that will serve to appease our people."

I glanced over at her and she shrugged. It was better than any other deal we'd been offered that day. I didn't dare ask Gan anything. No doubt, she was already thinking of step three of this plan - eliminate the Draculas, take over, and marry me.

Any way you looked at it, shit was not going to get any easier. It was like at some point I'd stepped into quicksand and, no matter which way I turned, kept sinking deeper into it. Goddamn it, when did life become so complicated?

Oh well, I pushed that aside for now. It was time to do something far less complicated - like charge into the fray where our choices were simple: live or die.

As far as Theodora was concerned, I could take anything that came out of my mouth and shove it back up my ass sideways. With Yehoshua, that was a different story, though. She obviously trusted him, or however close an ancient vampire could come to the concept. Thus, they took the lead.

We waited for a momentary pause in the onrush of Jahabich and then hit them hard from the side. Thankfully, those already inside were focused on Alex's group and continued onward, ignoring us as if we were of no consequence. Within moments, our group had cut off the charge and was busy hacking apart those trying to enter.

What Gan's blood lacked in strength compared to James's, it made up for in speed. I swear, I kind of had an inkling of what Spider-Man must feel like, taking apart foes who were practically standing still compared to him. If it weren't for the fact that I was terrified of adopting her craziness, too, I'd be tempted to ask for a few extra vials.

Even so, I was practically a clumsy kid with a hammer next to Sheila. One of these days I really needed to gain access to our fabled archives and see what they said about Icons. What she could do was kind of the equivalent of that "I know kung-fu" scene from The Matrix. She expertly weaved through our foes, cutting and feinting, almost as if she knew what her opponents were doing a second before they did.

OOF! A punch to the side of the head brought my attention back to the present. I quickly noticed the lack of my skull being split in half. That's because the fist that had hit me had been human in shape and hadn't struck home particularly hard.

"Hey, Farley. I see you've gotten a promotion to doorman."

A part of me was sure that when he spoke, all pretense of the inexperienced grunt would be gone - that I'd find we'd all been duped by a trained killer ready to spill my blood upon the ground.

Amazingly enough, sometimes expectations fail us in ways that don't suck.

"Shut up," he mewled, trying to sound tough and falling a couple feet short of the mark. "I knew we should have killed you when we had the chance, but the master didn't want it."

"Master? Let me guess...big guy, bitchin tats, tends to speak in long-dead languages? Sound about right?"

"Mock the true Freewill all you wish, imposter. He

will tear down the false coven and pave the way for the love of Ib."

"You do realize how stupid a name that is, right?"

"The true First is beyond names. I only wish I had known about the pure one before handing you all over to these scum. I could have delivered him to the master myself and been bathed in eternal glory."

"Wait...pure one?" The Jahabich had said the same thing about Ed. The fuckers obviously didn't know my roommate. "Vehron wants him too?"

Unfortunately, I realized too late that having an expositional conversation in the middle of a pitched fight was probably not the brightest thing. The sounds of battle from beyond the open portal caught my ear just as two of the Jahabich charged straight at me. Fuck!

Farley grinned and produced a handgun, pointing it my way. Obviously, he was of the mindset that three against one was a fair fight.

He was wrong.

46

THAT WHICH IS DEAD CAN
INDEED DIE

Under different circumstances, Farley and I might have had a decent slugfest...or at least a slap fight. He looked about as cut out for the life of a soldier as I was. Sadly for him, I was the Freewill and he was just some low level putz who'd...well...somehow managed to overcome the compulsions of the most powerful vampires in the world.

Okay, forget that last part. I still had no clue how the fuck he'd pulled that one off. What I did know was I was amped up on Gan's blood and he wasn't. Before he could so much as cock the trigger, I had grabbed him by the throat with one hand and lifted him off the ground - mainly because that move never fails to look cool in the movies. With my other, I grabbed hold of the weapon he held and crushed it...also probably awesome looking, but maybe not the smartest thing in the world. I could have probably used it.

Oh well, when in a pinch, sometimes one must make do with what's at hand. Interestingly enough, that happened to be my buddy Farley. I swung, using his body as a flail, and smashed both of the Jahabich aside. Judging by the sharp crack that sounded, I also pulverized Farley's legs in the process. Oh well, can't make an omelet without breaking a few eggs.

I continued forward, using him as my personal meat shield to ward off any attacks. Ooh...that was a nasty hit to his kidneys. That was gonna hurt in the morning. Too bad, so sad the Jahabich didn't seem to hold him in high enough regard to not pummel him into chopped meat in their quest to get at me.

"It makes my heart proud to watch you brutalize our enemies so," Gan said, stepping up to my side as we continued to gain ground.

A part of me was sure I would feel bad the next day, but for now, giving an asshole his just deserts felt pretty darn good. Whoever said revenge ultimately left a hollow feeling inside had apparently never given it the old college try.

Flashes of light out of the corner of my eye told me my squad-mates on this mission were dispatching Farley's buddies...probably with extreme prejudice. There were few things scarier than powerful vampires with bruised egos. Likewise, I turned and caught sight of the white glow of Sheila's faith aura flaring up as she swung her sword in an arc, taking out a Jahabich and two of the traitorous vamps with one swing.

I allowed myself a nanosecond to think *so fucking hot* before concentrating on our objective.

Gan pried a few of the monsters away from the hinges where they stood guard like living doorjambs, and then we were through. The scene in the room beyond was surreal. Piles of ash and discarded weapons lay everywhere, speaking to how the vamps on guard had been ambushed. Sadly, whatever was left in there didn't seem particularly friendly to our cause.

A column of both Jahabich and what I assumed to be

more traitorous vamps stood guard outside. Multiple heads turned in our direction, and they did *not* look happy. One of the creatures stepped from its line and pointed its clubbed arm at me.

"*Freewill. We shall enjoy this.*" Before my eyes, its features melted and deformed. Within a second, it had reformed into...fuck me...Mark.

"Never let a witch do a vampire's job," I muttered.

He grinned, revealing the blackened granite spikes of teeth in his mouth. "Kill the rest, but keep this one alive for questioning. He'll know where the pure one is hiding."

His vampire buddies, obviously holding a very liberal concept of keeping me alive, all raised their weapons toward me. They'd ditched the silver stakes in favor of semiautomatic assault rifles.

As for the Jahabich, about half of them took Mark's lead and resumed their alternate forms. Unfortunately, those who did had seemingly been cloned from some of our uglier enemies. About a dozen Sasquatches, all sporting stalagmite dentures, charged us.

Shit had just gotten surreal.

Shots rang out, and I wasn't taking chances that they were aimed at anyone else. I held Farley - still ineffectually struggling against my iron grip - up to block them, hoping maybe he'd dissuade their ire. Unfortunately for him, the poor dude just wasn't very popular and they peppered the fucker. Looked like silver too, from the way his extremities combusted. At least he'd had the foresight to wear a bullet-proof vest.

I dove to the side, out of the line of fire and, when I came back up, did my best Captain America imperson-ation - using Farley as my shield. I threw him with everything I had, nailing the vamps right in the middle of their lineup. Woo, bowling for assholes!

There wasn't time to gloat, though. What we were trying to do was painfully obvious, and our enemies closed in on us to put a stop to that shit. Theodora and Yehoshua took up positions to the left of me, engaging the Jahafeet - or whatever - while Gan raced forward on my right, intent on doling out some justice to the vampire traitors.

Two of the monsters, still in their rock forms, came straight at me, but they didn't expect me to come equipped with Gan's speed. My claws extended, I erased both of their faces before they could even properly raise their clubs against me.

I glanced over my shoulder and saw that Sheila had cleared the door of the last of the creatures blocking it open. We just needed to buy her a few more minutes.

I turned back to the fight at hand, thinking that now would be the perfect time to knock Mark's fucking head off his shoulders. I caught sight of his still grinning face, but he was backing up, letting the others swarm out before him. He was obviously trying to goad me into following, but as much as I'd grown to dislike him during our short acquaintance, I wasn't that stupid.

The four of us formed up into a loosely knit defense in front of the door, trying to keep anything from getting past us. Even with two Dracs on our side, though, that was gonna be tough.

Their initial clumsy charge repelled, the Jahabich began to line up in a formation similar to how they'd kept me and my friends penned down below - turning themselves into a living wall.

At least several bodies deep from what I could see, they began to press forward. Every time we'd smash one to bits, another would take its place. They weren't even trying to attack, just force us back - their goal obviously the opposite of ours, to keep the damned door open.

And they were going to do it too if we didn't hurry. As powerful as we were, they started pushing us back. Even Theodora's fury, tossing the monsters aside like they were ragdolls, didn't stem the tide.

A small breeze on the back of my neck caught my attention, and I glanced over my shoulder to find Sheila was pulling the blast door shut - the massive structure moving silently and without much effort.

"Wait for her to get it at least three quarters of the way," Yehoshua said from the far side of our line where he'd just put his fist through a Jahabich skull, exploding it like a freaky-ass pumpkin.

Unfortunately, I didn't think we were going to make it. Sheila was only about a quarter of the way there, and the enemy was rapidly gaining ground. We may as well have been trying to fend off an avalanche with a snow shovel.

It didn't help that we couldn't put our guard down to just push back either. The few vampires remaining on their end had regrouped. They were firing shots over the Jahabich, hoping for a hit on us - keeping us dodging and weaving...and occasionally throwing a severed rocky limb their way.

Bright flashes of white light lit up the room from behind us and I had little doubt of the source. They were trying to shoot Sheila too, but she was ready for them - her shield flaring up whenever they were spot on with their aim. That in itself was another danger. If one of us was too close to her when that happened, it was going to hurt.

Fuck me. Talk about choosing between the fire and the frying pan.

A bullet whizzed past my head and my hair was blown forward by the close proximity.

Wait, *forward?*

Just then, the shot echoed from behind me, followed by another and then another.

I glanced back into the auditorium and saw Alex leading a contingent of vampire guards toward us. Though he still held a sword in hand, the vamps following him had apparently ditched the ceremonial silver stakes for weapons with a bit more range. Beyond him, I could see the last of the survivors leaving through the exits.

He'd made good on his word. They'd fought their way through the monsters still in the room before we'd cut them off, and now he was actually coming to help us. As much as I hated the fucker, I had to admit it was good to see his arrogant asshole of a mug.

Whereas Farley's men had seemingly been mostly newbs, Alex's guards were not. Several of the traitor vamps took headshots and immediately exploded into dust.

Although bullets weren't great for killing the Jahabich, they weren't half bad for slowing them down. The monsters themselves didn't seem overly fond of taking a round in their empty glowing eye sockets.

It wasn't much, but it was enough.

A few seconds later, Yehoshua shouted, "Go!"

I didn't need to be told twice, taking off with Gan at my side. She quickly took the lead, and I understood why. The battle had finally taken enough out of me that her blood was wearing off, but I most certainly had enough left for one last super speedy sprint.

We raced through the rapidly closing portal with a few feet left to spare.

Theodora was next. She stopped behind us and turned. "Hurry, Joshua!" Gone was her typical arrogant tone. I was actually surprised to hear what sounded like genuine concern in her voice. Guess maybe some of the

Dracs still had a few of their emotion circuits plugged in after all.

The door's momentum was carrying it the rest of the way. Sheila let go and stepped to the crack of an opening, raising her sword. "Come on; I'll cover you."

At last, Yehoshua appeared in the doorway. He stepped through and...

Sheila's aura flared to life around her in a brilliant flash of white flame.

The crack of rifle fire sounded a scant second later, but I barely noticed it. Yehoshua had been too close to her. The powerful magic coursing through her flung him back, his body catching aflame as he flew through the last remaining feet of open doorway into the sea of angry orange eyes beyond.

Theodora cried out, but it was too late. The blast door shut and the hollow thud of the bolts engaging sounded throughout the room.

What happened next was quick, almost too fast to make sense of it.

I turned back to find one of Alex's guards still pointing his gun at Sheila, the barrel smoking. Before I could say a word, though, Theodora crashed through me and Gan, knocking us to the ground as if we were inconsequential. "You traitorous whore!" she screamed.

Dazed, I watched as Sheila raised her sword defensively. She spoke rapidly, telling Theodora it was an accident, but the ancient vampire was having none of it.

Thea swung her claws, connecting with Sheila's sword. Sparks flew, but she continued her assault, seemingly not caring when her hand ignited from the impact. She swung again and once more it was parried, if just barely.

The attack nearly knocked Sheila off her feet, her foe too strong even for her. She continued to give ground until her back was against the now locked portal.

"Stop," I cried, but it was too late. Her opponent cornered, Theodora leapt - no doubt intent on finishing things.

Sheila just barely ducked in time as Theodora's claws sank into the metal framework. She sidestepped, swinging with her blade, and nearly bisected the elder vamp with the blow. White fire exploded out from the weapon and Theodora instantly immolated from the inside out in a brilliant explosion of fire, sparks, and dust.

Within seconds, one of the oldest creatures on the planet was no more.

Gunfire caught my ear from behind and I spun to find Alex pointing accusingly at the guard who had fired upon Sheila. The other soldiers at his command emptied their weapons into their former comrade, destroying him instantly.

Alex's eyes met mine, but where I expected to see sympathy or perhaps confusion, he instead momentarily flashed me a confident grin.

It immediately became painfully obvious.

The whole ordeal had been a setup and we had played our parts as pawns perfectly.

47

DECK THE HALLS

I half expected us to be rearrested immediately. However, I'd forgotten there were still plenty of Jahabich left to deal with. Alex and his men, all apparently loyal to his cause, quickly vacated the room - the fight not over yet.

By the time I got back to my feet, only me, Sheila, and Gan remained in the auditorium.

Gan was dusting herself off, obviously only barely inconvenienced, but I paid her no heed. I stepped toward Sheila, who wore a shocked look on her face. Her sword clattered to her feet as she backed away from the pile of scorched remains that had been Theodora.

"What the hell just happened?"

"Alex," I replied, wanting to reach out and comfort her, but not quite daring to, as she was still aglow.

"Huh?"

"It is quite simple," Gan said from behind me. "Theodora has obviously been a thorn in Alexander's side for these entire proceedings. He could not directly punish her, but when he saw an opening to do so with minimal damage to his own reputation, he took it. I have to say I am impressed he was willing to sacrifice another of his council so easily."

"I don't think so."

"Oh, beloved?"

I opted to ignore her continued infatuation with me - instead mentally replaying the earlier memory of me clocking her. Oh, yes; that one was going to be a keeper every bit as much as Sheila in her towel.

I took a quick look around, confirming we were alone, and then replied, "Both Theodora and Yehoshua were working against Alexander."

"How do you know?" Sheila asked.

"They told me."

"Okay. Ask a stupid question..."

"They weren't open about it, though. I think they were relying on me to be an X-factor in Alex's plan. An agent of chaos, if you will."

Gan perked up. "You do excel at such, my love."

"Don't you have somewhere else to be?"

"Where else would I wish to be other than by your side?"

I pointed toward Sheila's sword, then at my chest. "Right here, if you'd do me the favor."

"The time of your destiny is not yet at hand, my love," Gan chided.

I gave Sheila the stink eye for chuckling, then tried to steer us back on track. "Anyway, I don't think it's a coincidence what happened. I have a feeling Alex purposely sent Theodora with us. Hell, he probably even assumed that Yeho...fuck it...Joshua would follow. In the middle of a battle, with those fucking monsters rampaging about, and the Icon smack dab in the midst of things, it would be a simple matter for something to conveniently go wrong."

"Or for Alex to subtly compel one of his guards to

shoot the Shining One, knowing how her power would react," Gan added.

"Exactly."

"But doesn't that weaken his position...or at least, the leadership of the vampires?" Sheila asked.

"Yes and no. Losing two ancient vamps is probably not going to be great for morale. On the flip side, getting rid of two conspirators is great for him personally. The fucker's so full of himself he probably thinks he can win the war alone."

"It would make sense to remove both," Gan added. "Should someone slay you, Dr. Death, my vengeance upon them would be never-ending."

She had a point, in her disturbingly single-minded way. It was painfully obvious those two had had a thing for each other.

"If Alex managed to off one, but not the other, he would be potentially looking at a vengeful lover to deal with. A pissed off, grief-stricken vamp would probably have no fucks left to give with regards to screwing over their tormentor as badly as possible. With both gone, though, he's pretty much free to do as he pleases. You saw the rest of them. Nobody there was willing to raise so much as a peep against Alexander. Even if they did, he has the perfect stooge to point a finger at and blame."

Sheila raised her eyebrow at that.

"In a manner of speaking, of course."

I glanced back at the blast door. I really hadn't known Yehoshua from a hole in the wall, but he'd been slightly less of a dick to me than some others. I could respect that. I found myself hoping his was a good death, because I shuddered to think of the alternative if he was brought to the Jahabich's lair and their glowing pool of goop.

Oh well, he was beyond our help now, but others weren't, and I for one had no intention of letting them down. "We need to find our friends, and then we need to figure out a way to get the fuck out of here."

As far as plans went, it wasn't much, but it was all we had to go on at that moment.

A small part of me was convinced I was going insane. With Gan's power rapidly draining away, I was easily the weakest of our trio. Thus, leading us back into the fray was probably one of the stupider tactics I could have adopted. Of course, I kept those little facts to myself.

I still could taste Gan's creepy little preteen tongue...ugh! Who the fuck knew what she'd try to do if she thought I needed another power-up.

Unfortunately, it was difficult for me to think of blood at that moment without also thinking of that human I'd drained.

I glanced back at Sheila, wondering if I was worthy of her anymore - a difficult proposition considering I wasn't sure I'd been worthy of her even before being turned into a bloodthirsty creature of the night.

"What is it?"

Oh crap. I'd been staring. Shit! I opened my mouth to make up some excuse or other - maybe rock monsters coming down the halls behind us. Instead, I surprised myself and said, "I've done some things lately that I'm not proud of."

"Huh?"

"I...I'm not what I hope to be. I keep trying to be a good person, but inside there's this monster..."

"You really want to do this *now*?"

"Well..."

She smiled and stepped up to me, putting a hand on my shoulder - one that wasn't currently burning with holy fire, thankfully. "We've all done some questionable things."

"But…"

"Myself included. I'm no saint, trust me. Besides, remember what you said when you first found me with the Templar?"

"That I was there to rescue you?"

"No. You told me that this world is what we have and it isn't a very nice place to be. That it was bloody and dangerous and only going to get worse."

Oh yeah, that. I'd just been blathering, not realizing anyone had been listening.

"I didn't want to believe you at first, but I've seen a lot more since then, and I think you're right."

"I am?"

"Yes. We're going to have to do bloody and dangerous things if we're going to have any hope of surviving, much less making things better."

"I want to make things better." I left off "between us" but hoped it was implied.

"Me too." Her grin widened. "But for now, you need to grow a set." She clapped me on the shoulder and let loose with a laugh as she strode in front of me.

I couldn't help but smile after her…not even staring at her ass as she walked - much, anyway.

"I echo her sentiment," Gan said. "Also, when you finally do grow *a set*, I would very much like to see them."

"Are you certain I cannot kill them?"

"For the last time, Gan, they're my friends. They're off limits."

"Very well. Their lives shall be my betrothal gift to you."

I caught Sheila's eye and mouthed "Kill me" to her, but sadly, no such luck.

It had quickly become obvious that my intentions to rescue my friends weren't worth shit in the maze of tunnels we attempted to navigate. We tried to avoid fighting whenever we could hear it up ahead but still wound up running into some of the creatures.

Thankfully, that was one area where Alex hadn't been full of shit. Fighting them was easier in a boxed-in area...at least it would be until our luck ran out and we ran into a large force of them - which I was sure we'd eventually do.

Much to my equal parts delight and chagrin, though, Gan was able to offer assistance right when I was about ready to give up. Her nose had proven freaky in its ability to allow her to track me down. She wasn't as intimately familiar with my friends, but had been around them enough to have a general idea of their scent. Even better - sorta - she apparently saved a special mental file for her enemies, and thus locked onto Christy's smell fairly quickly.

Now I just had to hope those two didn't decide to gut each other on sight.

It was hard to tell how things were going for our side - which wasn't really *my side*, but was as close as I was going to get in this prison. However, we passed many dead and dismembered Jahabich along the way - some in their natural states, others in whatever other form they'd chosen. It gave me hope that perhaps we were driving them back. Although after all was said and done, who knew what our fate held?

At last, Gan pointed to a reinforced door. "Her scent leads there. Beyond it, I cannot tell."

"That's as good as we're going to get, I suppose."

The door had an airlock crank on it. I grabbed the handle and gave it a try. It turned, which made sense. If this was indeed the prison cell where they'd been kept, there would have been no reason to lock it - nobody should've been aware they'd teleported back to it.

"Stand back," I warned, mainly addressing Gan. "If they're in there, they're with an angry, hormonal witch. Best not to *excite* them."

"If the mage attacks us, I will be forced to respond with deadly force."

"Hence why I want you to stand back. Let's not give her a reason." Duh!

I turned the handle and began to pull the door open. Just as the crack of an opening appeared, I shouted, "Don't shoot, it's m..."

Something akin to a runaway train hit the other side with tremendous force. Sadly, the hinges of the door were on the outside, giving it a full range of motion. It flew open and took me with it, slamming into the concrete wall next to it with enough power to ensure I would have an indentation of the crank in my chest for all of eternity.

"Sorry," came a cry from inside.

"S'okay," I gurgled, spitting up a generous amount of blood from my shattered insides.

Sheila and Gan grabbed the door and pried it off of me - stuck as I was like a bug on a windshield. I gave a thumbs-up once they were done and promptly passed the fuck out.

"Do not touch him, witch. His healing will suffice."

"She's not trying to hurt him, you little creep."

"I promise you, Gansetseg, this is only a little jolt to wake him up."

ZAP!

"Holy shit!" I sprang up to a sitting position, as if a

hornet's nest had just been shoved up my ass. Had I still a beating heart, I'm sure it would have popped out of my chest.

"Are you okay?"

I blinked, the light from the fluorescents of the facility a bit too bright for my tastes, and looked around. My trio had been augmented into a...um...sextant or something - whatever the fuck it was called. Gan had been right on the money with her nose.

She and Sheila stood to one side of me, but I got the impression Sheila was there in case trouble broke out. On the other side stood Christy and my roommates. Tom and Ed looked down at me as Christy and Gan busied themselves by glaring daggers at each other.

"Ah good, you are awake," Gan said, as if my being smashed to shit by a ton of door was an everyday occurrence. "I was just informing the witch of my displeasure at learning the whore had lied about her survival."

"Oh, believe me, the feeling is mutual," Christy shot back. "Next time you take a hundred-story swan dive, try a little harder to land on your head."

"Such heights are child's play for one such as me. Although if you would like to experience the sensation personally, it would be my pleasure to show..."

"Okay, enough," I croaked, my body still knitting itself back together. "We're on the same side here."

"I am not on the same side as this..."

"Listen up, Gan. If you want to hang with me, then you're on the same side. If not, you're free to catch the next plane back to the Gobi Desert."

"Very well, beloved. I will tolerate her continued existence on your behalf. What of her human paramour?"

"Him too."

"Thanks," Tom said, offering me a hand.

"Don't mention it." I got back to my feet, wincing. It

felt like all my internal organs were shifting around. Inclining my head toward the door, I asked Christy, "Same trick you used at your apartment?"

She smiled, obviously pleased at seeing her handiwork acknowledged. "A variation of it. I figured it would be more effective with this door."

"Trust me, it was."

"Wait, when did you…"

"Oh, Sally and me tried to break in last year around the time when you and Tom first started dating." Quickly glancing at Sheila, I added, "Don't ask."

Leaving them with appropriate looks of confusion on their faces, I stretched - feeling the last of the injuries healing - and addressed the group. "Glad to see that everyone is okay. It's still not safe, though." Considering where we were, I quickly added, "Even less safe than usual. We gave those fucking things a bloody nose, but they're still swarming the halls."

"You had to make a deal about not escaping, didn't you?" Christy asked with a sigh.

"Sorry. It was a heat of the moment type thing," Sheila replied sheepishly.

"It's not her fault," I said. "Alex had us by the short hairs. Still does…at least me, although I think he's broken the spirit of the truce, if not the letter."

I checked the halls in either direction then, seeing nothing but concrete walls staring back at us, quickly explained what happened back in the main courtroom - adding my own personal editorial touch to things. Fuck it, we weren't getting a fair trial during the proceedings. There was no way I was letting Alex off the hook without a little character assassination for his troubles.

"So he used you guys to ice two fellow Dracs just because they pissed him off?" Tom asked.

"More complicated than that, but in a nutshell."

"I guess I can see why James was acting all squirrelly back there," Ed commented.

"Me too. I'd been imagining being on the Draculas as one big party at the top of the food chain, but I'm thinking now it's just another level of being someone else's stooge."

"That will change when I am in charge, Dr. Death," Gan unhelpfully added.

I opted to ignore her little megalomaniacal proclamation. "James isn't our problem right now. Sally is. I want the rest of you to get the fuck out of here. Christy, teleport everyone somewhere safe. I need to find her, though."

"I will stay by your side, beloved."

Of course. What a surprise.

"I'm pretty sure you weren't on the invite list to begin with," Christy countered.

"Knock it off, you two," Ed said. "Fuck that, Bill. You know we're not leaving you behind. It's your word against his about what happened, and I'm pretty sure Alex would have a field day fucking you over on that one."

"Doesn't matter. I want you guys to get to safety."

"Where exactly is it safe out there?"

"I don't know. Maybe find another nuclear bunker...one not overrun with vampires and rock monsters. Also, Ed, you're not one to talk. Those fucking things are after you again."

"Oh great. What the fuck did I ever do to them?"

"I don't know. Everyone is irresistible to someone. You just got unlucky in your selection of soul mates."

"I'll stay too," Sheila said.

"No, you won't."

"I'm not your damsel in distress, Bill."

"Believe me, I know that." I held up my hands in a placating manner. "But even you have to admit this is probably the worst place in the world for you right now. Besides..."

"Besides what?"

"Well..."

"I believe what my love is trying to tell you," Gan said, "is he thought you dead once and it drove him mad with grief. Should it happen again, it would surely break him like the lovesick fool he is."

Oh, fuck me. "Not helping, Gan."

"However," she continued, "if I am reading him correctly, and I always am, I would say he has also recently developed feelings for his whore."

"What?!"

"Really?" Ed raised an eyebrow.

"No!"

"You cannot deny it, beloved. You are an open parchment to me. I must question your choice in paramours, however. The whore does not strike me as a particularly savory partner. You can do much better."

"Let me guess...you?"

"Of course."

Gah! "Christy, remember what I said about not blasting a certain munchkin in the room?"

"Yes?"

"Rapidly considering a change of mind on that one."

"Can we focus here?" Sheila asked, her aura flaring up for a moment. "We can discuss all of...*this* at another time, preferably not here and not in front of an audience."

Maybe it was me, but I could have sworn I caught the ghost of a blush on her face standing out against the white glow.

"Let's lay out what needs to be done. We need to find Sally, and we need to get out of here. There's strength in numbers, but according to Bill, these monsters are after you," she pointed a finger toward Ed, "for whatever reason."

Tom beamed at that. "Christy, any chance you can glamour us all up?"

A frown creased her face. "One or two people is easy, but I'm a little winded. I could maybe change our look, but if these monsters can sniff Ed out, that might be a problem."

"Just change him, then."

I let out a sigh. "So you want us to walk around with one member of our group missing, but a whole new guy with us, and hope they don't figure that out?"

"How smart could they be? They have rocks for heads."

"They're not the only ones," Ed muttered.

"The way I see it, we have a couple of choices," I said, trying to get us back on track. "We could all leave now. That saves our asses for the moment, but fucks Sally. I'm not willing to do that."

"The First Coven would be after you shortly regardless," Gan replied. "They already want the Shining One dead, and they do not take lightly to broken truces."

"Point taken. Some of you could *bamf* out of here. I can take the heat for that, but it still won't stop them from hunting down Sheila when this is over."

"You assume they'll leave the rest of us alone," Christy pointed out. "Not sure I trust that to happen."

Ed stepped forward. "Not happening anyway, bro. We're not gonna let you take the fall."

"Thanks."

"Besides, who knows when those fucking rock things will pop up again, looking for me. It pays to keep all of my super-powered friends in one piece, if you get my drift."

"That's all I am, a glorified bodyguard, eh?"

"More or less," he replied with a grin. Asshole.

"How about this?" I said at last. "I don't think all of us wandering the halls is a great idea. Too big of a chance of something happening. If they see Ed, we could be swarmed. They haven't found this room yet, and there's no reason to think they will before this is over."

"So you're splitting us up again?"

"More or less, despite all horror movie logic. It should keep you safe while not violating the truce. If things get hairy, step outside the door and teleport out of here."

"What if we can't get out the door?"

"You'll be able to because Sheila is going to stay here with you."

48

OLD BOYFRIENDS DIE HARD

"The hell I will!"

Needless to say, Sheila was none too pleased at my statement. A few unkind words were said about me being a sexist ass and her not needing a knight in shining armor, blah blah blah. What she couldn't deny, though, was that Christy was very pregnant. It was perhaps a low blow for me to point that out, but fuck that shit. Where chivalry fails, good old-fashioned guilt can work wonders.

Christy was powerful, but she was a sawed-off shotgun - nasty for a few blasts, but with limited ammo. If enough of any hostile force came after them, neither Tom nor Ed would be particularly useful if she clicked on empty. Ed's blood could pack a doozy of a punch against a vampire, but he had to spill it for it to be effective - not the most sustainable defensive strategy.

An Icon, on the other hand, was more than capable of defending a chokepoint like a narrow doorway. That logic, combined with protecting the unborn baby of a woman she was supposedly prophesized to destroy - a factoid I knew was eating her up inside - sealed the deal. I felt a bit bad playing the guilt card, but not nearly as bad as if any of them got hurt because we divided up the teams incorrectly.

That left me with Gan, the short end of the stick in more ways than one.

All of that settled, my roommates and I exchanged our customary insults toward one another's manhood - our way of wishing each other well. Christy then pulled me aside to have a few words.

When she was finished, she turned and headed back into the room, but not before saying, "May the White Mother watch over you."

"I'll take what I can get."

Sheila was the last to enter the former holding cell. We stood there awkwardly facing each other for a moment until I lamely broke the silence. "I should probably get going."

"Yeah. Good luck."

"You too."

I turned to leave, wanting to say more, but not quite finding the words.

"Oh, and Bill? Stay safe. You still owe me at least one awkward conversation."

"Huh?" I spun so fast, you'd have sworn that I was still amped up on Gan's blood, but it was too late. She was already closing the cell door behind her - no doubt taking up a guard position right inside.

Fuck! I so hated when women did that. How the hell was I supposed to concentrate on tying my shoes, much less surviving, with that one rolling around in my head?

"They'll be okay," I muttered, forcing myself to turn away again. "They have to be."

"Worry not, Dr. Death," Gan said after we'd turned a corner. "The Shining One is formidable. The only true danger to her are blades sanctified in the ritual of Baal, and most of them currently lie broken on the battlefield."

Wait, hadn't Alex mentioned something similar before mind-blasting Sally? "What are you talking about?"

"The darkened weapons and shackles that were used to hold the Shining One at bay."

"Oh. So what the fuck is a ritual of Baal?"

"It sanctifies the steel in the blood of the god of heretics."

"Wait. How the fuck can there be a god of heretics? By their very definition, heretics don't worship anyone."

"Some of the subtleties of the veil escape even my knowledge."

"Fine, the idiosyncrasies of ancient gods aren't really my concern anyway. Still, I'm not sure I buy it. Those things were pretty useless in battle."

"Indeed. The blood is a corrupting influence, making the metal brittle and unreliable. However, that same influence is what allows them to pierce the Shining One's defenses."

"How do you know this?"

"Any child of our history would know it. My father made sure all of his subjects were learned in our ways."

"Wait, James was one of your father's...err, sirelings, I guess. How come he didn't know about it?"

"The Wanderer? He is well aware. He studied from the same ancient scrolls as did I."

"Yeah, but Remington..." That made no sense. If James knew how to kill an Icon, then why did he send a group armed with the typical gear vamps used to hunt down other vamps? Was it a mistake? Could he have possibly set them up for failure on purpose? But why?

Unfortunately, that train of thought was sent hurtling off the tracks and down a canyon as Gan chose that moment to change subjects.

"You and the Shining One should consider being more direct with one another," she commented as we walked. "It will make your time together much more pleasant, at least until destiny forces you to kill her and become mine."

"Oh, shut up."

"Your whore is near."

One didn't need Gan's senses to make that guess. The sound of fighting had been growing steadily louder, echoing through the empty halls from seemingly all directions. That the body count had also been increasing was likewise undeniable. Dead Jahabich, piles of ashes, and the bloody remains of various allied creatures drove the point home. Needless to say, I didn't envy the poor schmucks whose jobs it would be to clean this place up once this was all over and done with.

I found myself idly wondering if it would be zombies or some vampire janitors. At least the latter could snack away as they mopped.

Such thoughts weren't particularly useful, but it was better than wondering if Sally would even let me help her. The truth was I knew very little about her life prior to me entering it. She always kept things close to the vest, seemingly living in the moment. However, from her various psychotic inclinations - such as opening a faux suicide hotline to draw in victims for our former coven - it wasn't a stretch to assume she'd been heavily invested in the vampire lifestyle. If she had reverted back to that, I...well, I might need for Gan to punch her out and explain things later when we were all safe.

Yeah, I was pretty well fucked no matter how you rolled the dice. But as long as she was alive, there was hope. That would have to be good enough. If I could get her to safety...

But then what?

How did one undo a compulsion of Alex's power? Even barring that, what about us? As much as I hated to admit it, Gan had a point. I'd considered Sally a friend even during my early days as one of the undead, her status quickly growing in rank to rival even my roommates. Now, though, I couldn't shake these other feelings I'd allowed myself to consider.

Personally, I blamed Robert. If he hadn't shacked up with Sheila, making her happy and all, then I'd have never opened myself up to other possibilities. The problem now was that once opened, that particular Pandora's Box - if you will - didn't seem to want to shut. Goddamn it! Leave it to the fucking accountants to screw shit up for the rest of us.

We rounded a corner and saw heavy double doors ahead of us. One was melted right off its hinges, little more than smoldering slag. It allowed us to see in to the room beyond where, judging by the sounds, screams, and bodies flying back and forth, a fight was going on.

"She is in there," Gan pointed out.

"Of course she is." I let out a heavy sigh, dreading this - not so much for Sally, but I had a feeling the first thing I'd hear upon entering would be Alex's smug voice.

Oh well, who wanted to live forever anyway?

I planned to sneak in along the wall and assess the situation before figuring out what to do - whether to fight or grab Sally and run, whatever looked the most likely to succeed.

That was my plan. Sadly, I didn't bother to share it with Gan, who seemingly had another strategy in mind. Standing beside me, she let out one of those battle shrieks of hers, hitting a pitch only prepubescent girls and trained opera singers seemed capable of. Rather than melodic, though, it was more like something you'd expect to hear during Ragnarök, right before the Valkyries swooped in and kicked the shit out of you.

Before I could say a word - not that she would have heard me anyway - she was off, a blur of motion, a tiny little whirlwind of teeth, claws, and crazy.

Well, I guess there was something to be said about the direct approach.

I followed, trying to keep an eye out in all directions. We appeared to be in a cafeteria, of all places. Though no stern-faced lunch ladies gazed out from behind pots of creamed meatloaf, it was fairly obvious - especially once an industrial-sized oven went flying past me to smash into a Jahabich closing in on my position.

I glanced to my right and saw one of the Draculas jumping back into the fray, the one Alexander had called Vargas. He seemed to be directing an attack by a contingent of vamps and a handful of creatures made of what looked like living flame. Wisps, if I recalled correctly from my time up in Canada. That explained the melted door.

Another of the rock monsters charged me and I ducked down, remembering one of my favorite wrestling moves. Once he hit me straight on, I straightened up and launched him over my back, nearly giving myself a hernia in the process. These things were a lot heavier than they looked, and I was currently my weak, pansy-ass normal self.

No offense to the vamps in the room, but I would need to remedy that if I wanted to survive.

There was no sign of the other Draculas. Alex had apparently split up his forces to better battle the threat.

Wherever he was, I hoped he was getting his fucking skull bashed into paste.

Bad karma thoroughly shared, I jumped into the fight, looking for my partner. The battle here seemed to be turning toward the side of the vamps. That was a relief - kinda. Unfortunately, no matter which way you looked at things, I was falling short on allies. I couldn't afford to lose those I had.

"Freewill!" a vampire shouted, running up to me. "Let us destroy these invaders together."

Finally, someone who was on my side. It was nice to see my reputation wasn't entirely tarnished. I grinned and he returned the gesture.

I turned away, looking for an enemy to engage, too late registering the obsidian smile flashed back at me. Oh fuck.

The fist that hit the side of my head was human-sized and shaped, but felt like it was made of rock - probably because it was. I hit the floor and slid across it to land in a heap against one of the serving counters. I shook my head to clear it as the faux vamp charged.

Crap! Maybe we weren't winning as handily as I'd thought. Thinking quickly, I reached up for anything I could use as a weapon, desperately hoping not to grab a handful of plastic forks. Instead, I brought down a shower of trays onto my head. Ouch! Make that a shower of those *metal* mess trays they used in the military.

Oh well, when in Rome...

I grabbed hold of a bunch with both hands and swung just as the Jahabich launched himself at me. I hit him in the face with a solid clank, doing little damage but knocking him to the side nevertheless.

Now it was my turn. I quickly rolled to my feet and threw everything I had at the monster before he could either get up or resume his true form.

Back in grade school, I'd always been picked last for soccer, and for good reason - I kinda sucked. I still wasn't in any danger of being recruited by Manchester United, but I did have the freakish strength of the undead backing me up.

I connected solidly with the fucker's skull, breaking at least one toe in the process - fuck - but it did the job. The monster went flying and crashed against the wall, landing in a heap.

I was on the move again before it got back up - mentally chiding myself to keep an eye on their teeth lest I get bamboozled again. Once more and I might not get so lucky.

All around me, creatures clashed. Some fought silently, others snarled like animals locked in a fight for dominance...

"Oh, you want a fucking piece of me too?"

But only one displayed that snark I was so familiar with - Sally!

Her voice came from deep within the kitchen, so I hopped the counter and went looking for her amongst the stoves, deep fryers, and counters once meant to keep high-ranking muckety-mucks fed while the world burned above them. Wow, this place made my old kitchen nook back in Brooklyn look like...well, exactly what it was - a shit box in comparison.

A clanking noise caught my attention and I spotted Sally at the far end of the room, near another door. She had one of those rock monsters on the floor and was busy smashing its skull to dust with a length of pipe. It reminded me to be ever so subtle in my approach to her. We were still friends, but she didn't realize it, and that could lead to an awkward reunion involving such unpleasant things as my head being pulverized.

Unfortunately, before I could reach her, another of

those creatures did. This one tackled her from out of nowhere, its momentum carrying them both through the door.

No!

I raced forward, diving over a counter that stood in my way and knocking over an old heat lamp assembly. I guess I wouldn't be getting fries with that after all.

Scrambling back to my feet, I heard her cry out, "Get off me, you fucking freak. I'm gonna tear your...what the?"

"Oh, Lucinda, my dear. You have the most intoxicating way with words."

"Mark?"

Oh shit.

49

QUIT YER BITCHIN AND GET IN THE KITCHEN

Coincidence is a bitch, although a part of me knew that had nothing to do with it. Those things were after Ed. The easiest way to find him was to find one of his friends...a prospective girlfriend being a good choice, although I tried to push that little detail from my mind. Talk about complicating matters. Comparatively speaking, fighting was so much easier.

Now all I had to do was hope Sally remembered this guy was plotting to make her his goo-slave, jump in, kill the asshole, and hope she didn't bash my skull in as way of thanks.

Piece of cake. Yep, that's what I kept telling myself in the hope that I'd eventually believe it.

I reached the doorway and flattened myself against the wall next to it.

"How are you alive?"

"You didn't really think your little cave-in would stop us, did you?"

"Cave-in? What are you talking about?"

"The one you and your Freewill friend caused."

"I don't know what friend you're referring to, but I just met the creep."

Creep? What a bitch!

"If you're trying to fool me..."

"The last time I saw you..." Her voice trailed off for a moment - almost sounding sad. "I'm sorry, but you didn't give me a choice."

"Wait, what are you referring to?"

"The Jahabich. I didn't want things to end that way."

"Hold on, you mean you don't remember...just a few days ago?"

A part of me wanted to spring into action, but I hesitated for some reason. Oh, who was I kidding? I wanted to hear what they had to say - to hear if Sally still had feelings for this guy. If she did...

"Everything is fuzzy. I remember killing Marlene, taking over Pandora, but it feels like there are pieces missing, like maybe I hit my head too hard." Her voice suddenly hardened. "I do remember you trying to gut me in the sewers, though."

The previously sarcastic tone of Mark's voice changed, dropping down to a soothing quality. "I will admit to overreacting."

"Overreacting?"

Heh, shades of *Kill Bill*.

"Yeah. Don't forget I also had Marlene's orders constantly ringing in my ears. Thirty years of compelled anger is hard to shake off. You know exactly what I'm talking about. Don't pretend you don't. I heard stories about Jeff."

"Don't remind me about that asshole. So how did you survive?"

"The Jahabich. They're not what you think and they have access to...well, it's hard to explain. All I know is they freed me. They could do the same for you. Think about it,

Lu - no more covens, no more being a slave to compulsion."

Oh fuck. It was the sales pitch - conveniently leaving out the fact that while in his blockhead form, he was pretty much just another node on the network.

"No more compulsions..." She trailed off, almost wistfully. It reminded me of how good I had it, never knowing what it was like to be mind-fucked by another vampire into doing whatever the hell they pleased. Sally wasn't usually one to let her guard down, and let me tell you, she had shields that would have made the USS *Defiant* jealous, but every so often, I caught a glimpse. It was brief and usually followed up by something sarcastic that would kill the moment, but I was finally realizing the real Sally was a lot more complicated than just painted nails, a great wardrobe, and an attitude problem.

"Exactly. No bending to their will ever again. And we're going to win too. The vampires and those hairy monsters are both full of themselves, thinking the world will fall to one or the other. They don't realize there are other forces at play - stronger ones. *Older* ones. We can remake this world into a better place. Come with me, Lucinda, and let me show you."

Sally was silent for a moment, sending my "oh crap" meter into overdrive. Surely she wasn't actually considering it. The Sally I knew wasn't so quick to jump into bed with anyone...well, figuratively speaking, anyway. Even so, I knew next to nothing about this guy. What had their relationship been? If there had truly been a bond of love between them...

"I said it once before, Lucinda is dead. My name is Sally, and if you think I'm trading in the small bit of freedom I have to be some granite-covered freak, well, then it's time you stayed buried in my past."

Or not. Fuck, yeah!

Mark chuckled in response, his voice growing cold again. "A small part of me was hoping you'd say that." The sounds of feet shuffling could be heard. The time for talking was done.

I stepped around the corner and found the two squaring off in a storeroom. Shelves reached the ceiling, stacked with boxes of presumably non-perishable foodstuffs.

"You guys have room for a threesome?" Hmm, that line sounded distinctly less creepy in my head. I really needed to work on that.

Sally dropped her guard to stare incredulously at me. "You again? Don't tell me you were eavesdropping because I am gonna rip your balls...ugh!"

Mark wasn't quite so sentimental about their past that he was willing to overlook the opportunity for a good sucker punch. "Freewill," he greeted, showing me his blackened teeth.

"Well, if it isn't the ex. Let's see if we can finally sign those divorce papers."

"We were never married, asshole," Sally snarled from the floor right before slamming a kick into the side of Mark's knee - a blow that...that did nothing. He barely budged, not even losing his footing.

He grinned even wider. "I may look like my old self, bitch, but believe me, I've been upgraded."

That was the last straw. Nobody called Sally a bitch except for me, and maybe my other friends, and probably any vampires who outranked us, but definitely no sewer-dwelling rock assholes. One had to draw the line somewhere.

Before he could make another move against my friend, I threw myself at him in a dive tackle. *Oof!* He was right. He might've looked like someone who wouldn't be out of place around my gaming table, but he definitely had the heft of something made from a half-ton of gravel. Even so, we vampires aren't exactly lightweights ourselves. I might have bruised my shoulder in the process, but we both went down with me on top.

Oh, yeah!

At least until he threw me off of him like I weighed nothing.

"You little punk. Even if I wasn't better than I was before, I'm still older and stronger than you."

"Maybe so," Sally said, rising behind him - whole, if limping a bit. "But I brought you into the underworld." She followed up with a swing of that pipe she was still holding. It connected solidly and Mark went stumbling across the room. "And I can sure as shit take you out."

She glanced toward me and, for a second, I was worried she might decide that two nerdy guys needed to die this night, but then said, "You gonna just stand there staring at my tits or do you want to help me kill this asshole?"

"You are so hot when you're..."

She flashed her fangs at me.

"Which I mean in a purely platonic way, of course."

Unfortunately for us, Mark was barely even dazed. A large dent stood out on the side of his head, but it rapidly filled in...and then kept going as his form shimmered and thickened, his eyes collapsing in on themselves until all that remained was an empty orange glow. "*We will enjoy killing you both. Then we will find the pure one and deliver him.*"

"Over my dead body, asshole," I replied.

"*Your terms are accepted.*"

Oh shit.

Sally tilted her head slightly to the side. "Pure one?"

"Long story," I said as we backed out of the room and into the kitchen. I glanced around, hoping for reinforcements. Sadly, neither Gan nor Vargas were anywhere to be seen - same with the other combatants. It appeared the fighting had moved on without us.

"*Tell us where the pure one is.*"

"And you'll let us live?"

"*No, but your death will be painless...mostly.*"

Hell, it wasn't an entirely bad deal compared to what else I'd gotten that day, but still... "I hate to break it to you, Rocky, but he's not all that pure."

"*Mother wants him.*"

"Mommy will have to find a new plaything...oh, crap!"

Mark had used my own ploy against me, letting me banter until he'd closed the gap. I so hated when the bad guys studied up on this shit. Why couldn't they just stick to their clichés and die when they were supposed to?

Such speculation would have to wait, sadly. Spreading his clubs out to the side so as to maximize his reach, he came right at us. Being a chivalrous fellow, I moved to shove Sally out of the way, forgetting that she'd been in her fair share of scrapes. Before I could reach her, she nimbly leapt into the air, cartwheeling over Mark and leaving me right smack dab in the way of his charge.

Fortunately, a nice industrial-strength grill assembly eventually stopped his momentum, allowing him to smash me against it in a not-so-gentle fashion. Ouch. The wind knocked out of me, Mark closed his arms around my midsection in the kind of gentle embrace an angry grizzly might make against a lost hiker. The razor sharp shards protruding from him immediately tore into me. It was like being hugged by a giant blender. Blood began to drip from my body as I was slowly shredded from every direction.

Mark grinned, the smile on his pumpkin head nearly a foot across, every inch of it filled with rock-like daggers. He opened wide and leaned forward. I wound up with my right and punched him square in the face, mindful of not feeding him my hand.

Yeah, it felt about as good as punching a concrete wall.

He tightened his grip, then, just as suddenly, spun us both around.

Before I could wonder what he was doing, I saw stars as something collided into the back of my head with enough force to make me momentarily forget my name.

"Sorry," Sally said.

I would've admonished her to watch her fucking aim, but the only thing that came out of my mouth was a bloody gurgle as Mark put on the pressure. He once more moved in to give me the last hickey I'd ever receive. I grabbed hold with my claws on either side of his head and kept him at bay, but just barely. I had no leverage and the best parts of me were currently spilling out in rivulets

"Let him go, Mark."

So nice to see she cared..."ARGH!" Something snapped inside, a rib probably. It wasn't the first time I'd experienced that, but what made this especially excruciating was the feeling inside of me. I'm no doctor, but if I had to guess, I'd say a broken shard of bone was the culprit. It was jabbing against something in my chest and it hurt...*badly*. I didn't think I could stand if it got worse.

Oh no!

A rattling cough escaped my mouth, but I cut it off halfway to scream out again as the shard continued to scrape against my heart.

This was it. I was going to stake myself from the inside out. What a fucking...*OH GOD!*...what a fucking way to check out.

"Let him go and I'll surrender."

"*You will be mine regardless.*" A deep chuckle escaped its mouth.

"And I'll throw in the pure one."

Mark cocked his head to the side as if thinking. "*You do not know where he is,*" he concluded, calling her bluff.

"No, but I can sniff him out."

Mark didn't let up on the pressure, but he stopped making it worse for a moment. How nice of him to give me a couple of seconds to enjoy the agony as my body did what no enemy had been able to do so far. "*We will find him.*"

"Don't bullshit a bullshitter, lover," she said. "You would have done so already. I can see you're a lot stronger now than you were, but I'm willing to bet you lost some things in the exchange." She tapped her nose. "Me, my sniffer works better than ever. I can find this pure one you're talking about. Then you'll have everything you wanted. You can take us down below and do whatever you want to us...*to me.*"

That last part had enough seductive intent to almost make me forget I was about to die horribly. She stepped up right behind me. I hoped it was to pry this fucker off, but she instead laid her head on my shoulder and...holy shit...ran her tongue down the side of my face ending at my earlobe. Of all the ways I'd thought I might die today, I'd never have guessed it would be with a mega-boner.

"What do you say?" she purred to him, her hot breath washing against my cheek. She reached around me and touched Mark's arm, running a finger across it, leaving drops of blood behind. "You'll have all eternity to prove to me you're as hard where it counts as the rest of you."

Mark's Jahabich form wavered. His body remained as it was, essentially a barbed-wire-covered vise grip that was currently crushing the life out of me, but his face changed back to its human guise.

He leaned forward, a sly grin on his face. "Oh, you have no idea the things I am going to do to you. If you thought I used to make you scream before, that will be nothing compared to what you are going to experience." The smile widened into something predatory. "But if it's all the same to you, I think I'm still going to kill this...guh!"

I drove my head forward into his, smashing my forehead directly into his nose. What's good for the goose is good for the asshole...or not. Mark might have looked human, but he wasn't soft and squishy like one. I nearly caved my skull in from the effort, my vision doubling and then tripling.

Three Mark heads swam in front of me, leaning back from the blow but looking a lot more pissed than hurt. Within a moment, they turned back into three wavering monster faces, their orange eyes...opening wide in surprise?

Just like that, Sally had used the distraction to leap over us and onto Mark's back. Ignoring the pain of being in contact with him, she extended her claws and drove both hands deep into his glowing eye sockets. These creatures didn't have eyeballs, at least none that I could see, but he still didn't like that - not one bit.

He threw back his head in a roar of rage...and then I was free, free to fall right down to the ground in a pool of my own blood. Yeah, that ought to do it.

I glanced up to see Sally holding on for dear life. The creature's girth prevented it from using its clubs against her for anything more than glancing blows. They probably hurt, but that was nothing for a seasoned vampire. The Jahabich freak next tried to spin its head around toward her, but she was wrist deep in its skull and had the leverage to keep it from doing so.

That left one thing for the monster to try...whirling around blindly in a rage and trying to smash her against whatever seemed solid.

There was no way she'd be able to hold on for long,

and then what? We'd be pummeled into pudding, that's what. On the upside, at least I wouldn't have to deal with Gan when she got back. It would also save me from further pontification by Alex. Maybe that wasn't such a bad...

No, that wasn't particularly positive thinking.

I wanted nothing better than to pass out for five or six days, but mind scrambled or not, Sally had still proven that, together, we were an unbeatable team. There was no way I'd let her down now.

Also, I had every intention of living long enough to recall the way her tongue had felt during my next session of *alone time*, if you get my drift.

I pushed up off the floor, once more crying out in pain as the shard of hurt continued to threaten popping the organ essential to my not turning into a pile of ash.

The sound of a collision caused me to glance over my shoulder. Sally still hung on, but Mark was pummeling her against every hard surface he could find. She was getting bloodier by the moment. There was no way she could hold out for long against such punishment.

I took a deep breath...well, really a shallow one. I was pretty sure I had a punctured lung in addition to all the other fun injuries my vampire healing was probably shaking its head in disbelief at. Gathering what little bit of power I had left, I crawled to the nearest wall and used it to brace myself as I clawed back to my feet. I lost my balance for a moment and found myself leaning against a massive steel refrigerator. Hmm, wonder if they had any cold cuts left. I sure as shit could've gone for a sandwich and a cold beer right about...wait a second.

A bloody smile crossed my lips. Fuck it all, it was worth a try.

"Yo, Marky Mark, let's finish this. The better man gets

to lay claim to your girlfriend, and I think we already know who that is."

He spun toward my voice, teeth grinding together and making a most uncomfortable sound. Sally's head also whipped in my direction, but I put a finger to my lips - hoping she took the hint and kept any snark to herself.

She didn't.

"When this is over, I want you to tear my panties off with your fangs and take me on top of this asshole's corpse."

Uh...okay.

With my current injuries, I really couldn't afford for blood to start rushing to my crotch, so I did my best to think unsexy thoughts...Gan handcuffing me to a bed...yeah, that did it.

Unfortunately, it almost did me too. Mark was rushing blindly toward my position, driven into a frothing rage by Sally's disturbingly X-rated taunts. A few more moments of daydreaming and I'd have been pulverized.

He was nearly within range, so I grabbed the back of the refrigerator and shoved...

...and it didn't budge. What the fuck?!

Oh shit, he was almost on me.

I quickly gave the fridge a once over. Was the fucking thing bolted to the floor? No, as it turned out, it was bolted to the *wall*. Goddamned nuclear bunkers. Did they need to take every fucking precaution under the sun?

"Any year now," Sally growled, trying her best to slow him down.

"Working on it."

I grabbed hold of the appliance again and heaved with everything I had, definitely not doing my innards any good. Motherfucking military-grade bolts!

Finally, though, a squeal of metal on metal rang out as the mooring started to pry lose.

Unfortunately, I was also out of time. Homing in on our banter, Mark took a massive swing, intent on making sure one couldn't tell where my head ended and the metal of the refrigerator began.

I ducked, and he hit it on the side full on - leaving a dent big enough to have fit my cranium had I been obliging enough to stay put.

He wasn't finished, though. Apparently tired of the blonde monkey on his back, he spun and slammed Sally into the front of the appliance with a massive crunch.

Oh no!

That was more than even she could take. Battered and bloodied, she started to lose her grip on his back.

He must have sensed this too, because once more, his form shimmered and, this time, his hands resumed their human guise. He reached back, grabbed a handful of her hair, and slammed her over his shoulder into the floor.

I still wasn't in very good shape, but I managed to stand up straight, ready to do whatever it took to save her. I stepped forward to engage him, only to receive a contemptuous backhand that sent me crashing into the wall.

Mark, his eyes now free of fist-shaped debris, completed his transformation back to his human-looking self. He glanced at me, chuckled, and then turned away as if I was no threat. Unfortunately, he was probably right in that regards.

"Now, little Lucinda, I believe you and I have a long overdue date with destiny."

I steadied myself for another charge, hoping maybe this time was the charm, when something out of the corner of my eye caught my attention. Holy crap. Whatever damage Mark had inflicted upon the fridge had actually freed it from its mooring. There was no time to lose.

I had no idea if she was still conscious or not, but I

couldn't afford to wait. I grabbed hold of the heavy structure and pushed with everything I had left. "Sally, move!"

Amazingly, she rolled to the side as Mark spun around just in time to see several hundred pounds of the finest in Uncle Sam's reserve of food storage devices topple down on him. He hit the floor, the fridge pinning him from the chest down, but I didn't have any delusions. That kind of weight might have crushed a human, but when dealing with beings of supernatural strength, such items were often a minor inconvenience at best.

Of course, even minor inconveniences could be fatal when a person such as myself, happily willing to take cheap shots at a downed foe, was around. Before Mark could topple the stainless steel box off of him, I stepped around and delivered a kick to his head that would've punted a Jeep onto its side.

Fuck me!

And pretty much broke all my toes in the process. It was worth it, though, as his head whipped to the side, stunned.

Limping badly, I debated my next move when I saw something being tossed in my direction. I caught it and looked up to see Sally had a similar hunk of metal in hand - having just torn the legs off a nearby table. She looked like hell - splattered in blood, clothes torn to shreds, and with numerous cuts and abrasions covering her. None of that diminished her in the slightest, though. She was still beautiful - perhaps more so than ever - her eyes shining with black fury as she stepped to the opposite side of Mark.

He blinked a few times, no doubt clearing the cobwebs, then focused on us just as she raised the weapon above her head.

"Consider this our official breakup, lover. Oh, and in case you were wondering, I faked every single time."

THE CLEANUP CREW

I felt safe in assuming that would be the last time Mark darkened our doorstep, unless someone happened to wander by with a shitload of industrial-strength epoxy. A part of me felt a bit of regret, though. Despite Sally's iron exterior, I could tell offing her ex had been more a necessity than something she truly wanted to do. I also doubted the Jahabich as a whole would be so easily dissuaded from coming after Ed, for whatever asshole reasons they had, but for now, I could at least try to be comforting.

As we limped away from the scene of the battle, I put a hand on her shoulder. "Hey, if you want to talk, I just want you to know..."

In one violent action, she grabbed me by my shirt and shoved me against the wall - hard enough to make me wish I'd waited until I was fully healed before saying anything.

"Just because we fought off my asshole ex together doesn't mean we're friends. I want you to listen and listen well. I am not a nice person. I killed my own sister, ripped her still beating heart out of her fucking chest. I have no problem doing the same thing to you if you piss me off."

Whoa. I didn't know that. Of course, she could have just been acting all tough to try to keep her bitch queen reputation intact. Still, something in her eyes told me I didn't want to pick that moment to push my luck.

"Do I need to repeat myself?"

"Nope." I held my hands up in surrender. "Heard you loud and clear." It wasn't that I was worried about her killing me right then, but she was in prime position to smash her knee into my two best friends in the world.

"Good, just so there's no confusion on the subject." She turned and took a few steps further down the hall.

"You really don't remember anything, do you?" It was a stupid question and I knew it. Alex himself had compelled her. If he had said her name was Bonzo the dancing monkey, she'd be doing cartwheels and begging for bananas. Even so, one couldn't blame a guy for trying.

"I..." Her eyes faded from focus for a moment, as if she was doing some internal soul searching. "I don't know. It's all a jumble. Some memories are clear as day, but with others, it's just fog. I do know one thing, though." She pointed a clawed finger at me. "I don't remember your face in any of them, and something is telling me to stay away from you."

"And you would be wise to heed that advice, my darling child."

We both turned to see Alex step round a corner. His outfit was smudged and his hair slightly mussed, but he otherwise appeared fresh as a daisy. He was also alone.

I stopped dead in my tracks, a deer in the headlights. Had I not gotten the piss recently beaten out of me, I was certain it would now be running down my leg.

"Lord Alexander," she said, dropping to one knee. I

found myself wondering if he'd had something to do with that as well. Under other circumstances, she'd have been about as likely to flip him off as curtsey.

"Rise, child," he replied dismissively, smiling at me. "As I was saying, this one is a sower of discord. Where he steps, chaos blooms. That he has allied himself with the Shining One is fair testament to that."

I stood my ground, my eyes darting left and right. Where the fuck was...

"If you are hoping for Lady Gansetseg's timely arrival, you can spare yourself the trouble."

"What did you do to her?"

"Do not be so melodramatic. Our attackers are being routed as per my strategy. I merely ordered her to assist Vargas in his continued offensive to purge them from these halls. Interestingly enough, the resolve of our foes seems to have wavered in the past several minutes. Nevertheless, I expect my forces to be busy for a while yet."

That was interesting. I knew they'd been after Ed, but I had to wonder how much of Mark's insane desire for revenge had been leaking upstream, polluting their network, and keeping them going even after it became obvious they had no idea where he was. "They'll be back."

"Oh, and you have some insight into this?"

"Not really, but I know assholes. They always seem to find a way to pop up again."

Alex actually chuckled, his knowing grin evident he most certainly got my little double entendre. "I have never lied to you, Freewill. What I said stands. Your unique way of communicating is truly a breath of fresh air."

"Yeah, and he seems to like doing it a lot," Sally commented. Bitch.

"Indeed."

"Oh, so you've never lied. Well then, I'm free to go?"

"How so?"

"Didn't you say you'd let us go if we went on your little suicide mission?"

"I said no such thing. I offered you clemency, if you will recall my exact words."

"Well, then..."

"And I believe I also stated our truce would hold only so long as none of our kind fell to the Icon's blade. I dare say, poor Thea might take offense if I were to fail to uphold that part of the pact."

"Yeah, but you're the motherfucker who..."

"Be mindful, Freewill. I am tolerant of you to a degree, but the First do not take lightly to accusations. We are above reproach."

Translation: *I am above the law.*

Goddamn it. Would any vampires even fucking believe me if I tried?

Sally? Maybe if she ever found all her missing marbles.

Gan? Fuck, she was so insanely infatuated I could have told her I hated corn and she'd have run off to Kansas and killed every farmer in sight. That was about it, though. At the end of the day, anyone else who had doubts would probably keep their mouths shut and toe the party line.

"So, I'm fucked."

"That depends on one's point of view. I still have use for your power. I suspect the beast inside of you merely slumbers, waiting for the right moment to awaken. We have lost much today, so I do not feel particularly selfish in claiming you as a prize."

I backed up a step. Oh crap.

"I believe an appropriate penance will be for you to resume your training from before you escaped the Chateau."

"What are you...?"

"Hush, child," he said dismissively to Sally before addressing me again. "Despite being under no pretense to do so, I will also grant you the boon of clemency I promised. It will be painless for your human friend and the Icon."

I raised an eyebrow to that.

"The witch," he continued, "sadly, she did not survive the battle, a story which will appease her people. As for the *oddity*, he warrants further study."

"I won't..."

"You will not what? Let me? Boy, you are alone against the First of the First. You have no chance of escape, no hope of victory, and no allies to call upon."

I brought up a hand and began to rub my right arm as if massaging my sore muscles. He was right on those first two, but maybe not so on the last.

"Only use it if you get in trouble."

"I'm not bringing you into a fight. That's final."

"Fine, then use it after you find Sally. That'll be our cue to get out of here."

That, I happily agreed to.

Christy had pulled me aside before Gan and I had left. I figured it was to wish me luck, thus I was a bit taken aback when she rolled up her sleeve and cut her wrist using a sliver of broken glass she'd procured from somewhere.

"What the hell are you doing?" I whispered. "I'm fine now. You don't have to worry about me..."

"Relax; I'm not. That room is warded. I can't send us to your location while we're inside, but that also means I won't be able to scry on you either to see if you're okay. I think this will get through, though."

As I raised a quizzical eyebrow, she dipped one finger into the blood and began to trace a symbol onto her forearm with it.

"I repeat, what are you doing?"

"Blood magic, similar to the wards I set up while you were at Sheila's place. Not my specialty, mind you. Most of it is used for...not very nice things, but I know a few tricks. It's powerful stuff; should be enough to get through even in there. Roll up your sleeve."

"Why?"

"Just do it and don't argue." Her voice had the tone of someone who would be just as happy to flash fry me than receive "no" for an answer.

"Okay, okay..." I did as she asked, ready for her to slice me too, but she merely repeated the action with her blood, drawing a matching symbol on me. "This isn't going to burn off my arm or anything, is it?"

"Hopefully not."

Yeah, that filled me with all sorts of confidence. I took a moment to look over what she had traced on my forearm. Odd - it looked vaguely familiar, as if I'd seen it or something similar before. I told her as much.

"Oh?" she asked, surprised. "You can read Enochian?"

"Enochian?"

"Angelic script." Seeing my eyebrows arch, she explained, "It's just called that. It's the secret language of spell crafters. We've used it for thousands of years. As for the angel part, you get a few normal people who see it written down, then watch us do our thing and they tend to jump to conclusions."

"Oh, that's kinda...disappointing."

"Real life often is, compared to fantasy."

I held my tongue from asking if that applied to Tom too. I had a feeling that would just get me another harsh glare. "So what's it do?"

"If something happens or you need us, smudge the symbol. It's my blood, so the sister ward on my arm will instantly react to it. Assuming those monsters aren't busy battering down our door, we can step outside and I can bring us right to you."

"It's too dangerous," I protested, which brought us full circle to Christy's plan for using it as our signal to vamoose.

Alex took another step toward me and I continued pretending to scratch an itch that wasn't there. I hated to bring my friends here, as this was even worse than the potential danger I'd been trying to avoid, but it sounded like they were up shit's creek anyway. Better to face our fate together than alone and not knowing what had happened to each other. Hopefully, they'd even agree with that logic.

I glanced over at Sally. Her eyes met mine and she inclined her head apologetically, not that I blamed her. There were some fights you took your chances with and others...well, others, you stepped aside rather than get steamrolled. At least she didn't look happy about things.

Come on, now's not the time to take the scenic route.

"I will offer you this, Freewill. Come with me now and I shall ensure the circumstances surrounding your arrival and detention are not entirely unpleasant."

"It can either be the easy way or the hard way, eh?" A twinkle of light appeared in my periphery, growing quickly until it surrounded us all. *Finally!* "Think I'll choose the hard way."

The lights coalesced into the forms of my friends. Even better, they were smart enough to realize they were probably heading into unfriendly territory. Christy and Sheila both materialized with their powers aglow around them - ready to rumble if necessary. Awesome!

"You rang?" Tom asked jovially - the doofus.

Probably my favorite part, though, was the momentary look of surprise that appeared on Alex's face. It wasn't much, appearing for just a moment, but I'd finally done something he hadn't been anticipating. I could die happy now, although, hopefully, that wouldn't be the case.

His eyes narrowed. Sheila and Christy had appeared on opposite sides, flanking him. Tom and Ed...well, they were smart enough to step back upon catching sight of who we were facing off against.

"Do you think this changes your fate in the slightest?" Alex asked smugly.

"I think this is us taking our fate into our own hands," Sheila replied, the white glow around her strong and steady.

Christy had appeared closest to Sally. She glanced at me and then at my partner. "You two okay?"

"Been a bit of a day," I replied.

When Sally didn't immediately answer, Christy hesitantly asked, "Sally?"

"The lights are on..." I commented.

"Fuck you, cock," Sally spat.

"As amusing as it is to allow you the illusion of superior positioning here," Alex said, "it is time to end this farce." He smiled and opened his mouth.

I felt the familiar sensation in the back of my skull, but where before it was usually a tingling, now began the tremblings of an earthquake - one that had the potential to shake my skull apart. Alex was about to send out a compulsion, one with everything he had by the feel of it.

Oh fuck!

"Lord Alexander!" a voice shouted from down the hall, startling us all.

Just as quickly as it'd started, the tingle died down as all of us, the mighty lord of the Draculas included, turned to find James striding down the hall in our direction. At his side were both Vargas and - of course - Gan. Two dozen vampire guards, with a few oddball creatures strewn about in the mix, followed.

I glanced back at my friends and, wisely, they stood down. Being all charged up with energy while surrounding the high fuck-meister himself probably would not do us any favors. Alone, we barely stood a ghost of a chance against Alex, but with reinforcements in the vicinity, that dropped to a big fat goose egg.

Gan ran ahead of the rest and practically threw herself into my arms - or would have if I'd bothered to catch her. Instead, the demonic little ankle biter latched on with a bear hug that rivaled what Mark had been trying to do to me. Fuck...and those ribs were just about healed too.

I tried not to look at my friends. Despite the dire seriousness of the situation, I knew they were all smirking like morons.

Gan pulled back and glanced around. "I am happy that you survived, beloved, and I see that you have found your whore."

"Hold on," Sally said, her eyes narrowing. "Are you talking about me?"

Thankfully, Alex spared us that ugly scene. "What is the meaning of this, Wanderer? I ordered...requested...that you take charge of the counterattack." His slip-up definitely did not go unnoticed. Was it possible the events of the day had ruffled even his legendarily stoic feathers?

Unfortunately, James decided not to acknowledge the snafu. "It is done. There are straggles of resistance remaining, but the others are hunting them down as we speak. The main force, however, is in retreat. I have to admit it's odd, though. One moment, they seemed resolute to fight to the last, and then the next, they had all but given up."

Alexander seemed to debate what to say next. He could technically still do to us whatever the fuck he wanted to and the others probably couldn't say shit. On the flip side, vampire politics were a fucked up lot - all sorts of bullshit ceremony and such. "Any victory should not be frowned upon."

"I agree, but it was a costly one."

"Indeed," Vargas agreed. "We haven't counted the dead yet..."

"Fodder is easily replaced," Alex interrupted. "Now if you'll excuse..."

"I beg to differ," James said. "We lost many dignitaries from amongst our allies, not the least of which were the humans." He glanced over at me on that one. I pretended to find something interesting on the wall to study. "They are even now demanding answers. Druaga himself..."

"Fled during the first moments."

"He has returned and is demanding to know who is accountable for the lapse in security when he was assured this facility was nigh unbreachable."

"I am not sure I like your tone, Wanderer."

James appeared to consider things. He glanced sideways at Vargas, who made it a point to look at his shoes. Finally, just as I was about to think he was gonna puss out, he said, "I believe the First have more important matters than tone to deal with, dear brother. Those recruits betrayed us. How is that even possible? They were insulated, compelled to loyalty."

"I am well aware of that." The cadence of Alex's voice was rapidly turning to one of annoyance. Despite his bullshit about the First being a council of equals, it was plainly obvious that was shit on toast. "Our enemy, The Destroyer, is..."

"Is simply not that powerful," James interrupted. A murmuring began in the ranks behind him. He quieted them with a glance, but I found myself wondering if both his appearance and choice of topics were not quite as coincidental as I had initially assumed.

"To defeat one...maybe even more of us...is conceivable. But to overcome our combined measures? That speaks of power that, even as a Freewill, he should not have in his possession. Then there is the concern of the Jahabich. They are creatures of chaos. Why did they attack us here, and how has Vehron allied himself with them?"

"We do not know that to be true, Wanderer. The traitors may have simply seen an opening and a mutual enemy."

"Then why didn't those assholes just steamroll Farley and his pig-fucker buddies?" All eyes in the wide expanse of hallway turned toward me. I really needed to remember to keep my fucking mouth shut during times like these.

Alex's eyes actually flashed black, but James spoke up before he could order the masses to shit-stomp me. "Dr. Death has a valid point, even if he expressed it a bit colorfully. This was an unforeseen alliance. It means all of our assumptions may have been incorrect. Our intelligence has been compromised, as has our integrity. The entire war effort is in jeopardy while..."

"Integrity, Wanderer?" Alex asked, an eyebrow raised. "A curious word to use. I would ask what you mean by it."

Oh crap. During the discourse, my friends had all gravitated closer to me. I glanced around and met the eyes of my roommates. They both echoed what I'd been thinking. Whatever James was doing seemed purposeful, but he'd possibly just taken it a step too far - shown his trump card before he was ready. He'd just potentially declared himself an enemy to Alex's cause - something that had already cost two other Draculas their lives today.

James seemed to realize his misstep. He paused just long enough to let doubt slip in to the crowd, but before he could say more, Alex continued. "While we speak of integrity, I am forced to question your own. Your arm. Have you forgotten your penance - your vow of absolution in the wake of your failure?"

Fuck me, but I am an unobservant dickhead sometimes. I hadn't even realized that James was sporting both of his arms again - the appendage having obviously grown back sometime during the fight.

That started the gathered masses muttering again. Vargas glanced sidelong at James and took the slightest step away as if distancing himself.

Just like that, Alex had turned the tide back against...

"I believe the Wanderer has earned his absolution in full."

The entire assembly turned at the sound. I was no exception, craning my neck to look past Alex. It wasn't possible. The voice that had made the statement belonged to a dead man.

Despite that certainty, Yehoshua strode down the hall toward us. He was battered to all hell, his clothes practically rags hanging from his body, but he walked tall and resolute. In his wake followed three more of the First and their own contingent of soldiers.

Alex was facing their direction, but I caught a look at his profile, and he was as utterly gobsmacked as the rest of us. Fuck, yeah. If I could bottle that look, I'd enjoy a glass of it on every holiday.

"You..."

"I am of the First. We do not die so easily," Yehoshua said.

Alex's mask of neutrality quickly dropped back down. "So I see."

"Hold on," I said, once more risking a beating for

interrupting dudes who outranked and outclassed me by a shit-ton. "I saw you fall into their arms. How do we know...?" I let the question linger even though I hated to do it. One didn't turn their nose up at a potential lifeline when it was offered, but I knew the tricks the Jahabich had at their disposal. If even one of them managed to infiltrate the most powerful group of vampires on the planet, we might as well all snap off broomsticks and shove them up our asses until they impaled our hearts.

"Jackass here is right," Sally said, her head tilting to the side as if remembering. "Those things can impersonate..."

"Be at peace, my friends." He smiled, showing off his teeth - his gleaming white, *normal* teeth.

I could have filled up one of the Macy's Day balloons with my sigh of relief.

"Landing in the arms of the enemy," he continued, "does not mean falling before them. It simply means one must prove their mettle that much more thoroughly." He stepped forward, joined by the others of the First. There were seven currently present, a majority. He stopped and faced Sheila. "What I find odder than my survival, however, are the circumstances which made it necessary."

"It was an accident." She opened her mouth to say more, but Yehoshua held up a hand.

"That I believe. I heard the gunshot before the door was shut upon me."

He turned toward Alex. "Curious that it came from one of our own while a truce was in effect."

"Yet another traitor," Alex replied. "He was immediately dispatched for his disloyalty."

"We seem to have a problem with traitors, I would say," James added, earning a nasty glare from Alex.

"Indeed," Yehoshua replied. "Even more so since none of our elite guard have been to the compromised prefecture. It is most concerning."

"What are you implying, brother?" Alex asked, his tone dangerous.

"Nothing, my friend. We are of the First and above reproach, after all. I do believe it warrants investigation, though."

"I would beg to differ. One lone dissident among the bunch shouldn't require such an expenditure of resources in these dire times."

"Perhaps you are right," Yehoshua said with a measured smile. "But we must not forget this day as we move forward to repair the bridges sundered."

And there it was. I was no mind reader, but I was pretty sure that Yehoshua and James had more or less just backed Alex into a corner. They were all "above reproach," as each had said, thus any divide between them - anything that could cause doubt within the masses - would be a massive blow to Alex's efforts. No amount of compulsion could contain that kind of dissent forever.

A moment passed, feeling more like an eternity, when Yehoshua asked, "Theodora?"

Oh fuck.

Alex immediately regained his composure. Though his expression was grim, his eyes sparkled as he delivered the news. "Slain..."

Oh shit!

"...by the Shining One."

Alex pointed a finger and a collective gasp rose from the crowd, except maybe from Gan, who continued staring lovingly at me - little freak. Unfortunately, there was that beyond reproach thing again, this time biting us right in the ass.

"I mourn for my sister, but I say it is fortuitous you

have all arrived when you did, for I was just informing the Icon and her thrall," Alex looked directly at me, "that her treachery effectively nullified our truce. You yourself saw us when you arrived, Wanderer, did you not? She and the witch were poised to attack, hoping to add yet another of the First to the scores of those slain today. Can you deny it, brother?"

I hoped to Hell James would, for once, drop protocol and tell Alex to go take a flying leap onto an eighteen-inch studded iron dildo, but he simply shook his head. "I cannot."

"Then I say, before we can move forward, before we can regain the trust of our allies, before we can once again reassure the world that the First are unbowed and unbroken, we must conclude the matter for which we have gathered. The Icon and, by virtue of their association, the Freewill, the witch, and the two humans must be judged. I say they are guilty. Who amongst you disagree?"

Fuck me. This wasn't good. Alex might be in deep shit, but he was still a good swimmer while my friends and I all had hundred-pound anchors around our necks. Worse, Sheila's aura of faith started to form around her. Don't get me wrong - I'd fight and gladly die by her side, but I really didn't want to...at least, not that death part.

No voices dissented, so I raised my hand in a desperate bid to do anything to change our course. "If I might..."

"You may not." Alex's voice was iron - cold, victorious iron. "You forfeited any say in the matter the second you allied yourself with this creature. And for what - love? An emotion for foolish children, nothing more."

Hey! I resemble that remark!

Sheila glanced toward me. Our eyes met and hers held resolve in them. I desperately mouthed "Wait" to her, hoping for some flash of inspiration, but I could see the sadness in her eyes as she gave but a single shake of her head.

"I sentence you to..."

"Wait!" Yehoshua cried, his eyes darkening and his fangs descending. "You speak of love dismissively, Alexander, but I know its wonderfully cruel sting. This abomination has taken from me one who was more than sister in darkness. I claim right of vengeance."

"Such is his right."

"I am well aware of our laws, Wanderer," Alex spat. He took a moment and composed himself again, but I could see it was taking some effort. "Vengeance is yours, Brother Yehoshua, so swears Alexander of Macedon. The sentence is death, but I grant you their execution. Dispatch them as you will."

Yehoshua stepped forward, eyes still blackened. Sheila raised her sword and her body erupted into white flame. I stepped to her side, close enough to char my skin. Ed took up a spot alongside of me, and Christy and Tom did likewise opposite us.

"It's been fun, guys."

"A fucking blast," Tom replied, grinning, of all things.

"I know this is bad timing," I turned to Sheila, "but before we die, you really need to know how much I lo..."

"I will not dirty my hands upon these creatures," Yehoshua said.

"What?" Sheila asked, her head alternating between the two of us.

"Huh?" I muttered, quickly averting my gaze from her piercing silver eyes.

Yehoshua took a step back and addressed the crowd. "Their sentence is death, but the method is mine to choose." He looked back toward us, and his eyes had turned back to their normal brown. I expected to see rage smoldering within them, but instead I saw...understanding. "I sentence the Shining One to death at the hands of Vehron the Destroyer. Let these two cancers destroy each other."

"What?!" Alex roared. "You cannot..."

"The right is mine, and my right is beyond reproach, Alexander of Macedon. Do you deny that? Do you break your oath?"

Alex's own fangs descended, but he held his tongue. All eyes, especially those of the present First, were on him and he knew it.

"Very well," Yehoshua continued. "Her allies are similarly sentenced. They will go forth and face the monster that has breached our walls today. May justice be served in whatever outcome fate so chooses."

Murmurs of assent were heard throughout the crowd. I couldn't believe it. In one fell swoop, we were back on the path we'd originally planned on, this time with the blessing of the folks in charge - sorta.

I turned to Sheila. "What do you say? I know you didn't want to do things this way."

She considered this for a moment before answering. When she did, it was slow and deliberate. "I didn't want to be the aggressor, turn into a monster. But if this vampire is the cause of all of this, then he's a threat to everyone - innocent or not. I say let's do this."

I smiled and made to give her a thumbs-up, but she wasn't finished.

"Also, I really want to hear the rest of what you were trying to say back there."

"Uhh..."

"Think about it. I'm sure the words will come back to you."

"This all makes for fine theater," Alex said, barely concealed contempt in his voice, "but we cannot trust them to stay true to their path. To let them walk free without..."

"If I may, Lord Alexander," James said.

"You wish to accompany them? I will not allow it."

"Nor would I ask it. There is far too much to be done. The First are no longer whole, and that must be remedied. I was simply going to nominate a trusted minder to oversee that the sentence is carried out."

Gan looked up at me, a big smile on her face. Oh no, not her.

"Sally."

"What? You cannot be serious," Alex spat.

"Indeed I am," James replied. "You yourself exonerated her, proclaimed her loyal to our cause. I will likewise vouch for her integrity. I dare say she is also experienced with the foes who attacked us today. Should they indeed be allied with the Cult of Ib, she will prove most useful in devising an appropriate response."

"Wait a second," Sally said, a wary look on her face. "I don't mean to be disrespectful, but I'm pretty sure I'm not the right person for this job."

"I concur with the whore," Gan added unhelpfully.

"Quite the contrary," James replied, ignoring the munchkin. "You are the perfect choice for all the reasons I stated."

"But..."

"As far as protecting our charge, would I be overstepping my bounds, Brother Yehoshua, if I were to include as part of their sentence that the accused are to make every effort to guarantee our emissary's safety?"

"Please indulge yourself, Wanderer."

"So be it." James turned to me. "Freewill, Icon, Magi, and...friends, know that should any harm come to Sally, whatever extension your pitiful lives have been granted, shall be immediately forfeit."

Maybe it was me, but I could have sworn James threw a quick wink my way. Whatever the case, I quickly nodded my assent. "I swear, my life for hers." Glancing back toward Sally, I saw her roll her eyes.

There was hope for us yet. It wasn't much and we were certainly walking into a far more dangerous situation than we'd originally thought.

Even so, it was better than nothing. We had a chance and I, for one, was going to take it.

THE MAGICALLY MYSTIFYING
EPILOGUE

I never thought I'd be so glad to sit on our cheap-ass couch. Once my ass was planted, though, I could have stayed there for an eternity. I really needed a shower, still clad in my burnt up body armor. My clothes smelled like they were close to gaining sentience, but they'd hold for a bit longer.

More bickering had ensued in the underground halls of the bunker, lasting long enough so that eventually more, including the rest of the Draculas, joined us. I wasn't overly pleased to see several other high-ranking dick-biscuits had likewise survived the onslaught, Colin and François chief among them, but that's the problem with bad pennies - they keep turning up. Maybe that wouldn't be the case for long, though. It was hopefully only a matter of time before someone remembered that Colin had been the one to coordinate our arrest - including the assignment of Farley and his buddies. I had a feeling that particular checkmark wouldn't look all that great on his undead résumé.

Couldn't happen to a nicer asshole.

Alex, unfortunately, would be a much bigger problem.

Though he'd been momentarily outmaneuvered by James and Yehoshua, I had a feeling any loss of face on his part would be temporary at best. From what little bit of history I'd read up on him, he was the type who made sure that whoever gave him a bloody nose got their face chopped off in return. If I hadn't made an enemy of him before, I sure as shit had now.

Sadly, a lot of questions were still left unanswered. I'd hoped for a chance to speak with James before departing, but Christy had ixnayed that. The moment the majority of the Dracs agreed to our *sentence*, she'd ordered us to link hands - making a point of grabbing Sally's, despite her protests. Before we'd even had a chance to offer the Draculas a complimentary "fuck you" as way of goodbye, she'd zapped us out of there.

I'd been a bit worried at first about our destination. We materialized in an empty room, standing in a metal circle inlayed into the floor. It wasn't until we stepped out in the hall that the familiar beaten-down wood paneling registered and I realized we were back home in Brooklyn.

Christy had been drained from the effort and needed to go sit down for a bit. I think she was also bummed to find the place empty - no sign of her new coven about. Seemed the Grand Mentor had been thorough in his attempt to fuck her over. It was small comfort, but at least Gan had made sure he died wishing he'd invested in a couple of horcruxes before showing up and pointing fingers.

Speaking of Gan, I was happy to say she wasn't one of the zappees who joined us in New York. Sadly, before we could disappear, she'd thrown out the threat that she'd see me again soon.

So I had that to look forward to.

The next hour or so involved us settling back in as best we could. Manhattan was still a fucking mess as far as my roommates could tell me, but life in Bay Ridge was relatively normal - comparatively, at least, and only so long as one was smart enough to only venture out during the day. Regardless, I'd take it.

Even better, I'd found a message waiting for us on our answering machine. It was from Kara. She passed on her greetings to her brother and left a pathetically thinly coded message - no doubt for the rest of us - about how she'd settled down in Sacramento with some *friends*. I guess the apple really didn't fall far from the tree.

I reclaimed my old bedroom, tossing some of Tom's shit out into our living room. It was decided the girls would share a similar apartment on the floor below ours for now. What a fucking odd couple pairing that was going to make - a brainwashed vampire, a hormonal witch, and their legendary enemy, the Icon. A part of me was tempted to set up a few cameras for my own personal closed circuit TV. However, I had a feeling that would just get me killed sooner than expected.

Oh well, it was only temporary anyway. The plan was to spend a few days getting our shit together and then trying to figure out what the fuck we were going to do.

As much as I wanted to curl up in my room and ignore the rest of the world, it wasn't wise to stay put for long. The Draculas would almost certainly keep an eye on us, even if we could somehow figure out how to unfuck Sally's brain.

There were also the Jahabich to consider. Mark and his insane need to be a psycho ex-boyfriend stalker might've been dead, but I didn't fool myself for a second thinking those monsters would stop. They wanted Ed for some purpose, and we had no reason to believe they'd give up anytime soon.

"You might've been better off letting the Dracs keep you locked up, dude," Tom said as the three of us discussed it in our living room over cold beers.

I could've shed tears of joy as I took a sip. Christy's sisters might have ditched us, but they'd left intact all of the magical trappings they'd put in place - including a weird glowing ball of energy in the basement that had somehow been wired into the main circuit breaker. I wasn't sure how long it would last, but it beat the piss out of having to gas up a generator every few hours.

"Yeah," Ed replied with a snort, "because being surrounded by a bunch of arrogant asses who would probably take it out on me every time Bill fucked them over would be loads of fun."

"Better than being tossed in a pool of orange goo," I remarked.

"Can't argue there."

"I'm surprised they even let you go," Tom said to him. "You'd have made a pretty good bargaining chip."

"I find that odd too," I added. "Hell, they could have at least ransomed your ass. Might've gotten five or ten bucks for it."

"Very funny." Ed took a long pull from his bottle. "I was wondering about that too. Truth be told, in those last few minutes, I was close to shitting a brick, thinking they'd let everyone go but me."

"Wouldn't have happened."

"Speak for yourself," Tom said. "I'm pretty sure Christy was done with that fucking place, no matter who was hopping on the bus."

"I'm glad we didn't have to find out." Ed leaned forward in his seat. "Honestly, I have no fucking idea why they let me walk out of there."

"Maybe we should go with Occam's Razor," I said.

"Oh?"

"The simplest answer is that maybe they just didn't know."

"How so?" Tom asked.

"Those things kidnapped Ed from Pandora, but none of us had a clue why - hell, we still don't. Bottom line, though, is that Sally and I were the only others to walk out of there. They never found Ed in their raid on the bunker, and the only one who talked about it was Mark. I honestly don't think the Draculas had much reason to even begin to suspect they were after you."

"Oh, then why was I made an honorary vampire?"

"That one is still bugging me. It's possible James was just protecting you until he could figure out *what* you are." I wasn't sure I believed that, though. Sally had told me James was also the one who'd originally assigned her to Pandora - primarily to keep the Jahabich in check. He knew about those things and had at least some inkling as to their threat. But then why would he purposely send Ed to a place within their reach?

I had no idea on that one. Again, I wished there'd been time to catch up with him before departing. Sadly, the chances of him talking freely while surrounded by thousands of years' worth of pompous douchebags was probably low.

We sat there in silence for a moment contemplating this. I was just about to offer the brilliant suggestion for another round of beers when the building seemed to rumble around us. It only lasted for a few moments, but a couple of items fell from their shelves, confirming it hadn't been our imaginations running wild.

What the?

"Earthquake?" Tom asked.

"No. It was too quick," Ed replied, his eyes opening wide. "I think that might have come from the girls' apartment."

There was a pause amongst us, no more than a second really. I'm sure each of us was thinking the same thing - just with different faces attached.

"Fuck! They've been roommates for less than an hour."

"I know," Ed said, getting to his feet. "We'd better get down there."

Each of the women in the apartment downstairs was capable of their own bit of violent mischief. The only question was who was to blame for taking the first shot.

As the lone member of our threesome with actual superpowers, outside of Ed's ability to bleed, I bounded down the stairs several steps ahead of my roommates.

Knowing the three inhabitants, I probably should have taken a moment and knocked. However, I panicked, thinking the worst, and grabbed hold of the doorknob just as it was opened from the inside. My momentum carried me forward and I ran right into Sheila, our faces ending up less than an inch apart...

For all of the second it took for her powers to activate.

Thankfully, my roommates were a bit slow in their charge downstairs, otherwise I'd have smashed into them with all the force of a speeding bus. Instead, I was *lucky* enough to hit the wall on the opposite side of the hallway - load-bearing, from the feel of it - making just as much of a racket as that which had brought us running to begin with.

"Sorry," Sheila said.

Maybe it was a good thing I hadn't gotten a chance to change my clothes yet. The cracked remains of the ceramic body armor absorbed at least some of the impact, making it just bone-jarring instead of bone-shattering.

"What happened?" Tom asked, ignoring me and

rushing toward the apartment. How comforting to know I had roommates who cared. Brought a tear to my eye.

Ed likewise raced past where I was stuck, embedded into the wall panels like some sort of modern art. At least I wasn't on fire this time. Guess Sheila's control really was getting pretty good after all.

Grumbling something nasty under my breath, I used my arms for leverage and heaved, freeing myself.

I got back to my feet just in time to hear Sheila say, "It's okay, guys. We're fine."

"Then why were you rushing out?"

"I wasn't. I was opening the door. Figured someone would be coming down to check."

"And blowing me up?" I asked.

"You surprised me," she replied sheepishly. "Bad timing."

"Story of my life."

"Okay, so what's going on, then?" Ed asked.

She stepped aside to let us in just as Christy emerged from one of the bedrooms.

"That was on me," she said, dusting herself off. "My bad."

"Are you okay?" Tom stepped up to her, grabbed her by her shoulders, and spun her around as if doing a half-assed medical exam.

"I'm fine. It was just a little magical feedback."

"A little?"

"The building is still standing, isn't it?"

"Where's Sally?" Ed and I asked in unison, both of us sounding a bit more than just curious.

"She's fine," Christy replied. "I was working with her, doing a little probing to see if maybe I could break the mental blocks Alexander erected."

"And that resulted in what...her blowing up?"

"Relax, Bill. It was just a reaction...kind of like playing with a microphone and getting feedback through the line."

I raised a skeptical eyebrow.

"Okay, maybe a bit more than that, but it sometimes happens when opposing forces meet. I had thought it was just a wall of sorts in her mind, something cutting off a part of her memories from the rest, so that's how I tried to hit it. Unfortunately, it turned out to be a bit more complex. He didn't just cause her to forget her past; he made her forget her association with all of us. The problem is that she hasn't spent all her time twenty-four/seven around us, so some of her recent memories are fine. She knows who she is and a good deal of what's been happening. In short, he didn't erect a wall as much a series of them all woven throughout her brain. It's pretty damn impressive."

"That's wonderful to know, but how is she?" Ed asked.

"She was confused and a little angry. She doesn't remember who we are, so she doesn't trust us."

"Assuming she trusted us to begin with," Tom commented.

"Speak for yourself, meatsack," I replied jokingly, then stopped myself. "Wait, what do you mean she *was* confused?"

Christy put her hands on her hips. "I didn't want to get gutted. I mean I'm worried about her, but I'm not stupid. So as a precaution before we started, I sorta knocked her out. I figured her subconscious mind might be more receptive to not lashing out. She's in there resting comfortably."

"Can I go see her?" Ed asked, the worry evident in his voice. I was tempted to follow his lead but still wasn't sure how to tread through that minefield.

Things were more complex than ever. To have feelings for two women...both of whom now, oddly enough, were under the same roof, was bad enough. That my roommate had eyes for one of them was gonna be tricky. Either way you looked at it, we had some onerous ground to tread in front of us.

Christy nodded. "Just don't disturb her. I have a feeling when she wakes up she's gonna be cranky."

He walked into her room alone, leaving the rest of us in the living room. Sheila shut the front door and joined us. "Do you think you can break through whatever he did to her?"

"Hard to say," Christy said. "I'm good with mind magic, but vampiric compulsions can run deep, and Alexander is insanely strong. I have a feeling it's going to be touch and go - me trying to drill small holes to get her to remember. There is some hope, though."

"Oh?" I asked, glad to hear something positive for a change. "Spill. There's been too much bad news as of late. Lay on with the good."

"She's a smart girl. She knows she's missing pieces and wants them back. That she was willing to let me try, despite her mistrust, is a good sign. Also..." She hesitated for a moment, her eyes darting between me and Sheila. "...when I was in her head, I sensed some...powerful emotions."

"Sally's never been one to do things in half measures," I pointed out.

"Tell me about it," Tom replied, eliciting a chuckle. Barely a meeting between them had gone by where she hadn't threatened to gut him or worse.

"There's a lot going on in there. Hate, anger, fear...but plenty of positive stuff too," Christy said.

"Like?" I asked.

She again hesitated. "Just complex thoughts...girl stuff. Anyway, the point of the matter is it's powerful."

I snapped my fingers, getting where she was going.

"And strong emotions can sometimes overcome compulsions. I've seen it before." Of course, I'd never seen it with a vampire as powerful as Alex, but I held out hope that it wouldn't hurt in her struggle to become herself again. We'd need her. Facing Vehron with Sally by my side was still terrifying, but a lot less so than going it alone - even if figuratively.

Sheila would be there too, but...well, I had to grudgingly admit she had a life, one that apparently didn't include me. As much as I would always love her, I wouldn't be the barrier that stood between her and happiness.

All of this assumed we would survive, of course - yet another thing to weigh down my conscience.

"Why don't we all go in and check on her?" Christy suggested.

"Yeah, who knows what Ed is doing in there to her by himself," Tom joked.

"Not if he wants to keep living."

"But what a way to go."

The four of us laughed, but when Christy turned to open the bedroom door, I hesitated. She and Tom stepped through, but I stopped in front of Sheila and said, "We'll be in there in a sec."

Christy nodded, but Tom's eyebrows raised. He looked as if he was about to say something dickish, but Christy - thank heavens - grabbed his arm and dragged him with her, letting the door shut behind them.

"That afraid of her?" Sheila asked jokingly.

"Yeah, pretty much. But I just wanted a moment." I turned away and stepped toward the couch, an even uglier affair than the one in our apartment. This place had formerly been occupied by an older couple - one with shitty taste, apparently.

I placed my hands on the back and leaned against it. I

wasn't sure exactly what I was going to say, but figured I'd let my mouth do the talking and try to keep my brain in neutral lest it take over and turn me into a blithering idiot. "I wanted to tell you that I'm sorry."

She took a step toward me. Thankfully, there was no corresponding flash of white fire. Odd that I'd almost come to expect it. "Sorry? For what?"

"For almost getting you killed."

"What? You didn't..."

"That whole freaking kangaroo court." I turned to face her. I needed to talk fast before I lost the nerve. "All of that back in the bunker, it was my fault. I led them to you. My precautions weren't enough. I should have left you alone, let you live your life, but I couldn't. Once I found out you were alive, I had to see you - make sure you were okay. It was stupid and selfish and I only realized that once it became clear you were fine. So you can blame me. I fucked it up, just like I seem to fuck everything up. Hell, the world is ending and you might as well blame me for that too, because yep, that one's on me as well."

Yeah, I was rambling. I could tell by the confused look on her face. I'd probably given one bizarre confession too many to make sense.

"You didn't lead anyone to me."

"Yeah, I did. I found you, then *bam*...just a short while later, they had you in cuffs."

"Short while? That was months. I don't know what you think you're blaming yourself for, Bill, but it was my fault, not yours."

"Don't say that."

"It's true." She threw up her hands and paced before me. "I got sloppy. I didn't see a single thing out of the ordinary for weeks after you left...no vampires, no anything. The problem was, I got antsy. I kept thinking of the sword, sitting there in the closet - thinking I should be out there using it."

"The sword *I* brought to you."

"It would have happened anyway. I was getting twitchy. The truth is, I like going out at nights - helping people. I tried to deny it, but it's there, nevertheless. Being what I am...it's weird, but it changes you. You don't look at things the same way. A quiet night at home is nearly torture once you know what the world is really like. The sword was just an excuse. I started going out on patrol again...at first, just here and there, but soon all the time. And I stopped taking precautions, not caring if others saw me or that I was getting mentioned nearly daily on the evening news. Didn't you see any of that?"

"Not much television in Vegas these days."

"Vegas?"

"Long story."

"Well, apparently, other vampires pay their cable bill on time. They set up a trap and I walked right into it. There was no one to blame but myself." She stopped and looked down at the floor, shaking her head.

I was almost afraid to ask the next question, but I did anyway. "Did Robert get away?"

"Huh?"

"Robert. They didn't...kill him, did they?"

I half expected her to collapse into tears at his name, cursing that she'd ever had the misfortune to meet me. The Draculas could be a heartless bunch when they wanted to be. I had little doubt they would have used a loved one against her, then disposed of him like rotten meat when they were done.

To my surprise, though, she burst out laughing instead.

"I have no idea. He dumped me."

Sheila explained how things weren't the same between them after my visit. How Robert had grown distant...*uncaring*, as she put it. A few weeks later, he broke it off, asking her to move out.

"It just wasn't meant to be."

I kept my mouth zipped shut. Bringing up my little compulsion didn't seem like the smartest thing in the world. Even so, I felt bad knowing that, despite her beliefs, I had definitely screwed up something in her life.

"I think maybe he sensed I had unfinished business elsewhere."

"Wait, what?"

She stepped forward, closing the gap between us. Then, before I could act like my typical self - aka puss out and find some interesting knickknack to look at on the wall - she reached out and took hold of both my hands.

I was sure they were sweaty enough to make the Creature from the Black Lagoon wince in disgust, but she didn't even flinch.

"I think it's time we cut the crap, Bill."

"It is?" My voice registered in my ears, but to me, it was like I was talking from the other side of a bad telephone connection. I was barely aware I was saying anything at all.

"Yeah, we have a lot to talk about, and I don't think either of us has any clue what the days ahead will bring, so I..."

And of course Tom picked that exact fucking moment to open Sally's door and stick his head out. "Jeez, get a room, you two."

I loved him like a brother, but right about then, I could have gladly gone all Cain on his Abel of an ass. "What the fuck do you want?" I hissed.

"Sally's waking up. Come in here and say hi."

I looked Sheila in the eye and she shrugged as if to say, "What are you gonna do?"

Yep, if that didn't sum up the entirety of our relationship, I didn't know what did.

"How are you feeling?"

"Like shit. How the fuck do you think?"

"Sorry. What I meant to ask is do you remember anything new?"

We were standing in the small bedroom, pretty cramped now that all of us were gathered around the bed. Sally was sitting up on it, looking about as cranky as usual, but otherwise, she appeared to be in pretty good shape - physically, at least.

Tom stood next to Christy, but I had maneuvered so that Ed was between me and Sheila. In the back of my mind, I was telling myself it was because I didn't want to get distracted from my friend's plight, but a small part of me wasn't sure. It was safe to say that, despite the aborted conversation from moments earlier, nothing was going to get sorted out for the time being.

"I remember lots of things, just not about any of you."

"Oh." I turned and saw my friends were all thinking the same thing. *Fuck!* This was not going to be easy.

"But I feel like I should," she added.

"What?" Ed and I asked simultaneously.

"Dude, do that again and you're buying me a beer," he said. "What do you mean by that?"

"Exactly what I said, fleshwad," she replied. "It's like I don't know who the fuck any of you are, but at the same time, I do. It's hard to explain. All I know for sure is I could use a case of aspirin."

"Let me guess," I replied, "and a bottle of tequila to wash it down."

She actually smiled at that. "Sounds like a plan. Just make sure it's not the cheap shit."

We all shared a chuckle at that, but then she got serious. "Hey, Freewill..."

"It's Bill."

"Whatever the fuck. I just wanted to say thanks for helping me out with Mark."

"Not a problem. Making sure assholes get what they deserve is one of the small pleasures in life."

"Mark?" Christy asked.

"Yeah, Sally's ex. Real piece of work..."

"Wait," she interrupted, holding up a hand. "He's still alive?"

"Not after we were done..."

"Hold on," Sally said. "You know Mark?"

"Yeah, from back when he took Kara..." She stopped midsentence, her head whipping toward Tom. "Cara...mel, I mean. That time he ordered his favorite drink, a caramel latte."

"Mark didn't like caramel..."

"Yes, he did!" Christy snapped at her. "He loved them. You just don't remember."

"O-kay."

"Never trust a monster with a taste for shitty coffee," Tom remarked, blissfully clueless.

That was a close one. On top of everything else, I wasn't quite ready to spill the beans on his sister.

"Shitty or not, I could go for a cup," Sheila commented.

"We might have some upstairs," Tom replied. When I glanced sidelong at him, he grinned. "What? I never claimed I didn't like the occasional shitty beverage."

"Sounds good to me," Sheila said.

"Okay, why don't you all go get some," Christy suggested. "I'm going to work with Sally for a little while longer, then I think we all need some rest."

There were nods of consent all around. A cup of overly sugared Joe, a long shower, and then passing out for several hours sounded like heaven to me after the past few days.

"Honey, would you mind bringing me down a cup?" Christy added.

Tom shrugged as if to say "whatever." He was apparently used to being an errand boy to satisfy his girlfriend's needs.

"One for me too, meatbag," Sally said, smiling.

I grinned. It was only a matter of time before she tried becoming master of this little makeshift coven.

The others left the room, but I hesitated for a moment, my grin faltering. Thoughts of both Village and Pandora covens swam through my head, including what we'd lost. Starlight was gone. James was a shell of his former self. Dave was missing. Tom's sister was thousands of miles away - her fate in the hands of someone I hoped Sally was right to trust.

The truth was I'd had more than enough. I didn't want to lose anyone else, especially someone I really cared for. What Alex had done to Sally ate at me, for him to so casually erase what she and I had - and to do it for no reason other than to spite me.

Christy must have read my face, probably not needing any magic to do so. She smiled at me before sitting down at Sally's side. "It'll be okay, Bill. I swear by the White Mother I will do everything I can."

"I know you will." I turned away, wanting to believe she'd succeed.

I was just closing the bedroom door behind me when

something she said struck a chord - stopping me in my tracks.

"I'll be up in a bit," I said to the others as I turned back.

"Don't be too long." Something in Sheila's tone made me silently vow not to be. God, just to share a cup of coffee with her again without something blowing up between us...

First things first, though, before I forgot again - not that I was likely to forget my adventures in the sewers beneath Vegas anytime soon.

"Listen," Sally said with an eye roll as I reentered the room, "just because I want my memories back doesn't mean I'm inviting you in for a threesome."

Christy's eyebrows shot up at that.

"Relax, bitchzilla." I turned to Christy. "Remember how I told you that symbol on my arm looked familiar?"

"The Enochian, yeah?"

"Angelic script?" Sally asked.

"Ancient Magi, actually," Christy corrected.

"Whatever," I said. "Anyway, that thing you just said about the white chick..."

"The White Mother."

"Yeah, her. It reminded me where I'd seen that stuff before." I reached into the front pocket of my body armor, where I'd deposited my phone while still underground and...and pulled out a piece of charred plastic. "Fuck."

Sally smirked. "Offhand, I'd say you're due for an upgrade."

"Real funny. Christy, do you have a cell phone with you?"

"It's in the other room."

"Could you go get it?"

"Why?"

"Hold that thought and I'll tell you." I extended my

claws and began to tear apart the melted device, peeling away first plastic and then the metal inside. "Come on...yes!" I was in luck. Though the outside of the phone was toast, the SD card inside appeared to be intact.

Christy, in the meantime, had come back holding an intact phone in her hands. She handed it over to me and I was happy to see it was an upgradable model. I pried the back off and installed the card. "Fingers crossed," I muttered, turning on the photo app.

"For what?"

"For this." I handed her the device, the series of photos from the Jahabich cave queued up on it. "This is where I saw it."

Christy stared at it for a few moments, casually flipping through the photos at first, but then slowing down as she began to study them.

"The witch who came with us - her name was Miranda. She said she thought there might have been a spell written on the wall, but she hadn't studied your history enough to know what it was. So I was hoping maybe you'd have a..."

"Is this a joke?" Christy asked, wide-eyed.

I glanced at Sally, but her face shown only confusion - the memory of our encounter down below obviously amongst those buried in her head like the Ark of the Covenant in the fucking well of souls.

"No,"

Christy stepped to the bedroom door and shut it, clicking the lock.

I was about to ask her what she was doing. Don't get me wrong; I normally wouldn't mind being locked in a bedroom with two attractive chicks, but one was mindfucked and the other heavily pregnant. I'm sure some dudes would have been all over that fetish, but it wasn't one of mine.

I started to joke as such, but it died in my throat when she turned back around - an angry red glow erupting from her.

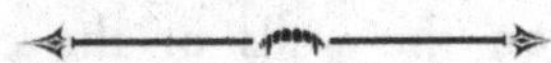

My first thought was to step in front of Sally. It wasn't so much to protect her as it was to keep things from escalating out of hand. Memories or not, she wasn't the type to take a threat lightly. Sure enough, a glance back confirmed her eyes had turned black.

"Where did you get this?" Christy snapped.

"Okay, can we all calm down for a moment?"

"I said, *where did you get this?*" Energy crackled around her, and red fire filled her eyes.

What the fuck? What the hell had set her off so? Pointing a finger at Sally, I said, "Stay!"

"You tell me where..."

"Okay, I heard you the first time," I snapped at Christy, hoping I wasn't about to be disintegrated. "We found it deep underground. It was in this big cave full of those fucking rock monsters. I think it was their home, or maybe their prison."

"That can't be."

"I think it was. There was this weird cave leading to it - looked like it had been melted open and..."

"No." The red glow began to dissipate and she slumped against the door, suddenly looking very tired. "The White Mother."

"Yeah. You said that earlier. It's what made me remember. Those goddamned weirdos had a statue that was..."

I trailed off as Christy reached into the top of her maternity blouse. She pulled out a pendent of sorts, hung by a chain around her neck. I stepped closer to take a look.

"What's going on?"

"Not now, Sally." I took in the shape. The pure white color, the outstretched arms, and the semblance of a dress...it was the same figure the statue had depicted - the same thing on the walls of the cave. "What the fuck?"

"It's the White Mother," Christy replied softly.

"Who..."

"One of the first of us...the best of us. She lived thousands of years ago. Legend says she was the first of the Magi to truly harness magic in ways other than hunting or waging war. She was the first to understand how it worked and how to use it to be in harmony with nature. Everything we hold dear is descended from her teachings. She is revered as a scholar, the first Mentor, the mother of kindness and knowledge."

"Okay..." I replied, not really understanding.

"Don't you get it?" she asked, tears now fully streaming down her face. "This thing...this *abomination*?" She threw the phone across the room where it hit the wall and shattered into pieces.

I slowly stepped toward her, mindful that she was a witch with enough power to blow a bowling-ball-sized hole through me. Carefully, I knelt by her side and placed a hand on her shoulder. "What is it?"

"The pictograph," she sobbed. "It says that she created those things. She called them forth from nothing, created life where there was none."

"So she..."

"It's a heresy! A crime against nature. The symbols tell of how she stole the souls of other living creatures and infused them into these...*freaks!*"

Whoa. That sure as shit sounded like a match with what we saw down below - creatures reborn as Jahabich soldiers.

"It's all a lie," she muttered, putting her face into her hands.

"So what?" Sally asked from where she sat. "So a long-dead witch fucked with nature. It doesn't mean..."

"Yes, it does!" Christy snapped, but this time when she looked up, I saw not anger or sorrow in her eyes, but fear. "Don't you understand? The matriarch of my people created those things. As far as both sides of this war are concerned, that will mean the Magi are responsible for them."

"That's stupid, they won't..."

Her eyes grew ever wider as she spoke. "We've lived for thousands of years under a guise of neutrality, but it's all been a lie. Those things not only attacked the vampire First Coven, they somehow allied themselves with that monster in Boston."

"Vehron?"

"The one and the same. That makes us an enemy of your people. That makes us an enemy to *everyone*."

"Nobody is going to believe that."

"You don't know how these things work, Bill. They snowball, spiral out of control. The souls corrupted by these things will want vengeance. They'll find a way. Soon the world will know of our part in this."

"I doubt that," Sally said casually. "Once we get finished with this Vehron asshole...well, dead vamps tell no tales."

"You just don't get it, do you? The Icon...she's coming with us. It's not just her destiny to face the Freewill. She's destined to destroy my kind as well." She put her hands protectively around her stomach.

"Sheila wouldn't..."

"She doesn't want to, but she will. She'll find out and it will turn her against us. She'll realize that if one of us can do this - can set forth these abominations against the world - then others can too. I don't know how it will happen, but it will happen. It's fate. I'm fated to die at her hand and so is...so is my baby."

She tried to say more, but the rest was lost to her sobs. I wanted to comfort her, but it wasn't exactly my strong suit. What was there to say? "There, there, I'm sure Sheila won't chop you to pieces with her flaming white sword"?

"Fuck fate."

"Huh?" I turned around.

Sally stood up and stepped forward. "You heard me. I don't remember either of you for shit, but that doesn't mean I don't know myself."

She knelt down on one knee and gently took hold of Christy's hands. Whoa. It was...almost human of her.

Christy looked up, her eyes shining with tears as Sally spoke. "You don't know how many times I've wanted to give up. I've faced disappointment, betrayal, violence, all of it. More than once, I've resigned myself to fate - to be a failure in my father's eyes, to be little more than a whore, to be a slave to Night Razor..."

On that last one, her eyes flashed black and her fangs descended. She gritted her teeth and I saw a thin trickle of blood run down the side of her lips. Obviously, the memory of Jeff was a potent one. She opened her mouth, perhaps to say more, but then a violent tremor shook her.

Christy reached out, but I was faster - using my vampire reflexes to reach Sally's side and steady her. After a moment, the spasm subsided.

She blinked a few times, shook her head, and looked up at me. "You were there, weren't you?"

"What?"

"At Jeff's death."

"You remember?"

"Vaguely...almost." I was about to say more, but she held up a hand. "Doesn't matter."

"The hell it doesn't."

"You're wrong," she said before turning back to Christy. "What matters is that each and every time, I refused to accept my fate. I told destiny to go fuck itself, that I'd make my own. If I can do it, you can too."

Christy and Sally stared hard at each other for several seconds. Finally, Christy broke contact to glance up at me, her eyes asking a question.

"Don't look at me," I said. "I've been telling the powers that be to go take a flying leap since I got bitten."

"So what do you say?" Sally stood up and offered a hand.

Christy looked at it for a moment, then grabbed hold as my partner pulled her up to her feet. "I've always been taught to respect destiny - that accepting it was the path to true happiness. But if what I thought I knew about the White Mother is false, then maybe that is too."

"You never know."

"But if we're wrong..."

I held up a hand. "We're going to be walking into a lion's den. You won't be able to throw a rock without hitting an enemy. If we're wrong, we're all dead anyway."

"You're not doing a very good job of making me feel better."

"But if we're right," I continued, "then who knows what awaits us in the end? I think we need to find out together. What do you say?"

Christy hesitated for a moment, but then she nodded, forcing a smile.

"I'm in. What the hell?" Sally said. "Beats the fuck out of being Alex's slave or, even worse, Colin's."

"You remember that asshole too?"

"Unfortunately."

I laughed at that and soon both of them joined in.

Fate could indeed go fuck itself.

I had no idea what the near future held, who would live or die, or even who truly held the keys to my heart, but I finally realized that maybe I didn't need to.

I'd just been witness to a minor miracle - a child amongst our kind shaking off a small part of the compulsion laid down by the most powerful vampire in the world. If she could do that, then couldn't we all do the same to the strings of fate guiding us? It was worth a shot.

Together, my friends and I would stride forward and make our own destiny.

The future was ours for the taking, and we'd do our damnedest to make it one worth remembering.

THE END

Bill Ryder will return in:
The Wicked Dead (The Tome of Bill – 7)

BONUS CHAPTER
THE WICKED DEAD

The Tome of Bill - 7

"Anything?"

"Yeah," Sally replied, holding up her glass. "This needs more vodka."

"I'm not talking about the drink."

"Sorry. The only thing I can concentrate on right now is what a shitty bartender you make."

Grumbling numerous unkind words, I grabbed the glass out of her hand and stormed out of the room - feeling her smirk following me all the while. As much as her memories might still be scrambled, deep down she was still Sally. That meant she'd quickly made a game out of her sessions with Christy, settling into a routine that was all about her. Christy would do the magical equivalent of entering my partner's head and rearranging the furniture, often exhausting herself in the process. Afterward, Sally would be the one demanding to be pampered for her *suffering* - refusing to cooperate until she was suitably mollified.

And yet for some reason I actually wanted her memories back. Hell, I was willing to do whatever it took to restore her.

I must have rocks in my head.

Slamming the door shut behind me, I let out a weary sigh. No, it wasn't rocks. There was something a lot heavier weighing me down. Some days I almost envied the older vampires. To them power and station were everything. Pesky crap like emotions were too petty a thing for them to worry about. I dare say a callous Vulcan-like attitude sure as shit sounded tempting lately. It would have made things a whole lot easier as I fumbled through the days - trying desperately to sort out my feelings for the women in my life.

I walked over to the kitchen nook, internally amazed at how life could sometimes hand you everything you ever wanted while still managing to flip you the finger.

Seriously, if you had told me even a few months ago that I was going to live in the same building as Sheila, the girl I'd been pining after for years, I'd have done cartwheels up and down the halls. That was shit straight out of my best fantasies. Sure, it was out of necessity as we prepped for battle - one that we had no guarantee of walking away from alive, but those were just the pesky details.

Allowing myself to have feelings for Sally had muddied those waters, though. A small part of me kept screaming that the whole thing made no fucking sense. Sure, physically, Sally was a dream girl for most heterosexual males, but her attitude was enough to drive any sane person to drink. She was an alpha dog to the extreme. In many ways the concept of just working with her was intimidating - much less doing anything of a more intimate nature.

In short, she was a threat to the manhood of any redmeat eating, tough-guy male - much less me - smart enough to give her biting wit razor sharp teeth and tough enough to let her fists do the talking if she needed to. Hell, she was out of my league on so many levels that I shouldn't have even been allowed to watch her play. All in all, there should have been enough red flags there to make me run off screaming. Yet, all of it had the opposite effect on me. I greatly respected her. She was strong even when she didn't have any reason to be and she'd stuck by my side during moments when I wouldn't have blamed anyone for running for the hills.

My thoughts trailed off as I looked through the cabinets in the little kitchen nook. Where was that bottle of vodka? More importantly, why was I putting even a modicum of effort into finding it? All so I could top off a concoction of orange juice and blood in the hopes that Sally would claim remembrance of something - *anything* that would give me hope?

Of course I was.

For the sake of our friendship alone I'd have done that and far more if it meant she remembered even a second of our past.

"Getting awfully dry in here!" her voice carried from the room.

Bitch! Yeah, I definitely had rocks in my head.

Speaking of crazy concepts, though, I really had more pressing ones to focus on. The truth was, worrying about any potential relationship with either Sheila or Sally was a luxury I didn't really have.

The end of the world was nigh, but there was a good chance we wouldn't even live long enough to see it. We'd been busy planning an assault on the Boston Prefecture - the heavily fortified former nerve center of vampire activity in the Northeastern United States. That in of itself was going to be tough enough, but it was just the tip of the fucking iceberg. Assuming we got in, we'd have to battle our way through an unknown number of vampires, zombies, and god-knows what else to reach our true target: Vehron the Destroyer - a nickname not earned due to his fondness for naval vessels.

Well okay, that wasn't entirely true, I considered as I found the bottle of Smirnoff Red in a cabinet above the sink. The whole part about him being a badass was, don't get me wrong. The untruth was that my friends had actually been the ones planning things. I'd made myself scarce the past few days. Worry over Sally had been a part of it, but there had also been some planning of my own - considering a desperate course of action that I knew to be borderline insane.

The others weren't pleased at me, thinking I was blowing them off. I couldn't blame them for that. After all, under any other circumstances that's exactly what I would've been doing. Instead, I'd been deep in thought, mulling the possibility of...

"I remember it all!"

Sally's cry brought me out of my reverie. Hope instantly filled me and I found myself actually taking a step toward the bedroom before stopping myself short. As much as I wanted to race to her side and confirm it to be true, deep down I knew I had to take care of one small bit of business first.

"What the fuck took you so long?" Sally asked, her tone betraying her irritation. "Were you out there playing with yourself? On second thought, don't answer that."

"Sorry," I replied, stepping into her room and closing the door behind me.

"Didn't you hear what I said?"

"Of course I did." I smiled and crossed over to the side of the bed where she was sitting. "Tell me everything."

"I'd be happy to, but first..." She trailed off and lifted a hand, palm up - the meaning clear.

"Yes, Your Highness." I handed her the now full glass. "Will there be anything else?"

"I'm good, for now at least."

"Great. So what did you remember?"

A smartass grin lit up her face. "Just that you were taking your sweet fucking time."

"Really?" I asked, through gritted teeth. "That's it?"

"Yeah, but you know how these things go. They take time. You need to have some patience." She lifted the glass to her lips. "Being a little less gullible wouldn't hurt either."

I stepped back as she took a sip. My timing was impeccable as the spot where I'd been standing just a moment earlier was immediately drenched in the spray that shot from her mouth.

"What the fuck?!" she cried, wiping her lips.

"I'd say I have the less gullible part down just fine, wouldn't you?" I ducked just as her glass sailed at me - missing and shattering against the wall instead. A few drops splattered my shirt, but it was worth it. "Oops, did I accidentally grab the vinegar instead of the vodka? Silly me, I'm always making that mistake."

She was up in a flash, her eyes black and fangs descended. Normally, I'd have backed off - enjoying my little victory while I could. This time, though, I stood my ground, looking down at her despite knowing she wasn't even remotely intimidated by my greater height.

"Look at it this way," I said, speaking quickly as I had a feeling I'd be eating a fist otherwise. "Obviously I'm well versed in your shit. If that doesn't prove we know each other, I don't know what does." I'd barely finished the sentence, when I instinctively brought my hands down to block the knee that I knew would be incoming. "See?"

I wasn't sure what would happen next. Memories or not, Sally could be unpredictable in how she sometimes reacted. To my surprise and relief, though, a ghost of a smile appeared on her face. "I guess I have been milking it a bit."

I held up a hand, two of my fingers an inch apart. "Just a little."

All at once the volume of her voice dropped, along with any attitude that had been in it. "I want to remember, Bill. Really I do."

She blinked and her eyes turned back to their normal dazzling green. I looked into them and could sense the confusion, desperation, and false bravery radiating from within her.

"I know and believe me when I say I will do whatever I can..."

The door opened and Christy appeared. "Everything okay in here? I thought I heard something breaking."

"Sally just had an accident with her glass."

"Yeah," she replied, turning away from me, her attitude back in force. "I accidentally missed his head with it."

Christy stepped out into the living room where I stood waiting for her. She put her hands on her hips and looked at me disapprovingly. "Really? Do you have to start with her?"

"Me?!"

"Are you trying to tell me you didn't?"

"Well..."

"I thought so." She turned to head back toward her bedroom.

"Wait."

"What, Bill? I'm tired." She had dark circles under her eyes that hinted at the exhaustion she was feeling. Mucking around in Sally's head, trying to undo the compulsion put there by Alex - quite possibly the strongest vampire on the planet - was difficult enough. That she was doing so while heavily pregnant was obviously putting a strain on her that she really didn't need.

Sadly, if I had my way, it wasn't going to get any easier for her.

I'd been putting off this talk long enough, busy debating with myself the downsides of my considered endeavor. I knew deep down, though, that no matter how long I hemmed and hawed over things, there was only one logical conclusion. It was time to stop pretending I had a choice.

The chances of Sally getting her memories back before we were forced to act were almost nil. Without her full facilities, she was at a disadvantage and we'd be heading north with enough of those as it was. It was time to add a few plusses to our column for a change - or so I hoped.

I stepped across the room, away from the door to Sally's room and beckoned Christy to follow - which she did with a sigh. "Listen, I'm sure this can wait until..."

"How's it going with her?" I asked in a whisper, hopefully low enough so prying ears couldn't hear me.

"You already know how it's going. You were just in there. We're uncovering bits and pieces, but it's one big jigsaw puzzle."

"You're making progress, though, right?"

Seeing that I wasn't backing down, she nodded and lowered her voice to match mine. "Yes. It's slow, but little by little I'm making headway."

"So you know what you're doing in there?" I raised a finger and pointed it to my temple.

"That vampire did a job on her, but I'm no slouch when it comes to mind magic. But you know this already. I've told you as much."

"You're right. Just double checking."

"Is that why we're whispering?"

"Not quite." I stepped closer to her, my next words barely audible. "Could you do it to me?"

"What?"

"Could you go inside my mind and do the same thing?"

"In theory, but you're not missing any memories so why would we even..."

"You're wrong," I replied, taking a deep breath. Oh well, in for a penny. "I'm missing three months of my life. That doesn't even count a big fight up in Canada and a battle with a bunch of Mongolian assassins, all of which are a blank for me."

For a moment she looked confused, but then her eyes opened wide with understanding. "What are you asking me to do?"

"We're in a bad spot right now. We have the Draculas threatening us with their bullshit death sentence. We try to run and they'll find us. The way forward might be even worse. There's Vehron, all the vamps he's swayed to his side, the Jahabich, and then there's all that business with the White Mo..."

She grabbed my arm, her grip surprisingly strong. "Don't say it."

"Sorry, but it's another X-factor...one that I'm willing to bet won't be in our favor." She nodded sadly and I went on. "We have a lot stacked against us and the hand we're holding isn't as strong as we're trying to fool ourselves it is."

"So you think you...*he* could..."

"Let me finish. We both know there's power inside of

me, a lot of it. I don't know if it's enough to even the odds, but I'd be willing to bet it would go a long way toward doing so."

"But he's a killer...a monster."

"I know and that's why I need you. I want to go deep inside of myself and wake up Dr. Death, but not in the way he wants me to. I need your help to lobotomize him, or whatever the fuck is the closest analogy. He's too much of a loose cannon otherwise.

I looked her deep in the eye. She was once my enemy, but she'd since become my ally - my friend. Now I needed her to go beyond even that. It was asking a lot for something that I wasn't even sure was possible. I had to try, though.

"We need his power, but I want you to ensure that I'm in control this time."

The Wicked Dead
Available in ebook, paperback, and audiobook.

AUTHOR'S NOTE

Whoever penned the phrase *no rest for the wicked* was right on the money. I find myself sitting here, mere weeks before the release of this book, wondering where the time has gone. It seems like just yesterday I'd released book five and was settling down to relax. Fast forward about ten minutes later and I was back at my computer, unable to get Bill Ryder or his friends out of my head. This is one of those stories that just poured out, almost as if I'd cracked open my skull and rammed a spigot into the opening - albeit slightly less painful.

Of course there's a vast difference between an inspired first draft and the final story you see before you. My first drafts have a roughness akin to chopping down a tree, running a piece of sandpaper across its length, and declaring it fine furniture. The actual art of polishing is what takes time and patience - working closely with my wonderful team of contributors. If you missed them, be sure to go back to the beginning of this book where they're all listed. Each of them deserves a round of applause for the effort - not to mention their patience in dealing with me. It is my sincerest hope that it was all well worth the wait.

I know it was for me. Though this book delves into dark places for our hero at times, I never once felt it. I had a grand time following Bill on his adventures and an even better time when it became apparent that nearly all of his "friends" would be making an appearance in this one. Some of these characters - I'm looking at you, Gansetseg - are such that I'll often get yelled at because I'll be typing away, fully immersed in their character, not realizing I'm cackling with glee like a madman.

I can only hope some of that joy has translated to the pages you have just read and, subsequently, to you, dear reader. If so, then this journey has been well worth the effort.

Until next time...
Rick G.

ABOUT THE AUTHOR

Rick Gualtieri lives alone in central New Jersey with only his wife, three kids, and countless pets to both keep him company and constantly plot against him. When he's not busy monkey-clicking words, he can typically be found jealously guarding his collection of vintage Transformers from all who would seek to defile them.

Defilers beware!

Also by Rick Gualtieri
THE TOME OF BILL
Bill the Vampire
Scary Dead Things
The Mourning Woods
Holier Than Thou
Sunset Strip
Goddamned Freaky Monsters
Half A Prayer
The Wicked Dead
Shining Fury
The Last Coven

BILL OF THE DEAD
Strange Days
Everyday Horrors
Carnage À Trois
The Licking Hour

www.ingramcontent.com/pod-product-compliance
Lightning Source LLC
Chambersburg PA
CBHW010534170726
48285CB00008B/2621